PRAISE FOR ROGER MacBRIDE ALLEN'S
THE DEPTHS OF TIME

"A tense tale of intrigue set in the far future of terraformed—and doomed—worlds." —*Library Journal*

"A highly readable balance of characterization, graceful and sometimes witty prose, and thoroughly, intelligently developed ideas." —*Booklist*

"I've read my fair share of Roger MacBride Allen novels over the years, and I'd have to say *The Depths of Time* is his best thus far. This novel has it all—hardcore science fiction foundation, a plot based upon a mystery that is guaranteed to drive you crazy trying to unravel it, and a deeply moving story." —Barnes and Noble *Explorations*

THE
DEPTHS
OF
TIME

First Book of the
Chronicles of Solace

Roger MacBride Allen

Bantam Books
New York Toronto London Sydney Auckland

THE DEPTHS OF TIME
A Bantam Spectra Book

PUBLISHING HISTORY
Bantam Spectra trade paperback edition published March 2000
Bantam Spectra mass market paperback edition / July 2001

SPECTRA and the portrayal of a boxed "s" are trademarks of
Bantam Books, a division of Random House, Inc.

ISBN 0-553-57497-3

Published simultaneously in the United States and Canada

Bantam Books are published by Bantam Books, a division of Random
House, Inc. Its trademark, consisting of the words "Bantam Books"
and the portrayal of a rooster, is Registered in U.S. Patent and Trademark Office and in other countries. Marca Registrada. Bantam Books,
1540 Broadway, New York, New York 10036.

PRINTED IN THE UNITED STATES OF AMERICA

OPM   10   9   8   7   6   5   4

To Eleanore and Matthew
mother and son
for creating a
past, present, and future
filled with wonder and joy

He hath set eternity in their heart, yet so that man cannot find out the work that God hath done from the beginning even to the end.

—*Ecclesiastes* 3:11

That which is hath been long ago; and that which is to be hath long ago been: and God seeketh again that which is passed away.

—*Ecclesiastes* 3:15

Wherefore I saw that there is nothing better, than that a man should rejoice in his works; for that is his portion: for who shall bring him back to see what shall be after him?

—*Ecclesiastes* 3:22

TABLE OF CONTENTS

x / Contents

ACKNOWLEDGMENTS

I would like to express my thanks to Pat LoBrutto, my editor at Bantam Books. His sharp eye significantly improved what you are about to read. Further thanks to him for allowing my ideas room to evolve, and for agreeing that an idea for one book was really big enough for two or three. Thanks also to Tom Dupree, who had a big hand in this book's early development. And, once again, thanks also to Eleanor Wood and Lucienne Diver, who were far more patient with me than they should have been, but definitely hard-nosed enough when it counted.

Thanks as well to my parents, Tom and Scottie Allen, who read over the manuscript and zeroed in on some significant flaws.

But thanks most of all to two people. First, thanks to my wife, Eleanore Fox, who read the first draft of this book and gave it no mercy at all. She was right, and I was wrong, about a lot of things.

And finally, thanks to my son, Matthew Thomas Allen. He had nothing to do with the writing or editing of this book, as he born after it was finished. But that doesn't matter. Thanks, Matthew. For everything.

Roger MacBride Allen
Takoma Park, Maryland
January 1999

DRAMATIS PERSONAE

A glossary and gazetteer appear at the end of the book.

Characters are identified in regard to their situation on first introduction in the story.

Wandella Ashdin—Historian and expert on Oskar DeSilvo.

Ulan Baskaw—Scientist who lived approximately five centuries before the main action of the story. Little is known about her—it is not even certain whether or not Baskaw was a woman or in fact a man. Baskaw invented many terraforming techniques that were later appropriated by DeSilvo. Baskaw also discovered certain mathematical principles underlying the science of terraforming.

Norla Chandray—Second Officer aboard the *Dom Pedro IV*.

Oskar DeSilvo—Architect and terraformist of the previous centuries, and director of the project to colonize Solace. He managed the centuries-long project by using cryosleep and temporal confinement, arranging to have himself revived from time to time in order to oversee critical points in the process.

Aither Fribart—Assistant to Grand Senyor Jorl Parrige.

Neshobe Kalzant—Planetary Executive, Solace.

Captain Anton Koffield—Commander of the Chronologic Patrol Ship *Upholder*.

Captain Felipe Henrique Marquez—Captain of the *Dom Pedro IV*.

Elber Malloon—Solacian farmer, caught up in the evacuation of flooded farm areas, and sent to SCO Station as a semi-involuntary refugee.

Mandessa Orlang—Director of the Greenhouse Institute.

Jorl Parrige—Grand Senyor, or senior senator, of the Planetary Council of Solace.

Dixon Phelby—Cargo specialist aboard the *Dom Pedro IV*.

Karlin Raenau—Station commander of SCO Station, orbiting Solace.

Hues Renblant—Propulsion and guidance officer aboard the *Dom Pedro IV*.

Ensign Alaxi Sayad—Watch officer aboard the C.P.S. *Upholder*.

Yuri Sparten—A young man working as an assistant to Karlin Raenau on SCO Station. His parents, as children, were refugees from the fall of Glister.

Milos Vandar—A biologist working on the project to revitalize Lake Virtue on the planet Solace.

THE TIMESHAFT WORMHOLE TRANSPORTATION SYSTEM

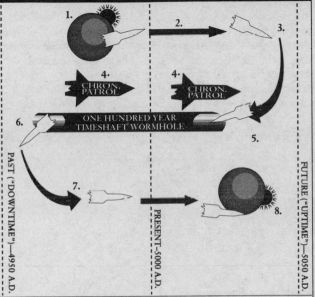

1. Spacecraft departs home star system, bound for target system, ten light-years away. Crew enters cryosleep hibernation and/or temporal confinement for duration of voyage.

2. Spacecraft travels for fifty years at one-tenth light-speed, thus traveling fifty years uptime and a distance of five light-years.

3. Spacecraft reaches timeshaft wormhole, midway between home and target systems. Captain is revived briefly to pilot ship through timeshaft.

4. Both uptime and downtime ends of wormhole are guarded by Chronologic Patrol ships.

5. Spacecraft drops through timeshaft and is propelled one hundred years downtime, into the past.

6. Spacecraft emerges from wormhole, fifty years before its departure from its home system and one hundred years before it enters the wormhole. Captain returns to temporal confinement.

7. Spacecraft onces again travels fifty years at one-tenth light-speed, again traveling fifty years uptime and five more light-years.

8. After traveling for one hundred years shipboard time, spacecraft arrives at target system a few days or weeks after departure in objective time. Crew is revived from one-hundred-year hibernation to find less than a month has passed.

THE
DEPTHS
OF
TIME

CIRCUM CENTRAL TIMESHAFT WORMHOLE
5211 A.D.

CHAPTER ONE

ASSAULT ON THE FUTURE

Brightness flared upon the face of the deep.

Alaxi Sayad, the most junior watch officer aboard the Chronologic Patrol ship *Upholder,* saw the dazzle of energy that appeared on her screens. She hit the alert button before she even had time to think—but not before the automatics had a chance to set off the alarms themselves.

She checked the drill-indicator, the one light on her board that would tell her if this was just old man Koffield running yet another dry run, another systems test. If this was a drill, the indicator would be a steady dot of green. The drill-indicator was unlabeled, and carefully positioned in the upper-left-hand corner of the display board so that only someone actually seated in the watch officer's chair could see it. Only the watch officers and senior officers were even supposed to know it existed.

Sayad had seen that tiny secret green light come on during a thousand drills, and she expected to see it now. But instead she saw a tiny, flashing dot of red: shocking and positive confirmation that this was not a drill. It was the real thing. Some damn fool was trying to make an unauthorized run through the timeshaft wormhole. Stranger still, if her displays were to be believed, they were going for the downtime, not the uptime, end of the timeshaft wormhole. They were trying, not to head from future to past, but attempting to dive *out* of the past and *into* the future.

Sayad allowed herself the luxury of a full hundredth of

a second of stunned disbelief. Such a thing had never happened, to the best of her knowledge, in all of Settled Space.

But it was happening *now*. She shoved feeling aside and let training take over. Seemingly without any intervention from her conscious mind, she started on step one of the standard operating procedure that had been drummed into her through all those thousand drills.

Confirm alert. Easy enough. There was no doubt this one was real.

Locate. That part was likewise quite straightforward. The blast of light had come straight from the timeshaft wormhole.

Identify. A far more difficult proposition. What in space could light up a wormhole like that? And why hadn't the *Standfast,* the downtime ship, sent some sort of alert through the shaftlink comm system? Even as she formed the questions, she got her answers. The comm system powered itself up and reported data streaming in from the downtime link. Seventy-nine years downtime from the *Upholder,* the *Standfast* had activated her comm system and started relaying through the shaft communications system. The signal had been flashed from the *Standfast* to the downtime stationkeeping laser relay. Then the stationkeeper had fired a repeater signal through the wormhole's signal portal, and to the uptime stationkeeper relay, which instantly passed it on to the *Upholder*.

The action-status display flashed to life, and Sayad expended five whole precious seconds studying the three-dimensional symbol-logic imagery the *Standfast* had sent milliseconds ago—or decades before, depending on how one looked at it.

She swore silently, but vehemently, as she struggled to believe what the display was telling her. Thirty—no, thirty-one incoming targets, sixteen of them bearing down on the wormhole, and the remainder diving straight for the *Standfast*. One of the targets bearing on the *Standfast* popped out of existence as the ship brought fire to bear. There was another flash of light, dimmer this time, as the blaze of the explosion lanced through the wormhole. That first light blast must have been another of the targets going up.

"Are they trying to kill the ship, or just trying to keep her busy?" asked a low, calm voice from directly behind her.

It took a major effort of will for Sayad not to jump half a meter in the air in surprise. It was Captain Koffield, of course. She glanced up at the small look-behind mirror built into her console, and there he was. Awake, alert, in a clean uniform. Sayad had been on the graveyard shift ever since coming aboard the *Upholder* and had rarely seen the captain. But every time she had seen him, the man had looked just as he did now—steady, alert, well rested, in control.

Captain Koffield was of average height, but thin and wiry enough that he gave the impression of being smaller than he was. His face was long and lean, his thinning hair dark brown. His eyes were brown, deep-set, bright, and expressive. He was clearly used to command, and used to his commands being followed. But there was nothing harsh, or cruel, or peremptory about the man.

Only the slight but unmistakable stubble on his unshaved face hinted that he had just rolled out of bed, wakened by the alarm. It was a small but telling detail, and Sayad found it reassuring. It said Koffield took care to be alert and professional, to get there first during an emergency, but that he was not fool or egotist enough to stop for a shave on the way.

But the captain was not a man who wasted much time with rhetorical questions. "I think they're making a try for the ship, sir," Sayad replied. "With velocities that high they won't have time to break off before impact—they're looking to ram her."

"Agreed. Either uncrewed missiles or remarkably well-motivated suicide crews."

Other members of the command-center crew were arriving, diving for their battle stations, getting their displays and systems on-line. Sayad paid them no mind. Let them do their jobs while she did hers. She was supposed to do more than see what was happening out there. She was expected to understand it, interpret it. "A saturation envelopment attack," she said. "Hit the *Standfast* from all sides at the same time and overwhelm her defenses. They want the ship. They've invested half their forces to go after her. That's too aggressive for it to be just a diversion. At least it looks like—wait a second." She put her hands on the display controls and checked the backtracks. "No. I was wrong. They want us to *think* it's a full-press attack and not a diversion."

"They've got me convinced," Koffield said. "But now you think otherwise."

"Yes, sir. The blips moving on the wormhole are maneuvering, seeking and zeroing in on the access nexi. That's not easy to do. But the blips moving on the *Standfast* are just boring right in, with no attempt to refine or correct their course."

"So they just want to keep her busy so their friends can get at and through the wormhole," Koffield said.

"*Through* the wormhole?" Sayad asked. "How the hell do they think they're going to do that?"

"I haven't the faintest idea how they'll do it," said Koffield. "But it's plain they *think* they can do it." He examined the symbol-logic screen. "Three minutes until they encounter the portal's event horizon. We'll find out then."

It was a startling thought, but why else would they be pressing home this attack? To hear Captain Koffield himself say the words made the idea seem much more part of the real world, something to consider in terms of practical detail. "They don't have the codes to open the access nexi," she objected. "There *aren't* any public codes for going uptime. Just the ones we used to move the *Upholder* uptime."

That the wormhole portal nexi codes were unbeatable, unbreakable, was an article of faith in the Chronologic Patrol, and among spacefarers in general. Only the Patrol knew the codes, and therefore only the Patrol controlled the wormhole portal nexi.

A portal nexus was a massively powerful gravitic distorter that, in effect, pushed aside the singularity's event horizon, opening up a hole in time through the hole in space. The nexi orbited at the fringe of the wormhole's event horizon, at hellishly fast velocities. Approach a time-shaft wormhole when a Chronologic Patrol ship had sent the proper code to open a nexus, and you dropped through the nexus, down the timeshaft, into the past. If the CP ship got the code wrong, or failed to send it, when the portal nexus controllers detected your ship approaching they would leave the nexus shut. Your ship would not go through the wormhole formed by the singularity's warping of space, but instead would spiral down into the black hole itself.

Koffield flipped on the ship's intercom, and raised his voice enough so that the bridge staff could hear him as well. "This is the captain. Our sister ship, the *Standfast*, is under attack, as is the downtime portal. We must work on the assumption that the attacks will succeed. If they do, we will be facing an assault coming from *inside* the timeshaft wormhole and heading out, rather than an assault from the outside in, toward the timeshaft. In other words, the exact opposite of what we've trained for. So let us prepare to face the situation. Bring all weapons to bear on the vicinity of the wormhole, and prepare to track and destroy evasive targets as they exit the timeshaft. You have two minutes. I authorize and order weapons hot and an unrestricted free-fire zone and unlimited target list. If it moves, shoot it. Koffield out."

The disorganized, uncertain bustle all about them suddenly gained focus and direction. The news was startling, and even alarming, but the captain had spoken. He had told them what was what, and what to do.

The crew of the *Upholder* set to work, making use of every one of the precious seconds they had. Energizers came on-line. The trackers took in the data from the *Standfast*'s datastream, interpolated probabilities on the egress trajectories for the attackers, and set aim at the most likely points in space. Damage-control teams went to standby. Hatches sealed. The battle lighting came on, a dim red glow that permitted one to see, but left one's eyes adapted to the dark of space and the glow of the display screens.

But none of that was the concern of Alaxi Sayad. Her job right now was to watch the *Standfast* and her attackers as they did battle, a fight to the death that was happening seventy-nine years in the past, and a heartbeat away, through the wormhole.

Sayad forced back the irrational wish that they could go look up what happened, and prepare for it that way. After all, the battle *had* happened nearly eight decades before. There ought to have been a way to know all about it, and be ready in advance to deal with the consequences.

But there wasn't, of course. The powers-that-be had quite wisely set things up to make such researches impossible. Indeed, the whole reason the *Upholder* was on station was to make them impossible. Her job, and the job of the entire Chronologic Patrol, was to ensure that the past knew nothing whatever about the future.

Their job was to protect causality, to prevent temporal paradox. The Chronologic Patrol went about its work with care and determination, and went to great lengths to keep the future as dark a secret as possible from the past— starting with how the uptime picket ships got to their stations. The uptime ships came from downtime, and thus knew nothing of events in the future of the downtime ship.

The *Upholder* might be in the year 5211 A.D., but she was far more connected to the world of 5132, seventy-nine years in the past. She and the *Standfast* had traveled to Circum Central Waypoint in convoy, relieving the two Chrono-Patrol ships that had been on duty. The *Upholder* had gone uptime through the timeshaft wormhole, while the *Standfast* had remained at the downtime end, but it could have just as easily been the other way around.

The *Upholder* had only two communications systems. One was a short-range beacon-interrogator that allowed her to challenge ships that arrived at the uptime end of the timeshaft and sought passage through. The other was the shaftlink comm system that *Standfast* was sending on. Both systems were, by design, extremely limited. Except in the most exceptional circumstances, the *Upholder* could not send messages at all, aside from clearances and portal-control commands. For the most part, she could only receive communications, and send them only in carefully proscribed circumstances. Every regulation, every Artificial Intelligence watching over the comm channels, every safeguard in the hardware, was designed to ensure that the *Upholder* did not send any information about the future into the past.

One of the most basic precautions was to see to it that she did not *receive* any information about the future. By design, the *Upholder* carried no long range comm system that might pick up transmitted information.

Timeshaft wormholes could only be located in the depths of interstellar space, far from the time-space distortions created by a star or even by a mid-sized planet. The Circum Central Waypoint wormhole was no exception to that rule. It was three light-years from the colony at Glister, and a good 3.5 lights from Solace, off in a different direction. Without a highly sensitive, precision-aimed receiver of exactly the sort the *Upholder* did not carry, there was no way to communicate with the worlds on the uptime side of the timeshaft.

A ship could in theory carry information to the *Upholder*, or even downtime into the wormhole. However, timeshaft-wormhole ships moved far slower than light, meaning that most information would be out-of-date by the time it reached a wormhole.

But precautions were taken nonetheless. An uptime picket ship would refuse transit rights to any ship that had been under way less time than half the chronologic distance of the timeshaft wormhole in question. Circum Central Waypoint, for example, was a seventy-nine-year timeshaft. No ship was allowed to enter the uptime end of the shaft until she had been under way for at least thirty-eight and a half years.

And, no matter what, no ship, aside from the arriving uptime picket, was *ever* allowed to enter the downtime end of a timeshaft.

Including this bizarre fleet of presumably uncrewed ships

that had just appeared out of nowhere. *Uncrewed.* They would have to be, and it wasn't just their apparently small size. How the devil would anyone find crews enough to fly thirty-two ships on a secret and criminal mission that was all but suicidal? But if no one was aboard those ships, what was the point of the attack? What value in sending a machine into the *future*? Why not just put the ships in storage and wait seventy-nine years? Alaxi stared at the sym-log display, trying to will the answers out of the cryptic indicators of heading, speed, projected course, acceleration, and weapons discharge.

The *Standfast* had been holding her ground, presenting a stationary target to her attackers. Now, perhaps too late, she got under way, even as she finally blazed away with her heavy weapons, the laser cannon and her steel-shot mag accelerators, firing at the incoming attackers.

"At last," Koffield said. "What the devil kept her from maneuvering before now?"

"They were taken by surprise," Sayad replied, though she had been wondering much the same thing. It was damned easy to let things get slack on garrison duty, and it looked as if it had happened to the *Standfast.* Sayad wondered if the *Upholder* would have done any better with zero warning. Besides, the *Standfast* had been watching for an assault coming through the wormhole, out of the uptime end and the future, not from out of normal space.

The *Standfast*'s heavy-weapons fire took a heavy toll. Three, four, eight of the blips diving on the ship blazed and vanished from the display. More, dimmer flares of light, flickered through the timeshaft.

But then the *Standfast* broke off and started maneuvering at flank acceleration toward the wormhole. The remaining ship-attacking blips did not pursue her, but instead kept on diving straight for the ship's original position. The *Standfast* had finally seen what Sayad had seen minutes before. The attack on the ship was a diversion, not a serious danger.

The diversion had served its purpose. The *Standfast* commenced firing on the blips moving toward the wormhole, but the incoming ships were already deep enough inside the wormhole's complex gravity field and moving fast enough that accurate targeting was all but impossible. Space and time were wildly warped and twisted by the wormhole's intense gravitation, sending laser fire and mass-accelerator fire skewing off in strange, unexpected directions. Even so, the *Standfast* scored a series of direct hits on the attackers. Whoever was in charge of those guns might have been slow to react, but he or she was a remarkably good shot.

Five, six, seven, eight of the attackers flared into nothingness as the *Standfast* raced toward them, all weapons firing. But that still left half the attackers coming on.

The closer the *Standfast* got to the wormhole, the more difficult it became to target her weapons. But she had to get closer, and closer still, if she was going to be able to bring her weapons to bear on the remaining targets. Another volley of fire, every shot a clear miss. And another volley, this time taking out two of the intruders.

"Oh, no," Koffield said. "Stars in the sky, *no!*"

Sayad had been concentrating so hard on the screen that she had all but forgotten Koffield was there. What had he seen that she had missed?

Then she saw. The *Standfast* was moving too fast, getting too close. She was going in, all guns blazing. She was redlining, headed down into the black hole's gravity well, past the point of no return. She would either have to go through the wormhole, or crash into the surface of the black hole.

And she was nowhere near any of the alignments for a safe transit through one of the approach nexi.

The *Standfast* made no attempt to save herself, but instead flew in closer to the intruders, setting up for one last desperate all-weapons volley, getting in under the six remaining targets, firing directly into their paths. She fired everything she had, and then, before her guns and laser even reached their targets, she fell in toward the black hole's event horizon, far, far away from any of the approach nexi.

She was too close, going too fast. The datalink died with the ship, but the suddenly blank screen told Sayad all she needed to know about what happened next.

Within a blink of an eye, the flicker of a moment, the *Standfast* had been destroyed, torn into a million, a trillion microscopic fragments, every man and woman aboard ripped apart with shattering speed, down to and beyond the molecular level. They had been ground up, shredded into subatomic nothingness by the gravitational vortex of the black hole before they even had time to know they were dying.

The rest was silence.

The crew of the *Upholder* stared at their screens in horrified, frozen shock. This wasn't supposed to happen. It made no sense. How could—

"They're coming through!" Koffield shouted into the mike. "All weapons, fire at will. The *Standfast* died trying. Don't let her down."

It was what the crew needed to hear. They shook off their shock and their horror and refocused on their duties.

Sayad blinked, drew in breath, and tried to do the same. No more data coming from the downtime feed. All right then, work from last positions and trajectories. Factor in projected paths of the access nexi. Feed it all to the battle-projection Artificial Intelligences that weren't designed to track targets coming up *out* of the timeshaft, and pray they could do the projections, and that the probabilistics projections weren't completely smoke and mirrors at the moment. She massaged and routed the data, and saw projected exit trajectories appear on her display. She converted them to firing solutions, and piped them to the weapons consoles.

It was guesswork piled on guesswork, but there was no time for anything better—and no way to produce it, no solid numbers to work from. It had taken precisely twelve seconds for her to go from raw data in to firing solutions out, but Sayad doubted she could have done much better work if she had taken twelve years.

"Well-done, Ensign Sayad," Koffield said. "Now we wait, if not for long."

"No, sir. Projected arrival in fifteen seconds—mark."

"Here comes our turn," Koffield said.

Right on schedule, a flare of blueshift light blossomed out of the event horizon, and then another, another, another, until all six of the surviving intruders had punched through. Sayad felt a sick knot in the pit of her stomach—the enemies had known the codes, and the *Standfast*'s last volley of fire, the one she had died to make, had been for nothing at all.

But then there was no time.

Weapons section took the conn, and the *Upholder* came about hard, placing the cylindrical ship's long axis at right angles to the wormhole, so as to bring the most possible firepower to bear. Her main weapons opened up at once, directing laser and railgun fire at the twisting, dodging intruders. Sayad checked her instruments and got her first direct mass, size, and acceleration readings on their uninvited guests. No doubt about it—those had to be uncrewed ships. They were too small and too dense to carry both crew and any sort of acceleration shielding, and they were accelerating hard enough to squash any human passenger into red paste with or without shielding, accelerating faster than any ship she had ever seen or heard of. It was precious little comfort that her tracking projections had proved accurate enough that the weapons systems were able to start targeting the moment the intruders emerged.

The *Upholder*'s lasers locked on to the first target, and chased it relentlessly as it dived and twisted and pinwheeled through a complex evasive-action sequence. The target held together far longer than it should have under main-laser fire, but whatever its very impressive shielding was made of, it couldn't protect the intruder indefinitely—not from the multigigawatt intensity of the *Upholder*'s firepower. A second bank of the main lasers locked on the target, doubling the energy being pumped into the intruder's hull. It flashed over, blowing up in a spectacular blaze of glory that blinded half the *Upholder*'s sensors and detectors for three very long seconds before the damper systems could recover.

The position-predictors did their best, but the surviving

five targets were performing evasive escape maneuvers. Even three seconds of sensor-blinding was enough to make the old tracking projections worse than useless.

The weapons systems lost five more irreplaceable seconds as they tracked and scanned for the surviving intruders. Sayad slaved her screens to the weapons display and watched their frantic search. Koffield stayed with her, watched the battle off her screens. No sense rushing to the weapons boards. He had already given all the orders he was going to give. All he could do was sit back and watch. He could do that just as well from Sayad's stations, without distracting the gunnery teams. But the gun crews weren't finding anything. Sayad flipped back to her own tactical search algorithms and ran them against the weapons-sensor data.

And found the intruders again. Or maybe the intruders had found *them*. "Bloody hell!" Sayad cried out. "Bogie, coming straight at us, right through the wormhole blind spot!" She thought at first it was a variant on diving out of the sun, one of the oldest dogfight tactics there was. The intruder had the wormhole directly astern, and was barreling straight for the *Upholder*.

But no. No, not straight for the *Upholder*. But near enough, only two or three degrees up-Y from straight-line on the wormhole. And almost certainly, the intruder had no detection gear capable of finding the *Upholder*. If the intruder had known where the *Upholder* was, it either would have revectored to ram, or aimed for just about any other spot in the sky. In fact, the intruder she was tracking had ceased evasive action. Either it expected that the *Upholder*'s detectors would not recover in time, or its automatic-sequencing system had told the intruder to do so. In either case, the intruder had not spotted them. Chance, damned-dumb chance, and nothing else, had sent the intruder flying right across the *Upholder*'s bow.

She checked range and rate on the new target. It was coming almost straight for them, all right, but it still had a long way to go before it reached them. It could be tough to fire on a target that was coming straight on, as opposed to traveling laterally. They had a good ninety-five seconds until it was within a prime firing solution. Sayad relayed the new tracking to weapons control, and saw by her boards that they had just located an intruder themselves.

She cleared her main board and brought up the symbollogic displays for the destroyed intruder's trajectory, the intruder she had found, and the one the weapons team had found. She studied the three, looking for relationships and patterns that might lead her to the other three that were still unaccounted for. She added her arrival projections, and the pre sensor–blinding tracks as well. The big screen was a tangle of traces and vectors, dots and lines, color-coded sym-log gibberish.

But Sayad could read it all. The incomprehensible mishmash made perfect sense to her. The pattern was clear. Whoever had sent these probes through the wormhole had set up pseudorandom evasive patterns that ended with the surviving intruders in a radial-symmetric dispersal pattern, each craft heading off in a different direction. She frowned, and thought fast.

Thirty-two attackers to begin with, but half of them diversionary. Sixteen actually attempted to get through the wormhole, but the *Standfast* had taken out ten of them, and *Upholder* had killed one. She had good current real-time tracks on two of the survivors, and she had no doubt the weapons team would take them out in short order. That left her with three intruders for which she had no reliable current track. She had lost them in their evasive-maneuver phase, thanks to that sensor-blinding explosion of *Upholder*'s kill. *Think*. Six intruders. Three accounted for. Three missing. Six out of sixteen intruders programmed to go through the wormhole and disperse. She worked her board controls, slicing up the sphere of space around the wormhole into sixteen pyramid-shaped sectors, the points of the pyramids meeting at the center, at the wormhole.

The geometry required mostly six-sided and some five-sided pyramids to allow an absolutely precise fit, but she ignored that level of nicety for the moment. She threw the tracks of the detected intruder up into her improvised radial-sector map, and was not in the least surprised to see it was easy to match them up with the centerlines of three of the sectors. Each of the known intruders was moving on a direct radial course out from the wormhole, each moving more or less precisely down the center of its assigned "slice" of space. It was so tidy, so accurate, that Sayad had not the slightest doubt that the remaining three intruders would likewise be found in the centerlines of *their* sectors.

That was a mistake on the part of whoever had programmed the intruders, and a big one. It meant she only had to search near the centerlines of the remaining sectors, thus eliminating about 99 percent of her search area.

Well, if the person who had programmed the intruders loved order so much as to be tempted into one mistake by it, maybe he or she had made another.

She had tracks for those three, but they were more than a minute old, closer to ninety seconds by now: far too old to be of any direct use. But they at least told her the arrival order for all six of the intruders that had gotten past the *Standfast*. She compared it against the known intruders' sector assignments.

And there it was. Breathtaking. Perfect. Tidy. And incredibly stupid. The intruders had been slotted into their sectors in order of their arrival, rather than at random. All she had to do was figure out where in the arrival sequence an intruder had been—something she could derive easily enough by noting the moment of each arrival—and she would know just about where to look along the lengths of the centerlines of three particular sectors of space, to find the missing intruders.

Her fingers danced over the controls. She focused the long-range detectors at the appropriate points in space—and was rewarded with almost immediate detection returns on three bogies.

"If that's not black magic I don't know what is," Koffield said from behind her. "Brilliant work, Sayad. Later you can tell me how you did it."

Sayad smiled at her board. "Yes, sir," she agreed as she routed the detection tracks to weapons. "I'll be glad to oblige." Later. Now there was far too much to do. The three new intruder tracks were on the far side of the wormhole from the *Upholder,* and doing their damnedest to get still farther away with every moment that passed. The *Upholder* was going to have a devil of a time pursuing any one of them, let alone pursuing, intercepting, and destroying all three. They would need smart tactics, and need them fast, to have any hope of blasting them all. She set to work gathering information, coaxing more data out of the pinpricks of light that were doing their best to escape.

A flare of light lit up the main screens, and Sayad was focused enough on her own work, she did not know at first what it was. Ah, of course. Fire control had locked in and blown out their second bogie. Sayad checked her displays. It was, not surprisingly, the one the weapons team had found for themselves. That left the one she had first spotted, the one bearing straight down on them. And fire control was already redirecting fire toward intruder three. She let them do their job while she did hers, and concentrated on intruders four, five, and six. The flare of the explosion had blinded her detection systems again, but this time it didn't matter. Bogies four to six weren't trying anything fancier than flying in a straight line.

And then, one after another, bogies one, two, and three each did something very fancy indeed. They started accelerating, putting on speed—and putting it on with a vengeance.

Sayad frowned and checked her displays. The numbers they were showing were impossible. *Accelerating* was too mild a word for what those ships were doing. They were doing hundreds, no, thousands of gees in acceleration. Even as she watched, the acceleration displays for each of them went off-scale high. No ship, not even an unpiloted ship, could possibly survive the thrust levels those ships were putting out, no matter what kind of acceleration buffers they had aboard.

And there, as she watched, one, two, three, the three bogies just—vanished. Gone. Did not show on any of her instruments. Her velocity meters showed why, and it was impossible to believe them. Light-speed. The damned intruders had accelerated all the way up to light-speed in the space of a few seconds.

And *nothing,* nowhere, could possibly travel at light-speed. That was an article of faith, an unalterable fact. That was the whole reason for the existence of the time-shaft wormholes—to serve as a creaky, awkward, difficult substitute for true light-speed and translight-speed travel. If you could go faster than light, you didn't need the wormholes.

So why in the name of the devil's chaos had the intruders just *used* a wormhole? And how did they jump to light-speed? And where the hell were they going? And what the hell was the *Upholder* going to do to stop them?

But then her attention refocused itself on the problem still at hand, the problem *Upholder* could still do something about. That one remaining intruder, the one just coming into range. She flipped back through all her data, through all her guess-upon-guess-upon-guess extrapolations. If she had it right, the one coming up on them right then was not only the last of the surviving six to come through the wormhole, but was to have been the last of the sixteen in the intended schedule. Whatever the first ones out of the chute had done was what this one was *about* to do—

She slapped a hand down on the comm key. "Weapons! Remaining target is about to commence massive acceleration and blow right past us. Advise you fire scattershot railgun rounds across its projected course! Fire now, now, now!"

If fire control was fast enough off the mark, they should at least be able to hit this one as it started its escape run. There was a faint *whir-thump, whir-thump, whir-thump* from somewhere belowdecks, a sound and vibration so slight she wouldn't even have noticed it if she hadn't been waiting for it. The railgun was firing. Sayad watched her screens and the projected course of the intruder, and the cloud of scattershot pellets expanding out from their dispersal point. They were no more than tiny balls of perfectly ordinary iron, but if fire control had done its job right, the intruder was going to pass through a cloud of several thousand such bits of iron at a minimum closing rate of ten or fifteen kilometers a second. And if the intruder started its acceleration run before it hit the cloud—well, the faster it flew, the harder it would hit.

Koffield leaned in over her and hit the comm button himself. "Captain to conn! Attitude X-125, Y-010, Z-220, full emergency thrust! Immediate action! Fire control! Saturation fire of scattershot across intruder's projected course! All hands! Impact and hull breach alert!"

The *Upholder* lurched crazily about on her long axis and fired her main engines. Sayad stared wide-eyed at her screens. She hadn't seen it. Thank the stars Captain Koffield had. If the intruder hit the scattershot and blew up, it would likely do so a mere five or six hundred kilometers from the *Upholder*'s present position. And when a target that big hit a cloud of scattershot at high velocity, it would fill all of surrounding space with shrapnel. The ship needed to get out of there, and fast.

The acceleration compensators bucked and shuddered as they struggled to correct for the sudden shifts in velocity. The whole ship creaked and moaned as her structure took up the acceleration.

"Defense systems!" the captain shouted. "Current status! How long can you hold a maximum electromag shield around the ship?" Most of the crew regarded the ship shields as more nuisance than protection. They sucked in inordinate amounts of power, jammed or degraded every detection system on board, and tended to scramble computer circuits that weren't shielded with absolute perfection. Worst of all, it was impossible to fire the engines with the shields up. But if the *Upholder* was going to be practically next door to a bomb that was about to go off, Sayad was ready to put up with any degree of nuisance.

"Ah, ah, estimate thirty seconds, sir," a nervous voice replied. Sheelton, it sounded like. "Twenty-five seconds with aft-enhanced deflection." Aft-enhanced shields would protect the whole ship, but focus a larger fraction of that protection across the aft section, which was going to take the brunt of the impacts with the ship in its present attitude.

"Very well." Koffield paused for something less than a

heartbeat, then issued his orders. "Rig for aft-enhanced deflection, maximum power, and stand by to activate on my command. Conn, prepare for emergency engine shutdown at my command. Advise me the moment engines are safed. Once that thing blows, we'll kill the engines, light the shields, and hang on. All hands, rig now for impact, collision, and hull breach condition one. I say again rig now for impact, collision, hull breach condition one." He shut off the intercom.

Hatches slammed shut, sunshields swung shut over viewports, alarms hooted. Rigging for hull breach condition one meant all hands not in pressure suits and not standing watch were supposed to dive for their suits and get into them—but everyone on the bridge was, of course, standing watch. None of them could be spared from their duties for the sixty to ninety seconds it would take to pop the suits from their lockers and get them on. No one on the bridge moved toward the suit lockers, but Sayad was far from the only one who glanced at the closest locker and did a quick mental rehearsal of the steps needed to get her suit on.

Condition one rules said the captain could suit up or not at his own discretion. And it would be easy to argue that a suited-up captain would be better able to maintain effective command during a hull breach. But of course, morale might be a problem on a bridge where the only one going for his suit was the captain.

Koffield made no move toward the suit lockers. As best Sayad could see, he did not so much as glance in their direction. She watched her screens for what she knew was going to happen—and felt her heart start slamming against her chest when it did. "Sir!" she called out. "Remaining intruder commencing acceleration run! No course change or attempt at evasive action. Intruder on collision course with scattershot."

"Time to impact?"

Sayad shook her head. "Velocity ramping up too fast for solid numbers. Estimate impact on scattershot in thirty to forty seconds."

"Damn it!" Koffield slammed his fist against the console. "We're nowhere near clear."

One glance at her screens had told Sayad that much. The *Upholder* would be well under a thousand kilometers distance away from the point of impact.

Koffield checked her displays. "No time to figure the rates and ranges," he said, half to himself and half to her. "We're going to have to do this one by feel." He flipped the switch on the intercom again. "This is the captain. Conn, you will perform an all-engines emergency throttle-down to zero power and safing when I call Mark One. Understood?"

"Orders received and understood, sir," a voice from conn replied.

"Defense systems. Activate maximum shields, aft-enhanced deflection, five seconds after I call Mark One, or five seconds after you see all engines stop or safe, or when you hear me call Mark Two. Whichever of those happens, activate shields. Repeat and confirm."

"Um, ah, yes, sir." Definitely Sheelton. Sayad could hear him forcing himself to get calm, get professional. "Go to, ah, full-surround shields, max aft-enhanced, at first of any three events: call of Mark One plus five, *or* engine stop plus five, *or* call of Mark Two. Received and understood."

Sayad understood the point of the complicated order. The impact was going to be almost unimaginably violent. With that much energy blasting out so close by, lots of things could easily go wrong. This way, if the intercom blew, or the repeater displays went out, or Koffield was killed before he could give the order, the shields would still come up. She was glad Koffield had ordered repeat and confirm. They all needed Sheelton to get this one right.

"Very good, defense systems. All hands, stand by. Any impact estimate update, Sayad?"

"Estimate still holds. Now ten to fifteen."

"Conn, defense systems," Koffield called out. "Stand by for my commands. Let's get this one right, ladies and gentlemen."

Koffield leaned in close, his face next to hers, and stared hard at the displays, watching the numbers change, the projections adjust, the variables shift. If he called his commands too soon, they would lose priceless seconds of escape acceleration time, and the electromagnetic shields might fail before the blast wave had expanded out past the ship. Call them too late, and the radiation and blast debris could catch them with the shields not yet activated and up to power.

"Verbal time in seconds to and past first estimate," he ordered, not taking his eyes off the patch of screen that showed the visible estimate.

"Impact first possible in eleven seconds," Sayad said "Ten. Nine. Eight. Seven. Six. Five—*It'll take more than five seconds for the engines to stop and the shields to come on,* she thought. *He's gambling on a late impact.* She kept up the count, keeping her voice steady, calm. Just say the words. "Four. Three. Two. One—"

"Conn, Mark One, all engines emergency stop and safe! Now, now, now!"

But the engines were dying before he was even done speaking the word *Mark,* the ship's frame shuddering and vibrating anew as the stresses rearranged themselves.

"Zero. Impact now possible. Plus one second. Two. Three. Four. Five."

"Engines all stopped and safed!" came the call from the conn.

"Defense systems—Mark Two! Mark Two! Shield full, max aft, now, now, now!"

And the lights dimmed and throbbed as the shields grabbed greedily at all the ship's power they could take. Sayad's screens flickered and distorted for a moment as the electromagnetic shielding pulsed up. Then her displays cleared, steadied. Sayad tried to hold herself steady as well. "Six," she intoned. Steady. Professional. "Seven. Impact detected."

But she didn't need to say that, no, not at all. A flare of light bloomed out in the darkness, blinding the *Upholder's* sensors once again.

"Shields at seventy percent. Eighty. Ninety. Ninety-five. Ninety-eight. Stability flicker."

"Hold at stable point!" Koffield called. The lights dimmed again, and the ship's fabric moaned and creaked as the shields took hold, wrapping a thick, clumsy wall of electromagnetic energy around her.

"Dropping to stable point. Holding at ninety-seven-point-five."

"Hang on!" someone on the bridge shouted needlessly. No one in the compartment was giving any thought at all to anything *besides* holding on.

The first radiation pulse had passed them with the light of the explosion, but the slower, heavier, more deadly radiation would be just a trifle behind it. The shields *ought* to be able to handle the heavy particles. But they would have to hold long enough to protect the ship from the larger debris, from the bits and pieces the size of molecules to dust particles to shrapnel to fist-sized chunks of metal. The debris moved slower than the radiation, but was still coming at them fast, far faster than rifle fire.

"Estimate, time until front of blast wave arrival!" Koffield called.

"Sensors blanked, sir. No current data." How hard had the intruder hit the scattershot? What was the closing rate and angle? She could have read all that off the lightblast, given time and sufficient data. But not in half a second, and not with her detectors blanked.

"Estimate and count to and past first possible moment, based on last data."

"Estimate first possible, twenty seconds. Nineteen. Eighteen—"

"Five-second interval," said Koffield, almost snappishly. "Hell of a time to go blind." He gave up staring at the displays. Old data could tell him nothing new.

"Defense systems!" he called. "Shield status, projected duration."

"Shields at stable point, drifting down to ninety-seven percent. They're taking a good peppering from the heavy particles, but holding stable. Projected remaining duration, twenty seconds."

"Fifteen seconds to first possible blast wave contact," Sayad announced.

Close. Damnably close. The shields would start to die just as the cloud of blast debris swept past them. There was not time enough to stop and restart the shields. It would be suicide to try, anyway. The heavy particles still streaming past would be enough to give them fatal doses of radiation sickness. Sayad could almost imagine that she could hear, feel, the heavy particles pinging off the electromag shields. But that was nonsense, of course.

"All emergency power to shields," Koffield ordered. Not that there would be much power not diverted to them already. Simply to function at all, the electromags needed nearly all of the *Upholder*'s power output.

But the bridge lighting dimmed by half. The ventilators cut off. The ship's ArtInts were stealing whatever little dribs and drabs of power they could from other systems. If the trivial amounts of power the ArtInts were stealing were what made the difference, then their chances of survival were very slim indeed. But there was nothing they could do but watch their boards and make their time reports.

"Fifteen seconds shield duration remaining. Shields at ninety-five percent," Sayad reported.

"Ten seconds to first possible impact."

And the bridge went silent with waiting. Time had been dragging before, but now it seemed to have ground to a complete halt. How long since that first blast of light through the wormhole? Five minutes? Ten? An hour? A day? Any answer seemed possible. It was as if time no longer had any real relation to the clock numbers that were beating down on them.

"Ten seconds of shields. Shield decay rate increasing. Shields at ninety-two."

"First possible impact in five seconds. Four. Three. Two. One. Ze—"

And it came down on them, a half heartbeat early. The ship lurched violently to one side, the shields holding, but only just, as the first wall of debris ripped past, hitting the shields a dozen times, a hundred times, in the space of a second. The ship fell into a violent tumble, pinwheeling across space. The shields weakened under the drumbeat of blast debris tearing into them, but still they held, diverting, deflecting, slowing the impacts. Something tore off a stanchion and crashed into the floor. The lights died, and alarms began to scream. Then came the horrifying, echoing bangs of impacts directly on the hull as debris penetrated.

In the darkness came the shriek of tortured metal, the sudden, terrifying first drop in pressure, the sudden cold feel of air being sucked away that told of a hull breach somewhere not far off. Death and terror seemed on all sides of Sayad in the lightless compartment. Another shriek of torn metal, another hull breach, and then—

The rest was dark and silence.

It was not until hours later, until the damage-control crews had sealed the hull breaches, until power was restored, until the ship's tumble was slowed and then stopped, that Captain Anton Koffield even had time to realize that Ensign Alaxi Sayad was among the dead.

He could read the story off the gouges cut out of his ship's bridge. A ricocheting piece of debris, a wedge-shaped piece of the intruder, a full ten centimeters long, had torn through the hull and bounced around the bridge interior, caroming a half dozen times off the decks and bulkheads before zeroing in on Sayad. It had caught her in the side of the head, stabbed deep into her skull. Death had come to her in the darkness, and in an instant.

It was not until later still, until thirty hours after the attack, after the initial repairs were complete, and he was sitting in the galley, staring blankly down at a stone-cold meal he could not force himself to eat, and could not remember preparing or ordering, that he realized how close that fragment had come to him. His head had been less than half a meter from Sayad's when that fragment had torn through the hull and into the bridge compartment. It so easily could have, should have, been him who was killed.

It took scarcely any imagination at all for Captain Anton Koffield to know there would be times without number to come when he would wish, most devoutly, that it *had* been him.

CHAPTER TWO
THE FOG OF TIME

Seven days after the attack, Anton Koffield sat in his working cabin, examining the ship's department reports with a certain degree of gloomy satisfaction. Things were getting back together. Life aboard the *Upholder* had returned to a grim version of normality. The hulls were patched, and the last of the "emergency" and "urgent" repairs were complete. Navigation, propulsion, defense, life support, and detection were all reported as operational again, though relying on backup systems in some cases.

Some damage could not be repaired until and unless the *Upholder* reached port, if she ever did. But there were still a thousand doable fixes to be made all over the ship, most of them minor things that could be done almost at leisure. Koffield was in a way glad of all those dents and dings and blown circuit breakers and minor breakages that needed attention. Work kept the crew occupied, kept them from brooding on the ship's near-dire circumstances.

Services had been said over the fallen, and the dead were all safely out of sight, the six coffins in cold storage, deep in the hold of the ship. Captain Koffield had briefly considered burial in space, but it had taken very little time for him to conclude it would be very bad for morale. Normally, a burial in space happened in the emptiness between the stars, out where the dead were truly consigned to the infinite and the empty. Inside a star system, however, spaceside burials were always targeted so the coffin and corpse would burn up in a planetary atmosphere or impact into the star itself, vaporizing instantly. That was clean, and quick.

But neither choice was possible in orbit of a wormhole. Given the *Upholder*'s circumstances, the dead would either have to be left in orbit around the wormhole, where the tracking team would be forced to monitor the movements of their dead comrades, for fear of their becoming traffic hazards, or else the bodies would have to be targeted to impact on the wormhole, and be absorbed by it. But it was the wormhole that had killed everyone aboard the *Standfast*, and destroyed the ship as well. It was bad enough that the crew could regard the wormhole, the thing they were there to guard, as a killer. Koffield did not want their thoughts moving in that direction. Giving them cause to think of the wormhole as a graveyard as well could hardly help matters. Better the dead remain aboard, awaiting a better time and place to be consigned to the dark and the deep. He had no doubt that the *Upholder*'s dead would be as eager as the survivors to get far, far away from Circum Central Waypoint.

In point of fact, Circum Central Waypoint was not central to anything, nor on any transit circuit. It had a grand sounding name, but Circum Central was no Thor's Realm, no Sirius Power Cluster Farm, with a dozen wormholes cross-linking thirty worlds. All Circum Central handled was the traffic for, and the traffic between, the new, small, and unimportant planets of Solace and Glister. There was not much traffic to handle. Circum Central wasn't even, properly speaking, a wormhole farm. It was a singleton post, with but a single timeshaft wormhole. Whoever had built it, long ago, had named it for expectations of wealth and growth and prosperity that had never been realized, rather than as an honest description of what it was.

But that was before the attack. What was Circum Central *now*? The scene of an invasion? But who was invading, and why? What had the intruders been after? He shoved his report pads to one side and stared sightlessly at the blank bulkhead that faced his desk.

It made no sense. No sense of any kind. Why raid a timeshaft from the *past* in an attempt to reach the *future*?

Settled Space was full of cryo-equipped ships that could simply *wait*, cruising through interstellar space as time passed. For that matter, there wasn't any need for cryosleep. The intruder ships had clearly been robotic. If they had needed to reach the future, all they had to do was put themselves in storage for seventy-nine years. Why attack a wormhole and lose ninety-plus percent of your force in a needless attack? What had it all been in aid of?

He had gone over it in his mind a hundred times, and still could see no explanation.

And what of those acceleration rates they had recorded? The intruders had put on speed at utterly incredible rates, and had at least *appeared* to reach the speed of light, vanishing off the detectors as they did so, as if they had just blown through light-speed and kept going, moving so fast the trackers couldn't even see them. But faster-than-light travel was impossible. Three thousand–plus years of space travel had taught humanity that much. Was that assumption wrong? Or were they misreading the data, seeing something that wasn't there, while missing things that were?

The door comm blipped, and Koffield pressed down the stud on his desk that opened the door, glad of the interruption. It was Lieutenant Sheelton, the defense systems officer, though today he was handling comm duties. Because Chronologic Patrol ships were deliberately designed to allow precious little communications, the standard patrol ships did not even carry full-time comm officers, but instead swapped the duty around the other departments.

But at the moment the *Upholder* had a great deal to communicate, and sending her messages, despite the complexities and difficulties, was a top priority.

"What have you got for me, Sheelton?" Koffield asked as he stood up. He returned Sheelton's nervous salute and gestured for him to come forward into the compartment. Koffield forced himself to smile, and forced the smile to look pleasant, sincere. Koffield knew he could not afford to let any member of the crew note his own worries, his own anxieties. He had to create and maintain the illusion that he was calm and confident. He knew damned well that if he crumbled, morale would plummet. And morale was dangerously low to begin with.

"Well, ah, good news, I think, sir," Sheelton replied, proffering a report pad. Koffield took the pad and sat back down behind his desk. He activated the pad and started to examine it before he glanced up and saw Sheelton still standing there. "At ease and take a chair, son."

"Thank you, sir," Sheelton said.

Koffield nodded absently as he scrolled and paged through the report pad's display. "Four serviceable courier drones?" he asked. "That's all we can manage?"

"We're lucky to get that many," said Sheelton. "I thought for sure we'd lost all eight drones when we did the first after action survey. The drone storage bay got hit hard in the last wave of impacts, sir, and that compartment took a big part of the electromagnetic pulse when the shields burned out. Sorry, sir."

Koffield didn't understand the apology at first—but then he made the connection. Sheelton had been operating the shields during the attack. He looked the young officer straight in the eye. "Sorry for what?" he asked. "Because the shields couldn't absorb and disperse ten times the energy and impact stress they were rated to take? The shields *saved* this ship, and everyone aboard her. I suggest you remember that, Lieutenant."

"Ah, yes, sir. I will."

"Let's get back to the couriers. You report four serviceable drones, assembled by cannibalizing the eight wrecks and by dipping into spare parts. How far into this will I have to read to find how serviceable 'serviceable' is?"

"I can tell you that right off, sir. You've got two courier drones that meet all specs and certificates, full backups to all systems. And you've two others that work, but with a few subsystems that are running without backup, or where main and backup systems are both a little chancy. They'd probably do fine on a routine flight—but, well sir, I can't promise you the couriers will *have* routine flights."

Koffield nodded thoughtfully. Considering how badly the *Upholder* had been chewed up, he was probably lucky to get one good drone, let alone two good and two fair. "Very well," he said. "Prepare to send all four of them out, at twenty-four-hour intervals. The first we'll release on this side of the wormhole, with the fullest possible documentation of the attack. Send all our data, copies of the ship's automatic and manual logs, everything. Use the better of the two substandard drones. Then send the other three downtime through the wormhole, into the past, with *nothing*, and I mean *nothing*, more than the allowed operational-rules data. We send to the past only what came to us *from* the past. That means recordings of the telemetry and other data we received from the *Standfast*, and nothing else. We do *not* send analysis, or narrative, or calls for help. Just the *Standfast* data playback. We clear on that?"

"Ah, yes, sir. But given how bad this was—"

"No!" Koffield cut him off. "No matter how bad it was, especially *because* it was so bad, we do it *by the book*. Our job here is to *defend* causality, prevent paradox, protect history from anyone or anything that might try and use the timeshaft wormholes to alter the past or the future. We can't do that if we start out by *violating* causality ourselves. I'm sure everyone on this ship has checked the operational rules by now. They allow us to send data from the past back into the past, and nothing else."

"Yes, sir," Sheelton said again, this time with a bit more spirit.

"Very well." Koffield didn't like explaining his orders, but he was no fool. Everything had turned upside down for this crew. Nothing like this assault had ever happened in all the long history of the Chronologic Patrol. There were going to be people in this crew scared enough, shocked enough, that they might try and convince themselves it would be all right to bend the rules. He did not dare let that idea take root. Knowing the rules still applied, that the captain meant what he said—that would help hold them together. "In any event, I don't think the drones will need to carry much more than the *Standfast*'s telemetry," he said in a more gentle tone of voice. "When the folks back home see the attack on the *Standfast*, they'll send every kind of support and reinforcement they can.

What more could any of us say that would make them send more than that?"

"Yes, sir," Sheelton said. "I hadn't thought of it that way."

No, Koffield thought, looking at the young man, and straining not to reveal how old, how worn, he himself felt. *You didn't think of it that way. And it hasn't really dawned on you, or on anyone else, that we're never going home. What happens when you realize that?*

The whole system of defense around a timeshaft wormhole was based on the uptime ship, the ship on the "future" end of the wormhole, being *in* the future, but not *of* the future. The uptime ship had no contact, no link, no knowledge of the uptime universe, or of the history of the years between the uptime and downtime ends. That willful ignorance ensured that the uptime ship had no hidden agendas, could not knowingly or otherwise exchange information with incoming ships, could not be suspected of manipulating events and passing the information to someone on the downtime side. A ship that arrived at the uptime guard post from the uptime universe would be utterly contaminated with all sorts of knowledge of the future, as seen from the downtime end.

But a patrol ship and crew that arrived at the downtime end and moved through the wormhole to the uptime guard post, and followed all the safeguards against receiving contaminated knowledge, could remain safely ignorant of the future during her tour of duty, and then withdraw back through the wormhole and go back home to the past, because her crew would know nothing of the future.

It was precisely because the *Upholder* had come from the past, and had prior contact only with the past, that the operational rules permitted her to send a courier drone bearing a sharply restricted report on downtime events. If the *Upholder* had been an uptime ship, even that limited contact would have been forbidden.

But the *Upholder* had seen the future and had acted to change it. She had become part of the future. By the act of doing her duty, she had been contaminated with information that could not go into the past, for fear of scrambling causality. Therefore, the ship could not return to the past, any more than she could send word of what had happened.

"Keep me informed of progress," Koffield said.

"Yes, sir." Sheelton shifted uncertainly in his seat, but did not stand up. "Sir, there is one other matter . . ."

"What, Lieutenant?"

"Well, sir—The intruders moved uptime through the timeshaft wormhole, instead of just waiting for seventy-nine years to pass."

Koffield smiled sadly. "That one I can't help you with, Lieutenant. I can't figure it out either."

"No, sir, that's not it. I mean, I think I *have* figured it out."

Koffield looked at Sheelton in surprise, and then damned himself for a fool. Why assume that he had the only—or the best—mind on the ship? "Go ahead, Mister. Tell me."

"Well, sir, the intruders had the portal nexi codes, or knew how to get around them. That gave them the *ability* to go through the hole. But why would they *want* to go through the hole, if they didn't need to do any time travel?"

"That's the question, all right," Koffield said. "I'd gotten that far by myself. Is there anything more?"

Sheelton reddened visibly. "Ah, yes, sir. I wouldn't waste your time if that was all I had. What if it wasn't travel—space travel, time travel, whatever—that they were interested in? What if it was the *wormhole* they cared about?"

That notion hadn't occurred to Koffield, but now the thought made his insides freeze. Now he could see what Sheelton was after, and he cursed himself again, for blindness far worse than his arrogance. "Go on," he said.

"A calibration run, sir. The only way to get exact, perfect data on a wormhole is to go through it, measure all the dynamics, and measure your exact temporal and spatial coordinates at either end. The *exact* data, down to the nanosecond and the micrometer."

Koffield nodded, still half in shock. Sheelton was right. It made sense. It was the only possible reason for making an uptime run through a wormhole. "Thank—thank you,

Lieutenant. That's a startling thought. But I do believe you're right. I do believe you're right."

"Thank *you,* sir," Sheelton said, smiling broadly. He stood up and saluted again. "I'll get to work on the courier drones at once, sir."

Koffield absently acknowledged the salute with a nod, and stared at the closed hatch long after Sheelton had gone.

Calibration run. That had to be it. But if that was it, then there was a world of fresh trouble brewing. No one needed to measure down to the nano and the micro in order to travel through a wormhole. In the scale of an interstellar trip, being five or ten minutes off in time, or a few hundred kilometers off target in space, was less than trivial. The intruders would only need that sort of precision data if they were planning to *retune* the wormhole, reaim it, change it somehow.

Timeshaft wormholes—their creation, control, tuning, and operation—were the exclusive province of the Chronologic Patrol. Before the intruders' assault, Koffield would have rejected out of hand the notion of anyone's seizing control of a wormhole. The idea that any group of outsiders would, or could, interfere with the Chronologic Patrol's monopoly was absurd, impossible, on the face of it. But the intruders had done a half dozen impossible things already. Koffield was fully prepared to believe they could do one more.

But. If they had made the uptime run to obtain the calibration data, that meant they intended to *use* that data in some way. And that clearly implied something that scared the hell out of Anton Koffield. He was the master of a ship that was half-crippled, nearly derelict, and very definitely time-stranded after her *first* encounter with the intruders.

And if the intruders were planning to make use of that calibration data—then that meant the intruders were coming back.

"All right," Koffield said, walking the circle of the operation stations on the bridge. "That was good—but let's see if we can do better. We'll run the simulation again. Reset to startup status and cross-check."

There was a low murmur of voices as the bridge crew reset their boards and did their cross-checks. Not to put too fine a point on it, Koffield was lying when he called the results of the last drill "good," and he knew the crew knew it. But it wouldn't do to tell them their work was "good under the circumstances" or "as good as could be expected." It would not do to point out that, if the *Upholder* had been operating with a normal crew complement, and all systems in good repair and in operation, the results of the last hostile-encounter drill would have been bad enough to put the entire bridge crew on report. But with half the external detectors blasted away, with three of the four laser cannon still out of commission, and a shortage of ammunition for the mass accelerator, there wasn't much hope of nominal performance.

Koffield stopped at the patched-together detection control station, where Sayad had been posted—where Sayad had died. Able Crew Member Ander Chasov seemed to be trying to sit at attention in front of the detection station, or what was left of it.

There were two officially qualified and rated detection officers alive and fit for duty aboard the *Upholder,* and Chasov was not one of them. But the two surviving watch officers could not keep heel-and-toe watches forever, not without being worn down by exhaustion until they were of no use at all. Koffield had similar problems at other posts. He needed chair-warmers for the detection station and other positions, crew members who, even if not fully trained to deal with an emergency, could at least stand routine watches and summon the trained personnel if and when a real alert happened.

"At ease, Chasov," said Koffield. "Do your work, and don't worry quite so much about your posture."

"Yes, sir, Captain," Chasov replied, as he drew himself up straighter, if such a thing was possible.

Koffield allowed himself the luxury of a quiet sigh. Chasov was not exactly the most promising candidate for detection officer he had ever seen, but there were precious few alternate choices available at the moment. Koffield didn't even have enough warm bodies. He had personnel shortages at nearly every crucial position aboard ship. With a half dozen fatalities, and twice that many seriously injured, there were more holes to fill than bodies to fill them with. He was relying on half-trained or untrained crew in every department of the ship.

"All right," he said, turning his back on Chasov in hopes of getting the poor devil to relax a bit, "we're going to take it from the top. Or rather, you are. Lieutenant Sheelton, please be so kind as to take charge of the training session."

"Yes, sir," Sheelton said. "Very well, then. Hostile-contact detection drill. Ship's computer will generate random simulated hostile contact sometime within the next half hour. This time I want to see sharper handoffs and tighter communications. Commencing randomizer *now*."

Koffield took his chance to slip quietly off the bridge and make his way back to his office, feeling a mixed sense of relief and guilt at having escaped the endless practice sessions. Koffield had not the slightest idea if the training would do any good at all, for he had not the slightest idea what, if anything, they were likely to face. If Sheelton's logic held, and the intruders had indeed been on a calibration run, it only made sense that they would be coming back. But logic was merely one tool of reasoning. Maybe they had missed some vital link, some clue that would have led them to a completely different conclusion. Maybe there was no other clue they could have found, but they had still gotten it wrong.

Koffield's thoughts went back to Sayad, as they had a thousand times since the raid. She had worked miracles on the detection board before she had been killed, working the scant data with remarkable speed and skill. Finding the intruders' far-flung ships in the depths of space, and in the midst of battle, should have been all but impossible. And yet she had done it with preternatural ease. Koffield reached for a record pad, but then pulled his hand back. There was no point in reviewing the action logs from Sayad's station once again. He had done it a dozen times already, and they had told him all they were going to tell.

But that same data had told Sayad a great deal more.

She had spotted some underlying pattern, some frame-work, even in the first incomplete wisps of data, that had told her where to look.

What had she seen that everyone else had missed? What could she have told them, if she had lived?

There was no sense chasing those ghosts again. But neither was there anything more useful that he could do.

He had directed that all the repairs that could usefully be done, be done. He had juggled the crew assignments and assigned substitutes as best he could. Now he had to hang back and let the crew and officers do *their* work. Breathing down Chasov's neck had done no good, and Koffield doubted if that sort of close-in supervision would help elsewhere. It might well do little more than give the crew and officers more of a chance to see through the holes in his performance, in his pretense of being confident. He had no wish for the crew to discover how unnerved their captain truly was.

He forced all that from his mind and tried to come up with something else to worry about. He smiled to himself. Finding worries wasn't likely to be a problem for him for a long, long time.

But most of his worries came down to timing. The odds on all the courier drones getting through were not good. The drones had been kicked around pretty badly in the attack, and they were being sent on long and arduous journeys. However, the odds that at least one of them would make it through were excellent. Koffield found himself wishing, not for the first time, that he had sent more than one drone to a Chronologic Patrol base on the uptime side of the wormhole. His ship needed relief—devil take it, his ship needed *rescue.* But duty and logic had told him the same thing—it was more important that the people downtime get the word. It was the downtime side of the timeshaft wormhole that had been left unguarded by the destruction of the *Standfast,* and it was the primary mission of the Chronologic Patrol to guard the past from the future. The downtime side of the timeshaft took priority.

But still, relief might come from uptime or downtime,

and it would be all to the good if it arrived before the return of the intruders, or else—

Koffield chose not to contemplate the or-else until he had no choice.

Nor was it simply a race between relief and the intruders. There was another variable to be considered in the timing: the regular merchant traffic that was the main reason for the existence of the timeshaft wormholes in the first place. He might not know *when* legitimate merchant traffic would be coming through, but Koffield knew it would come.

No one at a timeshaft wormhole could ever know for sure when a ship might arrive. In the first place, the basic principle of information-denial in and of itself meant no ship guarding a timeshaft was authorized to know anything of events in the future—and that very definitely included ship schedules. Secondly, timeshaft ship schedules were notoriously unreliable in any event, especially concerning arrival at a timeshaft. The distances were so vast, and the travel times so long, that a navigation error of one part in a hundred million could easily translate into an arrival-time error of a month or two.

Koffield, therefore, could not know for certain when a ship might show up. But all the willful, determined effort to retain ignorance of the future could not keep Koffield, or any good portal-guard captain, from noting patterns in the schedule of ships' arrivals. And one pattern in particular of ships in transit had stood out from the general flow of craft that came and went through the Circum Central Wormhole.

Four times in a little more than a standard Earth year, at more or less regular intervals, a flotilla, a convoy, of five cargo ships had come through. Four times the same five ships had arrived on the same trajectory when headed downtime, and then on opposite trajectory when headed uptime. The ships all carried cargo modules on the outbound leg, and towed huge strap-on cryosleep chambers on the return trip. That in and of itself was unusual. Timeshaft-wormhole ships, dropships as they were often called, almost always traveled alone. Aside from that, five ships making four round-trips in less than an objective year represented a remarkable effort. Each trip involved dozens or even hundreds of years of wear and tear, measured in ship's time, and meant crews kept in expensive, potentially hazardous cryosleep for nearly all of every journey. Someone was making an all-out effort. Judging from their trajectories, it was almost impossible to avoid the conclusion that the five ships were out of Thor's Realm, and bound for Glister.

Koffield had done several tours of duty in intelligence analysis before managing to draw command of the *Upholder*. He could not help but interpret what he was seeing. He knew that conditions on Glister had been deteriorating for years before he had drawn command of the *Upholder*. The news had been full of accounts of ambitious plans to reinvigorate Glister's climate. There had been much discussion of the fact that any such effort would put a great strain on resources, because the great Oskar DeSilvo's terraforming of Solace was not yet complete, and that project was still a net consumer of terraforming material.

The five ships that came and went told Koffield that the Glister Reinvigoration project had not succeeded. They were, he was certain, relief and rescue ships, bringing in yet more equipment, more supplies. He knew that much by watching them on their return trips, towing the jumbo-sized cryosleep modules. Nothing but supplies going in, nothing but people coming out. That could only mean things were bad and looking to get worse on Glister.

And that fleet of five ships was due anytime. They might even be within normal detection range already—except the *Upholder*'s detection gear was barely functional even at restricted range.

A great deal could depend on who, or what, arrived first. Koffield devoutly wished that both uptime and downtime relief ships would come before any other craft approached the timeshaft wormhole. He could use all the help he could get in dealing with the situation. Better still, let his relief face things on their own. He would be delighted to be ordered off station and to receive authorization to limp toward the nearest Chronologic Patrol repair yard.

In the meantime, all he could do was prepare for attack, for battle, for further disaster. While so doing, he would continue praying most devoutly, to whatever gods might be available out in that middle of nowhere that was the Circum Central Wormhole Farm, for nothing at all to happen for as long as possible.

And so things stood for the next nineteen standard days. The *Upholder,* while by no means in anything like good repair, held together, and little by little, the thousand small repairs that had to be made got done, each one a tiny lift to morale. Even if the detection systems would never be what they once were, unless or until the ship got to a repair yard, getting hot water back into the enlisted quarters plumbing loop could not help but be a major lift to the spirits.

Space around the ship was utterly, endlessly empty. No word came through the signal portal from the downtime side of the wormhole. Either no relief had yet arrived, or else the relief ship was not able to communicate with the *Upholder.* Koffield ordered all the subsystems for the link to the uptime relay checked and rechecked. Everything seemed to be working, and the relay itself reported in as healthy and as sending and receiving normal test pulses with the downtime relay. If the systems checks and telemetry were to be believed, then they had a solid comm link all the way through the wormhole, but no one had yet linked in to the other end.

The detection section was not in good shape. The watch officers were still struggling to get the semitrained crew members, who had been drafted into the job, up to some sort of half-acceptable degree of competence. They were just about to the point where they could work a routine ship arrival without direct supervision, and that was all to the good. But by using untrained personnel, they were increasing the odds of missing the beacon on an incoming freighter. It certainly meant they would be more likely to miss any intruder or raider that was so inconsiderate as to fail to transmit a beacon signal.

There were times when Koffield thought the waiting, the worrying, would drive him around the bend. And there were times, such as when the repair crews got the bridge ventilation system back up to spec, that he thought he could see an end in sight. When they got the main thermal systems back under control, so the officers' quarters cabin air temperature didn't suddenly spike fifteen degrees higher one hour and then crash down almost to freezing the next, he felt sure they had passed their low point. The worst was over. They were going to hold together until relieved. They were going to be all right. But then he received the chief engineer's final report on the condition of the main propulsion system, and he knew their troubles were far from over.

Koffield also knew that the main part of his job at this point was to stay out of the crew's hair. Once he had made his decisions and given his orders, there was not a great deal of useful work that the captain could do. He was careful to make himself visible. He performed inspections, listened to his crew—but it was easy to overdo that sort of thing. He did not propose to breathe down their necks. He kept himself out of the way, and kept to himself. He did what he had always done when there was little to do but wait for a crisis to mature. He listened to his music, read his books, quietly, alone.

Throughout Koffield's career, it had seemed to him as if the crises always hit quite literally at the darkest hour, during ship's night. As a general rule, things happened at 0200 hours, not 1000 or 1900 hours. They happened when Koffield was sound asleep, or about to sit down to a meal that had already been postponed three times. For once, all such rules were broken.

It happened at 1107 hours, right in the middle of the dayside shift, with a well-fed and well-rested Captain Anton Koffield on the bridge and at the conn, and Lieutenant Jem Sentar, the ship's best detection officer, on duty.

"Signal incoming through wormhole link!" Sentar called out.

Koffield was out of the command chair, on his feet, and standing over Sentar, right where he had been when a piece of shrapnel had killed Sayad. He half-consciously moved back a step, even as he stared intently at the repaired display screens. Sure enough, there it was. "Identify," he ordered.

"Data packet from Chronologic Patrol vessel," Sentar reported.

Koffield nodded in agreement. It wasn't much, but there it was. A minimal arrival signal, a Chronologic Patrol identity pattern on blank signal packets. Aside from saying *Here we are,* they were sending null data, not even so much as the ship's name attached. Clearly whoever was on the other end was under strict orders to keep intertemporal-information exchange to a minimum. There had been more than enough in the way of temporal violations already. But no matter how little the signal told them, it was enough, more than enough. They weren't alone anymore. "Confirm signal," Koffield ordered.

"Rechecking—confirmed," Sentar said. "That's a Chrono-Patrol identity signal."

"Excellent. Good to have someone watching the back door. Send mirror-reply signal." A mirror reply was simply the received signal played backwards and beamed back to the sender. A mirror reply sent no new information, but served to confirm accurate receipt of the sender's signal.

"Mirror reply sent," Sentar said.

"Very well," Koffield acknowledged. He returned to his command chair, determined to hide his sense of relief as thoroughly as he had hidden his worries and fears. He wanted to cheer out loud and announce it at once on the ship's intercom, let the whole crew know there was something to celebrate. But he couldn't. He dared not encourage them to get their hopes up, or let their guard down. Too much could still go wrong. The news would spread around the ship fast enough, and the crew would be glad to hear it. That way of getting the news would be far more appropriate than what would be touched off by a jubilant shipwide announcement. He sat back down with as much of an air of calm routine as he could manage. "Lieutenant Sentar, log my order that the detection and comm officer is to alert me if and when we get a new signal from the downtime relay. If we get a ready-on-station signal, I want to know the moment it arrives."

"Understood, sir. I have logged the order."

An incredibly complicated sequence of events had just concluded with the relief ship's arrival, and the complex motions through time and space that had brought the relief ship to the downtime end of the Circum Central timeshaft as soon after the *Standfast* disaster as possible. It had taken centuries of travel time to make it happen, but the relief ship had arrived in under three weeks of objective time.

And all that time and effort had been taken simply to allow the relief ship to send the least information possible. She had signaled her arrival, but it might well be some time before she signaled that she was on station and ready for duty. Whatever ship it was, she had merely reported herself to be in useful range of the downtime relay. She still needed to perform a series of navigation checks, secure from cruise mode, rig for patrol. It was possible, even likely, that she had not yet roused all of her crew from cryosleep.

Koffield devoutly wished the on-station signal would come soon, before anything else could go wrong. He tried not to remind himself that wishing rarely made it so.

The duty shifts rotated around through a normal day of ship's routine, without any further contact from the downtime side of the wormhole. The *Upholder* watched and waited.

The second alert came just over twenty-six hours later, at 1311 hours the next day.

Chasov had just relieved Sentar at detection and comm duty when the traffic contact alert buzzed. Chasov turned pale for a second, then checked his boards and started analyzing the contact. "Incoming traffic, sir," he reported.

"Very well," Koffield said coolly, as if this were normal routine and not a potential crisis. "Keep me informed. Work the contact by the standard procedures." If the new downtime ship was not yet fully powered up, operational, and prepared for on-station duty, she might not be in position to receive clearances on the ships headed downtime. If they were a bit edgy or trigger-happy aboard the downtime ship, and were surprised by the convoy ships coming through, things could get messy indeed. And considering that the new ship was replacing a craft that had been reduced to subatomic particles, they might have good reason to be edgy.

Standard operating procedure called for Chasov to summon Sentar back. Chasov did not have to wait long for Sentar to scramble back onto the bridge. But there was little for Sentar to do, other than watch Chasov work the contact and watch him send the standard mirrors back to the convoy ships. Sentar looked inquiringly at Koffield, who remained in the command chair. Koffield shook his head no, very slightly. Let the boy work the contact. It was routine stuff, after all, and if uptime relief was slow in arriving, Chasov might well have to do the job on his own before too long, without any backstop. Live work was always the best training.

Chasov quickly interpreted the contact and put it on the main displays.

It was a beacon signal, or rather five beacon signals. The signals carried little more information than that, but the ships' heading told them more. They were inbound for Glister, coming in straight down the heading from Thor's Realm. It was plain to see it was the relief convoy, just about on schedule, and inward bound for Glister.

"Verbal report," Sentar ordered.

"Five beaconed merchant ships, inbound on standard heading for Glister," Chasov promptly replied.

"Distance and time, Crewman Chasov?" Sentar asked.

"Yes, sir. Estimated range one billion four hundred six million kilometers. Doppler ranging shows targets to be decelerating, rendering arrival time uncertain. Using comparison to recorded similar flight paths, I derive estimated time of arrival at timeshaft-wormhole final approach cone at ninety-three hours, fourteen minutes."

Sentar nodded in satisfaction, and Koffield allowed himself just the hint of a smile. If Chasov's report wasn't word-for-word out of the detection officer's training manual, it was awfully damned close.

"Very well," Sentar replied. "It would seem that we'll have something to look at for the next four days. So keep an eye on those freighters for us, Crewman Chasov."

"Yes, sir!" said Chasov. It was obvious how proud he was of doing his job, of spotting, tracking, and analyzing the detection data.

Koffield was scarcely less glad himself. If the *Upholder* hadn't been so badly damaged, he would have regarded that detection range as scandalously bad. As it was, he was more than pleased. It went beyond knowing one crewman had been trained well enough to do the most routine part of a detection officer's job. It meant that the ship as a whole had demonstrated her ability to perform at least part of her mission. Spotting ships coming in, and shepherding them through the wormhole, was normal, expected. The simple fact that the *Upholder* was back on the job was bound to do great things for morale—and shipboard morale could use all the help it could get.

If he was the only one worried that the downtime relief ship had only four days to declare herself on station and operational before the convoy came through, that was fine as well. He had no desire to wish that worry—or any of his other worries—on anyone.

The ships came on, moving toward the timeshaft wormhole, and for the next four days everything went by the book. The convoy's sealed Chronologic-Patrol-installed transponders sent all the proper authenticator codes to prove the ships had not sent or received any illegal communications during transit. The *Upholder* acknowledged, and ordered the ships to a standard approach. The convoy ships obediently shifted course, and set themselves up on the proper vector, beads on a string that led straight for the timeshaft wormhole. All routine, all normal.

Except there was still no further word from the down-time relief ship, nothing at all but silence. Standard operating procedure called for the relief to maintain silence after the initial send-and-mirror until she was on station and fully operational. What had happened to her? Had the relief ship been destroyed in some further disaster? Was it merely some minor communications glitch? Was she sending the on-station signal, while the *Upholder* was somehow failing to receive it? The comm people checked the primary and backup gear again and again, but never found anything wrong.

Koffield spent his off-duty hours in his cabin, brooding, worrying over it all. Two days after they had detected the convoy, he was sitting at his desk, reading an historical novel. He gave it up when he realized that he had just read the same passage over a half dozen times, and yet had no idea what it said. He shoved the datapage that held the book away and stared at the bulkhead opposite his desk.

He did not know what to do. He could order the convoy ships to cancel their approach and simply have them wait until the downtime ship sent the all clear. Or else he could let them continue their approach and send the clearance codes through the wormhole at the proper time, activate the nexi and send the ships through, and simply count on the downtime relief ship to handle her end of things.

But it wasn't that easy or that simple. Once he cleared the convoy ships to final approach, and they committed to entering the wormhole, there could be no turning back. Once a ship was on final approach, it was impossible to abort, impossible to come about and escape the singularity. A ship on final approach was falling like a stone toward the singularity, and there was nothing that anyone could do to stop the fall. She would either go through the timeshaft wormhole, or she would impact the singularity that generated the timeshaft.

Ordering the convoy ships to standby orbits seemed the most prudent course. But they were not ships laden with expensive trinkets or luxury goods. The scale of effort was too great for that, the ships coming and going too quickly for it to be anything other than an all-out relief—or even rescue—effort. Delay the ships a day, a week, a month, waiting for the downtime ship to end its silence, and there would, almost certainly, be people dying on Glister, waiting for the supplies the convoy was bringing. Better to risk the remote chance of the downtime ship taking a potshot at one of the ships before realizing her mistake, than go with the near certainty that slowing the ships would result in greater suffering and death.

Or was he pushing his guesses too far? He could not know for certain the convoy was even bound for Glister.

It was a maddening temptation to bypass all the safeties, to order the comm channels open, to send a voice message in clear to the downtime ship, asking what the devil was going on, to hail the convoy ships and ask what their mission was, and how urgent it was.

But to do either of those things would be to violate the very core of the Chronologic Patrol's mission, its reason for being. The convoy ships had followed all the procedures required to keep them from gaining knowledge of the future before they dropped back into the past. He could not betray their trust. That the *Upholder* had been contaminated with knowledge of events on the uptime side of the wormhole, events that the convoy ships and the downtime relief ship did not want to know about, did not matter. It was his mission to ensure that the past remained ignorant of the future, that time paradoxes of any sort did not arise. It was his job, his ship's job, to see to it that nothing, including his own knowledge of the situation, could reach back from the future and derange the past.

That was why the *Upholder* could never go back to her own time. She could not spread that curse of forbidden knowledge to the others. It was Anton Koffield's sworn duty to prevent any such thing from happening. He could not, dared not, try to make contact with any of the players in the drama.

And what of the uptime relief ship? Why hadn't she shown up yet? Had the one courier drone sent out on the uptime side of the timeshaft failed to get through? But it was clear that at least one of the couriers sent through the downtime side had made it. A time-sealed message should have been put in storage for seventy-nine years to let the uptime side know.

Unless.

Unless, somewhere in the seventy-nine years that stood between the downtime and uptime ends of the assault, they had learned something. Learned the answer to what the intruders were, and why they had come. Or learned there was no reason to relieve the *Upholder,* no purpose to be served by the effort of sending a ship. Maybe the people on the uptime side already knew all would be well—or already knew that disaster of some sort was foredoomed, that any attempt at rescue or relief would fail, and that there was no sense wasting more lives and treasure.

Or else there *was* no Chronologic Patrol anymore, on the upside of the timeshaft. Eight decades had passed, long enough time for things to change, to evolve or collapse.

Or else—

Hell and damnation! He stood up and began to pace the length of his cabin—something he would never allow his crew to see him doing. There was no end to the *or-elses,* the *what-ifs.* He could speculate until the end of time itself and it would do him no good.

Time itself was the problem. He was caught up in the tangled complexities needed to prevent paradoxes. That irony was far from lost on him.

His ship was lost in the fog of time, hemmed in by the hidden past and the unknowable future. He and his ship and her crew were marooned on a tiny island of present and known events, but cut off from all other knowledge by the endless expanse of the ocean of years.

He might as well head back up to the bridge and see if anything had happened. It was pointless, of course. The bridge crew would have summoned him if anything had. But there were limits to how long he could stay in that cabin. Besides, if he were on the bridge when things happened, he would know about them that little bit sooner.

He stepped out of his cabin and headed toward the bridge, his mind still chasing the problem around and around. Even in the midst of so much uncertainty, there were things of which he was absolutely positive. He had no logical or factual basis for the knowledge, but still it was there, solid and hard. He was utterly sure that, when the time to decide finally came, he would know no more than he did right now.

And he knew, deep in his heart, deep in his bones, that no uptime relief ship would come.

The *Upholder* was on her own.

Of that there was not the slightest doubt at all.

CHAPTER THREE

LOST TO THE PAST

Time ground down on them.

Nothing changed but the time left until the convoy ships would commit to final approach. There was no further word from the downtime relief ship, and no sign whatsoever of an uptime relief ship.

Nor was there any sign of the intruders, or any clue as to who or what they might be. Koffield checked over every record of events since the first intruder alert and studied all the tracks and contacts and reports and false alarms from detection and comm as they came in. But it did no good, told him nothing he did not already know. There was no brilliant, long-overlooked answer to this problem, no sudden insight.

Koffield made sure to be on the bridge well before final-approach commitment for the first of the convoy ships. Three hours before the last moment when he could order an abort, he was in the captain's chair, hunched over its repeater displays, monitoring the situation.

He had to choose, but none of his possible choices was good. Again and again, the conundrum wheeled through his mind. If he ordered the convoy to hold on this side of the wormhole, he would likely be causing further casualties and suffering in the Glister system. If he let the ships through before the downtime patrol ship signaled that she was ready on station and ready to receive clearance codes, there was at least some danger that a nervous downtime ship would fire on the convoy. And even if he lost his nerve and tried to make unauthorized communications with convoy or patrol ship, it was all but certain the other ships would refuse the contact anyway.

Koffield knew perfectly well that the act of not deciding was a decision in and of itself. With every second that passed, the convoy ships got deeper into the wormhole gravity well. With every moment that passed, more thrust would be required for the ships to break free, and there would be less time to apply that thrust. The maneuver that was needed to abort from final approach would grow more violent and difficult with every moment that passed. In the last few moments before final-approach commitment, any potential abort maneuver would be so violent that it would likely wreck any ship that tried it.

With every passing moment, the simple fact that he had not yet ordered the convoy to bail out put more pressure on him to let them pass. If he ordered a bailout too late, he would be issuing death sentences for all aboard the convoy, and therefore might as well let them through to try their luck on the other side. There would come a moment when he would have decided by default, by *not* deciding.

But Captain Anton Koffield did not like the idea of letting things slide, of letting things drift, or allowing decisions to make themselves. He came out of his reverie and looked about him, at the bridge crew, tending to the stations and monitoring the incoming ships, at the silent comm systems, at the *Upholder* herself. They had all done their jobs. Now it was time for him to do his. He had to decide—and deciding was not going to be that hard. He would make his choice—and then hope.

He allowed himself one last scan of the repeater displays, and then spoke. "Comm, the five incoming ships have full and final clearance to enter the timeshaft wormhole. Transmit the appropriate signals. Execute and acknowledge."

"Aye sir," the comm officer replied. "Clearances transmitted. Standing by for mirror replies." There was a brief pause as the comm officer watched his screens. "Mirror replies received."

"Very well," Koffield replied, and leaned back just a trifle in the captain's chair. That was that. He had decided, as best he could, based on the information he had, and acted on his decision. He could do no better, and no more.

No more except wait, and watch.

The last hours of the convoy's approach passed without incident. Koffield remained on the bridge more out of a sense of duty than out of need. But endlessly watching nothing at all happen seemed a waste of valuable time. Koffield occupied himself with calling up his own personal work on his main repeater display. He caught up on the endless routine items that had gotten stacked up and shoved to one side since the intruders' attack: repair reports, inventory updates, duty roster changes, and the like. It felt good to work through the routine, normal stuff, to pretend, if only for a little while, that everything was the way it was supposed to be.

Koffield looked up from his work after a time and wondered, not for the first time, if the crew was pretending at normality as hard as he was. More than likely they were. They were not fools. They had, no doubt, worked out the logic of the situation, just as he had. Some of them, most of them, maybe even all of them, knew they were never going home, that the only things now left to them were duty and, if possible, survival. The Chronologic Patrol would take care of them—the CP always took care of its own—but even if the CP was generous beyond all imagination, it could not give them back their homes and families. And the crew knew that.

What scenes had played out, away from his view? Bull sessions in the mess compartment? Heated arguments in the bunk rooms? What had his officers wisely kept from his attention, knowing he would be forced to obey regulations and mete out punishments that could do no good to anyone out here? Koffield knew there could be no justice, no logic, no merit in punishing the crew for feeling the same terror he felt himself, terror that was entirely justified and rational. So long as the fear was kept in check, and his people did their duty, he would gladly turn a blind eye to trivia and trust his officers to bring him word only of things he truly needed to know.

Just let them all get through this. Let everything stay on an even keel until the convoy was through, and then—

"Captain, I'm getting something strange on long-range detectors," Sentar, the detection officer, called out.

"What is it?" Koffield demanded, snapping out of his reverie.

"It looks like a fast-moving gamma-ray source, real close in, but that doesn't make any sense."

And Koffield knew. There was no doubt at all in his mind. He had no proof, no evidence at all, but still he was certain, unshakably so.

"Moving toward what?" he asked, knowing full well what the answer would be.

"Still getting a vector—it's—it's headed straight for the wormhole."

Of course. Where else would it be going? "Look for others," he said wearily. "There will be two others, probably coming in on widely dispersed vectors, driving for the wormhole." *Of course they would come back. And of course they would come back now.*

The convoy. Whatever happened next, those ships had to get clear. "Communications! Flash alert to all convoy ships—abort, abort, abort. Cancel final-approach clearance. Break off approach and take up parking orbits. Send that in clear over all voice and data channels."

"Two more gamma-ray sources incoming!" the detection officer shouted. "Correction—three, four, five, *six* total sources incoming. All decelerating at extremely high rates, bearing in toward the wormhole from widely scattered vectors. All match profiles of the intruder ships that killed the *Standfast.*"

Six of them. The original three survivors must have had some way of building copies of themselves, or maybe each of the original intruders had been a docked pair of duplicate ships that was now split up. Or else three of the incoming intruders were some sort of decoy—or else there was some other explanation that Koffield was missing.

Whatever it was didn't matter. What mattered was that six intruder ships were there, and heading for the wormhole, and they could not be allowed to break through into the past, no matter what the cost.

"Battle alert," Koffield said, his voice flat and cold. "All personnel to battle stations. Weapons, what are our present options for attack on the intruders?"

Amerstad was working the weapons panel. "None, sir," she said, an apology in her voice, if not in her words. "They're too far out of range and moving too fast for us to hit. Even if our weapons systems were fully operational, we wouldn't be able to hit them."

"Will we have a shot if they decelerate to more or less normal velocity closer in to the wormhole?"

"Possibly," said Amerstad, studying her displays as she spoke. "We *might* be able to get a targeting solution with the laser cannon. But I doubt we'd be able to get off any sort of shot at all with the railgun. Even if we could, we'd have friendly-fire problems with the convoy ships."

"Can you give me meaningful odds on our chances of destroying some or all of the intruders?"

"Very roughly, fifty-fifty odds we can score a hit on one of them. Maybe one in ten that we could score hits on multiple targets. Odds on hitting and destroying all of them—I'm sorry, sir. Far less than one percent. Maybe one chance in ten thousand we could do it. Maybe a lot worse than that."

Koffield nodded to himself. Those were the answers he had expected. And those answers told him something else he had already known, deep in his soul. Defeat was all that was left to them. A defeat so vast, so complete, that it was terrifying to do so much as contemplate it. A defeat that would trade victory over the intruders for incalculably greater losses.

For Captain Anton Koffield still had one last weapon, one that was still undamaged, one that he could still use against the faceless and ineffable intruders. A weapon that had never been used, and scarcely ever discussed, in all the long history of the Chronologic Patrol.

"Very well, then," Koffield said. "If we can't shoot down the intruders, I don't see that I have any choice. I'm going to blow the wormhole shut."

The bridge went quiet, as silent as space.

"Our mission," he said, "the *sole* mission of the Chronologic Patrol, is to defend time. All of our wildly elaborate precautions, all of our careful procedures, exist for that reason alone. We are here to keep the future from interfering with the past, to protect causality from paradox. Those intruder ships have spent weeks in their own future. I suspect they may even be capable of faster-than-light travel, though I have no idea how that could be. There is no end to what they could have learned of past events in all that time.

"Now they are driving for the wormhole, and there is no realistic chance of our destroying all of them before they reach it. They waited until there was a convoy coming through, so that we would be occupied with other matters and, they hoped, less willing to put legitimate ships at risk. They sent in six ships at once in an envelopment maneuver, so as to overwhelm our defensive ability. They are plainly attempting to do what we are here to stop. And we will stop it."

The bridge was silent for five seconds, perhaps longer, before anyone had the nerve to speak. "Sir?" It was Sheelton, sitting at the comm station.

"Yes, Sheelton?"

"Sir, if we blow the wormhole shut, it can never be opened again! There's another hole, six lights the other side of Lodestar, that serves Solace, but Glister will be all but cut off from the outside universe. And the convoy ships will be stranded here, as cut off—"

"As cut off from the past as we will be—as cut off as we are already." *Why not admit it now?* he asked himself. "I am aware of the consequences, Lieutenant Sheelton."

"But, sir—"

"I'm sorry," said Koffield. "But I don't see any other option for us. The people on those convoy ships will suffer, perhaps die. The people of Glister will suffer. But the damage and chaos that these intruders could create, throughout all of Settled Space, would be far worse. Think of all the horror stories and nightmares we were trained on. They could go back in time and kill the parents or grandparents of important leaders. They could bring back stolen inventions, take advantage of market panics—or know how to cause panics they could then take advantage of. They could prevent the discovery of whole worlds, or claim-jump worlds no one has yet found. They could be bringing back anything from unknown technology to mutant viruses. We have to stop them."

"Captain, surely we need time to think it through, call a ship's council—"

"There is no time," Koffield said, and smiled at that irony. No time at all to consider how to guard time. "No time to call a council or consider the situation. We must act now, or let the enemy pass. Let the log reflect that this was my decision, and mine alone."

Again, the bridge was silent. Koffield let the moment last as long as he could. This was the moment to protest. No one spoke, no one argued or called out, and the silence became acceptance.

"Comm—any response from convoy ships?"

Sheelton swallowed nervously. "Mirror response from the lead ship, Captain. No other replies. No changes in course or heading as of yet."

"Keep me advised. Weapons—are we going to have *any* sort of firing solution?"

"The intruders' deceleration is so violent I can't get a good forward projection yet, sir. But we ought to be able to take a shot at one of them at least."

"Weapons, take full helm control. Do what you can to optimize your firing solutions."

"Aye sir."

Koffield flipped the comm, detection, and weapons displays onto his repeater screens and gave a moment's concentrated study to each, but saw nothing that his officers had not told him already. He relegated them to background displays and brought up the wormhole control interface. There were six layers of security clearance to get through before it was even possible to get the control screen up. The security mask rose up out of the arm of the command chair, and he set his face into its rounded black scanface. A pinprick on the side of his jaw for the blood-drop DNA and drug scan, a whiskery caress as the brainscan contacts worked under his thinning hair to rest on his scalp. A brief dazzle of light for the retinal scan. He wrapped his hands around the rounded exterior of the mask and let the finger- and hand-print scanners do their work. A tiny hidden ArtInt-driven speaker whispered intimate questions in his ear, and the voice systems listened, not just to the correctness of his answers, but to the stress levels in his voice and, of course, to his voiceprint as well.

It took less than a minute to satisfy the artificial-intelligence systems and the automatic machines that he was Anton Koffield, that he was sane, that he was not under the influence of any drug, and that he was not acting under duress. But it seemed infinitely longer than that. The wait seemed endless, but at last the mask's interior display flashed the words *cleared and approved*.

Anton Koffield pulled the mask away from his face—and was greeted by the sight of every single person on the bridge staring at him, watching him. "Return to your work," he said quietly, and they turned back to the screens and displays full of information that would do them no good. The security mask retreated back into its storage niche, and Koffield found himself wishing that he too had someplace to hide.

The privacy screens rose up around Koffield's displays, shielding them from anyone else's sight.

Koffield brought up the portal nexi status display. All systems functional, all security features up and running. For half a heartbeat, Koffield toyed with the tempting idea that the security locks might stop the intruders. But the intruders had already demonstrated their ability to get past the security controls. If they could force their way from downtime to uptime, he had to assume they could travel in the other direction.

There was nothing else he could do, other than shut down every single nexus, completely and irrevocably.

The timing. The timing of the thing. That was all he had left, the only thing he had a choice about.

He checked the convoy's status. All five ships were still on course for the timeshaft. The absolute theoretical point of no return for an ideal ship appeared as a red line on the display. Even as he watched, the first transport in line, the vehicle that the ArtInts had labeled Ship One, crossed it and redlined. Koffield cursed silently.

He could not blame that ship, at least, for disregarding his commands. He would not care to abort as close to the absolute line, even in the newest, most agile, most powerful, and most heavily armored ship—and the convoy ships were far from being any of those things. Ship One—indeed any or all of the ships—might well have passed their own structural redlines long before. Ordering them to abort as late as he had left the ships with nothing but bad choices. They could risk the run through the timeshaft in spite of Koffield's command or have their ships torn apart in doomed attempts to escape the wormhole's gravity well and reach parking orbits. Ship One had told him which choice she had made, by sending a mirror reply and continuing her run.

"Comm! Send the flash alert abort to all ships in the convoy again."

"I've been sending it on constant repeat, Captain. Stand by. Mirror response from Ship Five, the last in line. Additional response from Five, sir. Text message—'Will attempt to comply.' Stand by. Getting similar messages from Ships Two, Three, and Four. No further reply from Ship One."

"Very well," Koffield said, the automatic reply coming to his lips. But precious little was going well. The first ship was heading in, and now nothing could stop her. Perhaps there was still a way for her to survive. But he would have to be ready to shut the wormhole nexi down at precisely the right moment.

He activated the nexus control system and set to work getting through the deliberately long and complicated job of satisfying its security, an entirely separate system from the one he had just cleared. It would have been painstaking work under the best of circumstances, and these circumstances were far from the best.

The security ArtInt on the nexus control system concerned itself with questions of situation, rather than identity. It took a data handoff from the access security system, and thus satisfied itself that Koffield was Koffield and had the right and power to do what he wanted to do. The nexus ArtInt's job was to consider the situation Koffield faced and the regulations concerning the situation. It was a passive control system. The ArtInt could not take any action itself, or even suggest any course of action. It could do nothing but determine if whatever Koffield intended was legal under the regulations, then block any acts it determined to be illegal.

Like nearly all the ArtInts aboard ship, the nexus controller had been deliberately stripped as bare as possible of personality. It was not human, was not alive, and was not meant to be treated as if it were. Thus it was given no personality construct, no voice, no simulated face that could be projected on the screen. Both to keep it from being treated as human, and for the sake of security, the nexus ArtInt had been built without even the capacity for audio pickup. It was a quite sensible arrangement, but it could be a damnably frustrating one. In the midst of the greatest crisis Koffield had ever faced in his whole career, he could not talk to the machine he needed to command, but was instead reduced to typing out his commands and queries, and choosing his way through endless screen menus.

He ordered the ArtInt to pull in data from the comm, detection, and weapons systems, and instructed it to scan in the ship's log of the last month as well. It was a lot to take in, even for a machine, and pulling in the data was the smallest part of the job. The ArtInt had to evaluate the situation and see how the current, unprecedented crisis matched up with the rules and regs intended for a quite different situation.

He found himself glancing up at his repeater displays as he worked. Convoy ships Two through Five were beginning their aborts. The intruders were still decelerating at the same mad, impossible rate. Koffield couldn't see how his ship was going to be able to manage a shot at any of them, and the job would be made all the harder if the intruders performed anything like the evasive maneuvers they had shown on the way out of the wormhole.

"Come on, damn it," Koffield muttered under his breath. "Let me in." Time was slipping away. At last the nexus controller flashed CLEAR TO PROCEED on its main display. It was ready to accept and evaluate commands. Whether or not it would allow them to be carried out was another question.

Timing. Timing. He had to get this right. The last four ships of the convoy were on their own. There was nothing he could do for them. But the lead ship. It was at least possible that he could hold the nexus open long enough for her to make her run. The other ships had at least half a hope of aborting their runs, but if he had to shut down the wormhole before Ship One went through, then he knew, to an absolute certainty, that he was dooming, killing, everyone aboard her. He kept half an eye on the status displays as he started keying in the power-down command for the first nexus. Would the ArtInt accept the commands, pass them on for execution?

Execution. A chilling word to use, under the circumstances.

Koffield checked the navigation projections for Ship One. The time-on-target prediction gave a precise time for her to reach the event horizon, and her course and speed had been carefully timed to ensure that she would reach the event horizon just as an open portal nexus swept past in its orbit. He confirmed that her course and speed were right, and that Portal Nexus D would be in position for the timeshaft drop. Koffield sent the standard nexus-open command to Nexus D, programming it to open just seconds before Ship One arrived, and to slam shut moments afterward.

"Comm. Advise Ship One she is clear to proceed through Nexus D as scheduled without need for course correction. And wish her good luck. She's going to need it."

Koffield returned to the nexus control screen. Very well.

Leave Nexus D operational and programmed to open and close in nine minutes, 14.3 seconds, ship's reference chronology. That left Nexi A, B, C, E, F, and G to deal with. They all had to be destroyed now. He would take out D after Ship One got through. And he had to allow for the time it would take to enter all the commands by hand and get the ArtInt to process them. The system made sure there was no way simply to hit a repeat button. Everything had to be entered in full, and with exact correctness. Beyond that, he had to allow time for the ArtInt to evaluate each command as it came in. With each command, and each nexus that was wrecked, the consequences of each following command would be of greater and greater significance, and thus would take the ArtInt system longer and longer to evaluate.

He keyed in the first command in the kill sequence for Nexus A.

ANTON KOFFIELD COMMANDING UPHOLDER INSTRUCTS NEXUS CONTROL SYSTEM TO DEACTIVATE PORTAL NEXUS "A" PERMANENTLY.

The system replied after only a moment's hesitation.

nexus control system receives and accepts instruction to deactivate portal nexus "a" permanently. please confirm command.

Koffield keyed in the confirmation, cursing when he made a mistake and had to back up and correct it. He sent the confirmation and waited through a slightly longer delay.

ANTON KOFFIELD COMMANDING UPHOLDER CONFIRMS INSTRUCTION TO NEXUS CONTROL SYSTEM TO DEACTIVATE PORTAL NEXUS "A" PERMANENTLY.

Again, a pause as the ArtInt thought it through.

nexus control system receives and accepts confirmation of instruction to deactivate portal nexus "a" permanently. nexus control system advises that this will be the last chance to countermand the instruction. send second confirmation within sixty seconds. any other action or lack of action will result in cancellation of instruction.

ANTON KOFFIELD COMMANDING UPHOLDER SENDS SECOND CONFIRMATION OF INSTRUCTION TO NEXUS CONTROL SYSTEM TO DEACTIVATE PORTAL NEXUS "A" PERMANENTLY.

A still-longer pause, and then came the answer.

nexus control system has deactivated portal nexus "a" permanently.

The symbol-logic image of Nexus A flashed red, then vanished. The status displays for A all dropped to zero. It was dead.

Anton Koffield did not know whether to feel relief or horror. The system was accepting and carrying out his commands, allowing him to destroy the nexi. The ArtInt agreed that the situation was dire enough to require such action, but Koffield had been half-hoping that it would not. If it had refused, his judgment might well have been called into question, and he could have looked forward to eventual court-martial, assuming he survived that long. But court-martial would have been preferable to wrecking the sole doorway to an entire world. What he was about to destroy might well take years, even decades, to repair, if it could even be done at all. Imposing new nexi on a singularity was hideously complex and expensive in time and treasure. Sometimes reimposition was impossible, and it was necessary to create a new singularity at even more spectacular cost, easily enough to bankrupt a small planet like Glister.

And he, Anton Koffield, was the one deciding that Glister would be forced to pay that cost.

But the intruders had to be stopped. If they escaped into the past, the consequences could easily be far worse than merely bankrupting one planet. He set to work on Portal Nexus B, working his way through the same tedious sequence of commands.

He glanced up at the nav screens. Ships Two, Three, Four, and Five were all just barely starting their abort maneuvers, struggling to break out of the wormhole's gravity well. Koffield knew how deep and powerful the gee well was. He doubted any of them were going to escape it. And if they were doomed, Koffield knew who it was who would have killed them.

"Sir!" Sentar called out. "Three of the intruders have shifted course. No longer bearing on the wormhole."

"Where the devil are they going?" Koffield demanded.

"Stand by. Still shifting . . . Burning stars. Sir, track projections show intruders two, four, and six are on intercept courses with our ship."

Koffield felt as if he had been kicked in the side of the head. What the devil else could happen? What the hell was he supposed to do now?

Thought. Logic. Work it through, decide what it meant. Three of the intruders had survived the original run out from the wormhole. Everything about their behavior suggested a repeat of the tactics of sacrificing expendable duplicates in order to saturate and confuse the defenses. If each carried a full copy of whatever information they had gathered, but only one intruder got through, that one would be enough. But *one* had to get through, or all would be for nothing.

Now three intruders were still driving for the wormhole—but three were not. The original intruders had shown little or no capacity for tracking or detection. One of them had nearly flown up the *Upholder*'s main thrusters, apparently by accident. But now at least three of the intruders could and were tracking the *Upholder*.

If the only thing that mattered was that at least one ship got through, spending three ships to attack the *Upholder* was a waste of effort—*if* the intercepting ships were capable of getting through the wormhole.

Suddenly Koffield saw it. It all made sense—*if* he assumed that each of the survivors had spawned or built a decoy for itself—a decoy that could track ships and run intercepts, but *wasn't* capable of surviving a wormhole transit. If the duplicates could make the run, they would have been driving for the wormhole as well.

"Weapons, you have conn control. I want evasive maneuvers to avoid the intruders targeted to intercept us," Koffield ordered. "Do *not* waste ammunition or laser power on the interceptors. They are meant to decoy us from our prime targets. Don't take the bait. Fire only on the three intruders that are targeting the wormhole."

"Aye sir," the weapons officer replied.

Koffield checked the nav plots again. Three minutes,

nine seconds until Ship One entered the timeshaft—if she made it that far. Ship Two appeared to be using full thrust, trying to break free of the singularity's gravity well, but it was plain to see she wasn't going to make it. He felt a cold stab of guilt deep in his gut. That dot on his display represented a multimegaton ship, a ship whose name he did not even know. She carried some unknown number of human lives, some unknown but vitally needed cargo carried at great risk and great cost—and now that dot, that ship, was going to die.

And she was not going to die alone. Ships Three and Four were making barely better progress. Five looked to be the only one of the ships to have any hope of escape.

Murder. Cold-blooded murder. And he had no choice in the matter.

He turned back to keying in his commands to the portal nexus ArtInt. He made his way through the commands for Nexus B, and watched as the nexus died. He started on C, with the ArtInt delaying more and more after each command, as the consequences of each command grew more and more significant. It was nerve-wracking in the extreme—but he knew that it had to be far worse for those aboard Ship One, watching on their display boards as the nexi popped out of existence, one after the other. Well, they only had just under two minutes more before they hit Nexus D.

What about the intruders and the interceptors? He reluctantly expended some small fraction of the time he had carefully examining their nav plots. They had all completed their hellishly rapid deceleration, and were moving at high velocities, though no longer at impossible speeds.

Just then, his command chair slammed up into him as the *Upholder* jolted abruptly, making its first evasive action maneuver. He watched for the reaction, but the three intercepting intruders did not respond or shift course in any way, long after they should have been able to track the *Upholder*'s changed course. The other three intruders were still bearing down on the wormhole. It was going to be close. Horrifically close.

Koffield sent the last confirmation of the order to kill Nexus C, and waited for a half-minute that seemed like half a lifetime before the ArtInt accepted and executed the order. He set to work at once on E, watching on the repeaters as the last act of the drama played out around him.

"Ship One entering the timeshaft wormhole via Nexus D in thirty seconds," the detection officer announced, as if there were anyone on the bridge who wasn't watching a repeater with the same data on it. "Twenty-five seconds."

He'd leave D until last, until at least Ship One was through. Koffield typed the next command. ANTON KOFFIELD COMMANDING UPHOLDER INSTRUCTS NEXUS CONTROL SYSTEM TO DEACTIVATE PORTAL NEXUS "E" PERMANENTLY.

The ArtInt took so long to reply Koffield began to think there had been a system lockup. Then came the reply.

nexus control system receives and accepts instruction to deactivate portal nexus "e" permanently. please confirm command.

"Twenty seconds for Ship One. Ship Two is—oh, damn it! Ship Two off-screen. We're getting a debris-field bloom. Debris impacting event horizon. Hell and damnation! Detecting flare-out on port main engine for Ship Three. Thrusters overloaded and blown. She's pinwheeling. Ship Three—oh, my God, Ship Three off-screen with debris-field bloom."

Ships Two and Three were dead. There was nothing he could do. Nothing but press on.

ANTON KOFFIELD COMMANDING UPHOLDER CONFIRMS INSTRUCTION TO NEXUS CONTROL SYSTEM TO DEACTIVATE PORTAL NEXUS "E" PERMANENTLY.

No response from the ArtInt.

"Intercepting intruders have just changed course!" Amerstad, the weapons officer, called. "All three now bearing to intercept with *Upholder* if all craft hold present course. Commencing new evasive."

With response times that long, the *Upholder* would be able to dodge the interceptors for days. But this game was going to be over, one way or the other, in a matter of minutes.

"Ship One now ten seconds from timeshaft entrance," Sentar called from the detection station. "Nexus D showing nominal start to portal activation."

nexus control system receives and accepts confirmation of instruction to deactivate portal nexus "e" permanently. nexus control system advises that this will be the last chance to countermand the instruction. send second confirmation within sixty seconds. any other action or lack of action will result in cancellation of instruction.

At last. Koffield typed in the final kill command for Nexus E and waited for the ArtInt to respond.

"Ship One entering in five, four, three, two, one, zero— Ship One, nominal entry to timeshaft wormhole. All reading normal. Nexus D closing."

"Ship One into the timeshaft," Koffield said, half to himself. "At least one thing worked right today." In theory, it was already safe to kill Nexus D. Ship One ought to be through already, emerging into the past and taking her chances with the downtime relief ship. But that was theory. The ship was dropping back in time. How did you measure time while you were moving through it? Duration of transit through the wormhole could be zero or infinity, depending on how you computed it. He could not know for sure that blowing D at once could have no effect on Ship One. No one had ever blown a portal nexus shut with a ship in transit. Koffield pressed on to Nexus F.

"Ship Three's debris bloom expanding to Ship Four's position!" Sentar called. "I'm reading flashpoints. Impacts, multiple impacts on Ship Four. All engines stop on Four. I think she's tumbling. Ship Four in free fall to event horizon. Impact. Oh, for the love of God, Ship Four, impact on event horizon."

Ship Four's symbol-logic indicator faded from the repeater. It was like a chess game, a monstrous chess game, where the pieces were lives, and they were being swept from the board, one after the other, no matter what move he made.

"Sir!" the weapons officer called. "I think I may have a shot on Intruder Three if we can hold position and attitude long enough."

"Very well. Cancel evasive maneuvers until you can shoot. Keep us alive long enough to see this through."

"Yes, sir," weapons replied. "Coming about to firing attitude."

The ship pivoted about as Koffield worked his way through the kill commands for Nexus F.

"Nav plot now projecting that Ship Five will break free to a parking orbit," the detection officer announced. A halfhearted cheer went up from the bridge crew. Three convoy ships were dead, but two still survived.

"Interceptors have adjusted course once again," detection called out, squelching the celebration. "All three now targeted to ram *Upholder*. First projected impact in three minutes, five seconds."

"Weapons! How long until you have a shot on Intruder Three?"

"We'll close to within maximum range for laser fire in mark, sixty-eight seconds, railgun fire in mark, ninety-one," the weapons officer answered, her voice smooth and calm. "I'd like to fire the railgun first, though, so that any evasive action from the target would force it toward the laser. If we hold until mark, one hundred eight seconds, the firing aspect will shift enough for Intruder One to be almost precisely in line with my fire. There would at least be a chance that misses or debris from Three would strike One."

"Do it," Koffield ordered as he watched Nexus F die and fade from his displays. They would have at least a minute after the weapons officer got her shots off to worry about evading the interceptors. Plenty of time. Plenty of time. He started on the commands for Nexus G as the ship pivoted hard about to a new attitude that would bring the main weaponry to bear.

Again, he typed the same commands into the system and sent them to the ArtInt and waited for endless seconds for the ArtInt to acknowledge. It took a full minute for the ArtInt to grind through them all. Koffield watched Nexus G die just as the weapons officer came up on her firing sequence.

"Intruder Three targeted," she called. "Railgun fire in ten seconds."

Koffield had no time to listen. He started the kill commands on Nexus D, the last surviving nexus. If the ArtInt had hesitated long and hard before killing the others, it would take halfway to forever to approve the death of Nexus D. He sent the first command and settled in to wait. There was certainly enough else going on to occupy his mind.

"Rail fire in five. Four. Three. Two. One. Fire."

The *Upholder* thrummed and buzzed with the vibration of the railgun's rapid-fire mode, as the electromagnets accelerated thousands of steel pellets up to near-relativistic velocity and launched them out toward their targets.

"Railgun fire pattern away. Time to target twenty seconds. No evasive maneuver detected. Stand by for laser volley-fire pattern. Laser fire in five. Four. Three. Two. One. Fire." Even at the speed of light, the laser blasts would take long seconds to reach their targets. If the targeting computers had done their jobs right, the *Upholder* would have moved enough between rail and laser fire to keep the two shots from interfering with each other. The laser fire ought to strike first, with the rail pellets sweeping in right behind it.

The bridge lights flickered, almost imperceptibly, as the last of the laser-cannon volley drained the main power systems. That there was any noticeable power dropoff at all was a warning to Koffield as to how close to depleted their systems were. If the power levels dropped too low, there wouldn't even be enough to start the regeneration systems and reenergize the power cells.

But none of that mattered. What they had to do now was stay alive through the next few minutes.

"Interceptors closing, projecting three-way simultaneous impact on *Upholder*," detection called.

"Weapons!" Koffield called. "Confirm. Are all shots away?"

"Aye sir!"

"Very well. Evasive! Random heading, max acceleration. Now, now, now."

The ship surged again, heeling over to bear almost directly toward the singularity. Koffield swore. He should have known not to call for a random heading, given the sort of luck they had been having. They would have to break off acceleration very soon indeed if they wanted to avoid following the example that Ships Two, Three, and Four had set. "Conn! New heading, any heading that's minimum ninety degrees *away* from the singularity!"

The ship lurched drunkenly and swung about again.

"Interceptors still closing on where we were!" the detection officer announced. "No changes in course or velocity. Mutual impact in ten seconds."

That impact was going to throw a hell of a lot of debris around. Maybe that was the plan, to kill *Upholder* with the shrapnel from a three-way impact. But there was damned little he could do about it. He didn't have enough power to spend it on the shields, even if they had been functional.

"Detection!" Koffield called. "Time-on-target info!"

"Interceptor impact in five seconds. Laser fire to primary target in eight, rail to prime in nine."

"Interceptors impact!" the weapons officer called, though there was no need to do so. Every screen on the bridge lit up with the violence of the three-pronged crash. If much of the blast debris caught the *Upholder,* and caught her just right, it would be the end of things, and no doubt.

But there was nothing he could do about it, so he did what he could instead and slammed down the send key on the first confirm command to kill Nexus D.

"Laser-fire shots, rail-fire shots, clean miss on primary target!"

Koffield hadn't had enough faith in the shots to feel much disappointment. "Any chance of hits on the secondary?" he asked.

"We'll know in twenty seconds, sir."

"Do you have anything left for a second shot?"

"Insufficient power stored for a laser shot. We have rail pellets and maybe enough accumulator power for one more volley. And we've got a marginal firing solution in thirty seconds on previous primary target."

"Then let's not waste it. Shoot when you can."

"Aye sir."

What the devil was taking the nexus control ArtInt so long? Maybe the damn thing finally *had* up and quit on him this—

"Sir! Detecting impacts on secondary target! Four, five, strikes. She's tumbling off course!"

A cheer went up from the bridge.

"Good shooting, Weapons! Now do it again!"

"Aye sir. Setting up for final firing pass, sir. Stand by."

Final firing pass. That was true enough, and sobering enough. Even if they scored another hit, and thus managed to kill or cripple two of the intruders, there was still one out there.

Koffield studied the repeater boards, and spotted something the detection officer hadn't noticed yet. Ship Five, the last ship of the convoy, wasn't just sliding into a parking orbit. She was still accelerating at maximum, thrusting away from the singularity. She was, in plain fact, getting the hell out, escaping the chaos and destruction that swirled about the Circum Central Timeshaft. Koffield could not blame her. No matter what the outcome, there would be precious little reason for Ship Five to remain anywhere near the wormhole.

"Ship Five on emergency departure track," Koffield announced, and then forgot about her. Another piece swept off the chessboard. Later, if he survived, would be time enough to think about her, and about all else that had been lost and destroyed this day.

"Confirmed," the detection officer replied.

"Coming up on firing pass," the weapons officer called. "Stand by. Firing in twenty seconds."

"I've been tracking some sort of erratic venting from previous secondary target, and her tumble is getting worse," the detection officer said. "I think she's out of the game."

Koffield checked his repeaters and pulled up the full navigation data on Intruder Five—the Intruder they hadn't shot at yet. Even if their last blast of railgun fire took out Intruder Three, Five would still be there, barreling down toward the wormhole.

"Firing in ten. Nine. Eight. Seven. Six. Five. Four. Three.

Two. One. Zero." Once again, and for the last time, the fabric of the *Upholder* thrummed and thrilled with the rush of the railgun's fire. "Firing complete. All railgun pellets expended. Time-on-target, mark, thirty-two seconds."

Projecting their courses forward, Three would reach the wormhole portal in ten minutes, twenty-five seconds, and Five in twenty-three minutes, eighteen seconds. If they got lucky on this firing pass—

nexus control system receives and accepts instruction to deactivate portal nexus "d" permanently. please confirm command.

Koffield was sufficiently surprised to see the ArtInt's response that he nearly forgot to act on it. But then he blinked, nodded, and typed in the first confirmation command.

ANTON KOFFIELD COMMANDING UPHOLDER SENDS CONFIRMATION OF INSTRUCTION TO NEXUS CONTROL SYSTEM TO DEACTIVATE PORTAL NEXUS "D" PERMANENTLY.

"Sir! I'm tracking on the debris cloud from the interceptor. Some of it is going to catch us—estimate about twenty seconds."

"How bad?"

"Not very. Just small stuff, which is why it took so long to detect."

But even that small stuff could kill them if it hit just right. Koffield checked his displays. "Conn, all engines, full stop and emergency reorient. Ship to attitude three-two-zero, one-one-zero." That ship's attitude would point the nose of the craft straight at the debris cloud, presenting the smallest possible cross section to the oncoming shrapnel. Normal doctrine would be to aim the better-shielded aft end, rather than the bow, at the debris, but the *Upholder*'s main engines had absorbed a great deal of punishment already, and it had taken all they had to patch them up. Another round of hits on the propulsion system could wreck the engines for good and leave them stranded in orbit of the wormhole. Better to risk the weapons and detection gear in the nose. They had nothing left to shoot with anyway, and, for that matter, there was not that much left to see.

The ship heeled over hard to her new heading, and

Koffield watched the symbol-logic displays of the debris rushing toward them, and of their own weapons fire heading out. He looked to the two countdowns. The seconds remaining until debris cloud impact, and railgun time-on-target, clicked down almost in lockstep with each other.

Ten seconds. Nine. Eight. Seven. Six. Five. Four. Three. Two. One.

"Multiple hits on target—" the detection officer began, but with a crash and a thud, the lights died on the bridge.

Pitch-blackness blanketed the bridge. Voices—shouts, cries, calm, professional reporting—filled the darkness.

Nothing. There was nothing at all he could do. Not until there was light, and power. Nothing until—

The nexus control panel lit back up, a message already on it.

nexus control system receives and accepts confirmation of instruction to deactivate portal nexus "d" permanently. nexus control system advises that this will be the last chance to countermand the instruction. send second confirmation within sixty seconds. any other action or lack of action will result in cancellation of instruction.

The screen flickered once and then died again.

How long had that message been there before he could see it? How long had the display been blank, unable to show him the words? Five seconds? Twenty? Koffield fumbled for the control system keyboard in the all-but-complete darkness. Working blind, he laboriously keyed in the second confirmation. He could not see the words he was keying in. At last he had the command keyed in as best he could, but then he held back. He had no way of knowing if he had indeed keyed the command in properly. What if he had typed it in wrong, and the ArtInt refused to accept the scrambled message? How long did he have before the sixty-second countdown was over and the ArtInt canceled the deactivation sequence? Had the keyboard even taken his keystrokes, or had the power failure cut the keyboard as well? If the main lights would only come on, he could check the command and resend it. But if he waited too long for the lights, the system would cancel the sequence anyway.

How long to wait? Koffield decided to give it twenty

seconds, and counted it out to himself, doing his best to guess how long a second was. He hit the send key.

A few seconds, or a few years, later, somewhere deep in the bowels of the ship, a power relay reset, and the bridge bloomed back into existence as the emergency lights came on, turning utter darkness to a compartment half-lit, half-shrouded in gloom. Koffield blinked as his eyes adjusted, and then saw what he had sent on the screen.

ANTON KOFFIELD COMMANDING UPHOLDER SENDS SECOND CONFROMATIUON OF INSTRUCTION TO NEXUS CONTRL SYSTEM TO DEACTIVATE PORTAL NEXUS "D" PERMANENTYLY.

The indicators *showed* the system had received the instruction, but they had just gone through a major power crisis. Koffield could imagine a half dozen kinds of power failures, trips, and flares that could have caused the message-send to get scrambled or lost, or caused the system to show a false positive. The ArtInt system *ought* to be able to parse through and interpret the command in spite of the miskeyed words, but there was no way to know for sure. Typing in the command again would either reassure the ArtInt—or make it suspicious of a trick and cause it to abort.

There was, in short, nothing he could do that would not just as likely make things worse instead of better.

Leave it. Leave it alone. Nothing he could do.

There was no telling precisely how long the ArtInt would take to work its way through the complexities of the situation, but Koffield had no doubt this step, this last, irrevocable step, would take longer than any other. Every other decision the ArtInt had made included the possibility of stopping, of backing off from a full shutdown. So long as one nexus remained, the system could be rebuilt. But with the last nexus gone, there was no way back. The ArtInt would think longer and harder before launching over that precipice.

"Damage status?" he asked.

"Five small debris strikes to bow of the ship," the ship systems officer reported. "Laser cannon off-line but possibly repairable. Railgun system badly damaged. Detection system highly questionable but marginally functional for the moment. Main power system appears to be fully functional but is still recovering from power surges. No other damage reported."

"Very well," Koffield said. His displays finished rebuilding themselves as he watched. Even with the detectors damaged, he could see that Intruder Three had definitely taken at least one hit. The detectors were only rendering a flickering dot of light, but that was enough to tell Koffield a great deal. The dot was swelling and fading, while at the same time pulsing in overall brightness—the classic fingerprint of a ship tumbling and venting violently. Intruder Three was still headed straight for the wormhole, but unless it restored full attitude control in very short order, it would surely be torn apart by tidal stresses as it closed in on the singularity. It was as good as out of the game.

Even as he watched, new disaster overtook Three. It brightened abruptly, then flared over into blackness. Koffield needed only a moment to figure out what had happened. The debris cloud from the interceptor collision had just swept past Three, and punished it far more severely than it had the *Upholder*.

Now indeed was the chessboard swept clean. Ship Five was departing as rapidly as she could, under full emergency thrust, her engines no doubt scrambling all of her rear detectors and communications. She could not see what was going on astern of her course, and could not send or receive messages. She might, if she survived, serve as a witness to what had already happened, but otherwise her part in the disaster was over.

That left only two ships still in the game—Intruder Five and the *Upholder*. Everything and everyone else had been destroyed—smashed into rubble, or swallowed up by the singularity.

In a sense, even the *Upholder* was now out of the game. She had shot her bolt. Her weapons were spent or wrecked, her detection systems half-blind. There was nothing left that she could do to stop the last Intruder. Koffield didn't even have the engine power to come about in time and put his ship on a suicide intercept. Nothing left to do but survive.

All that mattered now was that the *Upholder* hold together until the nexus portal control ArtInt processed the last confirmation and acted on it, killing Nexus D, and closed the last door into the timeshaft before Intruder Five went through it, in twenty minutes and five seconds. Koffield could do nothing, dared do nothing, until the ArtInt had done its job.

Twenty minutes. Nineteen, now. Too short a time, and too long. Not enough time to act, but more than enough time to think, to reflect on what was to come. Either bitter failure, and Intruder Five proceeding through the wormhole despite all the lives and treasure he had spent—or else equally bitter victory.

Even if he succeeded in stopping the last Intruder, then what was there for him, for any of his crew? They could never go home into the past again. They might, after a long and arduous journey, reach a safe port somewhere here on the uptime side of the timeshaft wormhole. But then what? What lives could there be for any of them? What life especially for Koffield, the man who had ordered the destruction of the post he was meant to protect?

But first they had to stay alive, and keep the ship functioning long enough to stop the Intruder. Koffield brought up the ship-systems repeater and studied it closely for a moment. The ship's repair crews were working fast, putting the ship back together as best they could. They needed no guidance, no instruction, from him. Nor did any other member of the crew. He had made his bidding known, and they were doing it. His work was done. Nothing left but to watch its sequel unfold.

Fifteen minutes, five seconds left.

Here and there, slowly, fitfully, small parts of the bridge and the ship came back to life around him. Main power came back on-line. The ventilation came back to life with a quiet whir, though he had not even been consciously aware it had failed. Koffield had seen the repeater display report that the ventilators were off-line, but somehow he had not equated that with the too-still, too-stale air of the bridge.

Still fifteen minutes, five seconds. Time. Time was what he was here to defend, what he was sacrificing everything for. How was it that time had stopped? No. There. Time had started up again, never really stopped. Fifteen minutes, four seconds. Three seconds. Two seconds.

He stared at the clock, half of him willing time to move forward, while the other half wished most devoutly for time to stand still until the nexus control system ArtInt had processed the last command, compared it to the situation, and judged whether or not it should be acted upon.

Strange indeed that they had all almost ceased wondering who, or what, the Intruders were, or what they wanted, or where and what they came from. So far as the attitude of Koffield and the crew went, they simply *were*, like a force of nature. None of them had seen the Intruders as anything more than dots of light or symbol-logic indicators. They had no idea what the Intruder ships looked like. It took a real effort of concentration to remember the Intruders were directed by intelligence, rather than by some malevolent natural force. They were machines.

And now it came down to Koffield's machine versus the Intruders' machines. It was even something of a relief that it would come down to what the machine chose. If the ArtInt decided, at the last, that it could not, should not, close the final nexus, then Koffield would be delighted to be wrong. He knew he would likely face court-martial, prison, perhaps execution—but even that would be preferable to the doom and disaster it would unleash if the timeshaft was indeed slammed shut. And if the ArtInt did indeed destroy the final nexus, then, perhaps, he could convince himself that it was the ArtInt, and not Anton Koffield, that had done the final deed. A tempting and comforting notion, that.

But no. This was his doing, his responsibility. He hadn't sworn an oath, taken an officer's commission, and accepted command of the *Upholder* just to hide behind an

Artificial Intelligence. Right or wrong, win or lose, this battle belonged to him.

"Sir, we're picking up the fringe of some sort of radio transmission from Intruder Five," the comm officer reported. "High probability it's signaling Nexus D."

No surprise there, but it was not exactly encouraging news. What if the controller system aboard Nexus D decided to accept commands from the Intruder, and ignore those from the ArtInt aboard *Upholder*?

Koffield flipped his prime repeater display over to comm and shook his head in frustration. They were only just barely able to detect the presence of a signal at all. Probably the Intruder was sending on a tight beam. If they had still had the use of the detection equipment that had been destroyed in the first attack of the Intruders, and a modicum of time, the comm department probably would have been able to reconstruct the message in full. But half the ship's detection gear was shot away, damage-control parties were still at work, and there were only thirteen minutes, eight seconds left until the end of things, one way or the other.

The end of things . . .

For the first time, Koffield allowed himself the luxury—and the horror—of considering what might happen, what might change, if the Intruder got through to the past. All the history between the downtime and uptime ends of the Circum Central Wormhole was at risk. Every person born, every idea created, every human action of the last seventy-nine years could be turned upside down and inside out. And what was there to prevent this Intruder from replicating itself, or to prevent its creator from creating more? What to stop it from seeking out the uptime ends of other wormholes, back there, seventy-nine years in the past? And if the Intruder could punch through *this* timeshaft wormhole, what was to prevent its forcing its way through others? If it had the timeshaft-wormhole control codes, what was there to keep the Intruder from going back, and back, and back, to the very beginning of the timeshaft-wormhole transportation system?

Thousands of years of history, of triumph and failure, lay open and exposed to every danger. What was to stop the Intruder from dropping back far enough in time to prevent the building of the *Upholder*, or the founding of the Chronologic Patrol itself? The ripples of time paradox could send chaos sweeping down the years.

And there was nothing he could do. All his power spent, his last throw of the die already made, all Captain Anton Koffield could do was watch the minutes and the seconds die.

He stared at the displays, his gaze shifting endlessly from comm to detection to weapons to navigation, and then back to the only one that still mattered, back to the nexus control ArtInt. The bridge went quiet, almost silent, as the end drew near. Ten minutes. Nine minutes. Eight minutes. And still the ArtInt did not respond, did not act.

Again and again, Koffield fought back the temptation to relink to the ArtInt and reissue his instructions, or at least query on status. Everything he knew about ArtInts told him that any distraction, any interference, would likely be disastrous. The ArtInt had the data it needed, the data it expected. In a situation this complex, this unexpected, and this dangerous, giving it extraneous information could only add to the number of variables it had to juggle.

A flicker on the comm repeater display. The Intruder was transmitting again. "Comm," Koffield said, "can you make anything more of that?"

"Doing a pattern match. Stand by. Sir, maybe a little bit of good news. As best I can tell, that was a repeat of their last signal—and I haven't seen any sort of response from the nexus itself. It sends a mirror reply of any command it receives and accepts. The Intruder is having some trouble."

"Very good," Koffield said. "That's a very good sign indeed." It might well mean that the nexus ArtInt had put a block on Nexus D's communications system, ordering it to ignore commands from any other source. And that in turn would mean that the ArtInt had analyzed the situation properly, and would blow Nexus D in time.

It sounded hopeful, though it was a hell of a lot to read into a silence—but silence was all they had.

Seven minutes. Six minutes. The wait went on forever. Koffield's universe shrank down to nothing but his displays, and the numbers and logic symbols on them. The bridge, the ship, the exterior reality represented by the displays, all faded away. There was nothing but the shifting countdown numbers, the dot representing the Intruder creeping toward Nexus D, the blank status line on the nexus control ArtInt display.

It was a standoff, but a standoff that favored the *Upholder*. Intruder Five had long since gone past the point of no return. It was headed straight for the singularity, falling like a rock, and nothing could stop it now. It could no longer escape the singularity's gravity well. It was going in, no matter what.

Koffield had ordered the ArtInt to destroy Nexus D, wreck it, slam the door shut and seal it for all time. The ArtInt had not yet decided whether to send that order. Intruder Five was ordering Nexus D to open itself, and let the Intruder through. If the ArtInt sent the destruct command and Nexus D accepted it and refused the orders from the Intruder, the Intruder would crash into the singularity. If the nexus refused both sets of orders, it would remain shut, and the Intruder would still slam into the singularity to be utterly destroyed.

The Intruder could only win, could only cause the nexus to open and allow it through the wormhole, if the nexus accepted the Intruder's orders and refused those from the *Upholder*'s ArtInt. The logic sounded hopeful—but the Intruder had been doing all the winning so far.

Five minutes. Four.

Was there anything left undone? Anything left to do at all? Koffield could hear a stifled sob, and the sound of someone quietly weeping, somewhere on the half-darkened bridge. All his life, all his career, there had always been some action to take, some choice left. Nothing.

"Intruder sending commands again," the comm officer reported, even as Koffield watched the same information pop up on his repeater.

"Is it repeating the same sequence?" Koffield asked.

"As best I can tell, sir. Our aspect angle is shifting relative to the Intruder, and we're getting less of the transmission every time."

"Very well." Let the Intruder keep trying. In three minutes' time it would be too late. Nexus D would stay closed, the Intruder would impact on the singularity, and it would be all over.

Two minutes.

"Sir! Detecting response from Nexus D. Odds ninety-five plus it's a mirror reply to the Intruder."

The news was a sharp, hard blow to the gut. Where the hell was the ArtInt? Had it been blown away, wrecked or damaged by the last strike to the ship? Ninety seconds to go. Not even time left to restart the sequence of command and confirmation. The ArtInt should have responded, yes or no, Koffield decided. There was some malfunction. He would leave it as long as he could, and then try the restart, hope that the urgency of the situation would get the ArtInt to act faster. At the sixty-second mark he would try it again. His hands were poised over the keypad.

nexus control system reports unauthorized access attempt. stand by.

Koffield stared at the display, the sweat standing out on his forehead. Stand by? How long could he—He checked the countdown clock. Seventy seconds until Intruder Five hit the singularity. And who did nexus control think was unauthorized? Koffield or the Intruder?

nexus control system reports loss of control over nexus. attempting to regain control and deactivate portal nexus "d" permanently.

"Nexus D opening!" the detection officer shouted. "Oh, my God, it's opening. Nexus D open, stable, active, and operational."

Koffield pulled his hands back from the keypad, his eyes wide with horror. It was the disaster, the catastrophe, that all of the Chronologic Patrol had been built to prevent. And it had come to pass, here, on his watch.

Sixty seconds. The past would be attacked—by what or whom? for what reason?—in sixty seconds. The Intruder would get past the downtime relief ship. Of that he had no doubt. It would get past, accelerate to those same impossible speeds, and roam at will through the past, carrying detailed information—about what, for what, who could know?—from the future.

Try again. If the ArtInt had gone off script, he could as well.

ANTON KOFFIELD COMMANDING UPHOLDER REPORTS SITUATION URGENT AND DANGEROUS IN EXTREME. KOFFIELD ORDERS NEXUS CONTROL SYSTEM TO DEACTIVATE PORTAL NEXUS "D" PERMANENTLY AT ONCE. DEACTIVATE NEXUS "D" NOW.

portal nexus control acknowledging. attempting to comply. stand by.

Thirty seconds. Who would not be born who should have been? What invention would be left uncreated, or created in the wrong time or place? What tiny chance encounter would be altered, changing all that came after? What small cause would lead to huge effects, like a deflected pebble setting off a landslide? What paradoxes would be sent caroming through the years?

"Intruder Five on final approach," the detection officer announced. "Centered on standard insertion vector. Twenty seconds."

portal nexus control still attempting to comply with previous order. stand by.

"Fifteen seconds. Intruder entering timeshaft in ten seconds. Nine. Eight. Seven."

History itself was about to be attacked, and there was nothing to be done.

"Six. Five. Four."

portal nexus control still attempting to comply with previous order. stand by.

Too late. There wasn't time.

"Three. Two. One. Zero."

And it was over. It would take several seconds for the confirming data to reach them at the speed of light, but it was over. The Intruder was in the wormhole, dropping into the past. Defeat. It was over.

Koffield switched on an exterior-view camera and pointed it at the utterly invisible spot in the sky that was the singularity. Out there, an equally invisible Intruder had left this time and entered—

A sword of light, impossibly brilliant, flared out into the darkness.

"Telemetry from Nexus D is going crazy!" the detection officer cried out. "The readings are all over the place. I'm—I'm picking up a debris cloud coming from the nexus. Trying a pattern match. Stand by."

The story of my life, Koffield thought. *Stand by.* "What the devil just happened?" he demanded. "Comm! Do you have anything?"

"No, sir."

"Sir, all telemetry from Nexus D is at zero. No carrier, no signal, no data. It's like it's not there."

And then, another message appeared on the nexus control ArtInt's screen.

portal nexus "d" deactivated permanently.

Short, sweet, and to the point. "It isn't there," Koffield said. "Not anymore. I think—never mind what I think. Detection—where's that pattern match?"

"Sir, I'm only at about eighty percent confidence, but that debris cloud looks a lot like what we got when the other Intruders went up. I think it blew right inside the timeshaft wormhole."

The light flare faded away, to be replaced by flickers and sparks of light concentrated in one tiny point in space—debris reimpacting on the singularity. Bits of this ship and that, this Intruder and that, dropping down onto the event horizon of the wormhole, letting out a last burst of energy as they were torn to pieces by the massive tidal effects.

The nexus must have closed down, deactivated, just as Intruder Five was going through. With the protection of the nexus gone, the Intruder would have been shredded to bits in a nanosecond, setting off a half dozen kinds of violent energy release.

It was as close as Koffield ever wished to cut anything.

Another heartbeat, another millisecond, and the Intruder would have been free in the past, and all would be in vain.

But even if their losses had given them victory, still the price was far too high.

The past had been spared. But at what cost to the present, and the future, to the *Standfast,* to the *Upholder,* to the five convoy ships, to the planet Glister?

And, Koffield could not help but ask, in the very core of his soul—at what cost to himself?

What blood and doom had he just put on his own hands?

Four standard days later, the *Upholder* boosted away from the ruined domain of the Circum Central Wormhole Farm, into the uptime future where/when Anton Koffield had stranded her. She quite literally left nothing behind, as the singularity swept up the wreckage of the battle. Nothing at all but the singularity, that point of deepest, and most absolute, nonexistence, remained.

The crew spent the better part of the first two months' boost repairing their battered craft as best they could. Then, in groups of eight or ten, they entered their cryosleep canisters, each group assisting those who went before. They would sleep away the long decades until they reached the Solar System, and Earth.

If all went well, they would be ninety years in transit, ship's time. A run through the 89.8-year timeshaft at Sirius Power Cluster would bring them to the outer approaches of the Solar System in about three months, objective time.

Then it would be up to luck, and fate, and the crew members themselves to build whatever lives they could build, seventy-nine years uptime from where they had started. If all went well.

But Anton Koffield had no illusions. Bad luck and ill fate had already shaped the form of his existence in the future. He was, he knew, *marked* by what had happened, by what he had done. When every other fact about him had been forgotten, he would be remembered—as the man who blew the timeshaft, the man who killed the convoy, the man who had faced and fought and killed a mysterious force of Intruders.

No one, much as he might wish it, would ever forget what he had done. No one.

Least of all, Anton Koffield himself.

Grand Library Habitat Orbiting Neptune

Oskar DeSilvo stared thoughtfully at the spherical image of the planet Solace that hung before him in the center of the room. The image was not of the planet as it currently existed, but as it would be, decades from now. By then, his work, his creation, would be all but complete. By then, Solace—his world, his laboratory, his monument to himself—would have come fully alive, have bloomed and commenced to flourish.

Baskaw's ideas were working—though no one but DeSilvo need ever know the ideas were Baskaw's, and not DeSilvo's. Indeed, DeSilvo himself was close to forgetting himself that he had not thought of it all on his own. He saw no need to share the credit, or the glory, with a long-forgotten crackpot researcher who had been dead for centuries.

But he dared not forget that what he looked down on was not real. Not yet. Until the terraforming of Solace was largely finished and complete, there was precious little point in worrying over who would eventually get the credit—or the blame—for it. What he saw was a mere ghost of what might be in a far-distant star system. Solace was but half-built, still a dream, decades in the future and light-years away. Reality was a holochamber in DeSilvo's office, center, aboard the Grand Library habitat, orbiting Neptune in the outer reaches of the Solar System.

And there was much to do in that reality. Reluctantly, DeSilvo turned his back on the glory that was to be and stepped from the holoprojection chamber into his elegant, well-appointed office. Solace was well on its way, but there was still endless work to do. There was no point in reflecting overmuch on glories to be, though he was supremely confident of the outcome. Once Solace was complete, all of Settled Space would ring with his name.

DeSilvo sat back down at his desk, taking care to sweep his flowing robe up smoothly as he did so, to avoid sitting on it and wrinkling the splendid pale yellow fabric. Whatever others might say of Oskar DeSilvo, for good or ill, all would agree on the man's vanity, though of course his enemies were more likely to dwell on that aspect of his personality.

DeSilvo was of medium build, his bronze skin firm and his physique well toned. His thick shock of hair was jet-black, and showed no sign of thinning. He wore it to flowing shoulder length. He was clean-shaven, square-jawed, high-cheekboned. His bright blue eyes were set off dramatically by his thick black eyebrows.

It would be impossible to judge DeSilvo's age based on his appearance. Nearly every part of him, from his heart to his fingernails, had, in one way or another, been replaced or revitalized repeatedly over the years. Nor did DeSilvo make it easy to establish his own age. His biographies were quite vague on the point, and his extended use of temporal confinement, cryosleep, and timeshaft-wormhole transport had done nothing to clarify the point.

Still, even DeSilvo himself knew something in his appearance whispered that his seemingly ageless, vigorous youth was at least in part deceptive. His eyes were too bright, his teeth too white and perfect, his muscle tone too good. He was the product of regeneration, transplant, and stimulation therapy, rather than of healthy living and good diet. His appearance was meant to be of youth and vigor, but it was in fact the face of wealth and age. Oskar DeSilvo was far from the only wealthy old man who sought to buy youth.

A practiced eye would have spotted the signs at first glance. DeSilvo's skin was drawn too tight, and its slight yellowish cast was a clue that repeated skin regenerations were reaching the point of diminishing returns, where the regen damage was more serious than the cellular decay it was meant to forestall. Oskar DeSilvo was hearty and hale, but the hints were there for those who could read them. The very fabric of his body had come close to the end of its capacity for absorbing the stress and shock of repair.

They called it Gray's Syndrome, after some long-forgotten near ancient who had first described the process of sudden aging onset, when decades of decay seem to sweep across the body in hours or days. One day, in a year, or a century, some part of his body would decide to refuse further regen, and that would set the age toxins flowing. The collapse would come fast.

But for now, all was well, and DeSilvo cut a splendid figure in his scholar's robe—and knew it.

He leaned forward over the desk and studied a data pad that was displaying the Master Action List, the long list of items awaiting his attention. A hundred subprojects of the Solace project, each in and of itself an enormous undertaking, awaited his consideration.

He scrolled down the action list. Massive excavations, comet diversions, gigantic interstellar transshipments, the construction of whole cities. And, last, but far from least, the chronicling of it all, the setting down in history of how such great things were accomplished. There would be the true monument, in the history books. DeSilvo smiled at the list and reached out to touch it, almost caressing it.

It gave him vast pleasure to think on the incredible resources at his command. The energy sources, the political authority, the masses of powerful machinery, the army of workers spread out over the generations that were required to rebuild a world—all were at his command. It was satisfying indeed to have such facilities, such resources, such *power* at his personal disposal. There seemed no limit to what he could accomplish.

But there were limits. Yes. Things could go wrong. He considered the news reports concerning the conclusion of the inquiries into the *Upholder* incident. It was good to have such reminders. The datapages were full of her ordeal at Circum Central, of the way she had been marooned eight decades into her own future, and of her harrowing journey back to the Solar System. He had read somewhere that the ship's commander, Koffield, was to be assigned to some sort of meaningless desk job, pretending to do research, here, aboard the Grand Library.

DeSilvo stared out his private viewport at the spectacular view of Neptune. The mystery of what had happened at Circum Central would remain unsolved for a long time to come, perhaps for all time. As long as it did, and perhaps long after, the whisperers would point at Koffield. Not many would have much to do with the man who had destroyed a timeshaft wormhole and cut off a whole world from the outside universe.

Someone ought to help the man. Encourage him. There could be no doubt at all that Koffield was competent. And there was certainly work that needed doing. DeSilvo nodded to himself. Yes. He would approach Koffield. Invite him to join the project. Let the whisperers whisper. He would reach out to Koffield and allow him to work with Oskar DeSilvo.

DeSilvo puffed up his chest a bit, and smiled proudly to himself, congratulating himself on this latest act of goodness and charity. It would be a good and generous deed, one worthy of the praise it would no doubt inspire.

How lucky for humanity, for the universe, that there was such a splendid being as Oskar DeSilvo in it.

The speeches were over, and the guest of honor had received his award, and given his eloquent thanks. The ceremonies being complete, the informal part of the evening had begun. All around the newcomer, a splendid party, a sparkling celebration, was happening, swirling about its still center, a merry storm of light, color, and music that filled the largest and most ornate ballroom aboard the Grand Library habitat. But, there, at its center, Anton Koffield, recently promoted to the exalted rank of rear admiral, handsome in his dress uniform, stood alone, and still. All was quiet about him. No one went to him. No one even dared come near.

He was the silent eye of the storm, and, as he moved,

the quiet moved with him. Voices faded away, and knots of conversation dissolved at his approach. Even the robotic waiters seemed reluctant to tarry long in his presence, and scurried away the first moment they could.

He should have known better than to come, should have known this time would be no better than the last time, or the time before that. The fact that his actions had been officially approved and endorsed by the boards of inquiry made no difference. No one wanted to make small talk with a man who had blood on his hands. And Koffield could not truly bring himself to blame them. He knew what they saw when they looked at him. He saw it himself whenever he looked in the mirror. Guilt. Blame. Failure. No official finding could hide or disguise the shadows that hovered about him.

What, he wondered, for the hundredth, the thousandth, time, was the point of surviving an ordeal as harrowing as the return trip from Circum Central? Could there be any point when the only role life had to offer him was as a focus for the whisperers, the pointers, the ones who stared at his back as they listened eagerly to a friend telling the tale yet again? What point in determination, endurance, leadership, if the reward was this? The partygoers would look haughtily in the other direction if he, Koffield the butcher, had the temerity to so much as catch their eyes, return their gazes.

His crew had spoken well of him through all the inquiries. They had called him courageous, even heroic, and still spoke up for him, even if no one listened. But his crew were not here, and were not, in truth, even a crew anymore. They had retired or resigned or been reassigned. Scattered, as lost to him as the *Upholder,* and the *Upholder* had been written off as a total loss, not worth repairing.

He let out a weary sigh and decided to give it up. There was nothing for him here. He caught up with a passing service robot and set his drink down on its upper tray. Time to go. He started to make his slow and quiet way to the exit.

"Excuse me," a voice said behind him. A man's voice, the accent warm and sophisticated.

Koffield turned around to see a handsome man in a burgundy scholar's robe. It was DeSilvo himself, he realized with astonishment. "Yes?"

The scholar smiled, his teeth blinding white. "I am Dr. Oskar DeSilvo," he said, the needless introduction charmingly modest. "You are Rear Admiral Anton Koffield?"

"That's right," Koffield replied, bracing himself for whatever bit of theatrics this DeSilvo had in mind. He had been through it all by now. Would it be another drink thrown in his face? Another outburst of verbal abuse? This fellow didn't look the sort to splash simulated—or real—blood onto Koffield, but it was hard to know. But if DeSilvo had intended a direct physical attack, he wouldn't have gotten Koffield's attention first. And the man's manner was distinctly friendly. Koffield decided he could relax his guard a bit, at least. "What can I do for you?"

DeSilvo smiled again. "Possibly, quite a lot," he said. "I have a large project under way. I am here at the Grand Library to turn over my archives of the Solacian Terraforming project. I was wondering if you would care to help prepare those archives."

Koffield frowned in surprise. "I'm not quite sure I understand."

DeSilvo reached over and put his hand on Koffield's forearm. "Your help," he said. "I believe your record would make you well suited to a task, an important task, I have in mind. I could use your help."

And those were words that Rear Admiral Anton Koffield had never expected to hear again.

SOLACE
127 YEARS LATER
5339 A.D.

CHAPTER FOUR
LOSS OF CONFIDENCE

They were dying before her eyes. Neshobe Kalzant stood on the observation deck and watched the stampede for the last shuttlecraft. They were shoving, screaming, shouting to get past each other, clawing at each other in a futile attempt to win one of the pathetically small number of seats on the shuttle—seats that were already taken, and already being defended by determined men and women at the shuttle hatch. Neshobe had counted at least four people crushed to death already.

The proud citizens of Solace were trampling one another in the rain-darkened night, forcing past one another in a futile attempt to get aboard what was merely rumored to be the last ship out. The public-address system bellowed its promises that there would be more transport on the way, that the rumors were false. But the crowd could not hear, or would not believe, the mechanical voice.

The storm shouted and thundered over and around the mob outside on the spaceport landing pad, and the rain surged in harder, pummeling the observation-deck window, making it all but impossible to see the madness outside.

For one brief, cruel moment, Neshobe wished that she herself could be on that shuttle. She could do it. Neshobe Kalzant's word was law on Solace. She got what she wanted. Even now, at this late moment, she could give a quiet order to the spaceport guards, and they would bash through the crowd for her, let her take her place aboard that shuttle. She could get the devil off this miserable planet. Even in the midst of this mob, this chaos, none would have dared oppose her. No one could have stopped her.

Neshobe imagined the pleasure of getting herself into the ship and up into the clean sky, away from both the literal and figurative rot and stink of Solace.

She could leave. And she sorely wanted to do so. She all but spoke the words of command, almost made the gesture with her hand that would have summoned the nearest guards. But she stood silent, motionless, instead. If her word was law here, it was because she held the law in high respect. Neshobe Kalzant had sworn to govern her people, and keep faith with them. She would do so—even as her people scratched and clawed each other to get aboard a spacecraft that wasn't going much of anywhere anyway.

Neshobe felt ill. It had been a mistake to come to the spaceport. She had told herself that she needed to see this firsthand, but seeing the latest liftoff riot had served no useful purpose. Perhaps she had been attempting to assuage her own guilt. Instead, she had simply added a layer of shame and disgust over it.

There had been a run on the Planetary Bank of Solace two years before. The depositors had panicked because of their perfectly accurate perception that the bank's supply of a valuable resource—money—was in short supply. The bank had responded by acting as if its cash reserves were ample to meet any contingency and calmly paying out all withdrawal requests in full—while frantically scrambling in the background to come up with secret short-term credits and bridge loans from every possible source. Most of the planet's other financial institutions were happy to cooperate—for if the Planetary Bank had gone under, it would have taken a miracle to keep the rest of them from following her down.

The financiers met the shortage of natural confidence by manufacturing the artificial variety. *After* the immediate problem was resolved, after the institution had survived, they had started to worry about long-term survival and the need for reforms and tighter credit controls.

That was the way to go here, now, in this crisis. She turned toward the local guard commander. "Link me to Commander Raenau on Solace Central Orbital Station," she said. "Voice only will do."

The guard commander gestured to one of his troopers, who pulled a secure-line comm-pad from his equipment belt and spoke to it in a low whisper, doing call-and-response code clearances, working his way through the layers of subordinate humans and robotic ArtInts and intels that worked for spaceside ops.

Neshobe let the guard do his work on the comm-pad. She stepped forward closer to the reinforced glass of the floor-to-ceiling observation window and looked down on her people, looked down on the panicky rabble that was, sad to say, something close to a representative sample of the good people of Solace, or at least the working classes of Solace.

Solacian society was deeply stratified, and always had been, going back to the first days of the terraforming project. A small, well-to-do, and largely hereditary upper class of administrators, engineers, politicians, and space-based workers presided over a much larger lower class of less-educated small-plot farmers, semiskilled laborers, and, these days, a large leavening of Glistern refugees as well. Neshobe knew all about the history and traditions of her world, and how they had produced a strong tradition of paternalism in the upper classes, a sense of being obligated to the masses, while still being quite well aware of being superior to them. But knowing how her culture's social patterns had come to be did not make them seem any less significant or meaningful.

She was sworn to protect those scared, angry people out there. Mob or no mob, it was her duty to serve them, and by all the Gods of Legend, she would do it, even if it got her killed—and some of them killed too, for that matter. Hard to avoid that, if the members of her flock insisted on killing each other. The best Neshobe could do would be to keep the casualties to a minimum. And she thought she saw a way to do that.

"Commander Raenau," the guard said, handing her the comm-pad.

"Thank you, Corporal," she said, and took the pad. She pushed the stud that converted it to handset mode and held it to her head, the mike by her mouth and the speaker to her ear. "Commander, this is Planetary Executive Kalzant. We have a panic here. We need to shut it down."

"Yes, Madam PlanEx, I guess you do." The tone of his voice made it as plain as his words that he didn't consider the groundside situation to be of any concern for a man in orbit.

"When I used the word *we* I was including you, Commander. In fact, you're going to be the one who solves this problem for the rest of us."

"Ma'am?"

"The panic here was set off by the rumor that we were going to order an evacuation of the population from the flooded-out areas to orbit, but that we didn't because of a ground-to-orbit transport shortage. We need to convince the people it's not true."

"That might be a problem, ma'am. I can tell you right now that the part about the transport shortage is no rumor at all. Two of our heavy transports are in orbital drydock for maintenance checks."

"Get them out," Neshobe said. "Stop whatever work isn't needed for safe ground-to-space operation, and get them back in service, along with every other transport you have. Put them all into round-the-clock shuttle service. Anyone who wants to go topside can. Anyone who wants to go groundside can. Relax the safety rules, and clear anything that can fly to orbit."

"But ma'am—"

"And make it look easy, like your people aren't even making an effort. Go all out, but don't let the strain show."

"But all the spaceside habitats are close to carrying capacity already," Raenau protested.

Neshobe shut her eyes for a moment and let tiredness sweep over her. It occurred to her she had spent her entire term of office doing what she had just told Raenau to try doing—working like mad while making it look easy. "Get creative, Commander. Welcome anyone who wants to go topside—but don't make them *too* welcome, or *too* comfortable. Put them in nice, clean, safe, uncomfortable, unprivate barracks accommodations. Run the air pressure just a trifle thin, and the temperature just a little cool. Find some reasonable excuse for splitting up families—men in one tempo barracks, women in another. Don't let it get out of hand, but let your people overcharge the groundsiders just a bit. And make sure everyone knows the ships are flying back empty."

"I get the idea, ma'am. But it won't come easy, or cheap. It's going to run into a lot of overtime pay and emergency requisitions."

"Whatever it comes to is going to be cheaper than having Solace City Spaceport wrecked and riots downtown," she said. "Can you do the job, and get things coordinated with the groundside teams?"

Raenau sighed wearily. "Yes, ma'am. We can do it—but I can't promise we'll enjoy it."

"Just see to it that the clientele doesn't enjoy it either," she said. "Kalzant out."

She closed up the comm-pad, handed it back to the corporal, and turned her back on the view of the riot below. Without another word to anyone, she walked out of the observation lounge and back toward her private skycar. She stepped into the car, let the hatch seal shut behind her, and dropped back into the luxurious upholstery. Privacy.

"Transport destination, instruct regarding," the car said in the backwards syntax of Solacian ArtInts.

"Away," said Neshobe Kalzant. "Out. To someplace clean."

The car was tactful enough not to observe that that would require quite a long drive indeed.

Jorl Parrige told himself that he should have been a happy man as he knelt among his tomato plants and toiled in his garden. The sun was hot, the sky was blue and laced with lazy white clouds, the ground was warm and redolent of life and the smells of fertile earth and green plants.

Jorl Parrige, Grand Senyor of the Planetary Council and

Legislative Member for the Riket's Town Constituency, was a tall, broad-shouldered man, large rather than merely tall, his long grey-black beard adding much to his massively dignified appearance. Even now, kneeling in the dirt, wearing old gardening clothes and a battered, foolish-looking straw sun hat, his serious expression and deliberate movement preserved the aura of stateliness and steadiness he had so carefully built up around himself.

Parrige was a man who enjoyed his garden. There was peace in his garden, and life, and the comforts of home. But, unfortunately, there was also his personal assistant, Aither Fribart, standing just a meter or two away, wearing his formal working clothes and, worse, his formal working attitude.

"There was another altercation at Solace City Spaceport last night," Fribart said—or, more accurately, announced. There was always something judgmental in the tone of Fribart's reports, a disapproving note that seemed directed as much at Parrige as at the fools and yokels whose misbehavior had attracted Fribart's attention. Just about everyone was a fool or a yokel, or worse, in Fribart's estimation.

Parrige made no reply. The bees were not doing well this spring, but Grand Senyor Jorl Parrige almost did not mind. It meant he was compelled to hand-pollinate much of his garden, and he found the slow, delicate work to be soothing. Or he would have, if he had been permitted the chance to get on with it.

"I said there was another altercation at Solace—" Fribart began again.

"I heard you the first time," Parrige said, glancing up at the sticklike figure of his assistant. Fribart was actually something above average height, but so thin and wiry that people took him to be much shorter than he was. He was dark-skinned, and, today, as usual, wore dark, drab formal colors, his knee breeches and leggings and frock coat and blouse all one shade or another of dark grey or brownish black.

There was something about Fribart that put Parrige in mind of a black-feathered, long-legged, predatory shore bird, stepping through the muck and mire of everyday life with absurdly overdone care and exaggerated caution. He was a bird who moved slowly and woodenly, watching everything, but then stabbed his beak down hard and fast into any tempting morsel of news that was fool enough to attract his attention.

"Well, sir, you did not respond the first time. How was I to know that you heard?"

There was a bit of discoloration on some of the leaves on this plant. Parrige took up his pruning shears and carefully cut away the stem that bore the offending leaves. "I don't honestly care how you were to know," he replied. "I don't see that it makes any difference if I did hear or not."

"Sir! This was a major disturbance. It was—"

"It was widely reported quite some hours ago by every news medium. I can read, you know, and I am capable of operating a viewscreen and comprehending the images on it. In short, there was, as usual, little point in your coming here to report what I already know."

"But if you knew about it, surely it was your duty to act."

"Act?" Parrige repeated, allowing a certain testiness to edge into his voice. He stood up and regarded his assistant closely. "Act? And what was I supposed to do? Bustle out to the spaceport and slap the rioters on the wrists? Shake my finger at the corpses and say I hoped that they had learned their lessons? Show up at security headquarters and disrupt their investigation by calling in a bunch of reporters and asking them to avoid disrupting the investigation? I suppose there were a great number of things I could have done, but none of them would have been useful. Did you know Madam Neshobe Kalzant was on the scene, an eyewitness?"

"No, sir, I didn't."

"Which is my point. *She* went out there to see the situation for herself. When she saw she could do no good, she got out of the way, called no attention to herself, and managed the situation from elsewhere. I took my cue from her. I suggest you do the same in future."

Fribart sniffed audibly. "Forgive me, sir, but I do not regard Madam Kalzant as a role model. She is impulsive, and her actions are often rash."

"Quite right," Parrige replied as he moved along to the next plant. "And it is a good thing too."

"Sir!" Fribart was genuinely shocked, as if Parrige was voicing approval for Neshobe Kalzant being degenerate or insane.

Parrige let out a sigh. He often wondered why he employed Fribart, but in his heart, Parrige knew the reason. Ironically, it was for moments precisely like this one. Fribart was rigid and cautious—every bit as rigid and cautious as the average Solacian. His reaction served as a highly reliable barometer of the average citizen's reaction, whatever the circumstance. Oftentimes, as now, his behavior was immensely irritating, but it was at precisely those times that it was most informative.

Fribart's scandalized reaction served to remind Parrige of how even an offhand remark could cause trouble. Parrige could just imagine the sort of thundering editorials and headlines that would have poured out of the various infostream centers if he had said any such thing in public. PARRIGE CALLS KALZANT RASH AND APPROVES. PARRIGE CALLS FOR IMPULSIVE ACTION.

Parrige deliberately chose not to get out before the public very often. For the most part, that choice served him well. But there were times he could not avoid public speaking, and at such times, it was painfully clear how little skill and practice he had in the art.

Fribart, with all his rigid moods and prejudices, made a useful stand-in for the Solacian public. But it was best to remember that Fribart spoke to the public himself. "Perhaps," Parrige said, "I could persuade you to rephrase that just a trifle when you speak of Kalzant in public. Say rather that she makes choices quickly, and acts decisively."

"But sir—"

"I know this will be a novel concept for you, Fribart, but theory has it that, in your capacity as my spokesman, you are to express *my* thoughts, views, and attitudes—not your own. And I might also remind you to look beyond the end of your nose now and again. If Madam Neshobe Kalzant goes down, and brings the present government down with her, there will be chaos. I myself often do not agree with her. But she is all we have, and, for the moment at least, none of all her potential successors have anything like the political depth of support needed to build a new coalition." Parrige raised his hand, open-palmed, to silence Fribart before he could speak. "And before you tell me, once again, how I myself am best suited to succeed her, let me say that I include myself when I say no one has the depth of support to build a new coalition. I don't want her job, and even if I did, I would not be able to get it. Is that clear enough?"

"Yes, sir. But—" Fribart stopped, as if expecting to be interrupted again.

"Go on," Parrige said. It did not do to bully one's subordinates too far. Even ones like Fribart, who were so easy to bully, and who deserved it so much. The man had a right to say what he thought, at least now and again.

"Sir—I can say whatever you like about her style, her attitude. But—but, sir, she is sincerely *dangerous*."

Parrige looked at Fribart in surprise. It was rare indeed for anything to break through the man's control. Fribart was, quite suddenly, speaking with genuine passion—and genuine fear. "Dangerous how?" Parrige asked.

"Sir, I should think that was obvious. She has spoken many times, to many people, about the recent weather problems. She has said far too much. There is no doubt in my mind that she contributed to—perhaps even created—the panic that produced last night's mob."

" 'The recent weather problems,' " Parrige repeated. Remarkable what passed for thinking sometimes. "Is that how you refer to the situation? I should think 'ongoing climatic crisis' would sum it up better."

"Surely, sir, the worst is over and past."

"Is it indeed? That, I expect, will come as news to most of the climate people. Do you have any basis for that statement?"

"Things are bound to return to normal sooner or later."

"Possibly so. But there have been people on this planet

for something less than three hundred standard years, and it was only certified as fully terraformed a bit over one hundred years ago. There are researchers up on Greenhouse who would tell you the job still isn't finished, and that is why the climate is so unstable. What would you describe as 'normal' for a presently life-bearing planet that was a lifeless ball of rock for the first ninety-nine-point-nine-nine-nine percent of its existence?"

"I—I don't understand."

"I am glad to hear it," Parrige replied. "Please bear in mind that you do not the next time you feel the urge to discuss the matter with others."

"Sir?" The hurt on Fribart's face was plain to see.

Parrige sighed wearily. It was difficult to *avoid* bullying Fribart. The man all but invited it. At least he had broken through that barrier of haughty reserve. "Forgive me," he said. "That was quite uncalled for. But my point is a valid one. We have not been on this planet long enough to *know* for sure what normal is. The terraformed climate itself has not been here long enough to establish a valid baseline. Some of our scientists on Greenhouse say there is good reason to think that it could be years before the climate restabilizes properly in a state that we would call normal. We could well be in for a prolonged period of violent and unpredictable weather in many inhabited areas—including the food-production areas. Unless we take the proper precautions, the people of Solace could be facing famine. Should Madam Kalzant simply ignore the problem in the hope that it will get better by itself?"

"Well, perhaps it will," Fribart said. Parrige did not reply, but instead regarded his assistant with a steady and reproachful eye. At last Fribart gave in. "It's unlikely, I grant," he said. "And I suppose we can't govern the planet by wishful thinking. But I still believe it is irresponsible of Madam Kalzant to stir things up as much as she does. I doubt you can argue with me on that point."

Parrige bent down to collect his things. He put his trowel and his gardening shears back in his carry-basket, and straightened up. Enough for today. Best not to fuss too much over the flowers. Tend them too much and you could kill them.

He had not answered Fribart for the very good reason that he agreed with Fribart, and no doubt Fribart knew that he had scored a point. Madam Kalzant *did* stir things up too much. She *was* impulsive. But even if Parrige was unable to give Fribart any further argument on either point, neither could he give Fribart the satisfaction of hearing him concede.

"I'm done here," he said, brushing the dirt from the knees of his trousers. "Come with me back into the house."

Fribart nodded gravely and fell in step with him as Parrige walked toward the exit. Parrige paused a moment at the exit hatch. He always hated to leave his garden. It was not just that he regretted leaving the place where he was happiest. It was that the very act of leaving, the complicated process of going in and out, forced him to break out of his own denials and illusions. When it was time to leave, he could no longer pretend that all was normal, that the garden was as it once had been. He could no longer pretend he did not notice the bubble-dome, no longer pretend he could not hear the low hum of the atmosphere reprocessor.

Fribart stepped into the airlock ahead of him, and Parrige, reluctantly, followed him in, taking one last breath of the fresh, fecund, moist air, one last indulgence in the scent of green and living things. He sealed the inner hatch and waited as the force-filter field activated.

There was breathable air on both sides of the lock, of course—but the air inside the garden dome was conditioned, humidified, ion-balanced, invigorating. The outside air was none of those things—and Parrige had no desire to expose his flowers to the rogue microbes and molds and parasites that seemed to be evolving into new and crueler forms with every passing day. The filter-field airlock kept the inner and outer air away from each other with all but perfect efficiency.

He looked down toward the floor of the chamber as the

filter field came to life, a shimmering grey sheet of blankness that completely hid the bottom of the chamber from view. The filter field started moving upward, pushing the live air back up into the ceiling vents and back into the garden dome, and drawing in the dry, desiccated air of the outside world from the floor vents. The field flowed upward, looking like a pool of glassy-smooth grey water rising up around them. The field flowed around their bodies with the faintest tremor of contained power as the static charge flowed upward along with the field. The garden air rushed up around him, forced out by the filter field. Parrige watched as the field swallowed up his feet, his legs, his torso. It was impossible to force down altogether the sense of panic as the field rose toward his chest, his throat, his head. It was too easy to believe he was caught in the rising flood, that the water was swallowing him up and he was about to drown.

The field swept up over his face, and the feel of living air against his skin was gone. The harsh dry air of the outside slapped up against him. Parrige looked up to watch the field, still moving upward toward the ceiling of the chamber, where it paused, its work completed, before vanishing as if it had never been. The outer hatch swung open and the unfiltered light of the outside world poured in. They were out of the garden.

Fribart let out a sigh of completely undisguised relief and satisfaction as they stepped out into the too-harsh, too-bright, too-hot light of the unfiltered Solacian day and moved out into the death-dry air and the hot, dusty, brown landscape.

Was Fribart to be pitied because he preferred the harshness of the outside over the coddled confines of the garden dome? Fribart had found a way to pretend that the current climate suited him, and was the way it should be, even as he worried about its decline. Certainly that was foolish.

And yet, Parrige wondered, should he himself be the one to be pitied, or even reviled, for preferring to hide away in a simulation of the world as it no longer was, for pretending that all the world was as lovely as his garden?

"Tell me, Fribart. You don't really prefer this shriveled landscape over my garden, do you?"

Fribart offered up the slightest of shrugs, the tiniest possible gesture of apology. "I suppose I do, sir. It is what I am used to. Perhaps, once the local climate recovers its normal state, I'll find it too damp, too muggy—like your garden. If things had remained as they were, it might be that I would enjoy your garden. But whatever went wrong has already gone wrong. I have changed, and the world has too." Fribart looked up into the sky, and Parrige followed his gaze.

The fat gleaming dot of Solace Central Orbital Station was plainly visible in the western sky. As they watched, a dot of light flared and moved away from the station as a large spacecraft of some sort launched itself.

"Big," Fribart said. "Probably a timeshaft ship, a star ship," he said.

"We don't see many of those anymore," Parrige said. "I remember when there were ships coming every few days, not every few months."

"If only we could do what they do," said Fribart. "The timeshaft ships drop back in time. Wouldn't it be splendid if we could go back and fix the mistake or the problem, whatever it was that got us into trouble, and then come back?"

Parrige took an involuntary half step back from his assistant, as if he subconsciously expected a bolt of lightning to smite the man in two. "Dangerous talk, friend Fribart," he said. "The Chronologic Patrol has little sense of humor. Don't joke, even in private, about such things."

Fribart blinked hard in surprise and turned his attention from the sky to his companion. His eyes widened in alarm. "What? Oh! No! No, of course not. You're quite right, Master Parrige. Quite right. Forgive me."

"Let us be on our way, then, and hear no more about such things." Parrige was astonished by his companion's behavior. Fribart was a conformist, if ever any man had been such a thing—and his whimsical little idea about using time travel to fix Solace was as black a heresy as any could be. There could not be any more dangerous thought. In literal fact, the interstellar transport timeshafts allowed for travel back through time, that much was true. But that was not what they were there for. There was no blacker crime than attempting to use the timeshafts to make a purposeful, intentional trip to one's own past on one's own world.

Paradoxes, changes to history, unintended consequences—it was impossible to imagine the chaos that would be unleashed by such an act, however well intentioned.

Things were worse than he believed, Parrige told himself. They had to be bad when as unimaginative and rigid a man as Fribart started fantasizing about the commission of desperate crimes in the pursuit of magical answers to their problems.

But the worst of it was this: A man like Fribart would dare imagine such things only after he started to believe, subconsciously at least, that there was no hope outside of desperation and magic.

If even men like Fribart were starting to think that way, then, it seemed to Parrige, things could not hold together very much longer.

CHAPTER FIVE

SOCKS IN THE SOUP

"It's quite a terrible stink, isn't it?" the biotechnician asked, his voice apologetic. He stood on the moldering pier and looked down at the greasy green water of Lake Virtue, a body of water that wasn't remotely near living up to its name.

The slope of the shore was very gentle at this end, and the pier wasn't long enough to get out toward really deep water. The pier's boardwalk was all of a meter above the lake surface, and probably the water below it was no more than a meter and a half deep. But no one would wish to get closer to that water than necessary.

"No worse than I expected," Neshobe Kalzant replied. She turned to Parrige, a step or two behind her on the pier. "Though you'll agree that's not saying the smell is pleasant."

"That much is certain," Parrige replied. Dead fish, decaying vegetation, a rotten-egg stench—far from the most enjoyable of bouquets. He certainly felt no desire to experience it any longer than he had to.

"It was worse a month ago, if you can imagine that," said the biotech. Parrige concentrated for a moment on the pro forma introductions at the brief ceremony when their aircar had landed. Milos Vandar. That was the fellow's name. He was an amiable-looking sort of chap, tall and thin, long-faced, with an impressive hook nose that could have looked sinister if the man's expression had not been so open and friendly. He had nondescript brown eyes, and brown hair that had obviously been ferociously combed down into place for their arrival. By now, twenty minutes later, it was already wandering out of control, back to what was obviously its customary state: drifting into Vandar's eyes and starting to stick up around his ears.

"Mind you," Vandar went on, "it doesn't *look* any better than it did back then. Not at this shore. Not yet. But it *does* smell better here—or at least less bad. We're definitely registering improvement."

Improvement. There was a word Parrige had heard but rarely in recent times—and it was the word they had come in search of. He stepped forward a trifle and looked at the greasy water a bit more closely.

"So you're turning it around," Neshobe suggested.

Vandar shrugged, then squatted at the end of the pier, staring out at the greasy green scum on the water. "I suppose you could put it that way. Lake Virtue is so far down there's not much place to go but up. If there *is* any way to go down from here, I don't want to know about it. But yes, we've got some nice clear positive upticks. Oxygen levels, water clarity, populations of desirable species. We're getting there."

"That's what we're here to hear," Neshobe said.

Or, more accurately, that's what we're here to be seen hearing, Parrige thought, glancing toward the infostream service techs on the shore. The point of the exercise was to have Neshobe Kalzant shown in connection with an ecological recovery project. It almost didn't matter *which* project. At least it wasn't an act. Madam Kalzant was genuinely, even urgently, interested in the recovery program. He watched as she knelt at the very edge of the pier, staring intently at the green sludge below as the biotech explained something or other.

With Neshobe's back turned, Parrige half-instinctively took advantage of the moment to move back from the edge of the pier, and a bit closer to the shore. He had never much cared for open water, particularly water this foul. Fribart, who, it would seem, believed even less in the lake's virtues, waited on land, standing on the path leading to the dock, the news-service reporters standing behind him.

The wind shifted for a moment, blowing a particularly pungent gust of rancid lake air right into the knot of reporters. It was almost worth the inconvenience of the trip to see Fribart's expression at that moment.

But there were other matters to deal with. He turned back toward Neshobe and Vandar at the end of the pier. "So what went wrong?" Parrige asked, moving a cautious step or two back toward the pier's end.

"Classic socks-in-the-soup infestation," Vandar said.

"I beg your pardon?" Parrige asked.

"Sorry," said Vandar. "That's our slang term for it. Introduction of an uncontrolled organism. Someone drops their dirty socks with who-knows-what bacteria on them into the soup, the environment, and the bacteria start in growing. The introduced organism doesn't have any natural enemies or internal kill switches, so it's hard to repress, never mind eliminate."

Neshobe nodded thoughtfully, but Parrige was not much better off for having received that explanation. "I'm sorry," he said, "but I don't know what a kill switch is."

"You should," Neshobe said. "There's only one species of life-form allowed on this planet without one, and you're it."

"I beg your pardon?" Parrige said, more confused than ever, and now even a trifle alarmed. "Should I have one?"

"It's not you personally who doesn't have one," Vandar said, smiling. "It's all of us. Humans. We're the only species legally allowed on-planet without having at least one, and generally two or three, genetically engineered kill switches inserted into our DNA."

"Every other authorized species on-planet has some sort of booby trap built in," Neshobe explained. "Something that will respond to a certain stimulus by inducing death. Some way we can kill some or all of a species in a given area without having to kill anything else. Usually a very specific artificial toxin, but it can be anything from tuned hypersonics to a particular frequency of coherent light. Whatever the switch is, if it turns out we've made a mistake, and the species isn't right for whatever niche it's in, we can undo the mistake."

"But there's always something that gets in that isn't supposed to," Vandar went on, obviously quite unmindful that he was interrupting the planetary leader. "A bacterium that comes in on some spacecraft that doesn't get a proper decontamination, some vermin or another that hides out in a food shipment, some damn fool pet someone smuggles in. Something. And one of those somethings is the species of algae that's infested this lake. There's nothing in this lake that's willing to eat it.

"But the real problem is that by now it's embedded itself in the local ecosystem. It's too well established. There's no longer any way to eradicate it without killing everything else in the lake and the surrounding countryside. And even if we did that, it's probably hitchhiked on a bird or two by now, or else traveled via windborne transmission, or even had itself carried up in convected water that's already rained down somewhere else. Which means either it already has or it probably will spread from here to other lakes and rivers and so on. We have to assume that, from here on in, it's part of the planet's ecology, and we have to figure out ways to live with it."

"What have you brought in to control it?" Neshobe asked.

"Nothing too fancy. We sent samples of the algae and the water and so on up to Greenhouse, and they managed to locate several organisms they had on file that'd happily eat the algae in question. Two looked like reasonable fits into the local ecosystem, with minor modifications. Greenhouse modified the candidate organisms, ran mathematical simulations and real-life trials, and confirmed the fix would work. The modified rotifers and microshrimp will eat the algae and won't overbreed themselves. Greenhouse bred up a stock of the new species and shipped them to us. We've started introduction at the south end of Virtue, and everything seems to be going well. We'll let the first introduction run another week or so, and then perform wholesale introductions into the entire lake and connected waterbeds. And, of course, we have the needed mods of the microshrimp and the rotifers on file if we get another outbreak."

"Excellent," Neshobe said. "First-class work all the way." She stood up, turned her back on the lake, and headed back toward Fribart and the newspeople. The whole point of the operation was to have them see her here, to have them report back to the people at large that Neshobe Kalzant was there on the scene, learning all about the latest and most advanced techniques for rebuilding the Solacian climate. It would tell her people that she was doing something positive—and that something positive was being done. A good morale booster, and a good way to improve her image, which had gotten a bit roughed up in recent days.

Certainly such staged events were far from new in the world of politics, but they had never been seen before on Solace. Before Neshobe Kalzant, politics and government hadn't been particularly public.

But now the public was paying attention. Neshobe understood the importance of playing to the public, of putting her story before them. Thus today's visit to a malodorous lake. Parrige had set the whole thing up himself—and had done so, needless to say, over Fribart's vehement objections, on any number of grounds. It was his first venture into political theater, and, modest though the effort might have been, it had gone well. He was pleased with the result, and was already thinking ahead to what might be done next.

But there was another part of him that was less than satisfied. He stepped to one side to let Neshobe pass, and then fell into step with Vandar as the scientist followed her toward the press. Parrige put a hand on Vandar's arm, holding him back just a trifle, slowing him down. "It all sounds very good," he said. "But this *is* just one medium-sized lake with one relatively simple, even routine problem."

"What of it?" Vandar asked, his voice as cheerful and open as his face.

"Well, I have two questions, actually. It took a fairly large effort, and extensive resources, for you to be able to solve this problem. Does it always take that much time and effort to compensate for an algae infestation?"

"Sometimes," Vandar said carefully. "Sometimes it's a lot easier. But, on balance, I'd have to admit that this was a comparatively simple fix. There have been lots of others we've put more time in on."

"And there could easily be more and bigger problems in future. One only a bit more complex than this one could absorb all of your people's time and attention for an extended period. Even overwhelm you completely. Or you could just be caught by the fact that a planet is a big place. You could easily miss a crisis as big as this one, or even bigger."

"Right again," Vandar said. "We *have* missed crises worse than this. Plenty of times. We're only now getting good at detecting them early on." They had come to the end of the pier, and paused there. "What's your other problem?"

"I gather that you needed Greenhouse in order to do the fix at all. Is that correct?"

"Absolutely. I suppose we could have done it down here, but it would have been far more difficult. They're the ones with the resources and facilities and the controlled environments. What's your point?"

"Greenhouse won't last forever. DeSilvo's original terraforming schedule called for it to be shut down over seventy years ago. The engineers have performed all sorts of clever tricks to keep it up and running this long. They've done it so brilliantly for so long that most people just assume that it will last forever. The reality is that each time they patch it up for a bit longer, it becomes even more fragile. And most people think of it just as a research facility—not as a vitally needed repair center. What do we do when it finally gives out?"

Parrige had half expected Vandar to get defensive, or to

deny the problems were there. Instead the man smiled sadly at him and shook his head. "You're pretty good at finding tough questions, aren't you?" he asked, and then starting walking on toward Neshobe Kalzant and the newspeople.

TIMESHAFT SHIP
<u>DOM PEDRO IV</u>

CHAPTER SIX

OUT OF TIME

The *Dom Pedro IV* was a gleaming, featureless silver cylinder, dropping down out of the cold darkness of interstellar space, falling toward the still-distant realms of warmth and light ahead. By the standards of interstellar transport she was of modest size, but she was monstrously large when judged by any human scale. She was nearly a kilometer long from stem to stern, though only seventy meters in cross section. The physics and economics of the timeshaft-transport system required ships to be as small in cross section as possible, though they placed no limits on ship length. Hemispherical endcaps made up the two ends of the cylinder, and that too was dictated by the physics of the timeshaft system. Everything had been done to present the smoothest of exterior surfaces to the outside world, for it was far simpler to induce integrity shields around a simple shape than around a complex one.

The adaptations to timeshaft transit had their benefits in the transit across normal space as well, of course. The *Dom Pedro IV* traveled at a significant fraction of lightspeed. At such speeds, even a subatomic particle would impact with remarkable energy. A narrow cross section and an easily shielded exterior greatly reduced the danger of serious impact damage.

The *Dom Pedro IV* was nearing the end of her long journey, and the few subsystems that had remained awake for all of the trip now set about rousing the dormant, power-downed, and trickle-charged main systems that had drowsed across the light-years. Hatches opened, sensors extruded themselves. Antennae and thrusters and navigational detectors popped out of their hiding places. The powerful braces of the inertial manipulators swung themselves out and locked into position.

The two endcaps of the ship folded back to reveal the transparent observation dome forward and the main engines aft. Like a masquerader who peels off an expressionless mask and reveals a face of character and complexity beneath, the *Dom Pedro IV* transformed herself. The mirror-bright quicksilver spear shaft that had flung itself across the star-void was gone. In its place was a wakening piece of machinery of impossible complexity, its bristling surface forested with spars and dishes and thruster bulbs and optical clusters.

The ship came about, bringing her main engines to bear forward, directly opposite her direction of travel. The inertial manipulators activated, spinning a shimmering greygold cocoon about the ship, diminishing, but not entirely cutting off, her inertial relationship to the outside universe. The main engines came to life, but with none of the flame and flare of the rocket-reaction engines of an age so far distant that it seemed the stuff of legend. The only visible evidence of operation for these engines was the dull orange glow that flickered and flared over the surface of their massive thruster bulbs.

In less time than any of the ancient engineers of the proto–Space Age would have credited, the *Dom Pedro IV* decelerated. The main engines shut down, and the great ship came about, until she was pointed nose first through her direction of travel, and the center of the local star system.

The *Dom Pedro IV* had arrived in splendid style, moving with an artful and graceful precision through every step of the complex procedure that brought a ship back to life and slowed the craft to a reasonable speed. All of it had worked perfectly, smoothly, beautifully well.

And that was quite remarkable, given the degree to which everything had gone so utterly wrong.

On board the *Dom Pedro IV*, the ship's captain became aware of his surroundings—and knew, instantly, that there was something seriously amiss.

There were only three circumstances in which the temporal-confinement field was meant to cut off—arrival at a timeshaft waypoint, arrival at destination, or in a major emergency. But in any of those cases, the temporal confinement should have flicked itself off smoothly and completely. The walls, ceiling, and floor of the reserve command chamber should have come smoothly into view.

He should have seen the jewel-black interior of the field snap cleanly out of existence, smoothly revealing the command chamber beyond. Instead, the field seemed to shudder once or twice, lurching in and out of the external timestream, the command center visible through a grey haze. Then the field came back on—and immediately cut off again, leaving the containment chamber floating in the center of the room.

Captain Felipe Henrique Marquez knew the sloppy cutoff had to mean that something was wrong. Very wrong. But what?

The bone-chilling cold of the long-dormant ship wrapped itself around the containment chamber. The chamber's transparent cover was frosting over as the too-cold air outside warmed itself against the containment and gave up its moisture in the form of ice crystals that froze to the chamber. The cover's defrosting system came on automatically and chased the frost away by warming the transparency.

Marquez opened the spill valve, allowing ship's air into the containment, thus equalizing the temperature. He took in a breath of the frozen air and felt the knife-sharp stab in his chest as his lungs struggled to contend with the subzero cold. At least that much was normal. The ship was supposed to be cold in dormant mode.

People generally knew that ship captains wore pressure suits with helmets open when they went into temporal confinement. Few realized that they did so more for protection against the expected cold than for protection against some unexpected danger. Marquez left his helmet open but powered up his suit heater. Perhaps it would be some scent in the air that would tell him what was wrong.

Otherwise, he made no attempt to leave the containment chamber. Not yet. Not until he knew more. Suppose he left the temporal-confinement chamber and the temporal field came back on—trapping him outside, aboard a derelict ship somewhere between the stars? And suppose the malfunction had jammed the containment controls in some way so he could not get back in? No, thank you. Marquez would much prefer to be trapped inside the field under such circumstances. If the ship were that far gone, he was a lot more likely to survive long enough to be rescued if he were inside the containment.

Besides, there was no reason to venture out at once. The reserve control center was designed to allow him a clear view of all the vital system-status boards while still inside the temporal-confinement chamber. Marquez decided to take advantage of that while he tried to think things through. What had happened? What had gone wrong?

A temporal-confinement-field generator was vastly more expensive, complex, power-hungry, and heavy than the sort of conventional long-sleep cryo canisters in which a ship's passengers and crew slumbered away the journey across the star-void. But the cryosleep canisters worked by, in essence, freezing the passengers solid. It could take hours or even days to fully revive a long-sleep subject and have him or her recovered and alert. That, of course, was far too long to wait for human intervention in an emergency. Thus the captain of a timeshaft ship—and the captain alone—traveled, not under long-sleep, but inside a temporal-confinement field, where time itself was vastly slowed.

In a sufficiently powerful field, a century would pass in but a few apparent minutes. Captain Felipe Henrique Marquez had traveled inside just such a field. He also knew precisely what would have to have happened in order to interfere with it.

One temporal-confinement field could not exist inside another. If one field came into being around another, the two fields would try and merge into one another. Either the more powerful field would simply absorb energy from the weaker one, or else both would flare out, decanting whatever was inside the fields back into the normal timestream. Similar results were produced when a field that manipulated time-like effects was generated—such as an inertial-manipulation field.

But the ship knew better than to activate the inertial-manipulation system with the captain in temporal confinement. The *Dom Pedro*'s artificial-intelligence systems knew perfectly well that the two field systems were enough like each other that they interacted in complex and hard-to-predict ways, up to and including a high-energy temporal flare-out. And a sufficiently energetic flare-out could incinerate the reserve command center—or even vaporize the entire ship.

It would, therefore, take a hell of an emergency for the *Dom Pedro IV* to take such risks. But what in the name of chaos was the emergency? Marquez watched as the reserve command center's displays came to life before him. Nothing. No explanation at all. Everything seemed absolutely normal. No warning lights flashing or alarms hooting. There was something eerie, disconcerting, almost unnatural, about the normalcy on the situation displays. He shifted his gaze to the temporal-confinement status display. As he watched, the indicator screens flicked over into standby mode as the containment generators powered down. That was something, anyway. Once in standby, the containment generators would require several hours to come back to full power. The temporal confinement couldn't come back on unexpectedly. *Suppose the system was damaged?* he asked himself. *Suppose it cannot come back on at all?* But there was no sense dwelling on such thoughts. One way or the other, there was little he could do about it.

He checked all the banked displays one last time, then unlatched the top of the containment chamber. The reserve command center was always kept in zero gee. Its grav system was independent of the main ship's gravity system. He swung the top out and shoved himself gently forward, floating toward the control displays. The containment chamber's stationkeeping system corrected for the force

Marquez had imposed and held the chamber dead in the center of the reserve control center.

Marquez floated forward, grabbed hold of a stanchion with a gloved hand, and steadied himself as he checked over the displays in more detail. Normal. All was absolutely normal. The ship was in the final stages of moving from long-flight dormancy to full operational capacity. A fully normal power-up. Except for the fact that none of it should have been happening, everything was precisely as it should have been.

So what had prompted the ship to run the inertial manipulators with the temporal confinement running? The inertial manipulators were activated when the main engines lit. It took Felipe Henrique Marquez only a few seconds to check the automated-operations log and confirm that the engines had fired moments before.

But the ship should not have come out of dormancy or activated the inertial systems or fired engines unless and until Captain Marquez was safely decanted out of the temporal confinement, for safety reasons and so as to allow him to oversee the ship's operations.

Marquez finished his initial systems check and went back to the operations log, reset the display to show major navigation events only, leaving out all the endless housekeeping operations and nav checks and minor course corrections that even a dormant ship had to handle.

And he was suddenly aware of his heart pounding against his rib cage. The system reported only one event—the engine braking that had just taken place.

And that should not have been. Because if that was the only major navigation event, then the *Dom Pedro IV* was nowhere within light-years of where she was supposed to be. The flight plan had called for launch and acceleration from the Solar System, a braking, timeshaft transition, and reacceleration through Thor's Realm, Wormhole TR-40.2, braking at Heaven's Funnel, transition through Timeshaft Wormhole HF-TW/102, followed by a long cruise phase and subsequent arrival at HS-G9-223, the Solace star system. None of that had happened. Or had it? The log was blank. He could have no confidence in the event log—which made it difficult to have confidence in anything else.

The only way that the log could have been wiped that completely was if the ship had suffered malfunctions massive enough to wreck every primary, backup, and tertiary navigation system, along with all the alarms and alerts on board. But all ship systems seemed to be operating. Marquez checked over all of his displays again, looking over the data. Some of it had to be wrong. In fact, *none of* it could be right.

The time codes. Marquez checked the ship's chronometer display, and felt his heart go as cold as the ship around him. It was showing 0000 years, 000 days, 00 hours, 04 minutes, and 23 seconds. The damned thing must have started over from zero just as the temporal confinement had shut down. There was no way to know if he had been in temporal confinement for three months or three thousand years.

That settled it. If the clocks had scrambled, there had to be some sort of major malfunction. A bad one, albeit one that managed to keep from shutting off any of the systems. Main control. Up in the forward dome. He could check it out there. If nothing else, he could look out the damned window and see where they were. He checked the telltales by the hatch that led to the ship's main companionway. Air pressure near zero but rising, temperature 120 below but rising, gravity system just completing activation. He nodded. All of it perfectly normal for a ship just coming out of dormant mode.

He closed the helmet on his pressure suit and depressurized the reserve control center down to the corridor air pressure. He popped the hatch, left the reserve control center, and made his way toward the lift complex. He was in the elevator car and had punched the button for the main command level, and watched the doors of the lift car shut, before he even stopped to consider that the lift was not to be trusted any more than the rest of the ship. He could be trapped inside this car for a very long time if its mechanism had failed. Then the car started moving upward, the acceleration pressing Marquez's feet down into the floor of the car.

He smiled to himself. Ridiculous. The lift system, like every other part of the ship, had been built to last millennia, and built with an intricate system of fail-safes that ran a full safety check before each use. There was no need for him to find imaginary things to fret about. Not when there were so many real worries already.

He rode the lift upward, hoping against hope that something in the main control center would make sense to him.

Captain Felipe Henrique Marquez stood in the main control center of the *Dom Pedro IV*. It would be a long wait indeed before anything made much sense at all. The ship seemed to be functioning perfectly, but even that was incomprehensible. The ship could only have gotten to wherever it was through a series of massive malfunctions that should have left it a derelict, tumbling forever through the blackest depths of space, never approaching another star again. Space was, after all, vast and empty. The odds against getting this close to a planetary system by chance were quite literally astronomical. But though the *DP-IV* had violated every step of her flight plan, she had arrived in a planetary system, and had made what seemed to be a perfect initial approach to it.

Which brought Marquez to the question of where, exactly, "here" was. Since the one thing he knew for certain was that the ship's navigation system had failed to carry out the flight plan, it would perhaps be best not to rely on it to tell him where he was.

He looked up through the forward observation dome. The *DP-IV*'s bridge stood at the center of the dome, on a cylindrical raised pillar. Marquez stood in the center of a hemisphere of stars, the myriad points of light dazzlingly bright in the darkness of the void.

The sky of deep space was magnificent, but it also told him nothing at all. In theory one ought to be able to divine one's position in space by seeing what stars were in what position. But there were simply too many stars, and, as points of light, they all looked alike. There was an off chance that some pattern of stars would jump out at him, something as instantly recognizable as Orion or the Big Dipper as seen from Earth's sky, but Marquez was not really expecting that kind of luck, and he didn't get it.

There was, however, one point of light brighter than all the others, visible directly overhead. It was the star the *DP-IV* was approaching. The science of spectral analysis was thousands of years old, and the *Dom Pedro IV*'s instruments could generate a chart showing the brightness and intensity of every color of light a star put out, a chart as unique and precisely identifying as any fingerprint or retinal scan. Compare that scan against the ship's archives, and you could know at once what star you were looking at, or, at the very least, you could find out it was not in the charts.

Marquez sat at the pilot's station and activated the spectrographic imager. The spot of light dead ahead was a nice, bright target. It only took a handful of seconds for the system to produce a high-quality spectrograph—and only a few milliseconds longer more to produce an exact match.

Marquez swore under his breath. It was HS-G9-223, local name Lodestar—the star that shone on Solace. The star that had been their destination. They had gotten to where they were supposed to go. Which was impossible. The *Dom Pedro IV* had missed her timeshaft-wormhole transit, and had therefore never performed the post-transit course shift that should have aimed her toward Solace. She should have been trillions, quadrillions, of kilometers off course.

Marquez checked the data again. The spectrograph he had just made matched the reference spectrograph perfectly. The odds, he knew, were billions to one at best that the system had made a bad match. But on the other hand, there seemed to be nothing but billions-to-one-against odds in the whole situation. Best to confirm this was indeed the Solace star system. Obviously, the best way to do that was to find Solace itself. Marquez set to work on the problem.

Even with the most sophisticated equipment, locating a planet from tens of billions of kilometers away was no trivial matter—and the *Dom Pedro IV* didn't have the most sophisticated equipment. She was, after all, a freighter, not a survey ship. The point of light Marquez was looking for was hidden in the millions of points of light that shone down on his ship. Fortunately, however, there were ways to narrow the search area. Marquez took a series of spectrographs of the solar disk's edge and ran a Doppler analysis to derive the star's axis of rotation. Marquez was startled to get back a result of zero rotation. Either the star was not spinning at all, which was more or less impossible, or else, far more likely, the *DP-IV* had, quite improbably, come in exactly and precisely over one of the star's poles.

Well, what was one more improbability among so many? Marquez quit worrying about it. The Solace system was like 99 percent of all the other star systems in the galaxy: The planets orbited around the equator of the star. That meant he should be face on to the system's orbital plane.

With the data he had already, it was a trivial calculation to compute his distance from the star, and once he knew his distance and position relative to the star, setting up the search parameters was almost too easy. He fed the numbers to the computers and ordered ship's detection systems to start searching the toroidal ring of space that ought to contain Solace.

Then it was time to let the machine do the rest of the work. He would get out of his pressure suit, freshen up, and get something to eat. With all the ship's clocks reset to zero, he had no way of knowing if it had been a few months or a few millennia since he had last had a shower and a meal. However long it was, he knew he could use both right now.

The familiar routine of stripping out of the pressure suit, bathing, and getting into fresh fatigues served to comfort Marquez. A hot meal helped as well. But all the comfort and familiarity in the universe could not have distracted him for long. The situation was too serious for that.

He tried to force back his worries and take pleasure in his meal, but the puzzle of what had happened was too distracting. No matter how hard he tried to empty his mind and relax, the mystery of how his ship had gotten to where she was intruded.

Marquez no longer doubted that this was the Solace system. Somehow, and he had no idea how, the *Dom Pedro IV* had guided herself here in spite of massive malfunctions, and in spite of missing the timeshaft wormholes. Besides which, those massive malfunctions seemed to have healed themselves. Everything on board seemed to be working perfectly.

But if the chronometers had all failed, then perhaps the navigation event log had gotten scrambled as well. Maybe the ship had, somehow, negotiated the timeshaft on her own, and then lost the record of the event.

Marquez was heartened by the idea—more heartened, perhaps, than was sensible. If it was merely a question of the log recorder and ship chronometers misbehaving, then maybe everything was all right. Maybe the *Dom Pedro IV* was not only where she was supposed to be, but *when* she was supposed to be as well.

A chime sounded, interrupting his thoughts. Marquez blinked and came back to himself. He looked down and saw that his meal was stone-cold, and virtually untouched.

The chime sounded again, and he looked up at the closest status display.

The detectors had found something. Marquez scooped the remains of his meal into the recycler chute and hurried back to main control.

The visual-spectrum telescope had spotted Solace first, but even as he sat back down at the pilot's station, the infrared scope and the radio-band detectors chimed in, announcing their own discovery of the planet.

On a hunch, Marquez checked the planet's position and projected forward motion against the *DP-IV*'s current trajectory. It surprised him far less than it should have to find his ship was on a highly precise near-miss intercept course with the planet, just right for dropping into a polar orbit.

But there would be time enough to worry about the implications of that later.

It was comforting at least to know the planet was there. Solace was not just his intended destination, it was a place he knew. He had been to Solace just six standard years before, and back then it had—

With a start, Marquez realized it had *not* been six years before. He had no idea how long ago it had been. But now that he had a fix on the planet's location, he had a way he could find out.

Wormhole transit, long flight times, and relativistic time-dilation effects all render time measurement difficult during interstellar flight. For that reason, timeshaft ships were equipped to determine the precise time in a number of ways, ranging from measurement of the periodicity of calibrated neutron stars to the technique Marquez was about to use—planetary positional chronometry. He could treat the relative positions of the planets' orbital position like the hands of some impossibly huge antique analog clock.

Marquez instructed the ship's navigation system to get position locks on the other planets of the system. Having a precise lock on Solace itself allowed the navigation system to zero in far more precisely and rapidly on the other planets. Within eight minutes, the nav system had a positive track on six planets, and that was enough for a precise chronology fix.

Marquez looked toward the positional-calculation chronometer display just as the observational system completed its calculations and put the results up on the clock screen, numbers that placidly reported the time, the day, and the year.

Marquez was vaguely surprised that he had no reaction to the numbers. Perhaps it was some aftereffect of being in long sleep. Perhaps he had subconsciously been expecting such news and had refused to consider it for that reason. Or perhaps his subconscious knew it was wise to keep him from reacting, because the only rational reaction would be unbridled panic.

It did not matter. Nothing he could do would matter.

Their flight plan had called for the *Dom Pedro IV* to arrive at Solace somewhere between two weeks and two months after her departure from Thor's Realm.

No matter what reaction Marquez summoned up, it would not change the fact that they had arrived at Solace almost precisely one hundred and twenty-seven years late.

Marquez sat, motionless, for how long he could not say. It was the realization that he had no idea how long he had been there that brought him back to himself. He smiled without pleasure at the gallows humor of it all. He had already lost track of more than a century's worth of time. It would hardly do to lose track of more time again quite so soon.

You should have been prepared for this, he told himself. *It is one of the risks of being a timeshaft pilot.* Well, that was true enough—up to a point. Every timeshaft pilot had nightmares about the temporal confinement failing to deactivate, or about the ship missing a waypoint wormhole or its destination star system and sailing past into the infinite void. There had been ships that had simply vanished, and many had no doubt suffered such fates.

But this was different, somehow. This was no conventional doom. A disaster in space was not supposed to end with a ship that functioned perfectly, arriving at its intended destination with admirable precision, if not promptness. If your ship malfunctioned in the interstellar dark, then doom was supposed to be absolute and final. There was something downright disturbing about being only halfway doomed, of being marooned a mere 127 years in the future. That seemed too small a number, too reasonable a figure. It was absurd that such a knowable, imaginable length of time should cut him off from his life every bit as much as a million years would do. It was not the sort of disaster a timeshaft pilot prepared himself to face.

A mere century should have been as nothing to Marquez and his ship. The hull of the *Dom Pedro IV* was 8,362 standard self-chronological years old. A very few of her fittings had been salvaged from ships far older than that, though her interior appointments were of course but a few hundred self-chron years old, thanks to a refitting at a recent port of call.

The *Dom Pedro IV* had entered service 432 objective years before the date now displayed on her positional-calculation chronometer, and Marquez prided himself on her relative modernity. Marquez himself was fifty-two biochron years of age. He had never bothered—or perhaps never dared—to keep track of his own self-chron age. However, by that measure, he was far older than his ship. But how could such a statement be meaningful, when both captain and ship had lived through the same few hundred years over and over again? He himself had piloted her on all of her journeys, having learned his craft on a dozen prior voyages on a half dozen other timeshaft ships.

In terms of self-chronological time, Felipe Henrique Marquez was no doubt somewhat older than recorded human history. And that statement, while true, was so manifestly absurd that it did not bear thinking about. But he *had* lived that long, though he had spent 99 percent of the time in question in one form or another of suspended animation, and he had slept through the same few hundred years over and over again as the *DP-IV* had dropped down the timeshafts and then moved forward in time.

And yet, for all of that, a short 127 years of normal, conventional time was more than enough to strand Marquez and his ship, cut him off from all links to his old life. For the years he had lived in for so long were now irretrievably lost to the past. The Chronologic Patrol would never let him go back.

But then Marquez remembered something. Maybe there *was* hope. Maybe there was an answer, waiting, sleeping aboard his ship. The *Dom Pedro IV* was a cargo vessel. The main components of her cargo this time were Habitat Seeds and heavy-duty terraforming gear, along with various smaller items and a few luxury goods. She carried but a single passenger on this run. But that passenger had made a request before departure, and considering who that passenger was, the request was something close to an order in the present circumstances. In any event, it was a request

Marquez would be happy to honor: In the event of any unusual event at arrival, Marquez was to wake that one passenger as soon as the ship was secure. Marquez had not thought much of it at the time, but now he did. Plainly, his passenger had entered cryosleep with the expectation of facing trouble at the other end.

Marquez climbed up out of the pilot's station and headed aft toward the compartment that held the cryo canister. The mere idea of talking to his passenger got him nervous. Before departure, everyone had warned Marquez to treat his passenger with great respect, to be careful around him. All of the warnings had been completely unnecessary. He had heard more stories than one about the man.

Everyone had heard stories about Anton Koffield.

CHAPTER SEVEN

OUT OF THE COLD, INTO THE DARK

Rear Admiral Anton Koffield awoke from the frozen depths of cryosleep, his body and mind both seeming lost, cold, impossibly at a distance from Koffield himself, and from each other.

His torso spasmed and his jaw clenched shut as his arms and legs strained futilely to shake and twitch. Anton Koffield's body writhed in anguish, and yet it all seemed far off from him.

Every part of his body felt as if it were no part of him at all. The agonies seemed to be happening elsewhere to someone other than Koffield; and yet for all of that they battered Koffield with pain.

Even his own mind felt as if it were not his own. Someone other than Koffield was thinking the thoughts in his brain. He knew that was impossible, but impossibility seemed of little import. The weird detachment of thought and sensation seemed quite real enough, hallucinatory though it might be.

His body had spent more than a century of ship's time cooled down to temperatures that should have killed it instantly. The heroic measures required in order for the human body to survive such conditions were in and of themselves an all-but-unendurable punishment. Beyond that was the simple fact that he was awakening after decades of total sensory deprivation. It took at least a little time for the nerves to remember their long-disused routings and reorder themselves. It was inevitable that he would experience pain and disorientation as his body struggled to sort itself out. He had been through it all many times before, and knew that it would, sooner or later, pass.

But mere understanding of the phenomenon offered little comfort as the uncontrollable paroxysms of agony swept over him and then vanished, only to return again and again. After a time, he came back to himself enough that the pain was unquestionably happening to himself, and to no one else, but there was no joy in claiming undisputed possession of his torment.

There were stories about those who woke up and never had the pain fade. If it went on much longer, Koffield would start to believe he was of that number. It was as if his body *sought* death as an act of rebellion against the indignities it suffered in deep freeze. But the human spirit has too strong an instinct for survival to allow any such antics. The spasms gradually subsided into a perfectly ordinary case of violent shakes and shivers, the mortal anguish faded into mere pain, and his quaking limbs returned to some semblance of control. Koffield lay there, grimly waiting it out until his body recovered.

It was starting to fade. That was the main thing. He was something like himself again, enough so that he realized how bad a shape he was in, how disoriented.

Supposedly it was difficult for most people to judge the passage of time for a while after awakening from cryosleep. It was certainly true for Koffield. Hours, or seconds, or days might have passed since he had awakened. Had Captain Marquez been sitting there, in the revival control room, watching him, for endless hours, perhaps so long that he had gone off to other duties now and then? Or had it all taken but a few seconds?

Such thoughts always went through Koffield's mind when he woke up from cryo. But for some perverse reason, he had never made the trivial effort required to find out the answers, never asked how long it had taken to revive him. No revival operator had ever volunteered the information. Anton Koffield allowed himself few superstitions, but not asking about his own revival was one of them. Cryosleep was a close passage to death, and he had no desire to trifle with the rituals that had seen him through it so often in the past.

Finally the last of the pain faded away to nothing more than aches and stiffness, and the spasms subsided completely. His body was his own again. Koffield let out a sigh of relief and unclenched his fists, not even aware until that moment that he had had them clenched in the first place.

He risked opening his eyes, forcing the lids apart past the sleep grit and the last residue of cryosleep gel. There, above his head, were the blurry outlines of the revival chamber's overhead bulkhead. It was real, solid. Once again, he had made it back. He knew the odds were good that one day he would not. But at least that day was not today. That in itself was something of a victory.

He tried sitting up, moving slowly and carefully, and immediately regretted it. His muscles were not quite revived enough to manage much in the way of concerted effort. Koffield gritted his teeth and tried again, levering himself up onto his elbows and ignoring the blackness at the edge of his vision. A featureless blob moved through his field of vision and extruded a brownish-pink appendage that reached out behind Koffield and touched him, with the tenderest of care, on the small of the back, providing just enough support to hold him upright.

Koffield flinched back from the contact even as he felt gratitude for it. It hurt, it hurt like hell, but that was to be expected. Everything hurt after cryosleep. But whoever it was who was helping him to his trembling feet clearly knew that, and was touching him as little as possible while at the same time more or less holding him up.

By sheer force of will, Koffield caused his knees to lock, his aching back to straighten, and his iron-stiff shoulders to pull themselves straight. The supporting hands let him go, but stayed close, in case Koffield collapsed under his own weight.

Then it dawned on him. Weight. He had weight. He was not in zero gee. Being roused from cryosleep was an incredibly stressful business, made all the worse by putting stress on muscles and nerves that had gone unused for centuries of shiptime. It was, for that reason, standard operating procedure to waken cryosleep subjects in zero gravity, except in cases of emergency, when the several hours it often took to isolate the revival chamber from the ship's grav system for zero-gee operations could not be spared.

He had weight. He was, therefore, awakening to an emergency.

"Wha—" he tried to say, but his voice with creaky with disuse, and his throat was suddenly raw. He coughed wretchedly and accepted a sip of the vile restorative drink offered by the helpful, half-seen blob-person holding him up.

He forced a swallow of the stuff down with a grimace and found that his sight had begun to clear a bit. He could see the kindly, worried face of the man who was supporting him. It had to be Captain Marquez.

He tried to speak again, with a bit more success. "What's gone wrong?" he asked in a voice that was more croak than speech.

"Something big, sir. You told me to awaken you first if something unexpected happened. It has."

"Are they here for me?" Koffield asked. No doubt they were. He had more than half expected it. They would have examined the preliminary data he had sent along via the *Chrononaut VI*. Assuming the *C-VI* and *DP-IV* had both stayed on schedule, the *Chron-Six* would have arrived about sixty days before the *DP-IV*. Plenty of time for the Solacians to go over his preliminary work. No doubt they would be here for him—either so as to seek further information—or to have him arrested and his information suppressed.

But Marquez looked puzzled. "No one's here. Why would anyone be here? Did you think someone would meet us?"

"Yes," Koffield said. It began to dawn on him that he had read the situation wrongly. "Obviously I'm making bad assumptions. What—what is the problem?"

"There's been a—ah, navigation problem."

"We haven't reached Solace?"

Marquez hesitated for a moment, clearly unhappy about

what he had to say. He grimaced and shook his head. "I've checked it very carefully, sir. It's definitely the Solace system. That part is all right."

"So what isn't all right?"

Marquez hesitated again. "It seems crazy, sir, but—well, I've checked every way I know how, and I keep getting the same data. We've arrived at Solace a hundred twenty-seven years late. I don't think we ever went through a timeshaft."

Koffield swallowed and blinked again, and forced down all the denials and inane questions. Marquez was a superb pilot, and even the most hopelessly incompetent starpilot would be unlikely to confuse one planetary system with another. Marquez no doubt had his facts straight. Therefore, Anton Koffield would not allow himself the luxury of denial, of refusing to believe in something merely because it was unpleasant.

Koffield reached out and took the beaker of restorative drink back from Marquez, and forced down another sip of the horrid stuff, as much to stall for time and collect his thoughts as to clear his throat. Calm. Marquez was looking to him for guidance. Better not to show any outward emotion at all, rather than give vent to the swirl of confusion and fear and postcryo disorientation. "One hundred twenty-seven years," he said, recovering something like his normal low, thoughtful voice as he spoke. "That's not good."

"No, sir. Not at all. We're—we're lost in the future."

One hundred twenty-seven years! Koffield suddenly realized that his hands were trembling. Would Marquez think that the shock of his news had caused it, or would he simply put it down to postcryo reaction? Koffield himself wasn't sure which it was.

One hundred twenty-seven years. Gone. His entire world utterly and irrevocably gone. Again. Stranded in the future for the *second* time. How was a man supposed to react to news like that?

There was no way, of course. And that was the way Koffield chose. No reaction at all. That was the best. "All right," he said calmly. "Clearly we have some thinking to do."

"Yes, sir," Marquez said, vague disappointment in his voice.

Koffield looked at the man in mild surprise. Had Marquez somehow imagined that all one needed to do was wake Anton Koffield so that he could solve all problems with a wave of his omnipotent hand? There was much to be said for having a reputation, but there were limits. Still and all, Marquez's reaction was to be preferred to some of the others Koffield had inspired.

One hundred twenty-seven years—maybe, just maybe, he had *outlived* his reputation. There were lots of old sayings to the effect that there was a bright side to everything. Perhaps they were true after all.

"Very well," Koffield said. Suddenly the note of calm confidence in his voice was not quite as false as it had been a moment before. "Let's get me cleaned up, then get a look at the future."

It was a few minutes before Koffield felt strong enough to walk unassisted. When he did, Marquez walked him down the corridor and showed him to his cabin. "Refresh yourself, Admiral," he told Koffield as he opened the cabin hatch and gestured for his guest to step in. "Take as much time as you need. I will be in the command center whenever you are ready."

"Thank you, Captain," Koffield said. "I won't be long." He stepped into the cabin and shut the hatch behind him with a distinct sense of relief. He needed a shower and a meal, of course—but he also, desperately, needed to collect his thoughts.

Koffield stripped out of the thin gown he had worn in the cryo chamber, opened the cabin's refresher unit, stepped in, and powered up the pressure shower. The jets of hot water seemed nearly strong enough to push him back against the opposite wall of the compartment. It felt good. *My first shower in over a century,* Koffield thought. *I bet I really need it.* The weak little joke was no doubt as old as timeshaft transport, if not older, but it cheered him up a trifle all the same.

Anton Koffield was not a particularly impressive physical

specimen at the best of times, and times had not been good for him, even before entering cold sleep. He had entered the cryocan in a state of near exhaustion from overwork. The effort needed to complete his research in time for departure, the desperate urgency of his mission, and plain, old-fashioned fear of what he had found had combined to leave him completely drained. After the further stress of cryosleep, he was verging on the cadaverous. His cheeks were hollowed, his skin drawn tight.

The outer layers of dead skin disintegrated in cryosleep, turning into a grimy and unpleasant powder that covered the entire body and itched like the devil. He leaned into the jets of water and scrubbed as hard as his still-rubbery arms would let him.

Clearly the first step was to establish, to his own satisfaction, exactly what their situation was. Accepting reality was one thing, but there were also such things as confirming important data and gathering supporting data. Anton Koffield had faith enough in Marquez to believe him, but not so much faith that he did not want to verify it all. Trusting unconfirmed information was a shortcut to getting killed.

And, no doubt, Captain Marquez, being no fool himself, was more than eager to have Koffield check his work. The good captain would be delighted if Koffield found an error, but Koffield had no realistic hope of that and doubted that Marquez did either.

Hurry could kill them too. Fresh out of cryosleep—if *fresh* was the word—no one was ever in any condition to do precise work. He stepped from the shower, dried himself, and pulled underclothes and a pair of coveralls out of the cabin's storage locker. He pulled on the clothes and extracted a quickmeal module from the cabin's galley unit.

He folded the refresher unit back into one bulkhead of the tiny cabin and pulled table and chair down from the opposite bulkhead. He activated the meal module and waited for the unit to heat the food. His shifted uncomfortably on the chair. His coveralls were tight under the shoulders, and the fabric seemed awfully scratchy. His skin was always oversensitized after cryosleep. A faint odor clung to the cloth of the coveralls, a musty, damp smell that put him in mind of mold and the cellar under his grandfather's house outside Berlin. Did that house still stand, a hundred twenty-seven years since he had last seen it? No, it was over two hundred years now. He had been time-stranded again, cut adrift from even the weak and tenuous roots he had set down eight decades before, after the *Upholder* disaster.

The meal module chimed, signaling that his food was heated. He opened the module and looked at the meal inside. There was nothing readily identifiable. A bowl of thick brownish-grey liquid that might be soup or stew, some beige-looking stuff that might be mashed-potato substitute, and some sort of green puree.

No doubt it was all edible, and nourishing, and precisely what the diet specialists knew he would need after cryosleep, but none of that made it appetizing. Of course, the dieticians made the postcryo meals bland and soft on purpose, to avoid overworking jaw muscles that hadn't moved for decades, or overstimulating the senses of taste and smell after they had gone unused for just as long. Still, considering he was about to have his first *food* in over a century, it was something of a perverse accomplishment to sit down to a meal and not wish to eat it.

He allowed himself a small smile. Well, what could he expect? The food had been in cold storage as long as the coveralls, as long as he himself. He took the fork out of its compartment on the side of the module and began shoveling the nutritious glop into his mouth, eating mechanically, experiencing no more pleasure than would a machine taking on fuel, paying no attention to what he ate.

They were in trouble, very serious trouble. The situation was far more complicated and dangerous than Marquez could even suspect. There were wheels within wheels, hidden opportunities, and pitfalls. He continued to feed himself as he tried to work it all through, his mind as far removed from his body as it had been on first awaking from cryo.

Still thinking over the situation, he finished up his joyless repast as quickly as possible. He stood, folded up the table and chair, and put the meal module into the cleanup bin. He needed to go forward, see what Captain Marquez had found out.

Except that Marquez did not, could not, know the half of it. Koffield had already reached out for the handle to the cabin door when he forced himself to stop, to consider.

Anxious as he was to go forward to the control center and get a look at the data firsthand, it was starting to dawn on him that so doing might be a mistake. He made himself sit back down and consider. Think it through. Consider it as a chess game, and try to think at least a few moves ahead.

One hundred twenty-seven years was a long time in human terms. Things got lost, or forgotten, or thrown away. Even if his preliminary warning, sent on the *Chron-Six,* had gotten through and gotten to the proper people, *could* they have acted on it? *Would* they have?

In a cold, rational analysis, there was no argument that could be raised against his data. But who would abandon a planet based on nine pages of obscure formulae? Koffield had known the data itself would not be enough the day he had sent off his preliminary findings on board the *Chron-Six.* That was why he had booked passage on the *Dom Pedro IV* in the first place, so that he could speak for the data, work to see that it was read and understood.

Unless she had been lost in transit as well, the *Chron-Six* had arrived at Solace 127 years ago, and she had delivered his data. What had happened then? Had his preliminary report changed the history of this and other worlds—or had it been lost and forgotten? Was it enshrined in a place of honor in the archives, or had it never been set down in the public record?

What sort of planet was waiting for them, out ahead of the *DP-IV?* Marquez had told him nothing about the state of the planet itself, but had merely reported the bald fact that it was there.

He, Koffield, at this exact moment, had no knowledge whatsoever concerning the state of the planet. That might well prove to be an important point.

There seemed to be three broad possibilities.

One—he had been right, and they had listened, tested his data, seen it to be true, and abandoned the planet. If so, the *DP-IV* was now entering an all-but-lifeless star system, littered with abandoned equipment and populated only by the descendants of the inevitable lunatics who refused to leave their space habitats, and whatever motley crew of vermin and microbes had found some way of surviving on the planet's surface. It was unlikely, but possible.

Two—they had lost, ignored, disbelieved, disproved, or suppressed his data, and events had proved his theory wrong. In which case the *DP-IV* was about to arrive on the garden planet that DeSilvo and all his experts had predicted. The advanced terraforming procedures had been triumphant, and Solace was a paradise, and he, Koffield, was either totally forgotten or else remembered as a figure of fun.

Or, three—he had been right, and they had ignored his work at the time, and long since forgotten it, and there was a planet full of people dying out there. Given human nature, the third option seemed by far the most likely.

In that case—in that case he might well need some proof that he had made his predictions 127 years in the past, and that he had made them before he had any way of knowing what sort of shape Solace was in.

He stood up and found the intercom set in the usual place, mounted on the bulkhead just inside the hatch. After a moment or two, he figured out how to hail the command center and did so. The captain answered almost at once. "Marquez here. What is it, Admiral Koffield?"

Just for a moment, Koffield found himself wondering how Marquez had known who was calling. Then he smiled to himself. Who else could it have been? He wasn't going to get far thinking ahead in this chess game if he couldn't think any more clearly than *that*. "Captain, I'm sorry to call you back here this way, but I have thought of something that needs doing, and it needs to be recorded and witnessed. I can't tell you more than that just now. Could I ask you to come back to my quarters, and to bring a longwatch camera and a secured container—one large enough to hold a cryosleep personal pack?"

"Admiral, there are a number of ship's systems I haven't done checks on since arrival. I really do have a lot of work to—"

"This is important, Captain."

"Well, what is it?"

"I can't tell you until after it's done."

"Then why should I—"

"I apologize for not explaining everything now," Koffield said, smoothly cutting in, "but there was a rule of thumb in my old investigative outfit that the most objective witness was the one who knew the least and saw the most—and I need you to be objective."

The line was silent for a moment, and then Marquez spoke, making no effort to keep the puzzlement and annoyance out of his voice. "I am not in the mood for games, Admiral, and I don't have time for them. Your rank doesn't entitle you to give me orders on my own ship."

"I know, Captain. But my guess is you know enough about me to know I likewise have little time for games. But if you can take ten minutes of your time to witness something, there is at least a chance that you will be helping to save lives, a great many lives, on Solace."

"I can't quite see how that could be possible," Marquez replied, the disbelief plain in his voice.

"But it is, Captain, I assure you," said Koffield. "It is. I'll be happy to explain after the fact. Please."

There was a heartbeat's worth of silence before Marquez answered, a silence that could have meant a great many things. "Well, if ignorance makes a man objective, I guess I will be, because I don't know a damn thing. It'll take a few minutes to collect the equipment from stores. I'll be there as soon as I can."

CHAPTER EIGHT

HEISENBERG'S SUITCASE

From the look on Marquez's face when Koffield opened the cabin hatch, Koffield could see that he had come down more than a peg or two in Marquez's estimation. Never mind. There were other things more important than the captain's good opinion. "Thank you for coming, Captain," said Koffield. "If you could bring the longwatch camera and the secured container in here, we can begin."

"Whatever you say, Admiral," Marquez replied as he carried the equipment in. It was plain from his tone of voice that he was humoring Koffield.

"I know all this seems foolish, Captain. I'll bet you're wondering if I'm all the way back from cryosleep yet."

Marquez shrugged as he set the container down on the deck. "Some people *are* a little out of it for the first day or so after. Revival jag, they call it. Makes them act a little strange."

"I assure you, I'm not one of them. There's a reason for all this, and I'll explain it in just a few minutes. But for now—please activate the longwatch camera and place it where it will be able to see both of us."

"All right," Marquez said, still plainly far from convinced. He pulled the table open, started the camera, and set it down.

The camera was a standard unit, a rounded oblong black block, about ten by four by four centimeters. It had a lens stuck in one end, and a folding tripod and two or three kinds of built-in clamps attached to the base.

Longwatch cameras had on switches, but no off. Once they started sight-and-sound recording, they could not be stopped by any means, short of destroying the camera itself. They simply kept recording for a standard year, no matter what, and then shut themselves off. Though the camera itself could not be stopped once started, it was possible to access the stored sound and imagery from the holographic molecular memory whether or not the camera was still recording. The camera recorded infrared as well as visual light. Darkness was no shield against it. Marquez glanced at his wrist datawatch. "Camera activated at approximately day 223, hour 4, minute 16, second mark— *ten*—in standard year 5339," Marquez said, following the standard procedure for activating a longwatch. "Time coordinates approximate, due to equipment failure. Time as given derived from planetary positional fix. The camera is in Admiral Anton Koffield's cabin aboard the *Dom Pedro IV,* Captain Felipe Henrique Marquez commanding. Captain Marquez speaking. The ship is at present approximately two-point-three billion kilometers from the planet Solace, approaching the planet from planetary system north on a course exactly perpendicular to the planet's orbital plane."

"Thank you, Captain," Koffield said. He faced the camera and let it get a good look at him. "I am Anton Koffield, inactive-duty rear admiral in the Chronologic Patrol." He turned toward Marquez and thought for a moment. It was important that he phrase his questions in as neutral a fashion as possible. If this recording was used as evidence at some future date, it might well be vitally important to demonstrate that he had not led the witness. Strange to think in such terms. What sort of group, exactly, was going to see this record? he wondered. A scientific peer-review board? A commission of inquiry? A court-martial? A competency panel convened to determine if he, Koffield, were insane? All of them, perhaps. Assuming there was anyone left alive to staff any such groups in the first place. "Captain, you revived me from cryosleep, did you not?"

"Yes, I did."

"When?"

Marquez shrugged, a bit petulantly, and glanced at his datawatch again. "Let's see. I started the procedure about six hours ago. You came fully awake about ninety minutes ago, and were strong enough to leave the revival chamber about an hour ago."

"What did you do once I was strong enough?"

"I led you to this cabin. Mostly you were able to walk on your own, but I gave you some help."

"What did I do when I got here?"

Marquez looked at Koffield with something close to suspicion. "You *said* you were going to shower, dress, and eat. That's what most people do, and by the look and the—ah— smell of you, that's what you did. But I closed the hatch on you as soon as I delivered you and went forward to the control center. I have no way of knowing what else you did."

"Perhaps you do," Koffield said. "If this ship operates anything like a Chronologic Patrol ship, there is an automated event recorder that logs virtually every mechanical and electronic action on board, from main engine firing down to what hatches are open and shut, and air-mix and temperature readings in every compartment. The logs are quite useful in confirming maintenance, monitoring environmental systems, reconstructing accidents, and so on."

"Sure, the *DP-IV* has an event recorder. But the log file was wiped clean when I came out of stasis. Nothing on it about our trip here."

"But has it been operating normally since our arrival?"

"So far as I know."

"Please consult the log now and report on hatch status and voice and data communications from this cabin for the last six hours."

"Whatever you say," Marquez said, his tone of voice teetering on the edge of insolence. He operated the controls on his datawatch, linking it to the ship's computers and pulling up the information he wanted. "According to this, the hatch has only been opened twice—for thirty seconds at 0309 hours, and for forty-two seconds at 0413. No data communications via the terminal, and the voice-comm system was used just once, at 0402."

"Interpret, please."

Marquez looked puzzled. "Well, I guess, in other words, I led you here, you shut the hatch on me, and it didn't open again until I came back and you opened it for me. And except for calling me to come here a few minutes ago, you didn't use the voice-comm system, and you didn't use the data system at all."

"Very well. Please give the longwatch a clear close-up of your datawatch display."

Marquez took the datawatch off, shoved it in close to the longwatch, and then put it back on again. "All right," he said, "now what?"

"We're nearly done here," Koffield said. "Please answer a few more questions. I have either been in your presence, or in a sealed room, since revival. Correct?"

"Correct. Assuming you're not a magician, and the log has been working properly."

"And I have had no access to any source of meaningful information, except yourself, regarding present conditions on the planet Solace, or indeed on any other subject, since my revival?"

"Ah, right," Marquez said, clearly growing more cautious and more confused. "If the event recorder log is accurate, that's right."

"Please tell me all that you know about present conditions on Solace."

"How the hell would I know?" Marquez asked irritably. "We're a hundred twenty-seven years overdue. About the same as it was last time I was here, I guess. All I know is that it's still there, because I got a fix on it. Comm systems are all still locked out, and I haven't exactly had time to send in long-range probes. I haven't even sent in a query ping yet."

"You have no current information, and therefore could not possibly give me any. Is that correct?"

"Correct."

"Thank you. With all that established, I think I can now leave my quarters. If you could please take up the longwatch and keep it pointed more or less toward me, I'd like us to head back to the revival chamber now. I'll carry the secured container."

Marquez seemed past responding. He simply picked up the camera and did as Koffield asked, following him out into the corridor and back toward the revival chamber.

Koffield's cryocan was still there, hanging on the service support, a meter or so above the deck. The can was a long white lozenge-shape, the coffin-type lid still open, and a slight residue of cryosleep gel still clinging to the can's interior. The air in the revival chamber was redolent with the sickly sweet odor of oxidized cryosleep gel, gone bad the moment it came in contact with breathable air. The decomposing cryogel smelled exactly like rotting flesh. Memories of those nightmare times surged up into his mind, but he forced them all back down.

Besides, it was not the can's main interior that concerned him at the moment. There was a smaller compartment on the bottom end of the can, a forty-centimeter-wide pullout drawer directly below where the cryosleep subject's feet would be. It was, in essence, the luggage compartment for the can.

The use of cryosleep was not limited to space travel. Many medical patients used it to avoid further pain or physical degeneration during the months or years it might take to grow a replacement organ. Some overcrowded space habs might put a certain percentage of their populace on ice for a time—voluntarily or otherwise—to stretch food and air until new capacity could be built. Many military organizations trained their conscripted soldiers and froze them for the duration of their periods of service, reviving them only at the end of their conscription, or when and where a crisis developed. Ice soldiers, they called them.

There were many uses, licit and illicit, for cryosleep, but no matter what reason there might be for freezing a person, there were few potential victims of crime more helpless than cryosleep subjects—and, aside from ice soldiers, cryo subjects tended to pay for their own cryo. Only very well off people could afford the extremely expensive process. It tended to be rich people who used cryo, and that meant the personal pack of a cryo canister was a most tempting target for thieves. Personal-pack compartments, therefore, were very well protected.

Even the minimal drain of power on an electronic or photronic system could add up to a great deal of power, when multiplied over centuries of operation and the dozens or hundreds of cryocans that might be aboard a timeshaft ship. Personal-pack compartments were therefore usually sealed and locked by techniques and devices that would have been utterly familiar to any well-to-do citizen of nineteenth-century Earth. A dial-style combination lock and blobs of sealing wax might seem an incredibly old-fashioned, if not utterly antique, or even ancient, method of keeping valuables secure, but they worked.

Even if they looked antique, both lock and sealing wax were made of quite modern and sophisticated materials. Any energy pulse strong enough to break open the lock would destroy the personal pack, the cryocan, and probably the thief. The sealing "wax" was a high-strength memory polymer resin, by itself strong enough to resist any attempt to pry it off, melt it off, or chip it off. In theory, at least, the seals would dissolve in response to Koffield's thumbprint. On the other hand, 127 years was a long time for a memory polymer to remember a pattern. Sometimes the seals got temperamental after too long at low temperature.

Koffield considered. The storage compartment was well sealed, that was for sure. Very safe. Perhaps he should leave the compartment sealed. But Marquez would have to start reviving his crew soon. What was the point of going to extreme measures to prove there had been no tampering around the cryocan so far if he turned around and let a dozen people loose around it later? There was no practical way of getting the entire cryocan itself into a secure area. Besides, he would have to take his personal pack out sooner or later to transport to—to whoever was out there. No, better to do it now, while Marquez was still willing to record the proceedings.

"Captain," Koffield said, still speaking as much to the camera as to the man holding it, "what I need now is for the longwatch to record the present state of the personal-pack compartment door, to demonstrate that it is still sealed and locked. Then if you would be so kind as to record me opening it, removing the object inside, and placing it in the secured container we have brought along, we'll be done."

"Good," Marquez said. "Let's get on with it."

Koffield knelt in front of the door and pressed his right thumb into the first of the eight seals. It was supposed to take no more than ten seconds for the polymer to respond, and he could feel the seal starting to shift and soften under his thumb after only five. It dissolved into a gritty sand that fell away from the compartment door and dropped to the deck with a quiet hiss. Seals two through six were equally well behaved, but the seventh gave him a bad moment, flatly refusing to respond to his thumbprint until he had tried it three times and leaned his thumb in hard for a full thirty seconds. Even then, it only broke up into eight or ten larger pieces that shattered like glass when they hit the deck. Well, never mind. The seal had come free. The eighth seal functioned properly, and he started on the thirty-digit lock combination. It opened without incident.

Koffield glanced over his shoulder to be sure Marquez was still recording, then pulled the drawer open.

Two travel cases. A medium-sized brown one, bought on the civilian market, and a smaller grey Chronologic Patrol standard-issue suitcase, battered and slightly the worse for wear, but still in good condition. Koffield pulled them out and held both up to the camera. "This larger case contains a few changes of clothes and other unimportant personal items." He set it down and lifted the smaller case.

"This is the important one," he said. "Please observe that this travel case is sealed and locked, and that the seals are undisturbed and the locks are shut. Inside this suitcase is my work on the subject of forecasting the behavior of terraformed planets. It is stored in printed form on archival-quality paper, and in a standard static holographic datacube, a data-storage format designed to retain its integrity for at least fifty centuries. This case also contains a military-specification reader for the datacube. I hope and expect that the data on one or both of these two formats will have survived the trip without decaying or degrading. I will now place this case in this secured container, seal and lock the container, and attach the longwatch to the secured container in such a way as to give it a viewing angle of the locks and seals."

Koffield felt a trifle foolish as he spoke, and as he locked the travel case in the secured container, took the camera from Marquez, and attached it to the container. Once he had seen a small-town sleight-of-hand artist who took so long explaining his trick in such detail that the stunt itself was a letdown. Had it been worth all that rigmarole just to establish that the data in the suitcase was authentic, and did indeed come from the last century?

Possibly. He wouldn't know until he got a good look at Solace. Until he *did* get a look, he could at least hope that he was wrong, and that he had just wasted Marquez's time, and his own.

The secured container was designed to hold a standard longwatch camera on a special projecting clamp, and it didn't take long for Koffield to put the travel case in it, seal the container, and set up the camera. "All done, Captain. Thank you for your help."

"Wait a second," Marquez said. "You did a forecast of how their terraforming turned out? On Solace?"

Koffield felt a brief moment of satisfaction that Captain Marquez was quick to spot the one fact at the center of it all, the thing Koffield was trying to protect against any accusation of fraud or trickery. "That's right," Koffield said. "That's part of it. A big part of it. I was coming here to warn them about what I thought was going to happen. Is there some sort of safe or lockdown in the control center, Captain? I'd like to lock this case away."

"Yeah, sure," Marquez said. "There's a small safe in the watch officer's cabin. But the ah, whatever it is—you figure it's happened by now?"

"Yes," Koffield said. "Unless my figures were utterly, totally wrong, it's happened by now. I'd like to be wrong, but I don't think I am."

"And you've done all this to prove you did the work a

hundred twenty-seven years ago, and didn't fake it up some way. Is that right?"

"That's right."

Marquez frowned and nodded thoughtfully, then shook his head. "But I don't get it. If you're right about—about whatever it was—and it's already happened, it's too late. It doesn't matter, one way or another. Either you were right or wrong. Did we just go through all that recording nonsense so you could prove how smart you are if it turns out you were right?"

Koffield smiled without pleasure and shook his head. "No," he said. "My ego's not quite that big. I had a better, if grimmer, reason for playing games with seals and locks and cameras."

"What reason?" Marquez demanded.

Koffield had to say something, had to let Marquez know that his guesses were right, at least as far as they went—if for no other reason than to keep Marquez from getting too curious and to keep him from looking for answers on his own. Marquez deserved to know the whole truth. But the truth was bad enough that Koffield could not bring himself to tell it yet. Maybe he *was* wrong. Maybe he had made some blessed mistake. No. Leave the detailed explanations until they were absolutely necessary. "If my calculations are correct," Koffield said, "and if I can prove that I made them before—things happened— then maybe that will serve as proof that my techniques are valid." He bent over to pick up the secured container. "And then maybe they will listen to me when I warn them about what's going to happen *next*."

CHAPTER NINE

ARRIVALS

Marquez settled himself down in the navigator's station and gestured for Koffield to sit next to him, at the nav assistant's station. Better that than having the man standing behind him, breathing down his neck. Marquez felt edgy enough as it was without the added subconscious distraction of worrying about whoever was behind him.

The first step was to bring the ship broadside to her direction of travel. The long slender cylinder of the *Dom Pedro IV* was currently pointed straight through her direction of travel. Marquez swung the ship around ninety degrees, so that she was flying sideways. That allowed him to bring the aft sensor clusters and side sensor clusters to bear on the planet as well, and made it possible to use interferometry and other multiple-aperture enhancement tricks.

He checked over the control settings one last time, and satisfied himself that the detector and imaging systems were ready.

He activated the forward and aft long-range cameras, slaved the aft cameras to the forward cameras, and set the system to track on the image of the planet. He threw the visual image up on the main nav display and set it for maximum magnification. He was rewarded with a blurry, indistinct blob centered in the main display.

"Is that the best we can do?" Koffield asked. "Are we too far out to get a better image?"

"Give it a minute," Marquez said. "Maybe my gear isn't as fast or fancy as Chronologic Patrol hardware, but it works." He brought the enhancers on-line, activated the image-vibration compensators, and told the image processors to use the interferometry data to sharpen the image. The enhancement software needed a few seconds of baseline imagery data to work with before it could do any compensation or correction. It ran the cleanup through several iterations, each a slight improvement over the last.

The image of the planet shimmered down from a blur to a fuzzy ball. There was a pause, then the fuzzy ball became a reasonably clear image; another pause, and then another transformation as the clear image turned sharp as a razor's edge.

The subprocessors were already at work, their results popping up on the smaller displays below the main viewer. The cartographic systems locked in on visible land formations, did pattern-matching against the maps in the *DP-IV*'s computer system, and threw a latitude-and-longitude grid over the image of the world. The atmospheric analyzers began their spectroscopic studies and density columns and cloud-cover analyses. The thermal mappers began their work as well, developing a heat model for the planetary surface. The *DP-IV*'s data-integration system went to work with all the new datapoints, throwing up endless screenfuls of derived information about the planet Solace. Atmospheric composition and density. Estimated extent and depth of ice caps. Shifts in land usage since archived mapping scan. But Marquez didn't need to look at any of that. All he needed to see was the image of the planet itself, centered there in the main viewscreen. The view inspired him to a string of eloquent, despairing curses. Everything Koffield had said and done had warned Marquez that it might be bad. But he had never expected it to be *this* bad.

They were looking down upon the wreckage of a world. Even from here, viewing the planet at long range from the edge of the planetary system, the ruin of Solace was plain to see. This was no living world, but a dying one.

Humanity had found no living worlds at all, besides Earth herself. All the other inhabited worlds had been made, terraformed. All the new-made worlds had been created by humanity in some variant of Earth's own image and so shared a strong family resemblance. They were blue and white and green, the view of their surfaces artfully dimmed and obscured by the intervening cloudscape and their oxygen-thick atmospheres.

A lifeless world might look like anything. It might be a vacuum-locked place of hard edges, sharp craters, and cruel mountains, a world devoid of color or softness. It might be a banded gas giant painted in the gaudiest of hues. It might be a featureless monochromatic ball of lurid green or sickly yellow or sullen red.

But Solace looked like none of those.

Marquez had seen many worlds in trouble. Humanity had attempted to terraform nearly a hundred worlds, all told, and many of them had failed, in whole or in part. Terraforms on the edge of failure all looked the same. And the planet framed in the telescope view looked like every one of them.

He could see where the blue ocean waters had turned algae-green in one spot as the microorganisms bloomed out of control, then on to death-brown in another as the algae died, once they had consumed all the nutrients. He knew without examining the datafields that the glare-white of the ice caps was gleaming too bright, and had swelled too large, as the ice crept forward from the poles toward the equator. He knew the planetary cloud cover was being frozen and boiled away as the temperatures went to extremes, driving the water vapor out of the atmosphere.

Koffield was right. Solace was in bad trouble.

He turned away from the screen toward Admiral Koffield.

"Is it as bad as you thought it would be?" he asked him. "Or better? Or worse?"

Koffield was unable to tear his eyes away from the displays. His eyes flitted from the main viewer to the subdisplays, to the imagery, to the charts and graphs and tables of data.

"Admiral Koffield?"

"Hmm?" Koffield blinked and looked toward Marquez.

"Oh. Yes. Sorry." He let out a weary sigh. "Very much as I expected, I'm afraid. We're just getting rough data here, of course, and obviously I don't have access to my data or my models, but yes. This is what my research predicted."

Marquez looked back toward the main screen. He thought back to the last time he had been to Solace, and the time before that. How long had it been, in his own personal bio-chron time? How much time had passed in his life then? Six years since that visit, nine or ten since the one before that? How could so much have happened to the planet in that short a space of time? But then he remembered.

The centuries and the light-years had come back at him, with all the sharp suddenness of a slap in the face. Since he had last been here, millions had lived out their whole lives. Species had been created in the lab, then gone extinct in the wild, while he had sat in his temporal-confinement chamber.

Time had gone past, and he was part of that past.

He forced such thoughts from himself. There was too much else to do, too many decisions to make. Standard system-arrival procedure said they should send a hail to Solace Central Orbital Station, assuming it was still there. But it might not be wise to advertise the presence of the *DP-IV* just yet. Not until they knew a lot more. "Now what do we do?" he asked Koffield. In theory, and indeed in practice, as captain he was the absolute master of the *Dom Pedro IV*. But he would be a fool not to seek advice from such a source as Koffield, at such a time as this.

"I don't know," Koffield said. "You and I both need time to think." He smiled grimly. "We've lost so much time already it can't do any harm to spend a little more."

"One thing I know for sure," Marquez said. "We don't let them"—he stabbed a finger at the image of Solace—"know we're here until we know more. Places in as bad a shape as that aren't always the healthiest places to visit."

"You're right as far as that goes," Koffield said. "At the very least, we should listen in on whatever radio traffic we can pick up."

"But before we start in on that," Marquez said, "I'm

going to put on the brakes and slow us down. Until we know more, and we decide what to do, let's stay out here, where it's nice and dark and lonely and no one's going to notice us."

"Do it," Koffield said. "Let's park this ship right where she is until we've had a good long look at the situation."

"Right," said Marquez. "And as soon as we've done the braking burn, you're going to help me get the rest of the crew revived."

He gestured once more toward the image of Solace on the screen and shook his head mournfully. "That's one dark mess out there," he said. "We're going to need all the help we can get finding out about it."

Neshobe Kalzant knelt in the sparse shade of the brown and dying trees and scooped up a handful of the near-lifeless soil. She ignored the cockroaches that scuttled over her hand and dropped away, back onto the ground. The roaches were everywhere, after all. Any squeamishness she felt about them had long since been worn away. What disturbed her far more than the live roaches were the corpses of the dead ones. It was hard to pick up a handful of earth that did not contain at least a few of them.

"It looks extremely bad," she said, standing up, the handful of the dried-out soil still in her hand. The country residence of the Planetary Executive shouldn't be in this bad a shape. No place on the planet should be in this bad a shape. What was it like in places where they didn't try to coddle and cosset the plant life? She looked toward her companion. "How bad is it?"

"I assume you want to know about the report on the overall climate and not about conditions here in your own garden," Parrige said.

Neshobe allowed herself a small smile. "Both, actually. You're a real gardener. I could obviously use some advice."

"My first piece of advice would be to fire whoever is looking after the place," Parrige said, looking around unhappily. "Plainly that person is not doing a good job."

Neshobe laughed sadly. "Are you talking about the gardener in charge of this estate or the politician in charge of the planet?"

Parrige stiffened for a moment, then shook his head. "I was of course referring to the gardener, Madam. But it occurs to me that he might well be in the same position as the politician—as yourself, ma'am. Relatively new in the job, and having inherited a disastrous situation."

"Quite diplomatic," she said. "But what of the commission report?" she asked. "What will it say?"

"That the underlying ecostructure is in worse shape than it looks, in some ways, and better than it seems in others. However, how things are now is almost immaterial. It is the direction of the trend line that is worrisome, not our present position on that line."

Neshobe looked up at Parrige. Such a dignified, serious man. Put him in a plain brown robe and a skullcap, and he would be the perfect archetype for—for—what the devil was the name? Monk, or friar, or pope. Something like that. Whatever name it was the near ancients had given to their religious isolates, Parrige looked the part.

But Parrige was dressed in a sensible white tunic and an entirely conventional, even conservative, pair of full-length trousers. No knee breeches for him, no matter what fashion dictated. Parrige was what he was, and he wore what he wore, and he did not care what the world thought of him. Neshobe envied him that.

"In other words, your commissioners are past caring if it's bad now. The problem is that it's getting worse." She looked around herself at the parched landscape. Bone dry, all of it. Solace City Spaceport, the scene of the hell-storm rain and riot not so long ago, was only two thousand kilometers to the east. Why in chaos couldn't they tempt some of the endless Solace City rain to this place, where it might actually do some good? "It *is* still getting worse, isn't it?" she asked.

"Yes, ma'am. The ecostructure is collapsing at a faster and faster rate. The commission will recommend that we now divert all the resources directed at renewing and reviving the ecosystem toward an effort to conserve what remains. Given such a redirection of resources, the commission planning staff thinks we can stabilize the situation in the short term, but—"

"Stabilize it?" she asked, holding up her handful of dead soil. "What's the point of that, when even the cockroaches are starving to death? If all we do is stabilize the situation, sooner or later we all die."

There was a moment of eloquent silence. Her companion needed to say nothing at all in order to make a full response. Neshobe sighed wearily, dropped her handful of soil, wiped each hand on the other, and then stood up. She began to walk back toward the main house, Parrige falling into step beside her. "I know," she said. "In the long run, we're all dead. And I suppose if repairing the planetary climate is not currently possible, stabilization at least buys us time. Go on with what you were saying, Parrige."

"Yes, ma'am. You are quite right—judged on any long-term time scale, mere stabilization is futile. The planet, in its current state, cannot permanently support human life. And renewing the ecostructure is beyond our current capacity. Propping it up, trying to get it to hold together a while longer, is all we can do. Doing so could buy us enough time until we have greater resources and can work toward actual recovery. That, in sum, is the view of the commission."

Neshobe looked to Parrige, and then back down at the dying soil, and the wretched insects scuttling about on it. Humanity had made a mess of this world. Humanity had to at least try to set things right.

There was a low bench at the side of the path. Once it had stood in the shade of an elm tree, but now the tree was dead. Its trunk had been snapped in half about two meters off the ground, no doubt the work of some windstorm or another. Some termites had found enough water to survive and they were at work on it now, by the looks of it. The exposed wood was riddled with boreholes and looked soft and crumbly. There were puddles of sawdust nestled here and there at the base of the tree.

Neshobe sat down on the bench and looked back the way they had come. Once upon a time, there had been a fine view from this vantage point. Back in her predecessor's time, it had no doubt been quite pleasant to sit in this place and admire the rolling hills of lush green meadow and the small stands of trees, the blue-purple skies of Solace and the dramatic banks of clouds that rolled across them. But now the green was brown, and the parched sky was grey with dust and robbed of its clouds, and all was dead or dying.

It was quiet enough that Neshobe fancied she could hear the termites gnawing at the vitals of the dead tree, even if she could not see them.

But no, that was only her imagination. There was nothing of the termites themselves that she could hear or see. There was no sound. The planet's enemies were like that too—invisible, all but undetectable, but unquestionably there, and unquestionably impossible to root out, because they had burrowed their way too deep into the life they were destroying.

What were humans to this planet? Were they cockroaches, unwholesome interlopers, with individuals struggling to survive, but the species itself perfectly capable of adapting and surviving? Or were humans the termites here, still gnawing on the corpse of this world long after they had killed the body?

We are neither, she silently told herself, as forcefully as she could. *We are not noisome scavengers or murderous parasites. We tried to plant a garden, tried to bring life to a world, and failed. Surely that is not the same as killing the world outright.*

She forced her mind back to the issues at hand and looked back toward Parrige. "All right," she said. "We'll refocus our efforts on stabilization. But not exclusively. If we concern ourselves solely with the short term, we're not going to have a long term. I want people working on how we can develop the industrial capacity, and especially bioindustrial capacity, so we can go back over to the offensive. I want to rebuild Solace, not just keep more of it from falling to pieces."

"You bring us back to Greenhouse, then," Parrige said.

"Exactly. We've settled for a stabilized decline *there* for entirely too long. I don't think we'd be in as bad a shape as we are now if it had been maintained properly. We need it revived, upgraded, better than it ever was."

"That may be impossible," Parrige replied. "It would require a new SunSpot, and igniting a new SunSpot would produce a pulse of radiation powerful enough to kill everything on Greenhouse—and wouldn't do the living things in the rest of the planetary system a great deal of good either."

"Then we find another way," Neshobe said. "Otherwise, when the current SunSpot finally gives out, Greenhouse dies. And if Greenhouse dies—"

"Yes, ma'am. Then there will be no hope for reviving Solace. At best we'll be left with the planet as it is."

Neshobe nodded and stood up again. "Time to get back," she said, and starting walking briskly toward the house, not waiting for Parrige to fall into step with her. No point in continuing the conversation further. If the best-case scenario was a Solace no better than the half-dead corpse that now existed—if that was the best they could do, well, then, perhaps there was no point in talking at all.

The engines of the *Dom Pedro IV* throttled down to zero. Marquez checked the system-status boards one last time, then unstrapped himself from the pilot's station. The braking maneuver was done. Marquez hadn't even bothered with more than a first-approximation calculation of what orbit he wanted to achieve. He had simply swung the ship around so the *DP-IV* was traveling stern first, thus aiming the engines through her direction of travel. Then he had fired the engine until the ship was at a dead stop, relative to the planet and the inner system of Solace.

Of course, the ship would be pulled in toward the inner Solacian star system by the star's gravity, and start falling in once again. It would be a leisurely fall, requiring hundreds of years to complete. They would change course again long before then.

In effect, he was allowing the ship to drift for the moment. So far as Marquez was concerned, their present position, course, and heading were not matters of particular import. Later, when they had actually decided where they wanted to go, and how soon they wanted to get there, he would take more care in setting his course.

But there was something else about the ship's flight path tickling at the back of his mind. However she had ended up on her original course, she had been placed on it with almost preternatural precision, aimed for a perfect intercept with Solace. The odds against that happening by chance were remote enough that they might as well be zero.

That was part of why he had done the braking burn in such a slapdash manner. If their situation had been manipulated in some way, it was, he felt it prudent to move the ship off that course in an unplanned, near-random way. He did not wish to appear predicable.

In any event, with the braking burn over, it was time to turn his attention to the other jobs that needed doing. They had a lot of work ahead of them—not all of it particularly pleasant.

Marquez made his way over to the comm officer's station. Koffield was there, slowly and carefully working to disarm the lockouts on the various comm systems. As was the case on every timeshaft ship, the ArtInts that controlled the *DP-IV*'s comm systems, along with the comm units themselves, had been designed and installed by the Chronologic Patrol. They were designed to prevent any infraction of the Patrol's complex laws against unauthorized communication from the future to the past.

The comm units had a well-deserved reputation for being prickly customers, suspicious of any human operator. If, for whatever reason, the sealed system did not like the situation, or got it into its mind that there was some sort of attempt at illicit communication going on, it was capable of self-destructing—using a built-in explosive powerful enough to destroy the whole ship. Marquez, therefore, had been more than willing to take Koffield up on his offer to dicker with the comm unit.

In theory, the system was designed with enough flexibility to deal with emergencies and unforeseen situations—such as the *DP-IV*'s present plight. But the whole system was so heavily encrypted and festooned about with fail-safes and fire walls that Marquez always felt it was something close to a miracle if a ship actually managed to send a message without getting shot down or blown up.

"How is it going?" Marquez asked as he sat down beside Koffield.

"Reasonably well, for a wonder," Koffield replied. "The comm system seems as shocked as we are about how much time has passed. It seems to have had its internal clock zeroed out as well. But once it got a look at the positional data for the Solace system, it was ready to believe. I think it helps a lot that I'm a Chronologic Patrol officer. It was a lot more ready to listen to me once it heard a few recognition codes and scanned my retina."

"Is it going to unlock the system for us?"

Koffield nodded wearily, and yawned. "Excuse me," he said. "It's been a long, hard day. But I think the comm system will unlock for us. After all, it's programmed to keep us from going into the past and communicating information from the future. It isn't programmed to care if we work it in the other direction. The situation we're in is strange enough that the comm unit suspects it might be a trick of some sort. But I think I've offered it a compromise it can accept. It's been gaming my offer for the last few minutes, doing decision trees and running down all the permutations. I'm not sure how long it will take to work enough scenarios to be satisfied."

Marquez raised his eyebrows. He knew perfectly well how long that sort of processing could take. Taken to and past its logical extreme, that sort of open-ended analysis could wind up doing estimates on the time remaining until the heat death of the universe, or projected changes in the statistical distribution of atomic particles throughout the universe. Comm units had a reputation for paranoid thoroughness. They'd just have to hope this comm was prepared to be reasonable. "What's the deal you offered?" he asked.

"I doubt you'll like it much. The comm system lets us in, but in exchange it wants to do a total, irrevocable lockdown on communication on any time-hack earlier than the present here-now."

Marquez frowned. Logically, he had no reason to object. He knew damned well they were never going to be able to return to their own time. It wasn't giving up much to give up the chance to communicate with a past he could not go back to. But interstellar travel was not always absolutely precise. Timeshaft ships often arrived at their destinations a matter of a few days or weeks, or even months, downtime from when they had started. A ship might arrive in its own past, albeit tens or hundreds of light-years away from where it had experienced that past. A ship in that situation was expected to sit tight and wait until time caught up with her before communicating, but was allowed to call for help in an emergency. Koffield wanted to bargain that ability away. "I hope you were going to check with me before finalizing that with the comm unit," Marquez said. "This is still my ship."

"Yes, I know," Koffield replied, and rubbed his eyes with a weary hand. "I was going to. I should have cleared it with you before I made the offer in the first place. I'm getting a little punchy."

"We're both tired," Marquez said. "It's been a hell of a day for us both."

"It has," Koffield said. "Shall I withdraw the offer?"

Marquez thought for a moment, then shook his head. "No," he said. "It's a sensible deal. Once I had a chance to think it all through, I probably would have offered the comm unit something like that myself. I suppose I was just a bit thrown by being reminded that we're not going home, not ever. Besides, if you tried to cancel the deal now, you'd only make the comm ArtInt even more suspicious."

"All right, then," Koffield said. "We'll let it go." He reached for the control panel and entered new commands into the system.

An overhead screen came to life.

Comm unit hereby accepts Admiral Koffield's bargain, it read. *Comm unit will fully release control of communications during present period in Solacian system in exchange for total lockdown of all communications at any time in the local here-now past. Comm unit will initiate this agreement upon confirmation from Admiral Koffield and Captain Marquez.*

Koffield looked toward Marquez with a wry smile. "It looks like your comm unit wouldn't go along without your okay anyway," he said.

"So it seems," Marquez replied. Not for the first time, Koffield had put him just a trifle off stride, seemingly without trying, without even being aware of it.

"So it's all right?" Koffield asked.

"Hmm?" Marquez looked up. "What? Yes. Comm unit—this is Marquez. I concur."

"This is Koffield. I concur as well."

A new message popped up on the screen. *Agreement implemented. No communication will be permitted prior to the present recorded time. Full communications system released for use during present period in Solacian star system.*

The comm board's manual controls came to life, and Koffield set to work as Marquez watched him.

The man had a way of moving ahead, moving in, taking over, without ever seeming anything other than quiet, urbane, courteous. It seemed as if the choices he offered were never truly choices at all. At the end of it all, there was never more than just the simple, sensible way forward that he put right in front of you. Somehow, what he wanted was always reasonable, and the options never were.

Did you have to have a personality like that, Marquez wondered, before you were capable of destroying a wormhole and a convoy of ships, a wormhole that was a vital link between a half-wrecked world and the outside universe? Before you could sign a planet's death warrant in defense of something as unsubstantial as that holy of holies, Causality with a capital *C*?

Koffield double-checked his control settings then nodded to himself, satisfied with his own work. "That should get us started," he said. "I've set it to locate and monitor all the public broadcast channels it can find, and record both the raw results and summaries of what it finds. We can leave it running now, and we should have some sort of results by morning."

Marquez didn't bother to point out that it was his ship, and he could see how Koffield had set things without being told. "Very good," said Felipe Henrique Marquez as he stood up, forcing himself to be civil. "Then let's get a good night's sleep tonight."

Koffield stood as well and looked Marquez in the eye. There was something in Koffield's expression that made Marquez feel as if the man could see straight into him and know all that he wished to keep hidden. But Koffield merely smiled. "A good night's sleep tonight," he agreed. "Things ought to seem a bit more settled tomorrow. We'll try and have a day with no surprises."

Marquez chuckled to himself. Koffield cocked his head quizzically, clearly wondering what was funny. But Marquez granted himself the small luxury of not explaining. *No surprises.* If Rear Admiral Anton Koffield could arrange, by sheer force of his quiet, determined personality, for there to be no more surprises—well, on that matter, at least, Admiral Koffield would meet with no resistance at all from Marquez.

CHAPTER TEN

AWAKENED BY DEATH

Her body was not her own. Someone or something else had grabbed it away from her, torn it from her grasp. Demons were forcing it to leap and whirl, buck and sway, as they danced to hideous music that blared and moaned, screamed and gibbered, all about her.

Norla Chandray, second officer of the *Dom Pedro IV*, woke up halfway through her nightmare—and realized that the nightmare was real.

Long sleep. Cold sleep. Cryosleep. Hibernation. Whatever name you called it by, she had been in it, and she was coming out of it. The trainers at the merchant's academy had warned her, over and over again, that it would be bad, that she would waken with no control over her own body, that she would waken in the midst of something very like an epileptic fit.

But they could tell her anything they liked. It was nothing at all like *doing* it.

It's my first time, she protested to the gibbering demons, and to whatever other forces or powers that might be willing to intercede. *It's my first time. Can't you go easy on me?*

Irrational, all of it, above and beyond the fact that she was trying to bargain with imaginary beings. Because all the training and medical people had told her the first time was the worst. Everyone had been more than eager to tell her that.

Some small fraction of the population couldn't handle

the shock of revival and just plain died halfway through waking up. Others lived through it without any physical harm, but never recovered mentally from the ordeal. To hear some of the old hands tell it, there were nonreturnables loitering around every port city in Settled Space—people who had meant to make a round-trip on a timeshaft ship, but could not face another cryosleep revival, nor even bear to get back into a cryo canister. Rather than face it, they spent the rest of their lives stranded light-years from home, watching the shuttles lifting for orbit, never daring to board one.

Her legs jerked back and forth and her stomach muscles spasmed violently. *Is that going to be me?* she wondered. *Am I going to be a nonreturnable?*

"Easy now," said a man's voice, an older man's voice, speaking in gentle, calming tones. "This is no fun, I know. I did it yesterday. We had a slight problem reviving you, and it's not over yet, but you should be all right."

Norla blinked and cleared her vision—or at least tried to do so. Neither her eyes nor her eyelids seemed to be working properly yet. She could make out a faint man-shaped blur standing over her, but that was all.

Norla tried to speak, but her voice was so garbled she couldn't even understand herself. *What's all the noise,* she tried to ask. It came out as something like "Wuz—wuz guggle naz?"

It was not until she heard herself asking the question that the conscious part of her mind even realized the screaming from her dreams was still happening, and apparently quite real.

"I have to go," the voice said, calm and yet hurried. "Someone else needs—needs—never mind. I'm going to give you an injection, a neural stimulant. Your body isn't reviving quite as fast as it should. There's nothing all that dangerous in slow revival, but it's best to get it over with. The stimulant will help you recover faster. The spasming is going to get worse, but it shouldn't last too much longer. But we have to leave you strapped down until we're sure the spasms have stopped. I'll be back when—when I can."

"Bownt eav me. Pease bownt eav me!" Norla cried out,

and this time she was in conscious—if imperfect—control of what she was saying. Just as she was about to open her mouth to try to speak again, a strong, gentle hand grasped her jaw and eased her mouth open. She felt something being put in her mouth, and firm, insistent, careful pressure on her jaw. "It's just a bite guard," the voice said. "To stop you biting your tongue off or cracking a tooth if the spasming gets too bad. I'm going to have to tape it in place." She could see blurry movement and feel the adhesive tape being strapped down on her face. "It's all right. It's all right," the voice said. Even in the state she was in, Norla couldn't help wondering whether its owner wasn't trying to reassure himself as much as her. That thought, all by itself, was terrifying.

But there was nothing she could do. She felt the icy pinprick of a pressure injector on the base of her jaw, just under her left ear.

But the voice and the man were already gone.

Whatever the neural stimulator was, it seemed to go to work fast. Suddenly her head cleared, and her mind felt sharp, alert. Her vision snapped into focus, and the ceiling over her head was no longer a muddle of fuzzy white, but instead a gridwork of sharply delineated panels. But the same stimulant seemed to encourage every muscle in her body to spasm and cramp even harder. Her stomach muscles clamped down so hard she thought she was about to crack a rib. Her legs and arms arched up against the restraints. Her breathing turned shallow and rapid.

And the screaming went on and on.

Screaming? It dawned on her fully for the first time that the horrible sound was outside of herself, and not some invention of her cryo-muddled head. She realized that she could hear others' voices as well. Two men, talking in urgent tones, struggling to make themselves heard over the dreadful shrieking of a soul in mortal agony. The calm, urgent voice of the man who had spoken to her, and another voice, deeper and more guttural, more emotional. She could hear nothing but snatches of their words to each other.

"—out of control—"

"Hold him dow——straint is coming loose—"

"What's gone wro——"

"Hold him! Hold him!"

"The spasming is getting—"

"Lord's sake! Hold him!

"He's going into sho—"

The screaming grew louder, drowning out all other sound for long seconds. Then came a loud, sharp banging noise, of something hard slamming into a solid surface again and again and again, the screams cutting off with every bang before starting up again.

"His head's loose of the restraint!"

"He's going to smash his brain out!"

"Hold it down before he breaks his—"

And with the hideous, sickening *snap* of breaking bones, the screaming stopped again, this time forever.

Norla wanted to scream herself, scream and run away, to tear the bite guard from her mouth and the restraints from her body and run, run as far as could be from that hideous noise, and the horrible after-silence that was somehow louder than any scream.

But the bite guard stayed in, and the restraint held, and she could feel the neural stimulant digging in and taking hold. Her mind sharpened along with her fear. *Will that he me?* she asked herself, *Will I be next?* She was suddenly aware of sweat pouring out of her body, of her forehead damp with perspiration and her eyes blinking back the stinging salt of tears and sweat commingled. She felt as if she were burning up. The ceiling was looming in closer, and sounds took on a strange and eerie timbre. *Just the stimulant,* she told herself. *Just side effects of the stimulant.* At least that's what she hoped.

But then the spasms took hold of her again, with greater cruelty and violence and pain than before, hitting so hard that fear of her senses betraying her, fear of death itself, seemed trivial by comparison.

Her body was not her own. Trussed up and tied down, her body awash with revival drugs and cryosleep reaction, there was nothing, absolutely nothing she could do.

With a muffled sound that could have been a sob, or a moan, or a prayer, she gave herself up to it all.

"You gave us a scare," the voice announced out of the soothing darkness.

It took a moment for it to sink in, but then Norla came to herself enough to realize she was awake, and alive. She reached up her hand to her face—and nearly slapped herself, her long-unused muscles and reflexes still not quite all the way back to normal. Moving her hand and fingers with slightly exaggerated care, she touched her face, her jaw, her mouth. She could feel the tender places where the bite guard had been taped down, and sense the ache in her jaw and the roof of her mouth from when her jaw had clamped shut and stayed that way for minutes—or seconds, or hours—on end. "I was pretty scared myself," she said.

"You had every right to be," the man's voice said.

Norla realized that she had yet to open her eyes, and wondered for a moment why she hadn't. What was she scared to see that could be worse than what had just happened?

She forced her eyelids apart. Discovering nothing more terrifying than the painted-metal ceiling of a ship's cabin, she sat up halfway in bed, bracing herself on one elbow. She winced as a half dozen sets of muscles protested. Her body was a mass of twinges and tender spots and sore muscles, as if she had being doing hard exercise all the day before. But such slight pains were as nothing at the moment. There was something welcome and comforting about a sensation as normal as feeling stiff and tired. It was a commonplace, everyday sort of sensation, one her body recognized and knew how to deal with.

She had made it.

"Is it always that bad?" she asked. *Is that what I'll have to go through with every revival? Can I be a timeshaft flier and get into a cryocan if I know I'm going to wake up in hell at the end of every trip?*

"No, praise the stars," the man said. "It's rare. Very rare.

But it was bad for everyone this time. I've done enough time drops to build up a fair amount of resistance. Even so, I had a pretty rough ride—though nothing like yours."

"You're the paying passenger," she said, apropos of nothing. "You're Admiral Koffield."

"That's right," he said, a faint smile on his gentle face.

"Someone else died during revival," Norla said. "I heard it happen," she added, to make it clear it was not a question, and to make it clear she was recovered enough to be told the truth.

Koffield looked her right in the eye, long enough that she started to wonder just how ready for the truth she was. Then, at last, he spoke. "Yes," he said. "Two died, actually. Sub-Officer Yacobs, the one you heard, was the second. Sub-Officer Lastiz died first. The usual mortality rate is under one in five hundred. We don't know why there were two dead, or why the revivals were so rough on all of us. It might just be bad luck, or maybe there was a malfunction. We don't know yet."

Yacobs and Lastiz, Norla thought. Just hours before they stepped into the cryocans, the three of them had been laughing and joking about how the first-timers had to stick together. The three of them had gone through cryo orientation at the same time, and spent endless hours in each other's company. Joah Yacobs had been so excited over the idea of his first interstellar trip, so proud to have passed all the tests so young. Zara Lastiz had been proud and excited as well, of course, but she had worked hard to keep it hidden. She was a great believer in self-control. Both Joah and Zara had earned their starfarer's rating before their twenty-first standard birthday. Norla was ten years older than Joah and Zara, just old enough for her to find herself playing mother hen to them now and then. Unconsciously she had taken it upon herself to look after them, and unconsciously they had accepted it.

And now they were gone, past care, past everything.

She looked up at the kindly face that watched her. Koffield had to know. From what she knew of the man, Koffield was not likely to be a man who acted without preparation, or spoke without knowing the facts. He knew that something had killed not just two victims at random. It had killed two first-timers and nearly killed the third. He knew they had all been friends. He knew he was telling her she was alone, and that the wings of the angel of death had brushed close to her.

But she could not believe he would tell her such things so soon after the fact, when she was scarcely out of shock, unless—unless she *had* to know such things right away, know everything about the situation right away. Unless they were in trouble so deep that they didn't have the luxury of time enough to worry over the sensibilities of someone who had nearly died in the act of waking. "We're in trouble," she said. "Something bad has happened, something very bad."

Koffield raised one eyebrow slightly and allowed one corner of his mouth to move in the direction of a smile. "You're not slow getting off the mark, are you?"

"I'm right?"

Koffield nodded reluctantly. "Quite right. Captain Marquez is going to brief the crew in about twenty minutes' time."

"Then I'd better get up," Norla said. She sat up completely in bed, then swung her feet around and planted them on the deck. Just that simple act was enough to set her head reeling and put black spots before her eyes. She grabbed the edge of the bunk with both hands, as hard as she could, and braced herself up.

Koffield watched her carefully, but made no move to help her. That all by itself sent a clear message. *We're in an emergency situation,* Koffield was saying, just by sitting there, hands folded. *We can't spare the time and energy right now seeing after invalids who shouldn't be out of bed in the first place. There's no sense encouraging you if you can't manage on your own.* "Do you think you'll be in good enough shape to attend the meeting?" he asked. The words he spoke were gentler than the message Norla imagined, but the intent was the same.

Norla sat there for a moment, trying to get her head to

clear. She could not, would not, let her first act after revival be a decision to give up without a fight. "No," she
said at last. "But I'm going to be there anyway."

"That about sums it up," Marquez said, switching off the
last of the display devices. "Beyond saying that I will conduct a memorial service for our fallen comrades in two
hours, there is little else left to report. Now you know as
much as I do about our situation. For reasons I cannot explain, we're where we're supposed to be, but over a century late. And, just to be absolutely clear, there's no going
back. The Chronologic Patrol would blow us out of the
sky if we went near the uptime end of a timeshaft and tried
to head downtime."

The main table in the wardroom was round, with just
enough room about it to accommodate the full crew of the
Dom Pedro IV. But two members of the crew were back in
their cryocans, dead, in storage, until Marquez could figure out what to do with them. No one seemed pleased
about the extra elbow room.

Marquez considered the faces about the table. Koffield
sat directly opposite him; Norla Chandray, the one who
had nearly been their third fatality, sitting on Koffield's
right. The rest of the crew, all twelve of them, took up the
remaining seats. Thirteen crew and Koffield—and he knew
most of the crew no better than he knew Koffield. That
could be a problem. Timeshaft crew tended to be free-
lancers, signing on for one or two voyages at a time, rather
than remaining with one ship for years on end. It was not
unusual for a timeshaft ship to have some of her crew re-
cruited at the last minute. But there were only three in this
crew Marquez had ever shipped out with before, and he
had done so only once with each.

Well, they were stuck with each other now. The *Dom
Pedro IV* was a century out-of-date. Would he, Marquez,
even be able to find the command center on a modern
ship?

One of the crew—Smillers, that was the name—raised
his hand. "Yes, Smillers, what is it?"

"Sir, beg your pardon, but how the hell did this happen?"

"We don't know," Marquez said, and looked at all the other faces around the table. "Why didn't we enter the wormhole or even fly toward it? Why didn't my temporal-confinement field shut down when it was supposed to? Why did the clocks zero out? How did we get to our destination at all, instead of sailing past into space? Why was cryogenic revival so bad for everyone? Why did cryogenic revival kill two people? I can give you the same answer to all of them—we don't know."

"Sir?"

Marquez turned toward the new speaker. He was a young man Marquez knew only slightly. Normally cheerful, he looked as worried as everyone else did at the moment. Dixon Phelby, the cargo specialist. "Yes, what is it?"

"I think I can help out with part of the last, sir," said Phelby. "I've shipped a couple of times on big colonist-transport ships, sir. Four times the size of this ship, and no cargo holds—just cryostorage for humans and animals. They might fly with three or four thousand passengers. They don't even use individual cryo canisters on those ships. They just put a hundred people in one big chamber, and freeze the whole compartment. They do it wholesale. Forty or fifty multicans like that per ship."

"What's your point?" Koffield asked, speaking for the first time.

"Well, sir, on a ship like this"—he gestured with a wave of his hand to indicate the *DP-IV*—"there's only healthy crew of adult age on board, and most of them have cryo experience that's on the shipboard computer file. The ship can't afford a full-time med staff, and doesn't really need one. No high-risk cases on board. So you stick your arm in the cryomed detector. It does some scans, takes skin and blood samples, looks up your onboard med history, and issues you the right types and dosages of cryomeds. The automatics are all you really need to deal with the limited-population universe. No muss, no fuss."

Phelby shook his head. "But you can't do it that way on a colony ship. You've got older people, people with medical conditions that would scratch them from starside service, teenagers, pregnant women, people with bad or missing or inaccurate med files, and so on. Colony ships have to go to the expense of keeping medical staff in temporal confinement. The doctors wake up every year or so to check on everyone, and the med-monitor ArtInts can wake them in an emergency.

"Anyway, I learned a couple of things. One is that the meds they give to the cryosubjects on a colony ship are very carefully tailored, both for the individual and for the duration of the trip. On a cargo ship, we tend to let the medical systems do the worrying. The crew members take the meds the automatics give us, and we don't much think about it. The flight plan called for us to be in cryo for about eighty ship-years on this flight, and we were dosed for that. There's a big margin of error in those dosages—but we were on ice for an extra forty-seven years.

"The other thing is that young people are more susceptible to revival shock. They let pregnant women go cryo, because the mother's body protects the fetus, but anyone from newborn up to about thirteen they don't let into cryo, period. An immature human body can't handle the stresses. After about age fourteen, children can manage cryo—but they have to make age adjustments to the standard meds, and increase the dosages, up until about age twenty-four."

"So what you're saying is that you were all on the ragged edge of depleting your cryogenic support medications—and the two who died did so because they were young and consumed their cryomed dosages faster than the rest of you," Marquez said.

"Yes, sir. We were all at dosage exhaustion. None of us would have come out alive if we had been on ice much longer."

Marquez looked around the table at everyone else. He had been the only one in temporal confinement. If Phelby was right, and they had traveled much longer, all the other people here would have been dead. He would have awakened to a ship full of death and corpses.

"That's all theory, and nothing else," said Hues Renblant. Renblant was officially first officer on the *DP-IV*, but he had signed up just before the *DP-IV* launched. Marquez barely knew him. He had hired Renblant for his skills in propulsion and guidance, and had not worried much about his command skills. There was something in Renblant's tone of voice that made it clear that someone as low-ranking as Cargomaster Phelby wasn't qualified to have opinions on such subjects. "I for one don't plan on getting back in a cryocan until we have something more."

"Fair enough," said Phelby, his tone quite relaxed. "I wouldn't want to bet my life on my explanation either. Not without checking it out. But it's a place to start from."

Marquez drummed his palm on the table. Renblant looked as if he'd be interested in arguing the point further, but Marquez cut him off. "Let us remain calm," he said. "Cargomaster Phelby raises some interesting possibilities, but we have to find out everything we can. The bodies of our unfortunate colleagues are in storage, and will remain there until we have a far better understanding of what has happened. If we reach some sort of facility where it's possible, we'll have full autopsies done. We have the revival-sequence medical information on all of us, and I want everyone to have a full medical scan as soon as possible, so we have some postrevival data."

"The automedics can do the scans, but who is going to interpret the data?" Renblant asked.

"I haven't the slightest idea," Marquez said. "We might have to educate ourselves to read them—in which case we will be here a while. Probably we will obtain some sort of local assistance, but that is by no means certain. Admiral Koffield will address that point in a moment. Before turning to that issue, however, let us remember there are more mysteries than those surrounding the deaths of our colleagues. Something, somehow, went terribly wrong with our ship. We have to find out what went wrong—and even if we are not competent to interpret medical scans, we had damned well better be able to understand a timeshaft ship! We must examine every system, every unit, every component on this ship. I will not trust her beyond the simplest of maneuvers until such time as I understand what happened. I will meet with section chiefs in my cabin at eighteen-hundred hours to discuss strategies and schedules for ship inspection."

Marquez looked around the table and got the nods and mutters of agreement he was looking for. It was important to be firm now, hard-edged, assertive. This crew had signed on for a routine cargo run that should have had them back in home port only a month or two of self-chron time after departure. Instead they were hopelessly marooned in the future, two of their number dead, face-to-face with the unknown. Such a situation required tight discipline for the crew.

But such a situation also engendered fear, anger, perhaps even panic. Renblant in particular would bear close watching. The man was too tightly strung for Marquez's liking.

"That all being said, I now call upon Admiral Koffield to brief us on the situation in the Solacian system."

"Yes, sir," Koffield said, in brisk, military tones. He nodded once sharply, and seemed to draw himself up a bit taller in his seat. Perhaps, Marquez thought, he was trying to remind the crew that a polite request from Marquez should be treated like an order from the ship's captain. "Before I begin, I should point out there are some guesses and some assumptions in what I am going to tell you. They are educated guesses and informed assumptions, and I think I can safely say that my information is essentially reliable. I am probably wrong on a few small details, but I very much doubt that I am wrong about the general situation."

He looked around the table, as if daring anyone to protest, then went on. "We have been monitoring whatever communications we could pick up from the Solacian system—commercial broadcasts, ship-to-ship radio, radio traffic in the clear, video news reports, and so on. None of what we have heard or seen gave us direct information on the matters that interest us. No reporter came on the screen and announced that a drought had started twenty years before, or broadcast a detailed account of Solace's history over the last hundred and thirty standard years.

We haven't seen statistical reports on population decline or infectious disease. What we have seen is normal, routine, everyday information, the sort of thing that assumes the person getting it knows the general background and just needs a quick update. Obviously, we don't have that background.

"What I have tried to do is study the daily news and other routine broadcasts to see what they can tell us about the background situation, or else to take note of the information that the sender does not even know is there."

"Sir, I'm not sure I follow," Phelby said.

"Let me show you one quick example," Koffield said. He flipped open a recessed panel on the table and punched a few buttons. Two-meter-wide panels on the four walls of the conference room slid open, revealing large flatview screens behind them. The screens lit up, each showing the same images. It was of an outdoor scene, a protest rally of some sort, angry people shouting and waving banners. Koffield let the imagery run without sound for about ten seconds, then froze the shot. "This was broadcast at local noon from a town on the southern continent, where it is currently summer. The protest was about some group of farmers doing too much overtime and for too little pay. It is what we can see behind that protest that is of interest. According to the archive data we have on file regarding general planetary climate, it should be hot and muggy there, with heavy afternoon showers nearly every day. Note that the people are wearing heavy clothes, more suited to late fall than midsummer. Note that the sky is deep blue directly overhead, while the horizon is a muddy brown, suggestive of a dry climate with a lot of dust in the air. Note that all the trees are bare, and the grass is brown. Not a very fruitful summer."

The room was silent, and Koffield pushed more buttons to make the screens vanish. "Those for whom the broadcast was intended would pay no attention to any of those details, because they would be aware of them beforehand. They would not notice that the information was there. Clear enough?"

Phelby nodded.

"Very good. We have developed a lot of information by using similar techniques with other forms of communication. We have combined that with data from direct observation of the planet, and with data from on board this ship. We have used the information from all these sources to develop what we believe is a plausible synthesis."

Marquez watched Koffield carefully. The man was playing tricks, using misdirection, hiding what he was doing by getting them all to look the other way. He had said nothing about his predictions, nothing about the warning he had been trying to carry, nothing about the contents of that personal pack he had gone to such pains to protect. But Koffield knew that Marquez knew of such things, and Koffield had to know that Marquez would notice the omissions. Did Koffield expect him to play along? What was he hiding, and why?

Koffield went on. "To state the situation in very broad terms," he said, "the Solacian system is in crisis, said crisis being brought on by major climatic problems on the planet. It's raining when and where it shouldn't, and not raining where and when it should. There are places where summers are too hot, and winters too cold, and others where just the reverse obtains. The ice caps are growing and the seas are shrinking.

"All this, of course, means the land is less productive in terms of food production. That in itself shouldn't mean much. The planetary population is only a few million. Even if crop yields drop further, far below what they are, there is plenty of land available for cultivation. But it is extremely difficult to prepare new cropland on a world terraformed as recently as Solace was. It takes a great deal of human and mechanical labor simply to waken the soil. The massive climate shifts now going on mean that it is unlikely for any crop field to be available for more than a few seasons before it is destroyed by drought or washed away by floods, or succumbs to some other climatic disaster."

Koffield went on. "Obviously, the climatic crisis on the ground has had its effect off-planet as well. It would seem there is some sort of evacuation going on at the moment, with large numbers of people being transported from the surface to the orbital facilities. News reports put the number at something like a hundred thousand."

"No one builds that much spare habitat space," Renblant objected. "How the devil could they have enough extra capacity in orbit to handle that many?"

"They couldn't," Koffield said. "Either someone is deliberately lying for some reason, or a reporter got his facts wrong, or there is something we've missed. A lot of the refugees are already returning to the ground, which would account for a lot of it. But even a much smaller number of refugees taken to orbit could be enough to seriously disrupt an orbital station or habitat. We don't know how much trouble they've caused."

And who is "we"? Marquez wondered. The man was making it sound as if a staff of fifty had been working around the clock. Collecting as much information as he had would have been an impressive accomplishment for fifty, but it had just been Koffield and the comm center, no one else—and Koffield had spent most of the morning with Marquez in the revival room. How had he learned so much so fast?

"So," said Captain Marquez, "this star system is in a hell of a mess."

"That just about sums it up," Koffield agreed.

"What about technology?" Phelby asked. "It's been a hundred twenty years. How different are things?"

Koffield frowned and drummed his fingers on the tabletop. Marquez got the impression he had been hoping to avoid that question. "It's strange, but nothing seems greatly different," he said at last. "Some refinements here and there. Of course, I haven't checked all the data, and there's more information coming in all the time, but so far, I haven't spotted anything so advanced it's unrecognizable, and I should have. Sometimes technology plateaus for a long time. Maybe that's what happened. But I don't know."

It was, Marquez noticed, the first time Koffield hadn't

spoken in the plural first person. *It that it?* he wondered. *Is it "we" who have successes, but "I" am the one who fails?* Marquez wondered. "Thank you, sir," Marquez said to Koffield. "Keep us informed."

"I will do so, Captain. But if I might ask, sir—can you tell us what you plan to do? Clearly it is only prudent to inspect the ship, but what is our next step after that?"

The room was deadly silent for a moment. Marquez could not help but wonder why the man who had commanded *Upholder* would ask such a question of a ship's master at such a time. No doubt he had a reason for such a serious challenge to the captain's authority. But what was it? "There is no doubt a great deal more for us to learn—and that is what I propose to do—wait and learn. I certainly don't intend to make ourselves known to the Solacians until we know more."

"Sir?" Koffield asked. "What do you mean?"

"I mean that this ship and her cargo are valuable, and that there are desperate people down there. We could certainly improvise some reasonably powerful defenses, given time, but this ship is essentially unarmed. If someone wanted to take the *DP-IV* from us, they could do it. What if, for example, we were docked at Solace Central Orbital when someone down there—the legal authorities or a mob, or anything in between—announced that desperate times called for desperate measures, or that we had no right to deny the use of our wealth to others during a time of crisis, or whatever other rationalization they cared to use. What could we do to stop them? Ships have been seized before."

"I have seen no indication that things are anywhere near to such a state down there, or that—"

"You have just gotten through saying you had not seen everything, Admiral Koffield. I do not intend to risk my ship to the mob."

Koffield looked at him steadily, but did not speak. The silence held for a moment, until Phelby spoke up. Either the man was oblivious to the tension in the room, or else he did not care about it. "Excuse me, sir, but if we're *not* going to make ourselves known, what—what are we going to do?"

"Hide," Renblant put in.

"Quite right, Mr. Renblant, but I'll thank you to allow me the luxury of answering questions for myself. We are, indeed, going to hide, Mr. Phelby. At least until we know more. Any action, any action at all, that we take now we would take on the basis of ignorance. Should we stay here, or head for Earth, or for some other port of call? What sort of place is Earth these days? Every star system we know of could have changed beyond recognition. And what of the ship? How did she fail us? Would she do so again? What of the cryosleep systems? Is the explanation as simple as what Mr. Phelby has suggested, or is there something deeper at work, some other malfunction? Should we choose to remain here, at Solace, for a time—or forever? Perhaps this is the best place for us, or perhaps our spacecraft is unrepairable."

"You're saying we can't go out and we can't head in," said Phelby. "We can't trust the cryo systems without a thorough checkout. Maybe we can't ever use the cryos again. But if we can't use them again—well, I don't know, but no matter how bad it is down there, it has to be better than being marooned at the edge of the system for the rest of our lives. We can't stay parked up here forever."

"You are wrong. We *can* stay up here forever," said Marquez. "Or at least for the rest of our lives. I do not wish to do it, and it might not be the most pleasant existence, but it would be possible, and probably much to be preferred to living on a planet facing famine. We have power and life support and food-generation systems."

"Many things are possible in theory, but madness in practice," Koffield objected. "We must go in. The whole purpose of our—of my—mission is at stake."

A tiny little break in the armor there, thought Marquez. "I am not proposing that we *do* stay here. There can be no doubt it would be a grim life—but when you say you don't know about how bad it could be down there, you are speaking more accurately than you realize. You *don't* know. I *do* know. I've seen it. I have three times before seen planets in the process of climate collapse."

"I know you've seen it," Koffield said. "But still, we must go in."

And suddenly something connected. Marquez looked up at Koffield, and he could read it there. Somewhere in the man's calm, emotionless expression, he could see it. Marquez had seen climate collapse. *That was why Koffield had chosen his ship.* There had been other ships headed for Solace, but Koffield had pressed hard to get a berth aboard the *DP-IV*. If things had gone as planned, and they had arrived at Solace in the previous century, before things had started to go wrong, Koffield would have faced a planet full of skeptics. It would have helped to have a climate-collapse survivor on his side, someone who knew what the nightmare would be like. Someone who could believe in the danger, could visualize it, and knew how to be afraid of it.

But now the very fear, the very caution, he had sought out had turned against Koffield.

"Ah, excuse me, Admiral Koffield," said Phelby. "Maybe you *had* reasons for coming here, but we are over a century late. Whatever it is can't still be urgent, can it?"

Koffield looked at Phelby, but did not answer. But it was easy to read that cold, hard expression. *It is not wise to meddle in my affairs.*

Phelby swallowed hard and looked down at the table. "Well, yeah. Okay. Never mind."

Koffield turned his attention back toward Marquez. "The captain understands the purpose of my journey here," he said. "He will understand that it has become more, not less, urgent."

"I cannot risk my ship and my crew," Marquez said. "The *Dom Pedro IV* will go into hiding, and remain there until such time as we have checked over the ship and studied the local situation. At our present distance from the inner system, we can avoid detection without much trouble. We can reduce power consumption to cut our heat signature, reduce our visual and radio cross section as much as possible, maybe hide behind some uncharted comet core, and play a few other tricks. No one in the inner system will stand a chance of finding us—even if they knew we were here, or where to look."

"Then let me go in on my own," Koffield said. "Let me go in on one of the auxiliary craft. We can arrange precautions that will keep the *DP-IV* from being detected, keep them from tracing back from the auxiliary craft."

Marquez had half expected Koffield to make such a suggestion, and he was ready with objections. "The *DP-IV* only carries three auxiliaries—two small cargo handlers that would not have range for such a mission, and one larger craft, a modified Corona Interspace Mark 300 lighter. The Corona shipyards make good ships, but their main market is for interplanetary ships, and interplanet controls and defaults aren't much like those on interstellar ships. Are you rated or licensed to pilot Corona Interspace lighters?"

Koffield smiled thinly. "I expect all our various licenses and certifications and ratings have expired by now—but no, I have never trained on any Corona-made spacecraft. But I expect I would have no trouble once I was checked out on your lighter. I have a general interplanetary license and an unlimited interstellar rating."

That inspired a flurry of awed murmurs around the table. There were damned few unlimited interstellar ratings in Settled Space. Even Marquez did not have one. But Marquez made sure not to seem impressed. "I have no doubt of your general skill, Admiral, but surely you would agree that it would be far safer for the lighter to be flown by a pilot trained for that particular craft? And if you are to take the lighter, what lifeboat capability would we have? If this ship fails altogether, would you have us left stranded here?"

Koffield frowned. "I hadn't considered the lifeboat issue," he admitted.

"Ah, sirs, excuse me," said Norla Chandray. "According to the ship-maintenance documentation I read when I came on board, the two cargo handlers got lifeboat capability installed at their last upgrade. They can be rigged to carry the whole crew between them, and even if they can't do the round-trip, they'd have the one-way range to get us to the inner system."

Damnation, thought Marquez. *So much for that bluff.*

Well, someone was bound to have read the documentation. "Quite right, Chandray. I had forgotten." A lie, but a captain needed to save face. "But that still leaves Admiral Koffield without a pilot. I'm checked out on the lighter, of course, but I doubt anyone else is. I had planned to run some of you through qualification training on her during approach to the inner system. Clearly we could still do that, but obviously doing a thorough safety check of the *Dom Pedro IV* will have to take precedence over—"

"I'm checked out on Corona Interspace ships. The Mark 250, 300, and 350-a," Chandray said.

Again, a heartbeat and more of silence around the table. Marquez looked at Chandray in astonishment. Interstellar crew looked down their noses at interplanet fliers, and interplanetary crew deeply resented interstellars. Both sides knew that interstellar was the elite, and that nine out of ten of the people in interplanet service got there by flunking out of the exams for starside service—or by not taking the exams because they knew damn well they were going to flunk out. Marquez had known, vaguely, that Chandray had done in-system work when he checked her service records before signing her up, but it would not have been seemly for him to look into the matter too deeply. She had her starside certificate, and she was willing to work cheap, and that was all he needed to know.

But now. Now, here among the elite, she was freely admitting that she was planetside trash. No one would put it that way in public, but there it was. She had been tricking the starside elite into treating her as one of their own. Just by opening her mouth, she had just changed her relationship with every member of the crew, now and for all time. Renblant in particular looked annoyed and put out.

It took Marquez a moment to recover. "I can't order you onto a mission like this. I promise you, the inner system is not going to be a safe or pleasant place."

"You don't have to order me," she said. "I'm volunteering. I signed up for starside so I could see new places. I won't get to do that if the *Dom Pedro* spends the next six months hiding behind an outer-system iceball."

"Thank you, Second Officer Chandray," said Koffield. "But, ah—"

"Captain Marquez." Koffield's voice was calm, firm, commanding. "I need to get where I am going. My errand has become more urgent, not less, as the years have gone by. You know this. Please let me go in. I do not ask this lightly."

Marquez glared around the table. He had been outma- neuvered. He could see that now. He could have sat on this if Koffield had asked for it privately. He could have kept Chandray from volunteering if she had talked to him without the crew watching—or at least he could have talked her out of it. He would have had more time to think of reasons to say no. But not when things happened this publicly. "I don't like this, Koffield," he said, quite deliber- ately leaving off the "Admiral."

"No, sir," said Anton Koffield, his voice quite calm and reasoned. "But it is necessary. And, sir, I might add, we will be able to develop more and better information about inner-system conditions if we have people in-system. I'm sure we can work up a way to communicate that data to you without giving away the *DP-IV*'s condition or posi- tion."

The hell of it was that the man had a point. If he was even halfway right about his climate-collapse theories, Solace wasn't just going through a bad patch—she was dy- ing, right now. The people down there had a right, and a need, to know that, and it would be criminally immoral for Marquez to keep that information from them, just to keep one miserable old obsolete timeshaft ship from possibly imaginary harm. And hell, they *did* need more and better information about what was going on down there.

But he didn't care for being tricked, or bullied, or maneu- vered into a decision. And he definitely did not appreciate Koffield so blatantly challenging his command authority. The man was pressing hard, very hard, risking a lot to get what he wanted. Marquez would be within his rights to confine the admiral to his quarters indefinitely.

On the other hand, there was such a thing as facing up

to the inevitable. They needed information. Maybe they'd learn something on Solace.

"Very well, *Admiral* Koffield," he said at last. "Go ahead. Go do whatever it is you intend to do."

As if, Marquez told himself, there was any way to prevent the man from doing exactly that.

AUXILIARY LIGHTER
CRUZEIRO DO SUL

CHAPTER ELEVEN

WALLS OF
GLASS AND STEEL

"Midflight checks complete," Norla announced. "All systems normal, and we are on course."

"Very good," Koffield replied, his voice coming through the intercom. And his voice made it clear he was not paying much attention.

Second Officer Norla Chandray spun around in her command chair and looked through the glass wall of the pilot's station. Koffield was reading, seated in the lounge area on the other side of the ops deck of the lighter *Cruzeiro do Sul*. With the pilot station's access hatch open, they didn't really need the intercom. They could have shouted to each other, or even just raised their voices a bit.

The *Cruzeiro* was essentially a fat cylinder, fifteen meters high and twenty in diameter. Topside was the docking system, and the flat upper deck, open to space so that the *Cruzeiro do Sul* could carry bulky cargo, that would not fit inside the ship, strapped down to her upper deck. The main deck, the ops deck, was little more than one big open compartment that could be rigged as any combination of cargo space or passenger facilities. Below was the systems deck, and below that, at the aft end, the main ship engines.

This trip out, they had rigged the ops deck with two small private cabins, one each for Norla and Koffield, and a large open area that served as a combined lounge and wardroom.

The pilot's station was built up against the hull between the only other two permanent structures on the deck—the gangway leading down to the systems deck to the pilot's left, and the main airlock to the right. The airlock was an oversize job, to allow for trips when the *Cruzeiro* carried bulky cargo in the main deck. For this trip, however, the central deck space was wide-open, the gunmetal-grey deck plates a broad and cold expanse between Norla Chandray and Anton Koffield.

The lighter had four portholes set into the hull at equally spaced intervals. These gave the pilot's station, the lounge, and each cabin a view out.

So far as flying the ship was concerned, the pilot's porthole wasn't of much use, because it looked out the side of the ship. For most operations, the ship's pilot relied on external cameras, radar, and other sensor systems that put information on the displays. But even if the porthole wasn't much use for piloting per se, there was good psychology in giving a ship's pilot a way to see out.

In the two days they had been aboard, neither had ventured near the other's cabin, let alone knocked on the hatch or gone in. They had their meals together, but there had not been much in the way of real conversation. Norla was starting to think she might as well carry the transparent walls of the pilot's station around the cabin with her, for all the contact she had made with Koffield so far.

The arrangement felt strange, uncomfortable, as if they had carved up the ship's interior into sections of private turf and neutral territory. Which was not to say that Koffield had behaved badly. Far from it. He was always gracious and polite, but still reserved and distant.

Well, never mind. She had work to do. She spun back around in her chair and started resetting the controls from diagnostic to operational.

The pilot's station consisted of two command chairs and control equipment inside a transparent cubical box. At the moment, the pilot's station was retracted into the hull. But merely by sealing the hatches on the transparent exterior shell and the transparent interior bulkhead, and pressing a button or two, the pilot's station could be sealed tight and raised up and airlocked out of the hull to the topside face of the cylinder. When the pilot's station was extended, Norla had an unobstructed view in every direction but straight down. The command chairs could be rotated to any orientation, pointing her straight at whatever she needed to see.

It would be nice if she could get a clear view of Koffield just by sealing a hatch and pressing a button. As she finished reconfiguring the controls, she found that, once again, her thoughts were turning back toward the mystery man she traveled with. Despite her best efforts, she could not keep her mind from the puzzle that was Koffield.

Norla Chandray finished the reconfig, flipped the master to standby, stood up, and stepped out of the pilot's station. She stood at the station entrance for a moment and considered Koffield as he sat in the lounge-area sofa, reading. A strange and haunting song, sung in no language she had ever heard, played over the wardroom speakers.

He had not done any of the things she had expected of him on this voyage. The nonsense about his not being rated for this type of spacecraft was just that—nonsense. After ten minutes of familiarization, it was clear that he could fly the ship as well as she could, or better. She had expected him to act on that, to plant himself in the copilot's seat of the *Cruzeiro do Sul* and stay there, watching her like a hawk—or, more accurately, like a flight instructor. It would not have surprised her overmuch if he had simply ordered her out of the pilot's station for the duration of the trip and done all the flying himself.

Instead he hadn't set foot in the station, once he had confirmed that he could handle the controls in an emergency. Beyond that, he had barely paid Norla a moment's attention since they had boarded the lighter.

Instead he had idled over his meals, by all appearances doing his best to savor what there was to savor in flavor and texture of shipboard food. He had brought along a large number of downloaded books from the *DP-IV*'s library. From what Norla could see from looking at the titles, his choices were either eclectic in the extreme, or else had been made totally at random. And if there was anything beyond random selection in the music he played, Norla was unable to divine it. She recognized hardly any of it. Some of it was, to her, heart-stoppingly beautiful, but just as much of it was indistinguishable from noise.

There was something disturbing behind his calm, his detachment. Something that also whispered of the condemned man's last meal, a man bidding a last fond farewell to all the things that made life worth living. But that was not quite it. There was something in what Koffield did that told her he was familiar with the patterns of the things he was doing, that he had done these things before, and in the same way. The meals, the books, the musical pieces were part of some ritual he had performed many times.

Norla was finally coming to understand what was going on. Koffield was preparing himself for battle, enjoying one last time the things of civilization, the things that made battles worth winning.

Anton Koffield was doing what he did when he knew it might be the last time. He was saying good-bye, bidding a ritual farewell to all the things he loved. Anton Koffield was savoring, one last time, not merely the things of life, but the things of peace. Whether or not he came back from whatever fight he expected, he would start the struggle with the fresh and clear memory of the things that made fighting worthwhile.

But if Koffield was going into battle, then she was too. And if he felt the need to be prepared, then so did she. She needed to know things. And there was only one way she could see that she was going to find them out. She crossed the deck and sat down in the chair opposite him, regarded him closely. It took a moment for him to look up from his book and notice her. "What is it, Officer Chandray?" he asked.

"That was what I was about to ask you," she said. "What's going to happen? What is it you're getting ready to face? Is there going to be a fight? A battle? If there is going to be, I should know about it, so I can get ready too—and get the ship ready."

"This ship was not built to fight," he said.

"No, sir. She's not armed. But even if it meant standing on the hull with a hand weapon, I'd rather go down fighting—if we are going to fight. When I see a man going through his prebattle ritual, I like to know what it's about. Are we going to have to fight—and if so who, and over what, and where, and when?"

Koffield glanced down at his book, then closed it and set it down on the sofa next to him. " 'Prebattle ritual,' " he said. "I've never thought of it in quite those terms, but I suppose that's what it is." He pulled a pocket controller out of his breast pocket and pressed a button. The music stopped. "I have every expectation that I will be in a fight," he said. "But it will not involve you. It will not be fought with guns or bombs or laser cannon, but with words—at least at first. I doubt I will be killed, or even injured, even if it goes badly—but I could very well be arrested and thrown in some sort of jail or concentration camp—or mental institution."

Norla thought back to the scuttlebutt she had heard aboard the *DP-IV:* third- and fourth-hand stuff about what one crew member had heard about what another crew member had said about what the captain had said in an unguarded moment. "The story going around is that as soon as you were revived, before you knew what had gone wrong, you were expecting to be arrested—for warning the Solacians that their climate had gone wrong."

"Yes. I expected to be arrested for predicting disaster."

"Are you still expecting that?"

"In a way, yes."

"Even though what you predicted has already come true."

"Partially. Not all of my predictions have come true—yet. According to my studies and researches, the worst is yet to come."

"You don't think the planetary ecostructure will recover," she said, careful not to make it sound like a question. "But I don't see why that should be such shocking news that you'd be thrown in jail for saying it. If things are as bad down there as you say they are, surely someone has thought of that—and said it—already."

"Quite true," Koffield said, his face revealing nothing.

"But if that was all there was to it," Norla went on, "you wouldn't have pushed so hard to go in-system. Why risk being thrown in jail for the rest of your life, just to tell them what they already know?"

"You are quite right once again."

"So what is all this? You know more than you're saying."

Koffield shook his head no, back and forth one time, as if to deny that he knew more—but then stopped, and let out a weary sigh. "And why I do keep hiding it all? That's the logical next question. And the best answer I can offer is force of habit. Fear of spreading panic, of getting rumors started without any way of stopping them if—or rather when—the story goes out of control. Maybe there's some part of me that still believes in magic, that thinks that if I don't say it out loud, it won't come true. But you're right. I know a lot of things. And I haven't even told them to Marquez. He *thinks* he knows it all—and what he knows is bad enough. But he doesn't have the whole story." Koffield paused a moment, and considered. "That was a mistake, probably. If something happens to me, there will be no one left in a position to press on. I should have taken the time, convinced him. Too late now."

"Perhaps so, sir. But you still haven't told *me* anything."

Koffield laughed, and there was even something careful and reserved about the way he laughed. "You don't miss much, you know how to put the pieces together, and you're damned persistent. Those are good traits to have, Officer Chandray. They'll serve you well."

"Well, sir, I'd like it if that started happening right now. Talk to me. What's going on? What is the big picture? *What is this all about?*"

Koffield sank back on the couch, rubbed his face with his hands, and let out a sigh. When his hands came down from his face, it seemed almost as if he had peeled away a mask. Suddenly the weariness showed, and the worry, and the anxiety. He was letting her see. "What's it about?" he asked, echoing her words. "Disaster. Long-range, full-blown disaster for our entire civilization—and our species as well, for that matter."

Her eyes widened, and she stared at him. His tone of voice, his expression, made it impossible not to believe Koffield. He wasn't spouting hyperbole that made him feel big and important. He was speaking the truth. That it had taken so much effort to drag it out of him only made him seem more convincing. He meant what he said.

"Tell me," she said.

Koffield stared at her for a moment, and then, at last, nodded. "All right," he said. "All right." He stood up and paced back and forth a time or two across the wardroom-lounge area. "It's hard to know where to start," he said. He paused and looked out the wardroom porthole. "After not speaking for so long, it's hard to start at all," he admitted.

He stared out at the cold stars for a long time, his thoughts seemingly as far from Norla as the stars themselves. Suddenly he turned toward her and spoke. "I suppose the best way to explain it to you is to explain how I got involved," he said. "I expect you know—you know what happened—what I did—at the Circum Central Wormhole Farm?

"In general terms," she said. I don't know every detail." *I know they curse your name at Glister, and the mere fact that the Chronologic Patrol approved your actions was enough that, before the collapse came, Glister's government ordered all Patrol facilities in the system closed, and ejected the entire Patrol contingent,* she thought. *They'll never trust the Patrol, or any outsiders, again.* But was that true? Never was a long time—and the incident was now a century and more in the past. What was Koffield to Glister now, today? A name that rated a footnote in the history books, or still a monster whose name would echo down the ages? "I—I suppose I know as much as I need to know."

"Hmmmph. You might—or might not—need to know a great deal more about it in future. But that's to one side. Circum Central is not what I want to talk about now."

Or ever, Norla added silently. If that blood were on her hands, she would not want to talk about it. "Go on, sir," she said.

Koffield sighed, turned his back on the porthole, leaned up against the outside bulkhead, and folded his arms wearily. "The Circum Central Incident. That's what it ended up being called, for the most part. I will tell you it in brief. Some of what I'll tell you I knew at the time, and some of it I knew later. I'll tell it as short and clean as I can. There was a standard defense arrangement on the time-shaft wormhole. One ship, the *Standfast,* on the past, or downtime, side of the singularity. Another ship, mine, the *Upholder,* that had transited from the downtime side, to the future, or uptime, side of the wormhole. The *Standfast* was jumped by thirty-two uncrewed intruder ships that seemed to come out of nowhere, and maneuvered and accelerated at very high rates. Sixteen of the intruders were decoys, meant to occupy the *Standfast* while the others got through the wormhole. The *Standfast* was destroyed while killing most of the sixteen intruders that were trying for the wormhole. Six of the sixteen got through—how, no one knows. The codes and control systems were supposed to be completely unbreakable.

"My ship, the *Upholder,* killed three of those six intruders, and was severely damaged in the process. I—we—lost six of our crew. The other three intruders escaped, and *seemed*—I emphasize that word—*seemed*—to accelerate to and past light-speed as they did so.

"Two relief ships—the *Guardian* and the *Watchkeeper*—arrived at the downtime end of the wormhole, and sent an extremely minimal signal to my ship, the *Upholder,* to report their arrival. I mistakenly assumed that only one relief ship would come from downtime, while the other would arrive from the uptime end. Once I destroyed the wormhole, of course, there was no point in sending any sort of relief craft, from past or future, to the uptime end of Circum Central. But I'm getting ahead of the story.

"The original plan had been to send the *Watchkeeper* through the wormhole to the uptime side while the *Guardian* remained on the downtime end. However, before the *Guardian* could rig for duty stations or the *Watchkeeper* could revive her crew and make the wormhole run, a new crisis erupted.

"Sometime after the first intruder assault, a convoy of five ships filled with relief supplies and bound for Glister came in on a standard approach toward the uptime end of the wormhole. Just as they were commencing final approach, six of the vehicles that came to be called Intruders with a capital 'I' entered the system as well. Three tried to ram the *Upholder* and so destroyed themselves. We destroyed two Intruders before they could reach the wormhole. The third was destroyed inside the wormhole as the wormhole nexus shut down with the ship inside.

"Once the wormhole was destroyed, and it was clear that no relief would be coming, I decided to head for home. The *Upholder* traveled back to the Solar System, using other timeshafts so as to arrive without getting thrown farther out of our own time. The ship was not in good condition even before we started the trip. Suffice it to say it was not a pleasant journey."

Koffield stopped talking and stared, unseeing, out across the compartment, at some dark and quiet place beyond. Norla had read enough about the Circum Central Incident to know that the return voyage of the *Upholder* was a saga in and of itself. She did not speak and waited for Koffield to start again. At last he did, but said no more about the *Upholder*'s return.

"One ship of the convoy, the *Herakles IX*, got through the wormhole. Three were torn apart by the singularity as they attempted to abort their approach. The fifth and last of the convoy ships, the *Stardrifter Gamma*, aborted successfully and left—or perhaps, or more accurately, escaped—Circum Central immediately, to be marooned on the uptime side of the wormhole. Merchanter's law puts priority on reporting an incident over delivering cargo eighty years late. The *Stardrifter Gamma* limped to Thor's Realm Wormhole Farm and reported what she had seen.

"However, Merchanter's law and Chronologic Patrol rules place defending chronology above anything else. That meant that the ship that made it through the wormhole could not report on the events she had seen until the events had in fact happened. As is and was standard procedure, only the captain of the *Herakles IX* had been revived for the pass through the wormhole. The rest of the crew had slept through the whole affair. But the captain, and the ship's data-recording instruments, had seen a great deal in the future. The Chronologic Patrol had to do two things. First, the Patrol had to prevent any description of the incident from getting out before the time in the future when it had happened. No one, not even the Patrol, could be allowed to learn more about Circum Central, before the incident took place. Second, the Patrol had to secure that information and get it to Patrol Headquarters as soon as possible after that moment had passed.

"Because the wormhole had been destroyed, the *Watchkeeper* could no longer transit through it to relieve my ship. She was, therefore, sent in pursuit of the *Herakles IX* in order to accomplish those goals. As is normally the case with a timeshaft ship's flight plan, it had been arranged so that the ship would arrive at her destination some month or two after her original departure. Thus, she was a month or two out from Glister when she reached her original departure date, and about forty years downtime, in the past, of the Circum Central Incident.

"A prize crew from the *Watchkeeper* boarded the *H-IX* before the captain came out of temporal confinement, took him into custody, and did a full data download of everything in the ship's computer and ArtInt system. Then the prize crew wiped the ship's memories clean of everything that had happened after her arrival at Circum Central. They put the data and the captain in a temporal-containment unit and sealed them in. Once everything was impounded and erased, they revived the first officer, informed him that the captain and the data had been unintentionally involved in a 'time-displacement incident,' and left the first officer to bring her ship in to Glister as best she could. For what it's worth, the *H-IX* arrived safely, though without a captain, and with her operational logs blanked out."

"Almost sounds like what happened to us," said Norla.

Koffield frowned in surprise. "So it does. I hadn't even thought about that aspect of it."

"Is that what happened, do you think? Did the *Dom Pedro IV* accidentally witness something? Did her instruments record something that forced the Chronologic Patrol to board her, blank her memories, and target her toward Solace without a timeshaft transition?"

Koffield shook his head. "It's possible, I suppose. I'll have to think about that one—but somehow, it doesn't quite feel right. It's not the way the Patrol does business. They don't like creating any more mystery than necessary. They leave a message, or make a statement, when they intervene. They made it clear to the *H-IX*'s first officer that the ship and the captain had broken no law, committed no crime, but were just in the wrong place at the wrong time. They do that to keep people from speculating and inventing conspiracies. If they hadn't said something to the first officer, then everyone in Settled Space would have spent the next forty years dragging the captain's name through the mud."

The way they've dragged yours, Norla thought. But best not to explore that area, just at the moment. "So what happened next?" she asked. "To the captain and the data."

"Well, they were in the temporal-confinement unit aboard the *Watchkeeper*. Think it through, and you'll see that, by chasing the *Herakles IX,* the *Watchkeeper* had marooned herself forty years into her own future. She couldn't go back. But her captain didn't want to go any farther forward either. Not if he could help it. He plotted a standard timeshaft transit flight plan back to the Solar System. They did a standard cryosleep flight through the Sirius Power Cluster Farm, and got to the Solar System about a month or so objective time after departing Glister. They turned the captain and the data over to Chronologic Patrol Headquarters and went on to other duties. CP HQ kept the captain of the *Herakles IX* and the data recordings in time containment until the objective-time year, day, minute, and second of the ship's uptime-end entrance into the Circum Central Wormhole.

"At about the same time, my ship, the *Upholder,* arrived back at the Solar System, and the *Stardrifter Gamma* arrived at Thor's Realm. For getting on eighty years, the only information on the Circum Central Incident had been the bare-bones account my ship had been allowed to send downtime—nothing more than a playback of what the *Standfast* had sent uptime. And that information, I can assure you, was kept very tightly under wraps. The only other information anyone had was that four out of five ships in that Glister convoy had vanished, along with the *Upholder*. By the time we returned to base, the story, and the mystery, had more or less died of old age—except on Glister, I suppose.

"Then the *Stardrifter Gamma*, the *Upholder*, and the information from the *Herakles IX* all popped up into view, one after another. Rumors started to float around. Crew from the ships circulated and started to talk. The messages relayed from Thor's Realm to the Solar System and back leaked here and there—and of course the data on the Intruders floored everyone. The whole tale came back to life. Everyone and everything sprang into action, trying to solve the mystery of the Intruders. Patrol Intelligence interrogated the captain of the *Herakles IX* for three days straight, just for starters, and went over every bit and byte of the *Herakles* data. Then the Patrol got their hands on the *Stardrifter*, and on the *Upholder*—and me.

"The interrogations, the debriefings, the analyses went on forever. They studied everything, and then studied it again. They even examined the piece of shrapnel, assumed to be part of one Intruder that blew up, that sliced into my bridge and buried itself in my detection officer's brain. But the sample was too contaminated by explosion and impact and all the ricochets it had taken bouncing around the bridge. It told them nothing. Nothing told them anything. The mystery came alive after eighty years of waiting, but it died again.

"Except on Glister. Glister had been in bad shape when I killed the convoy ships. Eighty years on, it was teetering on the ragged edge of final collapse. And suddenly, with the more complete story of Circum Central coming out, they had someone to blame. All of their bad decisions and budget cuts and bad luck didn't matter anymore. *I* did it. Because of me, four ships out of five in a convoy eighty years before never arrived. And because of that, because of all the magically potent and powerful cargo that was supposed to be on the other four ships, everything had gone wrong. *I* had killed their planet. Complete nonsense, of course. They were not utterly cut off. There were other routes—albeit more difficult and expensive routes—to and from Glister. Supplies and people could get through."

"But not easily," said Norla.

Koffield paused a moment. "No," he said at last. "Not easily. Circum Central was in the optimal location for transport to Glister. With Circum Central operational, it was an eighty-year objective-time trip to Earth. Without it, the next shortest routing turned it into a hundred-and-forty-year trip. That nearly doubled the wear and tear on the ships, made cryosleep far more dangerous, and made it massively more difficult to transport the biological material that Glister needed. Fewer ships were willing to make the run to Glister, and there were more casualties among those that did. That, I'm sure, did make things far more difficult for Glister. For that, I suppose, I could be blamed.

"But the ironic thing, from my point of view, is that the Intruders, whatever or whoever they were, or are, were never blamed. *I* did it. Not the ships that attacked me. To Glisterns, the Intruders were incidental to the whole story. Maybe I would have destroyed the wormhole even if they hadn't existed, out of sheer spite. Maybe the Intruders didn't exist. Maybe I had faked them, somehow, to provide an exculpatory motive for my crime against the good people of Glister.

"Aside from the Glisterns, most people were at least somewhat more interested in the Intruders than in what I had done. The moment the Circum Central story came out, there were any number of false sightings of Intruders coming in and out of every wormhole in space, circling every planet that experienced bad luck. Anything from a patch of bad weather to a currency collapse could be blamed on the Intruders. There were endless guessing games as to what they were. Alien beings, the nonhuman intelligences we've never found. A covert operations team sent by the Chronologic Patrol, or by nearly any other organization you can think of, to perform some mysterious and complex mission. They were a bizarre natural phenomenon, and their seemingly intelligent behavior was all explained away by invoking some little-known—and nonexistent—physics and mathematics.

"But there were no answers, and so, after a while, most of the questions and theories and sightings faded away, though there was still a sort of background-noise level of theory-spinning and lunatic-fringe research, the way there always is when something big and inexplicable happens.

"But they still had me. I was someone—something—they could point their fingers at. I learned very quickly that there was nothing I could say, nothing I could do, that would make it go away. I gave up trying. Silence seemed to make more sense."

"But what about the Chronologic Patrol?" Norla asked. "You followed their orders, did what they asked. Didn't they support you?"

Koffield was silent for half a minute. "The Patrol," he said at last. "They were part of my silence. They certainly sent plenty of signals to the effect that I should keep quiet. I'm sure they hoped that I would vanish altogether."

"But they promoted you. Decorated you. Told everyone you were a hero."

Koffield nodded. "There are times in any organization where the higher-ups will support a subordinate, back him to the hilt in public—but treat him very differently in private."

"They punished you?"

"My superiors backed me up in private just as much as they had in public. And, frankly, so they should have. What I did at Glister was absolutely, one hundred percent, totally in line with Patrol policy. The whole *purpose* of the Patrol is to see to it that what could have happened at Circum Central, what nearly *did* happen, never does happen. What took place—what I did—was terrible. The alternative would have been infinitely worse—and my superiors knew it. The core reason for having a Patrol at all is so what I did could be done."

"I heard the arguments on both sides of that point after—after the incident," said Norla. "Everyone did." *And which side of it did you come down on?* she asked herself. She had never been sure of her own answer to that one.

"Inside the Patrol, there was no argument, could be no

rgument," Koffield said, his voice still quiet. "There was nly Patrol doctrine—and I followed it, and the Patrol acked me up, in public and private."

Koffield went silent for a moment, and Norla knew that he would have to urge him on before he could say whatever it was that came next. "But?" she asked. "There's a but' in there, isn't there?"

"Yes," Koffield said. "They backed me up, in public nd private. But." He turned back toward the porthole, nd once again looked out at the stars. "But. There is such thing as realism. And there are such things as whispers, nd pointed fingers, and stories that get more overblown rith every telling. And for a senior officer there are such hings as official receptions, visiting delegations, courtesy alls on other commands, public occasions of all sorts.

"My superiors knew, and I knew, that, after Circum Central, I could no longer hold a command. Not for a long me. Maybe not ever. Because sooner or later someone important and official would throw a drink in my face. Or ome Glistern with thoughts of revenge would make a try or me with a pistol or a knife and get himself killed by my ecurity detachment—or try it with a suicide bomb attack nd get a few hundred innocent bystanders killed. Or maybe here would be something as trivial as a crude, loud, abusive runk cursing me at a party. Even something as minor as hat could develop into a very bad situation if it happened in he wrong time and place.

"Wherever I went, whatever I did, whatever orders I was iven, Circum Central and the collapse of Glister would be here, getting between me and whatever job I was supposed o do."

"So what did they do?"

"So they gave me a medal and made speeches they eemed to be embarrassed to be making, at a public ceremony that was kept very quiet and held where no one ould get to it. And then they took me off the operational-ssignment list and set to work finding a job for me that vould keep me busy, and keep me quiet, until the worst of blew over."

Koffield shrugged. "They put me on a shelf. And I

stayed there until Oskar DeSilvo reached up and took me down from it."

Norla was duly impressed. "You met Oskar DeSilvo?"

Koffield laughed, with more bitterness than humor. "Yes," he said. "Oskar DeSilvo. The great man himself." He walked to the wardroom porthole and looked out. The planet Solace was visible, a tiny blue, green, and brown ball hanging in the darkness. "The man who built Solace. Who made it what it is. Made it all that it is, for better or worse."

Anton Koffield turned from the porthole and looked at Norla. "Excuse me just a moment," he said. "There's something I want to get. Something I'd like to show you."

With that, he walked into his cabin and shut the door behind him. Norla shrugged. Even when he was explaining things, the man didn't give much away. Patience was quite a valuable virtue when dealing with Anton Koffield.

She stood up to look out the porthole. There was Solace, drawing closer. With a little luck, they'd be docked at Solace Central Orbital Station in another day or so. Or was SCO Station there anymore? It almost didn't matter. There would be some sort of station, and they'd dock with it, and arrange for passage down to the surface. Norla would get to see her first terraformed world.

Though, judging by the way Koffield spoke, she didn't get the sense it was going to be much worth looking at.

CHAPTER TWELVE

WORLD ENOUGH AND TIME

It was coming on toward night, and a group of refugees, all of them men, had decided to head out of Ring Park and stretch their legs out on the Long Boulevard of Solace Central Orbital Station. Zak and some of the others came by Elber's campsite and urged him to come along.

Elber would have preferred to remain in the camp in Ring Park with his wife, Jassa, and their baby daughter, Zari. Elber was reluctant to leave Jassa on her own. She still grieved over the death of their son, little Belrad, who had died the year before. He was buried in the now-flooded fields of their farm, out behind their snug little house, back on Solace. Grave, house, farm—all of it was washed away now, lost in the floods and the endless rains.

But Jassa had urged him to go out with the other men. "Get out of the camp for a while," she told him, sitting by their tiny fire in the chill, cavernous darkness of Ring Park. "It drives you mad, just sitting around night after night with nothing to occupy your mind. Go. Try and enjoy yourself."

Maybe, he decided, it would do *her* some good if he could get his mind off his own troubles. He knew it broke her heart to watch him brooding, night after night. So he had followed along with Zak and the others, hanging back just a bit as the group set out for the Park exit.

Three or four of the louder and more boisterous ones were passing a bottle they had gotten from somewhere and trying to get the rest of the group to join in a song, a bawdy old ballad about drinking and farm girls who were no better than they ought to be. Zak was singing loudest of all.

Nearly everyone else joined in at the chorus, as they came up toward the exit from the Park, but Elber couldn't bring himself to sing. He didn't care for that sort of song, and he wasn't at all comfortable with the idea of leaving Ring Park so late in the evening. There had been trouble already, and there was bound to be trouble again.

Elber had not met any of his fellow refugees before chance had thrown them all together in this strange space-station place. But that did not matter. He knew them all. They were all like him. Their story was his story. They had been farmers, and they had lived by an unspoken bargain with the upper-class, big-city, educated outside world. *Take care of us, keep us safe, and we will do the farming and the hard work.*

But then the bad-weather times had come, and their farms and their fields had washed away, dried up, frozen, baked, or just plain died. They had looked to the government, the Senyors, the uppers, to take care of them, and got no useful help. With their farms destroyed, the dirt farmers had retreated to the cities, and found no welcome at all.

Then had come the scares, the panics, the riots, the rumor that the uppers were taking everyone off-planet. And, somehow, Elber and his family had gotten caught up in it, become part of a loose group of refugees who had decided to take the offer to get off the planet and out of the endless rain of Solace City.

So now Elber Malloon and his family were refugees, swept up out of the rain, up into space, not quite sure how it had all happened, how they had decided to come to this strange place. He was, they all were, gluefeet, stuck in SCO Station, in space, no longer on the world of Solace at all. Instead they were in this weird, inside-outside place where walking in a straight line would as like as not turn out to be a circle that brought you right back to where you started. Lost and confused, Elber and his family, and all the other gluefeet, were hunkered down in Ring Park, the only place they were allowed to stay, up in the middle of the sky.

It was hard to believe they were in space, off the world, but Elber had managed to catch a glimpse through one of the big viewports in Ring Park, before SCO Station security had posted guards around all the 'ports. He had seen the world, the planet Solace, there far below. It was all true.

His fellow refugees were decent fellows, for the most part. But they were scared, confused, with no idea of what happened next. Some of them tried to hide their fears by talking big, by swaggering. But they weren't the ones who caused trouble, not really. It was the angry ones, like Zak, who started things. Zak frightened Elber. He was always saying how PlanEx Kalzant and the other big shots had let them down, had tricked them and cheated them. The uppers were the ones in charge of the weather. It was the bad weather that had ruined their farms. So why didn't the PlanEx and her gang give them new farms, instead of locking them up in this place?

Elber was no deep thinker, but even he knew that sort of talk was dangerous. It sounded like it made sense, but it didn't, not quite. And it could stir up frightened people, turn fear into anger, make people think they had rights to things they had no right to at all, and no hope of getting.

And it was even more dangerous to talk that way to men who had lost everything, who had no work to occupy them, who were trapped in a new world they did not understand—in a world that did not want them there.

The people of SCO Station had been more or less welcoming, at first. But then more refugees had come, and more, and more. The station had grown more and more crowded, more dirty. Machines started breaking down. Supplies ran short. The air stopped smelling nice. And still the refugees came, none of them knowing the first thing about life aboard a station. Elber, at least, could read, but many of the others could not. He was pretty sure Zak couldn't.

The knot of ten or twelve men reached the exit of the Park and set forth down the walkways of the Long Boulevard.

Elber did not understand the Boulevard. The shops full of precious things no one could truly ever need, the restaurants and sidewalk cafes that worked so hard to serve such little servings of odd food, the people that seemed to go there, not to do anything, but to see and be seen. It was a fairy world, a made-up place, a toy that others played with, that did not suit Elber. It was a place for the uppers, and not for the likes of him.

It was clear to Elber—if not to Zak or some of the rowdier members of their group—that the shopkeepers and patrons of the Long Boulevard felt the same way. He could see the eyes following their group as it moved up the walkway. It took no effort at all to notice the big, tough-looking men that stood at the doors of most places. Bouncers, enforcers, muscle to keep the riffraff out.

And Elber could see the shops and restaurants that were empty now, or boarded up, that had been open for business not so very long ago. The windows of one place across the street looked as if they had been blackened by fire. He noticed workmen installing heavy metal grillwork over the display windows of the store next to the burned one.

"Let's stop here!" Zak called out. Elber, looking everywhere but straight ahead, hadn't been paying attention to where the group was going. Zak had stopped them at the entrance to a very posh sidewalk cafe, a place with tiny white tables and chairs that looked too delicate to hold the weight of burly workingmen. But the first of their group was already staking out chairs, shoving tables together, laughing and calling to each other, treating the place as if it were a farmers' lunch counter, back home. Elber took a seat toward the edge of the group, as close to the exit as he could manage.

Zak plopped down in a chair that nearly gave way. He took a pull off the bottle he'd been carrying, drained it, and dropped it negligently to the ground. It landed with a heavy thud, but did not break. "Let's have a drink," he said loudly, looking around for someone to serve him. It was plain to see Zak was drunk already.

But the man who appeared at his elbow was no waiter. Waiters weren't that big and didn't look that mean. "Get your stinking, dirt-farmer, shiftless, peasant butts out of those chairs," the enforcer said. "This is a class joint for uppers, not the likes of you."

"We got the same rights to be here as anyone," Zak said, his voice angry, his eyes narrowing.

"The hell you do, gluefoot," the enforcer growled, leaning in closer. "This place is for station people, uppers with money, people who take baths and don't smell. And none of that is you. Now beat it."

Everything went quiet. "No," said Zak. "We stay."

"Leave now," said the enforcer, "or later you'll wish you had."

Zak stood up slowly and shoved his chair out of the way. Somehow the discarded bottle was back in his hand, held by the neck. He stood in close to the enforcer, nose to nose. "We stay," he said again, his voice hard and harsh. "Now tell someone to bring us all a drink."

The enforcer's hand came up, but Zak was faster. The bottle got the enforcer square on the side of the head, hard.

The enforcer staggered back, then shook it off and propelled himself forward with a roar, slamming his fist into Zak's gut.

And in the blink of an eye, the fight boiled over. Three more private enforcers and a whole squad of Station Security appeared from out of nowhere, and every gluefoot on the block was suddenly in the cafe, shouting and cheering and cursing, or else launching directly into the melee.

Every gluefoot but one. Elber slipped away out of the sidewalk cafe and back down the street toward the Ring Park entrance. He wanted no part in such things. His world had trouble enough already.

A siren began to wail, and Elber upped his pace to a jog, and then a run, back to the camp, back to Jassa and Zari, back to the two people who were all that was left of the life he used to have.

He got away clean, before the lockdown or the security sweeps got started.

It wasn't until the next morning that they heard the riot had spread far enough to shut down all of the Long Boulevard.

A good twenty minutes after he had stepped into his cabin, Anton Koffield reemerged, carrying something, a framed 3-D photo or image of some sort.

"Find what you were looking for?" Norla asked.

"Yes," Koffield said stiffly. He sat down on one side of the galley table, and Norla sat opposite him. He set the photo facedown on the table, giving Norla no chance to see what it was.

"I'm surprised it took you this long to find it," Norla said, trying to keep her tone of voice playful. "I didn't think you had packed that much."

"I packed very little," Koffield said. He frowned for a moment, and shook his head. "Thinking on it for a moment, it occurs to me that I *own* very little. I can't imagine that the items I put in storage before I set out on the *Upholder* are still there. And even if they hadn't been discarded long ago, they can't really be said to be in my possession, not all those light-years away. Really, I suppose, the only things I truly own are what's in that secure container, and what's in my travel bag in my room. And, of course, this," he said, patting the back of the picture frame. "It took me all of thirty seconds to find it. The rest of the time, I must confess, I spent staring at it, thinking about it—and working up the courage to show it to you. Other people have seen it, of course. But I didn't have to explain it to them. *You* need to understand."

He turned the photograph over and slid it across the table to her.

It was a perfectly ordinary full-depth photo of two men at a party, with other partygoers behind them. Both men were holding drinks and smiling at the camera. One of the men was Anton Koffield, in the full-dress uniform of a Chronologic Patrol rear admiral. His smile seemed forced, unconvincing, and he held his drink tightly, in both hands, as if frightened it would get away.

The other man was strikingly handsome. He wore a long, flowing academic robe. He held his drink casually, lifting it in salute at the camera, with his other hand on Koffield's shoulder. His smile was as inviting as an oasis in the desert, as warm and honest as sunshine in the morning.

There was an inscription along the bottom of the photo, done in a firm, very legible hand. *Best wishes to Anton Koffield, Oskar DeSilvo.*

"Taken by his staff photographer, the night we met. It was delivered to me the next morning, signed and framed. No doubt he had his picture taken with dozens of other people that night. No doubt they got theirs delivered the next morning as well.

"DeSilvo had a whole office whose sole job it was to handle distributing photos and sending out thank-you letters and so on. I knew all that at the time. But for all of that, getting this photo meant a lot. I hung it on the wall of my office as a memento of the night in question. After a while, when the bloom came off the rose, so to speak, I kept it more as a souvenir of times and feelings past.

"Later still I kept it for other reasons. Back when I was running investigations for Patrol Intelligence, I did what a lot of cops and agents and detectives have always done. They hang up the best photo of their prime suspect dead center on the wall they look at most. A photo gives you a focus, reminds you that your suspect, your quarry, your enemy, is a real person, and not a stack of allegations and file entries. That one photo you're holding became my rogues' gallery, all by itself.

"But—and this is the part that I had to work up the nerve to explain to you—the other reason I've kept this photo was to remind me of my own foolishness. My capacity for being seduced, taken in. Oskar DeSilvo tricked me into liking him, respecting him, even loving him, at least for a while. To know that, to admit that to you, is deeply humiliating for me. Think of the loyal wife who would not believe all the evidence that her husband was philandering. Think of the confidence trickster's victim, who can't bear to go to the police because it would mean admitting to being a gullible fool. That's what that photo is to me. When I feel that I have been clever, or insightful, or think I have understood everything perfectly, seen through all deceptions—then I look at that photo for a while."

Norla stared at the picture for a moment longer, then put it down, shoved it to one side. "Tell me about it," she said. "Tell me about meeting him."

Koffield nodded. "It happened when I was assigned to do general research at the Grand Library. When they asked me where I wanted to go, I think I chose it simply because it happened to be the first on the list of things they offered me. I was in bad shape, past caring about most things. So they packed me off to the Grand Library habitat, orbiting Neptune. It was a posting that kept me close to Earth, to home, so they could keep an eye on me. But it was also a post that didn't make me *too* visible. Just right for the sort of message they were trying to send."

"So you took the assignment. What then?"

"Then I met Oskar DeSilvo." He stood up and looked across the cabin, over Norla's shoulder, at nothing at all. "I'd heard of him, just as you had. That is—was—his great talent. Making sure people knew who he was, and thought they knew what he did."

"*Thought* they knew?" Norla asked. "He was a terraformist, right? *The* terraformist. He planned and oversaw the terraforming of planets."

"That's right. At least that's what he did in theory."

"I don't follow. If he only did terraforming in theory, what did he do in practice?"

Koffield shook his head sadly and sat down on the couch opposite Norla. "In my opinion? The one thing he was brilliant at was convincing people he was brilliant. In any event, DeSilvo had heard about me, and approached me at that party. He was the only one at the party who deigned to speak to me. It caused quite a stir in the crowd when he came over to me—and it touched something in me I didn't even know was still there. The gesture of very obviously speaking with me in public hooked me in, as it was no doubt intended to do. Sending the photo to me was more of the same.

"He'd donated his papers and files and so on to the Grand Library, and he was overseeing the cataloging of all the material. That sort of summed DeSilvo up, in a way. Breathing down the necks of all the specialists, making sure they did it his way, because only his way could be right, making sure that his work was noticed, acknowledged, honored."

"DeSilvo was better at claiming credit than doing work," Norla suggested.

"That's what I have come to believe. To terraform a planet is to rebuild it completely, in all its myriad complexity. No one man can claim it as his own. Such a thing is too impossibly complicated for one man to be master of it all. The task is too great, and takes too long, for one man to oversee it all, or even comprehend it all. It is a task for generations, a job handed down from parent to child, again and again and again."

Koffield paused for a moment, and chuckled to himself. "And it was a job that DeSilvo himself had *never actually done* before Solace. He never thought of himself as an engineer, as a builder, as a doer. He was far too lofty for such things. He was a *thinker,* a theorizer, an idealizer. He was the one who saw how things ought to be. He put his finger square on all the crucial mistakes made in the past—right back to the beginning, to the disaster of the first Mars terraforming attempt. He identified the precise points where all the great terraformists had gone wrong.

"So he said—and he said it often enough, in a grand enough way, that everyone believed him—and came to believe in him. Half a dozen terraforming projects called him in as a consultant, and listened to all he said, and believed him.

"He had never worked, in any capacity, directly on a terraforming job. He had never held responsibility, never been forced to concern himself with the results of his actions—and yet, no one seemed to notice that glaring omission. He was handsome, he was refined, he was elegant. He was charming and had the knack of making his own words sound like wisdom.

"And they all listened, and the more they listened, the

more he had to say. His opinion became doctrine. His vague notions became absolutes. His half-thought-out philosophies became unchallenged certitudes.

"The people who actually did the work came to sit at the knee of the man who seemed to know their profession, their vocation, better than they did. They, who remade old worlds into new, listened to the words and took the advice of a man who had never turned over a spadeful of dirt."

"In other words, he became the grand old man, and no one noticed there was no particular reason for it," Norla said. "I can think of a few professors from my old school like that."

"Exactly. I'm not saying he didn't have skills. He could do the calculations. He did understand the incredibly complicated theory and practice of terraforming. Drop a stack of datapacks about some work in progress in front of him, and he'd master the material, tell you what was working, tell you what was wrong. But DeSilvo was no genius. He couldn't do what had not been done before. What he could do was *find* geniuses, and make them feel useful—which only makes sense, as he used them relentlessly.

"But some people started to notice, and even to whisper to each other, that he was all talk and no action: The Master Worldbuilder had never built a world. And some of the geniuses he hired and used started to mutter about him taking entirely too much credit.

"Then, long, long before I met him, he found the perfect genius to use. One who would not talk back. One who would not elbow her way forward to grab some of the attention. A nice, well-behaved, quiet—and very dead—genius. A genius whose name I am quite sure you never heard. Even on Solace, the world built on Ulan Baskaw's vision, I'll wager that it's difficult—in fact, impossible—to find any reference to her in the public libraries, let alone find any monument to her. And you certainly wouldn't have heard DeSilvo talk about her.

"DeSilvo found Ulan Baskaw in the reference grids of the Grand Library. She had died centuries before DeSilvo was born, but her work—what there was of it—was still there. Just three books, short books, small ones. The first was of no great consequence, but the second seemed a jewel beyond price. The answer. From it sprang Greenhouse and the SunSpot, and the entire Solace project. And the third turned the answer upside down."

"The answer to what?" Norla asked.

Koffield laughed, and actually smiled. "The answer to that age-old question, the stumbling block of all terraforming projects: How do you get something precious, delicate, and rare across a wide and stormy ocean? It turns out the answer is: You don't. You get it across a small, calm, artificial pond instead. It's much safer and easier."

"Now I really don't understand."

Koffield shrugged. "It doesn't matter," he said. "For the purposes of my story, Baskaw's idea, in and of itself, is almost a side issue. Suffice it to say the most challenging part, the limiting factor, of any interstellar terraforming job, was the transport of large numbers of living things, enough to seed a terraformed world, across interstellar space. She found a solution to that problem, a solution that came to be known, in the Solacian system, as Greenhouse and SunSpot.

"Greenhouse was nothing but a barren ball of rock, a satellite orbiting Comfort, a gas giant planet in the outer Solacian system. They built vast numbers of habitat domes on the surface. They hung SunSpot in an orbit of Greenhouse that matched the Solacian day. SunSpot was—is—a massive fusion generator built into a massive adjustable parabolic reflector that could be focused and aimed, so that none of its light and heat is lost to empty space, but all of it could be directed down to the satellite below. It was, quite simply, the largest spotlight ever built. Once its fusion reaction was ignited, it shone down on the surface of Greenhouse with the same intensity as the local sun provides at Solace. It orbited Greenhouse once a day, providing light and heat to all the habitat domes.

"The domes could be used to build up large populations of whatever living things were needed. Without something like Greenhouse, the terraformers would have to rely on small, fragile breeding groups aboard the operations ships, or on the uncontrolled surface of the planet, that would have to be released at just exactly the right moment, with little or no margin for error. With Greenhouse, the terra-formers could grow a large, resilient, better-controlled, and healthier mixed population of many interacting species that could be held in readiness and sustained until the planet was ready.

"They could fine-tune the relationships, experiment, and adjust before releasing a single specimen into the wild on Solace. More importantly, the living things could be shipped direct from Greenhouse without recourse to the cryogenic or generation-ship techniques required of biota shipped from Earth.

"I could spend days discussing the details of why, but suffice it to say that the Greenhouse technique made logistics so much cheaper and easier that it had the potential to shave the thousand-year job of full terraformation down to only a century or two. Ulan Baskaw never found a way to implement the idea. But DeSilvo found a way—in the Solacian system."

"And is that why you wanted to go to Solace?"

"Indirectly, yes. But there's another part of the story I haven't told you yet. DeSilvo found Baskaw's book—or at least the datacube that preserved the words of her book—more than four hundred years ago."

Norla frowned in confusion. "But I thought you said that you had met him," she protested. "How could he have been alive four hundred years ago? How could he live that long?"

"Because, perhaps, DeSilvo did have one other sort of genius. He was able to convince people of things—starting with his own indispensability. Baskaw's methods would make it possible to terraform a planet in far less time—but, even so, the task would not be complete within a normal human lifespan. A *normal* one. DeSilvo decided that his lifespan would not be normal. He went cryo. Repeatedly. In and out of the cryocan, or in and out of temporal confinement, when he could manage it, but mostly in cryo. One year out, nineteen years in, on average. With a lot of Solace's senior terraforming staff doing the same thing."

Norla thought of her own revival and shuddered. To go through that time and again, over and over again. The very thought terrified her. But then she was brought up short with the realization that her own chosen career meant she would have to do much the same herself, over and over again. Would she have the strength of character for it? Or was she a nonreturnable, a stay-behind? When the time came, would she have too much fear—or too much sense—to go back into the cryocan?

"It's not as bad after the first time, and your first time was far worse than most," Koffield said. "The body adapts. It's never pleasant, but I promise it isn't always a passage through hell."

She looked at him in surprise—and then realized it couldn't have been that hard to read her thoughts at such a time. "They—they say that—but is it true?"

"It's true enough," Koffield said. "At least on average. This last revival was pretty bad for me too—maybe because of the dosage exhaustion Phelby was talking about. Or maybe because of something else entirely. I don't know. We might never know."

Norla found herself trembling a bit, just thinking about it. "Please—please," she said. "Don't talk about it. Talk about something else. Tell me more about DeSilvo—and what he has to do with you. So he took cold sleep over and over again—then what?"

Koffield looked out the porthole, a thoughtful expression on his face. "The idea of taking cold sleep over and over again was probably DeSilvo's single greatest contribution to terraforming technique," he said. "That idea, combined with a shortened terraforming process, meant a job of terraforming could be done within a somewhat prolonged human lifetime.

"DeSilvo never got tired of telling people what a revolutionary change it was. And maybe he was right. Look through the history books, and you'll see how many terraforming jobs failed because the dream died in the third generation, or because the fourth generation rebelled, or because the fifth was simply so weakened and impoverished by the task that they couldn't go on. But DeSilvo changed that. There wasn't any need to enlist or train—or forcibly recruit—generation after generation of specialists.

Just freeze the whole team, and revive the staff you need at any given time.

"It made good sense. Most of the job of terraforming consists of waiting for the effects to become apparent. Drop the seeded algae into the upper atmosphere and allow them to reproduce for thirty years. Shift the orbits of ten or twenty comets so they'll hit the planet and bring in water, and then wait the hundred years until the last of them hits, and another decade or so for the dust to clear and the atmosphere to restabilize. Set an army of robotic labor to work seeding a desert, and check back in fifteen years to see how they're doing. Between the times they're needed, the workers stay in cryo."

Norla frowned. "But not everyone could do that. There would have to be a certain number of people—probably quite a large number—whose work didn't allow them to do that—mostly lower-status jobs, I'd guess. Then there would be a certain number who were supposed to sleep and wake, sleep and wake, but who discovered they couldn't or wouldn't be able to endure that much cryo. There would be a huge class division, maybe a permanent one. A long-lived upper class that doesn't get its hands dirty, and a lower class that doesn't live as long and is expected to do all the dirty work. Assuming that most people who rebuild the planet stay to live on it, that sort of system would have profound effects on the planet's social structure."

Koffield laughed. "Quite right. Quite right indeed. Though what you spotted in thirty seconds, it took the social scientists generations to notice—and then they called it an unintended consequence. It shaped Solacian society, down to the present day, judging from the broadcasts I've monitored.

"But, in any event, DeSilvo was convinced he had the One True Way to do terraforming, a plan and a process and a way of working that solved all the old problems and conformed to all of his platitudes and airy theories of ecological esthetics. And he sold the devil out of it to everyone who might be willing to join in the funding—and so they let him have a crack at Solace. And he remade that world, in his own image—and was alive to see—and be lionized at—the official inauguratory ceremonies, when Solace was declared habitable, though of course there was still much to do. He was, well and truly, the Grand Old Man at last."

"And then?"

"And then he discovered there are few places worse than a recently terraformed planet in which to be a Grand Old Man of Terraforming. You never really finish terraforming a world, after all, any more than you ever really finish building a city—or even a house. There's always something that needs doing, some change that ought to be made, some mistake to be fixed. Details, fiddling details, and somehow there was always someone who thought he should be consulted, he should decide. But he was interested in grand visions, not detail work.

"Worse than that, Solace was a backwater. No one of any importance went there. Certainly no one of any importance to DeSilvo's ambitions. Nor had he ever much cared for life on the frontier, for getting mud on his boots and dirt under his nails. Strange tastes in a man who was supposed to be building frontiers for a living, but there it was. So he started looking for an excuse to leave Solace—and then he found an excuse, and he took it."

"Donating his papers to the Grand Library."

"Which, by remarkable coincidence, put him back in the Solar System, right at the center of things once again, where he could hold court and welcome admirers, advise students, pose for the cameras—all of that."

"And that's when and where you met him," Norla put in.

"Yes," Koffield said. "When his triumph at Solace was just a few years old, and my disaster at Glister was only a few months in the past. When he was at the apex of his career, and, in many ways, I was at the bottom of mine. Probably if that hadn't been true, then I never would have gotten to know him. Never would have gotten swept up by him. Connect all the dots, knock over all the dominoes, and my guess is that I wouldn't be here right now." Koffield looked at Norla closely, as if he were seeing something he had not seen before. "Nor would you, for that matter. The Glisterns would have had to seek their revenge some other way. My apologies."

Koffield went quiet. *Does he blame the Glisterns for what happened to the* Dom Pedro IV? she asked herself. *Just when I thought I'd broken through all the silence and the mystery, he starts in with puzzles.* She tried to get him talking again. "However it happened, we're both here now. But what happened with you and DeSilvo?"

Koffield didn't speak for a time, a long enough time that Norla started to wonder if she had offended him. Koffield just sat there, absolutely still.

At last he spoke. "What happened? I was a fool, that's what happened. I was a fool, and DeSilvo seduced me just as he seduced everyone else. Except with me he did it not by flattering me, or making a fuss over me, or making it seem like I was special and important. He did it by not knowing—or perhaps simply not caring—who I was.

"There was a grand reception for DeSilvo one night. Not the first in his honor, and not the last. I received a courtesy invitation, on account of my rank. There were a great number of receptions and parties and conferences and dinners held in the Grand Library habitat. Some for fun, or for private socializing, but most with some sort of agenda for someone. And I did not fit most agendas. As you might imagine, therefore, I didn't receive many invitations, and most of the ones I did get seemed to be the sort where I was supposed to have the good taste to understand that it would be awkward indeed if I actually accepted or showed up. I knew well enough when I was supposed to send my regrets and thus avoid causing a scene. What I didn't know about reading between the lines, I learned pretty quickly.

"But the invitation to the party for DeSilvo wasn't like that. No one called me two hours after it arrived to ask me to take a duty shift so he could go to the same event. None of my fellow officers just happened to stop by to say that this or that politician would be there, broadly hinting that it would be unpleasant if anyone caused a scene.

"So I went. It was the first time I had really been out to that sort of event since—well, since before Circum Central. There were speeches. Some functionary or other got up and told us how wonderful DeSilvo was, then handed DeSilvo whatever trinket it was—a plaque, a medal, whatever. Something he could hang in his trophy case. DeSilvo got up and accepted the award, then made his own speech—and it was a very good speech, a very compelling and moving and clever speech, all about how the new terraforming methods were going to revolutionize everything, turn the status quo around, get humanity back on the move. Now we'd be able to expand ten times as fast, to ten times as many worlds. Loud cheers and applause for that remark, and no one stopped to ask if establishing ten times as many under-populated, isolated, expensive backwaters was such a grand idea.

"I didn't think of any such questions myself, not that night. DeSilvo was a good speaker, and I got swept up in his words, the same as everyone else there.

"After the speeches, DeSilvo worked the room, smooth and thorough as any politician, making sure everyone there got a special hello, a personal greeting. And it so happened he came to me, and it so happened that, for whatever reason, it seemed as if he took a special interest in me."

Koffield went silent again, but Norla did nothing, said nothing, to urge him on. Somehow she knew that she could only reinforce this silence, that came at the exact moment when Koffield himself entered the story. She had to wait it out, let the time go by until he had no choice but to speak. This man had built a wall of silence around himself, and only he could pull it down. Never had he revealed the slightest detail about himself. Now he had no choice but to do so.

At last Koffield went on.

"For whatever reason," he said, "DeSilvo singled me out that night. Maybe he wanted something that he thought I could get for him. Maybe it was that he was a good talent spotter, and sensed, somehow, he could make use of me.

"If that last was it, the man's intuition was right. He used me, all right. He invited me to tour the suite of offices he was using in the Grand Library, and I went there first thing the next morning. After giving me the full tour of his operation—all the archives, all the info-storage nodes, the retrieval systems—he explained in detail what he wanted.

The details of it don't matter so much. What it boiled down to was that DeSilvo was trying to produce an absolutely complete record of the terraformation of Solace, and the Chronologic Patrol's archives had information he wanted, about the initial discovery of the planet by telescopes from thirty light-years away, about the first probes sent to Solace, and about transport services provided by the CP during the project.

"It was something to do, it was research, and it was, perhaps useful. I could imagine some Solacian child one day sitting down to learn about the founding of her world and reading about the information I had tracked down. I liked that idea. I set to work finding the references and getting the clearances. Because I was CP, it only took a few days for me to do the job. It would have taken a civilian months or years to track through all the red tape.

"That's how I got started. I found the history of the Solacian terraforming project fascinating—and, naturally enough, that pleased DeSilvo no end. I decided to write a history of the Solace project, something for the average reader, rather than for the scholar. It seemed the perfect project for me. It was a complex enough job to keep me busy for a good long while, and it would keep me quietly out of the way in the meantime. I'm sure it was just the sort of thing CP HQ had hoped I would decide to do.

"As it happened, starting my book project meant I would be the first person to use the archive DeSilvo was preparing, before it was even complete, and that, needless to say, appealed to his vanity.

"He wanted to assist me in as many ways as possible, but I did my best to keep him at arm's length. The truth be told, I didn't want him too close, because I wanted my book to be something a bit more objective than DeSilvo's version.

"I don't want to give myself too much credit. I hadn't yet started to notice the errors and inaccuracies in the official version, let alone the pattern behind those not-so-innocent mistakes. But there was something else I *had* spotted. Nothing that was terribly dramatic or underhanded. But, after all, the archive workers had all worked on the Solace terra-forming job, most of them directly under DeSilvo. They were, understandably enough, putting together an archive, a historical source, that reflected DeSilvo's agenda.

"I didn't go *looking* for the gaps, the hidden files, the things swept under the rug. But I had served for years as a CP intelligence officer. It was second nature, an automatic reflex, for me to find the holes.

"It was subtle stuff. I'll just give you one example of the sort of thing they were doing, and leave it at that. The cross-reference links—the archive's main index—had a lot more reference links to the successes of the project than links to the failures and mistakes. Any historian who relied on that index to locate information on a given subject, instead of searching the source material directly, would be getting very biased information without even realizing it. There were dozens of such subtle manipulations.

"At the time, I didn't think much of it. At the time I put it down to optimism and pride, an unconscious impulse to remember the good and forget the bad. The other researchers simply weren't objective. But I soon came to doubt it was anything so undeliberate or benign. I think DeSilvo was quite deliberately reshaping the record and steering his assistants to do the same, to the full extent that he could, in order to make the Solace Archive a more fitting monument to himself.

"As I got further along in my research for my book, I noticed more and more such holes and gaps and omissions. I found myself half-consciously tracking them back, for no better reason than that it was habit. It was automatic in me to want to know what a person was hiding. So I ran down the missing references, read the texts myself, and compared the indexes against them. When I found out how incomplete the indexes were, I set to work building my own cross-references. And don't think that is a small job either, no matter how intelligent your automated assistants are. They invariably find too much or too little.

"I found myself spending more time filling in the holes in the official history than I spent writing my own. And then I found it—found the key to it all, the hinge that everything else turned on. I found a cross-reference to a book by someone named Ulan Baskaw, a reference they had failed to expunge. The name meant nothing to me—and that in itself was remarkable, considering the amount of time I had spent reading through the archive files. By that time, I had become so distrustful of the archive project that I would have double-checked a reference to Earth's sun rising in the east.

"It should have taken no time at all to track down any and all references to Ulan Baskaw. The Grand Library's search system should have popped up a full set of information and cross-references to that name, and to variants on it, in the time between two heartbeats. But it didn't. It quite literally drew a blank. Nothing. Nothing at all. But I knew from the cross-reference number I had stumbled across that there had been at least one Grand Library reference to that name at some point in the past. The fact that it had turned up missing was, in and of itself, prima facie evidence, if not hard-edged proof, of a crime. *Nothing* is ever supposed to go out of the Grand Library. It is supposed to be the ultimate repository, the safe refuge for all knowledge. Once an item has a GL reference number, it is *not* supposed to go away."

Koffield frowned deeply. "But it did go away. DeSilvo erased it. That might not seem like much of a crime, but in the world of academia, in his world, altering or tampering with the Grand Library is—well, is sacrilege. Profaning the holy places. I couldn't even imagine a motive strong enough to make a man like DeSilvo do such a thing. But he had a reason. A reason more than big enough to make library-tampering worthwhile."

A beeper went off on Norla's control panel. The sound was not an alarm warning, not even an alert, but Koffield's mood, and the tone of his story, had put her on edge, and she was halfway across the deck before she was even consciously aware of the sound. She dropped into the pilot's chair and checked her board, then looked up to where she had expected Koffield to be, hovering over her shoulder, seeing the codes for himself. But he wasn't there. She looked across the deck to see that he hadn't made the slightest move. He was still in the wardroom.

Damn the man. What was it he had in his veins besides ice? "They've spotted us," she announced, raising her voice so it would carry across the cabin. "Solace Central Orbital Traffic Control is querying us for identity and flight plan. Looks like an automated transmission."

"Answer it," Koffield said, his voice already more distant and distracted than it had been. "But don't answer too thoroughly. If we go into any detail about who we are and how we got here, we'll spend the rest of the flight giving our life story over and over again to every office and section and department head. Just give ship's name and registry, and request a flight plan to Solace Central Orbital. See if that's enough to get us clearance. If it isn't, and they want more information, work on the same principle. Don't give them more than they ask for."

"Yes, sir," Norla said. "Setting up my reply now." Secretive sort of a fellow, that was for sure. What did it matter if they had to tell their story a dozen times as they worked up the chain of command? What else did they have to do?

Koffield stood up, crossed back to the table, and collected the photo of two smiling men, of Anton Koffield and Oskar DeSilvo. He looked out the wardroom porthole. "I'll be in my cabin for the remainder of the evening," he said, and turned toward his cabin door.

Norla finished feeding her reply to the comm system and looked up. "But, ah, sir—you haven't finished telling me about—about the . . ." Koffield stopped and looked toward her. The expression on his face made her give up before she had even fairly begun. His jaw was set, and his eyes, normally so warm and kind-looking, were suddenly cold and hard as blast-proof glass.

"I don't wish to speak about that matter anymore at present," he said in a voice as hard as his expression. Then his tone of speech softened just a trifle. "Another time, Officer Chandray," he said. "If they have found us, things might well start happening rather quickly. There is a lot for me to think about, to have worked out, before we meet the Solacians. It would be best for all concerned if I concentrated on what might happen next, rather than being distracted by things that happened quite some time ago."

"Understood, sir," Norla said, though she understood very little indeed.

"I promise, Officer Chandray, that you will know all you need to know before you need to know it." And with that, Rear Admiral Anton Koffield nodded toward her, once, very slightly, and vanished into his cabin.

All you need to know before you need to know it. How could he be sure *he* knew all that was needful? Even if he did, how could she possibly learn it all in time? Norla shook her head. Anton Koffield might be a man of his word, but the promise he had made would be tough for any man to keep.

And even harder for a man who was already a hundred-plus years behind schedule.

CHAPTER THIRTEEN

BURSTING THE BUBBLE

"SCO Traffic Control, this is *Cruzeiro do Sul*. We report engines off. Circular parking orbit in equatorial plane, as instructed, ninety-nine-point-nine-plus match with assigned orbit Easy-27-44. Over."

Norla killed the mike and glanced over at her companion. The man was making her nervous. She knew damned well she didn't have Admiral Anton Koffield close to figured out. He had told not a word more of his story since the first hail had come in. What was he waiting for?

She had no idea. But she had at least thought she had worked out his attitude toward the lighter *Cruzeiro do Sul* and her trip in toward Solace. She had thought he couldn't care less. He had, after all, paid not the slightest attention to her operation of the ship during the first two and a half days of the journey. She had expected him to keep that up, and pay no attention whatsoever right on through to the close of their journey. But she wasn't that lucky. He was right there, next to her, in the copilot's station. And the only thing he was doing was watching.

Which was just about all he had done since Solace Central had first hailed them. Watching. Observing. Checking his recording devices now and again to confirm they were getting everything. Sitting there in the copilot's chair with his hands folded, watching every move she made, listening to every hail and reply back and forth between the *Cruzeiro* and Solace Orbital Traffic Control.

She supposed it made sense, when she thought about it. He knew all about the *Cruzeiro*, and he knew that Norla was a competent pilot. Therefore, there had been no need to keep watch. But he knew next to nothing about current conditions on Solace, or in the Solacian system. At any moment, some vital bit of information could go past, something that might be the crucial piece to a puzzle, perhaps even to a puzzle they did not yet know existed. He *had* to take in everything that concerned the unknown.

"*Cruzeiro do Sul,* this is SCO Traffic Control." It was a young man's voice, worried-sounding, but trying to put on a show of calm and professionalism. "Maintain current orbit. Do not maneuver until instructed to do so."

"SCO Traffic Control, this is *Cruzeiro do Sul*. Instructions received, and will comply. We are standing by for maneuver instructions." Norla killed the mike. "That was the first voice I've heard from SCO Traffic that didn't sound automated," she said. "Do you think we got bumped up to actual human attention?"

"Probably," said Koffield. "If I were an ArtInt, this is about where I'd kick it upstairs to a human. It would seem they're starting to wonder about us."

"Well, it's not exactly like we're on their current registry," Norla replied. "I'm surprised we got this far."

"That's the advantage of not volunteering information," Koffield said with a chuckle. "It keeps people from getting curious about all the things you're *not* telling them."

"So now what?" she asked.

"Now we do what the man said," Koffield replied. "We wait. And don't ask me how long. Might be hours, or longer. Depends on what sort of bureaucracy they have these—"

"*Cruzeiro do Sul,* this is SCO Traffic Control. Please reply."

Norla grinned. "A pretty efficient one, it looks like." She flipped her mike back on. "This is *Cruzeiro do Sul,*" she said. "Go ahead, SCO Control."

"*Cruzeiro,* we've getting some strange data from your autotransponder. Are you aware it is running on a very out-of-date frequency? Over."

Norla raised an eyebrow and looked at Koffield. "It doesn't surprise me. Over."

"Ah, yeah. Well, the frequency's not the only thing out-of-date. Our ArtInts had to dig way back into the archives to find the registry data. We have you listed as a lighter off a larger core vessel. Can you confirm that?"

Core vessel? She hadn't heard that term before, but it was easy enough to figure out what it meant. "That is correct. Our core vessel is the *Dom Pedro IV,* Earth registry." She was tempted to tell him more, but Koffield shook his head. "Over" was all she said.

"Ah, right," the young man's voice replied. "That matches our archive info. Except the *Dom Pedro IV* was declared as lost with all hands, ah, one hundred twenty-two years ago. Ah, over."

That matched. They usually gave an overdue ship five years to show up. Norla shrugged. "Well," she said, "I guess we were lost, but we're found now, SCO. Over."

"Stand by, *Cruzeiro.*" The line should have gone dead at that point, but the controller apparently forgot to cut his mike. Koffield and Norla could hear two or three voices whispering urgently in the background. Finally the controller came back on. "Hell, my mike's still open. Ah, *Cruzeiro,* please advise. Where is the *Dom Pedro IV?*"

Norla looked toward Koffield again. He mouthed the words *Just tell the truth.*

"*Dom Pedro* is in-system, SCO Control, in a distant orbit. Our captain figured it would be smart to send in a, ah, scout ship first to see what the situation was. Given the circumstances. Over."

"Right, *Cruzeiro.* I can understand that. I think. Stand by."

This time the controller did cut his mike. Koffield shook his head and smiled sadly. "Now it begins," he said. "We're public. I wonder if they'll think we're freaks, or quaint survivors, or historical treasures, or suspect us of being part of some vast secret plot."

One thing was for sure. The man certainly knew how to put a positive spin on things.

After a brief delay, the controller came back on the line.

"*Cruzeiro,* SCO Traffic Control. Just so we're clear on this. You're saying that your core ship, the *Dom Pedro IV,* has just arrived, one hundred twenty-seven years late?"

"That's correct, SCO. We don't understand it either. Not yet. But that's what happened."

"Very well, *Cruzeiro.* Stand by one more time." Again the line went dead. But it didn't matter. Now they were public. Now the outside universe knew they existed. The outside universe suddenly had the capacity to reach them, to affect them, to hurt them or help them.

And now, at last, they had reached out *to* the outside universe. Before this moment, Norla could pretend that it was all a bad dream. There had been a bubble of unreality around them, because the outside universe did not know they existed. Now the bubble was burst.

Then, at last, the call came. "*Cruzeiro do Sul,* this is SCO Traffic Control. Please respond." It was a woman's voice this time, older, more confident and authoritative.

"Looks like we've been bumped up one more level," Norla muttered, and then flipped on her mike. "This is *Cruzeiro do Sul.* Go ahead, SCO Traffic Control."

"*Cruzeiro,* if the ArtInts and automatics are giving us straight data, it looks as if your autonav systems are about eight generations back. We're supposed to be backward compatible, but no one here wants to bet on eight gens of bug-free programming. We'd like you to fly a manual approach, rendezvous, and dock. Do you concur? Over."

"That makes sense to me, over."

"Very well. Is anyone aboard qualified for manual flight ops and docking? If need be, we can fly a pilot out to you."

Norla was about to take offense, but then she realized it was a perfectly sensible question. They were, after all, a hundred and twenty-seven years late getting in. The *Dom Pedro*'s crew could easily have taken some casualties— as indeed they had. There was no way for Solace Central Orbital to know whether they were alert and healthy and trained, or just barely alive and limping in on luck and automatics. "No need for that, SCO Traffic Control. We have two pilots aboard, both fully trained and qualified on this craft. Though I guess our licenses have probably lapsed by now."

"Well, we'll waive license requirements for the time being, *Cruzeiro*. We're sending your flight plan up on sideband two now. Please examine it and respond. Your maneuver window is ten minutes, five seconds, and it opens in forty-six minutes, seven seconds, mark. Please advise in ample time whether or not you concur with flight plan. Over."

"Understood, SCO Traffic Control. Flight plan is on my display now. Stand by just a moment." Norla looked over the flight plan and nodded to herself. No problem. A conservative transfer orbit and a very straightforward direct approach. Not the fastest way to get them there, but they had lost any right to be in a hurry about a century or so back. At a guess, SCO was making things easy on her just to be on the safe side. How sure could they be about what a ship from out of the last century could do? "SCO Traffic Control, this is *Cruzeiro do Sul*. The flight plan is fine. Will commence initial maneuver at start of window. *Cruzeiro do Sul* out."

Norla didn't have any way of knowing how they did things these days, but back in her own time, it had been surpassingly rare for a pilot to get a chance at a manual-approach maneuver, to say nothing of final rendezvous, or doing the actual docking. The automatics did it all, and the pilots sat on their hands, mere backup systems for the machinery that never failed. Pilots were there for the unforeseen, the unforeseeable. But after thousands of years of space travel, there was not that much left that could be unforeseen. Everything had happened at least once, and been recorded in the memories of the infallible machines.

Except what had happened to them. *This* crisis was not for the machines to deal with. This was hers. She was going to fly this sequence, and do it right, and enjoy it.

Because she might not get another chance. That joke

about their licenses being expired was no joke at all. Every thing she knew was a century-plus out-of-date. Would she even be able to recognize a modern pilot's station? Maybe ships these days didn't even *have* pilot's stations. She'd be lucky if they allowed her aboard a modern spacecraft, and never mind flying one. And if she could not serve on a space crew, what would she be good for? What work would she be qualified for here and now?

Besides, it wasn't as if flying the approach on manual was going to be all that manual. The way she was getting worked up about it, an outsider might think she was going to have to get out and push. When you came right down to it, all manual operation really meant was that she pro grammed the computers, rather than letting the station do it for her by remote.

Unless—unless she elected to do it by *true* manual. Cut out all the automatics and fly the flight plan herself, right off the controls. She felt a sudden thrill of excitement. Well, why the hell not? She had been instructed to fly on "manual," and she was certainly capable of doing the job.

She felt a strange thrill of rebellion, a pleasurable sense of thumbing her nose at the authorities, the rules, as she cut every level of automatics and took hold of the manual controls for herself. She glanced at Koffield, expecting ei ther a sharp protest, or no reaction at all. As usual, she got something completely different from what she had antici pated.

The man was smiling, almost laughing, the humor in those warm, kindly eyes plainly visible for the first time in many days. *He's a pilot too,* she reminded herself. *He probably hates all the automatics at least as much as I do.*

Sparing no more thought for what anyone else might think of her, Norla ran through the premaneuver checklist, set up her attitude and her thruster levels, and settled back to wait out the countdown.

Considered as a piece of interorbit transfer flying, it was nothing special. The engines fired briefly. Then they waited two hours, fifteen minutes, and nine seconds, until the ship was in position for the second burn. Another brief shot from the main engines, and the job was done.

The second burn put them in an almost perfectly matched orbit, five kilometers astern of Solace Central Orbital. They were in a very slightly lower, faster orbit, closing very slowly on their target. If Norla performed no further maneuvers, the *Cruzeiro do Sul* would make a closest approach of exactly one kilometer to the station and then pass it by.

Or at least that was what her instruments told her. But Norla wanted to see for herself—not just to confirm the instrument settings, but because she wanted to take a look.

"All right," she announced, as much to herself as to Koffield. "I'm extending the pilot's cabin now. Initiating autoextension procedure."

"Very well," Koffield said.

"Initiating," she announced. Norla confirmed that the station's inner pressure doors were sealed, then flipped up the safety cover and jabbed her finger down on the autoextend button, a bit harder than strictly necessary. The pilot station's outer pressure door slid shut, the movement of the transparent door panels barely visible. There was a low-pitched hum as the air pumps cleared the small amount of air between the inner and outer hull of the pilot's station. Then a moment's silence, then a deep and resonant *clunk* from overhead.

Norla looked up to watch the two halves of the upper hull hatch split apart, revealing the dazzle-bright sunlit face of Solace, seeming so close and sharp she could have reached out and touched it. The upper hull hatch opened fully, and, with a low hum and a clatter and creak or two, the pilot's station began to raise itself out of the hull.

Like some long-forgotten god or devil moving out of the underworld and ascending to heaven, the pilot's station rose up out of the darkness and into the light, out of the belly of the ship and into the sky.

Norla squinted and blinked in the sudden brightness. "Bright-tracking glasses," she said. She pulled open a small compartment on the control panel and took out two pairs of what appeared to be plain-glass spectacles of a sort that no one had worn for at least a millennium or two. She handed one pair to Koffield, and they both put them on.

The glasses sent a signal to the pilot station's hull photonics control system, indicating exactly what direction the wearer was looking in. The photonics system could then selectively and instantly darken the variglass of the station's hull if a blinding-bright object appeared in that part of the sky. The system made sure nothing was too bright to look at.

Solace bulged huge and bright, directly overhead, and she took a moment to admire the view. The sunlit side of the planet dimmed to a comfortable level the moment she had the glasses on. The planet's terminator was almost precisely over their heads, slicing the planet into dark and light.

Solace was big, bold, bright, a spectacular sight. But even from high up in space, it was plain to see there was something wrong with this world. A living world was a place of cool colors, blue and green and white, of vistas softened by clouds and moisture. Solace was hard, and bright, the land painted more in reds and browns and greys than green. Even the blue of the oceans was not quite right. It was too dark, too murky, the color of water that was full of dead things.

Easy now. She was reading too much into it all. They needed knowledge, not poetry; facts, not fantasy. She was painting the whole planet with Koffield's pessimism. Maybe things were nowhere near that bad. Maybe the light from the local star was just a shade she wasn't used to seeing. Best she should admire the incredible view, and leave interpreting it to others. Any planet viewed from low orbit was a fantastic sight.

But there would be plenty of time to look on Solace later. Right now she had other work to do. Norla adjusted the attitude of her chair so that she was lying flat on her back. She threw the switch on the heads-up display, and the upper face of the transparent cube that was the pilot's station hull lit up with a half dozen information displays

She cut out everything but the data on rendezvous with Solace Central Orbital. Most of the blizzard of numbers faded away from the transparent hull, leaving just the range and rate, orbital velocity, and approach vectors.

A white targeting circle lit up around a piece of sky over the nightside of Solace, pinpointing Solace Central Orbital's position. But even at this range, Norla didn't need the help. SCO was plenty big enough to see with the naked eye, a white cylinder off in the middle distance, slowly spinning in the sky. A station had to be plenty big for it to be easier and cheaper to spin it for gravity, rather than operate the sort of gravity generators used aboard ship. But SCO Station was that big, and then some.

SCO was made up of a series of flat disks, stacked one on top of the other, each disk with a hole in its center. For reasons lost to the depths of antiquity, the basic design concept was called a lifesaver stack. The stacked-disk design made it fairly straightforward to expand the station, simply by putting additional disks on either end of the stack. The hole through the center of the stack greatly simplified the movement of spacecraft in and out of the station. Ships simply matched spin with the station and went in one end and out the other, rather than having to go through all the complex and tricky maneuvers needed to match up with an off-axis external port on a spinning station.

The design had its drawbacks in other respects, but from a pilot's standpoint, a lifesaver-stack station was close to the ideal. Nice, direct, on-axis approaches, with none of the madly complicated corkscrew maneuvers required by stations designed by spatial architects who worried about being advanced, or sophisticated, instead of efficient.

Norla realized something was missing. Something wasn't there that should have been. And then she realized what it was. *Traffic.* Her displays showed no other ships on approach to the station, no craft departing. Maybe trade was slow, but more likely, SCO Traffic Control had simply warned everyone else off while the strange spaceship from the past made its slow, careful, manual approach.

SCO Station swelled up in the sky, growing from a toy,

a long thin top spinning slowly on its axis, into a massive world in the sky, a tower of gleaming metal and plastic and glass whirling silently through the darkness.

Now it was plain to see that SCO Station was not a simple cylinder, but a cylinder with all sorts of structures sticking up out of its outer hull. She switched on the long-range cameras to get a better look. Dozens of gleaming spires and complicated latticework structures thrust up from the circumference of the central disks. Dark turretlike buildings—if you could call them buildings—sprouted up from the hulls of the outer disks, alongside things that looked like the skeletons of parabolic antennae. Several of them looked broken, and a closer look at the turrets revealed several had portions of their outer skins stripped off. She realized that a good number of the extruded structures were showing signs of long use. The more she looked, the more she saw wear and tear. Missing parts, lost insulation, repair patches that did not quite match the original. Something like one in ten, or maybe even one in five, of the exterior structures had some sort of defect plainly visible even from long range.

According to the information in the *DP-IV*'s library, SCO Station was a four-disk stack, with some discussion of expansion to six sometime in the future. None of the images she had seen of the place had shown anything built up out of the hull.

But the station she was looking at was very plainly an eight-disk stack, and the four disks in the center of the stack looked distinctly older than the outer ones, their insulation sun-darkened and worn. If nothing else had convinced her that time had passed, those extra disks, and the towers, both shabby and gleaming, would have done so.

She did not have long to spend on counting disks. They were getting closer and closer to the station, their view of it growing more and more foreshortened as they drew nearer and their orbital paths aligned. At last all they could see of the huge cylinder was the aft end of it, a wide flat disk hanging in the sky, straight ahead of them and slightly higher than they were.

Norla looked down at the planet below. What was it like down there? What were the people doing?

The *Cruzeiro do Sul* moved in slowly, until she was only a kilometer astern of the station. She checked her displays. One minute away from the final matching burn that would raise the *Cruzeiro*'s orbit just a hair, slowing it to match the station's orbit precisely. The disk of SCO's aft end was growing larger and larger, swallowing more and more of the sky as they grew closer. Now the hollow at the center of the disk-stack was plainly visible, a gaping mouth that seemed about to swallow them—as indeed it was.

Norla brought the ship around to the proper attitude for the final burn, swinging the ship about to face away from the station. She checked her boards and repeaters one last time and watched the countdown clock. She blipped the auxiliary engines at three percent for two seconds, and they were perfectly matched with the station. Norla worked the attitude controls again and spun the *Cruzeiro do Sul* about to face forward, into the direction of flight. The ship came about smartly, and stopped her rotation with her nose pointed straight at SCO Station.

And then they were there. A bare hundred meters from the aft end of the station, perfectly aligned with the center point of the station, hanging right over the central access tunnel, looking right down it, right through it, the stars in the sky beyond it plainly visible. Perfect.

The next step was to match spin with the station. She switched the thrusters from attitude mode to spin mode and gave the clockwise thrusters the gentlest of taps, keeping her eyes glued to the aft end of SCO Station. She gave the thrusters another tap, and then another. As the *Cruzeiro do Sul* came closer and closer to matched spin, from where Norla was sitting, it looked instead as if the station were spinning more and more slowly.

Only the stars and planets, wheeling unimportantly in the background, in the periphery of her vision, betrayed the illusion. Another love tap on the spin-mode thrusters, and another. And they were locked, aligned, spin-matched, and at stationkeeping. She could see straight down the kilometer-long interior of the central access tunnel, watch the stars spinning in the piece of sky behind the station.

She felt a sudden sense of disorientation, and knew what it was, even as it scared her silly. Her subconscious mind could not make up its mind on the very important question of which way she was looking. One moment her hindbrain had her flat on her back, staring up at the massive tunnel shaft directly overhead and about to fall in on her. Then, in the blink of an eye, she was hanging off the ceiling of some vast imaginary room, looking *down* into the bottomless depths of that tunnel, so deep it had stars at its bottom, and she was the one who was about to start falling. Then, somehow, it all went horizontal, and she was sitting upright in a perfectly normal chair, looking straight through a perfectly flat tunnel ahead of her, and no one was going to fall into anything.

She resisted the temptation to cling to that last idea. Hang on to the comforting illusion, and things will only be worse when something shatters it. Better, far better, to grasp on firmly to the reality of a spinning city in space. Seize on to the strangeness, *accept* the strangeness, and it cannot hide behind the comforting fictions, or leap out at you when least expected. She took a good hard look at the central access tunnel of Solace Central Orbital Station.

The tunnel itself was 150 meters in diameter, and ran the kilometer length of the station. Its surface was a perfect forest of complicated shapes wrapped around the inside of the tunnel. The station's spin, naturally enough, produced simulated gravity, courtesy of the centripetal effect. Down was out, toward the exterior of the station, and up was in, straight toward the centerline of the cylinder. The horizon was, in effect, wrapped around itself. In the outer decks of the station, out toward the outer rim of the cylinder, the simulated gravity would be pretty substantial, but the gee forces on the cylinder's inner surface weren't anything much. But they were enough to hold things—all sorts of things—to the curving wall of the tunnel.

Part of the world was right-side up, part was upside

down, and the rest was on its side: landed ships, stored cargo, work lights, spidery manipulator arms, free-flying utility robots, and tiny space-suited figures kneeling here and standing there, doing whatever jobs could not be done except by human hands and human eyes, right there on the spot.

She could easily see the joins between the eight disks that made up the cylinder. It didn't take a very sharp eye to see that the inner disks were the oldest ones, or that a lot of ships had paid a lot of calls here. The inner disks were darker with age, with more cuts and gouges and dings knocked into their armored hulls. Here and there were scorch marks left behind by thrusters fired a bit too hard a bit too close to the deck.

But what about the station's docking system? Norla thought back to her briefing books. Primary Transporters, they called them, robotic arms mounted to carrier cars. The cars moved on monorails that ran the length of the station. Her briefing books said there were two monorails, 180 degrees apart from each other, but Norla saw four, oversize I-beam girders running the length of the station, equally spaced around the interior of the tunnel, each painted bright red to make it as visible and noticeable as possible. It was, once again, easy to tell the old pair, dinged-up and worn-looking, from the new pair. The Primary Transporter Arms' carrier cars rode on over-and-under wheels that held them firmly to the monorails as they rolled up and down the length of the station.

It was hard to see at this distance, but it looked as if two of the arms were at present stowed away and powered down at the far end of the station. The third was doing some sort of lifting job about halfway down.

And, she suddenly realized, the fourth was coming straight at her, riding its carrier car down the monorail, unfolding itself out as it came, like the leg of some absurdly overgrown monster spider. The carrier came to a smooth stop at the end of its rail, and the arm slowly extended itself beyond the station, lazily reaching for the *Cruzeiro do Sul*.

Norla had to resist the temptation to grab for the controls

and back the ship away, fast and hard, from the big, cruel-looking arm. This was what was supposed to be happening. The docking probe was on the end of the arm, its six capture petals opened up like a big hungry mouth, the two remote cameras on either side of the probe looking for all the world like the eyes of an insect monster that was closing in to devour them.

Norla forced herself to settle down. Five minutes ago she had been patting herself on the back for chasing away her imaginary fears. It wouldn't do her self-respect any good at all for the illusions to have the upper hand again so soon.

The arm stopped its motion with the docking probe fifty meters short of the *Cruzeiro do Sul*. Norla let out a sigh of relief in spite of herself.

"Looking good," she announced to Koffield, more for the sake of having something to say than out of any need or desire to communicate. She looked over at him again. He was staring intently at SCO Station, not paying the least attention to her. The bright-tracking glasses only made his expression that much harder to read. Damn it, didn't the man ever feel the need to *speak*? "We're ready to dock," she said, hoping to get his attention.

"Yes, we are," Koffield said, quite calmly.

"How does it look to you?" she asked, struggling to get some reaction from him. It was an important moment. It wasn't asking too much for the man to have at least *some* sort of reaction.

"Risky," he said. "Not the docking. I'm sure that will go fine. Once we're aboard, however—well, we'll be in their hands, won't we? And, from what I can see of the station so far, I don't know how comfortable I am with that thought."

"Sir?" What the hell was he talking about? What was he seeing that she was not?

"Proceed, Officer Chandray. Carefully. Just don't stop being careful once we're on board."

"Right," she said, utterly mystified. "Absolutely."

She checked her displays and confirmed that the ArtInts

aboard the *Cruzeiro do Sul* and SCO Station had satisfied each other's data requests. The station knew everything it needed to know about the ship, and vice versa. SCO Traffic Control had cleared her to perform the final docking maneuver. She checked her aft radar display, and saw four ships moving in on approach to SCO Station, and a fifth commencing maneuvers even as she watched. All of the ships were moving at far greater accelerations and in far faster flight paths than what she had been assigned. Quite obviously, they had cleared incoming traffic to make room for the fossil-ship that had arrived out of nowhere.

But that the other ships were now moving told her that even SCO Traffic Control was ready to concede that the *Cruzeiro do Sul* had made it in, and flown in safely. *Now comes the easy part,* she told herself. No need to be nervous about it. Nothing to be scared of. Nothing she hadn't done a thousand times before. The only thing different was that she was light-years from home, and marooned in the wrong century, and the unknown, the future, was waiting for them. Koffield was right. It wasn't the docking she should be scared of. It was what came afterward, once they were aboard the station.

Understanding that helped, somehow. Her lips had gone dry, and she ran her tongue over them and swallowed. She gimbaled her command chair around until the ship's docking probe was over and in front of her left shoulder, right where she could see it. She flipped the main video screen to the probe's camera, and was rewarded with a straight-on view of the PT Arm. She flipped her thruster controls back from roll to maneuver, and tapped the rear jets at minimum power for a quarter second. The ship moved slowly forward, straight on for the PT Arm's docking probe at a meter a second.

She watched her lineup indicators, and saw she was drifting just a hair high in y-axis. She blipped her side thrusters, killing the drift. The y-axis-up adjustment had put her perhaps three or four centimeters out of perfect alignment with the docking probe, but she made no attempt to correct it.

She was well within tolerance, and any attempt to compensate would likely produce an overcorrection, and lead to repeated over-and-under shots that could lead to a lot more trouble than being off center by four centimeters.

She drifted in slowly, watching the docking probe move closer. At fifteen meters out, she killed most of her forward motion, bringing it down to a quarter meter per second.

The PTA's probe was close enough now that she was no longer seeing it straight on. It was coming in toward her left, toward the *Cruzeiro do Sul*'s own docking probe. The closer it got, the bigger, the crueler, it seemed to be, its jaws gaping wide to seize at her ship.

Slowly, she drifted in, tapping out another bit of braking thrust at five meters, slowing to a bare eight centimeters a second. She checked her translations. She noted with a nod that the y-axis-high drift seemed to have solved itself, and they were right on target. If she had tried a correction, she would only have made things worse.

She pulled her hands away from the controls. She was exactly where she wanted to be. There was nothing to do but look out the port side of the pilot's station and watch the two probes close in on each other.

It took just slightly over a minute for the *Cruzeiro do Sul* to cross that last few meters. Strange to be moving so slowly aboard a ship that could go so fast, that could go from the outer reaches of the system to Solace in a matter of days.

And strange that a minute could seem so long.

She watched as the claw of the PT Arm docking probe drew closer and closer to her ship. Terror grabbed her, and she did not know what scared her—and then knew that it was the unknown itself that she feared. The outside world, the present-day universe, was closing in on them. Until they were docked, until they were in the station, they were not truly part of the future. They could at least imagine drawing back, safe into the vanished past. The last few seconds in which they were part of the past, part of the life and time to which she could no longer return, were evaporating before her eyes.

The ship's probe and station's probe moved closer,

closer. They touched. The jaws of the station's probe closed upon the *Cruzeiro do Sul,* and the whole ship shuddered slightly at the contact. The docking autostop thrusters killed the last of their forward momentum.

The future had caught them.

CHAPTER FOURTEEN

JONAH AND PANDORA

Anton Koffield watched and listened as an alert tone sounded and lines of text appeared on the *Cruzeiro do Sul's* pilot station's display.

POWER-OFF ALL ATTITUDE CONTROL, ALL PROPULSION SYSTEMS. EXTEND SHIP LANDING GEAR. WILL NOT PROCEED UNTIL COMPLIANCE DETECTION.

The syntax was a little odd, but the intent was clear enough. SCO Station didn't want powered ships flying around inside itself.

Anton Koffield looked to Norla Chandray, and nodded at her unspoken question. She let out a worried sigh and flipped the appropriate switches.

COMPLIANCE DETECTION. PT SYSTEM NOW WILL TRANSPORT TO SHIP BAY GAMMA TWO (G2). MAINTAIN PASSIVE STATE.

Interesting. There had been no noticeable shift in language or context when Second Officer Chandray had been talking with the human controllers. Why would an automatic system use such strange phrasing?

Koffield looked at Chandray again. The woman did not much like the thought of powering down her ship. Well, he could not blame her. Even under normal circumstances, no pilot liked to cede control of her craft—and these were far from normal circumstances.

The PT Arm folded back on itself, pulling the *Cruzeiro do Sul* toward the station. Koffield peered into the station's central access tunnel and saw their PT Arm's carrier car starting to roll forward, hauling the arm and the *Cruzeiro* along. There was a creak and a groan from the docking system's load-bearing structure as it took up the towing stress. Then the ship started moving slowly forward toward the station.

Koffield checked his recorders again and confirmed they were working, then concentrated on seeing everything, noting everything, that he possibly could.

The carrier car moved steadily forward, the PT Arm and the ship trailing along behind. It was hard not to imagine the open end of the central access tunnel as a giant mouth swallowing them up, and the tunnel itself as a gullet of some monstrous beast. Jonah being swallowed by the whale. Well, Jonah had come out of it all right. Perhaps they would be equally lucky.

The *Cruzeiro* passed out of sunlight into the shadow of the station, then entered the station's access tunnel. Without taking his eyes off the tunnel, Koffield removed his bright-tracking glasses and handed them to Chandray. She removed hers and put both pairs back in their storage compartment.

Koffield's attention was focused on the interior of Solace Central Orbital Station. The place had doubled in size in the last century. That in and of itself was not remarkable. It was the *way* that time and use had made their mark that told him what he needed to know, and that gave him reason for alarm.

They passed by a loading bay that was stripped down to its structural members, wall panels pulled out more or less at random, and some of the structural hardware missing as well. What looked very much like the same type of wall panels had been used to add an extra repair bay in a nearby yard. A beat-up old orbital tug in that repair bay was half-disassembled, but whether it was being taken apart or being put back together was impossible to tell. There were no work lights on, no cables strung, no test equipment running, no workers on duty. Koffield got the very strong impression that no one had worked on that tug, or in that yard, for a long time.

A quarter rotation around the cylinder, a new, bright, gleaming repair yard had all lights on and a full staff in pressure suits, swarming over a gleaming-new atmospheric shuttle.

That was the pattern, writ small. The old was not preserved, or restored, but left to fall into decline and decay, scavenged and stripped for parts. The newly built sections and systems were not integrated into the old, but simply slapped into place over them. It was not a rational way to do work, or an efficient way. And things would not be the way they were unless someone, probably a large group of someones, generations of someones, benefited in some way from doing things in that irrational way and had the power to make things happen to benefit them.

In other places, in other circumstances—on the surface of the planet, for example—abandoning one old loading crane where it stood, while building a newer, bigger, more powerful one a hundred meters away would not have held so much significance, or served as a warning sign of larger problems. But things were different in the tighter quarters of even a large orbital station. "They've doubled the size of the place," he said to Norla. "But half the place looks close to abandoned. What does that say to you?"

"I don't know, exactly, sir," she replied. "Maybe they're bad planners, or maybe it's just plain old corruption. Or maybe the old guard just refused to rebuild or improve, and the up-and-comers left them where they were and went around them."

Not for the first time, Koffield mentally gave Norla high marks. She was not a trained observer, but she was sharp, and she knew how to interpret what she saw.

As they were drawn in toward the older central disks, the pattern became more obvious and more extreme. Wrecked service bays, no busier than ghost towns, were side by side with bustling supply depots. Brightly lit VIP observation windows stared into the ports of darkened, smashed-out fueling stations. That too seemed to be part of the pattern. Not just the vibrant new next to the impoverished old, but the prosperous luxury establishment next to the bankrupt essential.

Not good. None of it was good.

The PT Arm towed them smoothly past it all, past the center point of the station and toward the far end of the cylinder. They came to the forward docking complex, and were greeted by the sight of a quite different sort of pattern—or perhaps, Koffield reflected, merely a variation on the same theme.

Every docking bay was full, and that made no sense. If there was one thing not in short supply, out in space, it was space itself. At every other station Koffield had ever seen there was a very simple way to deal with overcrowding. If a bay was needed, one simply waited until the ship in it was finished unloading, then undocked it and left it in a matched parking orbit close to the station. Assuming one took basic anticollision precautions, and assuming the ships had sufficient propulsion power and life support, there was no practical limit to the number of ships one could stack up, and no purpose served by leaving ships at their bays. Koffield peered down the forward end of the access tunnel, toward open space. Even just with the naked eye, he could see a good ten or twenty ships—interorbit jobs, mostly—of one sort or another, all plainly in just that sort of standard stationkeeping orbit. They used the normal techniques.

Then why were SCO Station's docking bays filled to bursting?

Koffield found his answer by noting what sorts of ships were in the bays themselves. Atmospheric transports, nearly every one of them. All of them of vaguely futuristic design, as seen from the perspective of a century and a quarter in the past, and nearly all of them showing signs of long and hard use. Few showed anything more than minimal interior lights through their portholes. Few had propellant lines or personnel access tunnels running to them—but all of them had what looked to be life-support umbilicals hooked up. Only a few had their locator lights blinking, and no pilot liked to power down those unless absolutely necessary. Yet a few ships had their beacons going, so there couldn't be a local prohibition against running lights. Then why shut them down, unless—

Second Officer Norla Chandray was a step ahead of

him. "I think there must be worse trouble on the planet's surface than we thought," she said. "Those are all ground-to-orbit ships, not orbit-only craft. That's why they've got LSUs running to them, but not propellant lines or personnel access tunnels."

Koffield nodded. He had read it the same way. The ships down there didn't have enough power reserves or propellant to get themselves back, so they had to stay docked. The station was feeding them power and air because the ships didn't have enough of their own. And the Personnel Access Tunnels weren't extended because a PAT gave, well, personnel access. And for whatever reason, SCO Station didn't want anyone from those ships getting into the station. The passengers and crew of the distressed ships were trapped there.

So why didn't the station refuel them? None of the three possible answers Koffield could come up with made him feel any better. Either the station didn't have the fuel to give the ships, or the ships couldn't afford to pay for it, or the ships were refusing to take the fuel, for fear of being sent back.

But who would fly from the planet's surface to SCO Station under such circumstances unless—

Unless things on the surface of Solace were getting very bad indeed.

"How's *our* propellant holding out?" Koffield asked. He could have checked for himself, but he couldn't tear his eyes away from the grounded hobo fleet spread out before his eyes.

"Tanks at just under eighty percent full," Norla said. "We can get anywhere in the system, or get back to the *Dom Pedro* with no problem, if we have to."

"The *Dom Pedro* sounds good right now," Koffield said. "But I can't think of anyplace else in this system I'd much like to go."

"I'm right with you there, sir," Chandray replied. "What I'd like to know is, where are they going to put us?"

"You saw it on the heads-up," Koffield said. "Docking Bay Gamma Two."

"Yes, sir. But it looks as if someone is there already." She pointed over his shoulder. He looked in the direction she was pointing. He hadn't been watching for the marking placards, but clearly Chandray had been. And there, very plainly, was the sign indicating G2. And just as plainly, there was a ship already there, a cone-shaped ballistic atmospheric lander that was plainly too large to share G2 with a minitug, let alone an intersystem transport the size of the *Cruzeiro do Sul*. The name of the ship, the *Pilot's Ease,* was painted in bold letters on the side of the ship

The answer to Chandray's question came almost before she was finished asking it. The PT Arm towing the *Cruzeiro* slowed to a smooth, steady halt, and the *Cruzeiro*'s superstructure creaked and moaned as the stresses readjusted. Another PT Arm rolled up on its carrier car and came to a halt just ahead of the *Cruzeiro do Sul*. The second PT Arm swung down over Docking Bay Gamma Two and connected its docking probe to the docking probe in the nose of the *Pilot's Ease*. The arm pulled the *Ease* straight up out of the bay and brought it to the centerline of the station. The arm rotated its docking collar about until the base of the ballistic ship was pointed straight at the forward end of the station, the end opposite to the one through which the *Cruzeiro* had entered the station.

The arm moved forward, pushing the *Pilot's Ease* ahead of itself. Arm and ship moved forward, toward the end of the tunnel. Twenty meters or so shy of the tunnel's end, the arm let go, and set the *Pilot's Ease* adrift. The big ballistic ship sailed slowly out into open space. So far as Koffield could see, she made no effort to adjust her course or slow her forward motion relative to the station. The PT Arm hadn't pushed her hard, but it had put a few meters per second of speed into the ship, enough to shift her orbit somewhat. If she did not slow her forward motion, the *Ease* would stay in her slightly variant orbit, gradually drifting away from the station. Koffield could not see any nav locator lights or interior lights on the *Ease*.

Chandray and Koffield looked at each other. Was the captain of the *Pilot's Ease* just being extremely—even insanely—economical of his onboard power, or had they just seen a ship being deliberately set adrift, made a derelict? Had there even been a crew aboard that ship? And if there had been crew aboard, were any of them still alive?

Had SCO Docking Control just performed a routine bit of ship-handling—or had they just seen a corpse thrown overboard to make room for the new arrival?

There was no time for such questions. Their own PT Arm had started moving again, swinging the *Cruzeiro do Sul* through ninety degrees so that her base and her landing jacks pointed straight at Docking Bay Gamma Two. The arm started lowering the ship down toward the deck of the docking bay, setting the *Cruzeiro* into her docking bay, a pawn being set down on a giant chessboard. But what of the *Pilot's Ease*? Had they just seen some other pawn sacrificed so they could take its square? Would they sacrifice the *Cruzeiro* just as casually, should that suit their purposes?

It seemed to Koffield that he had been moved about by others, often by forces he could neither see nor understand, moving without any real choice of his own, for far too long. Ever since Circum Central, or so it sometimes seemed. Games within games. Who had maneuvered him to this place and time, and why? And what, exactly, did the position of the pieces on the gameboard that was SCO Station tell him? What game were they playing here, and what, exactly, was the state of play?

With a sudden, sharp *thud,* the *Cruzeiro do Sul* landed on the docking bay deck. They had arrived.

It was, Anton Koffield realized, *his* move now. And he hadn't the slightest idea what the rules of this game were.

It should have been the climax of their trip. A few quick housekeeping chores to secure the piloting station and power down the ship's propulsion and nav systems, and then should have come the big moment when they stepped from the *Cruzeiro* into a Personnel Access Tunnel, and from the PAT into Solace Central Orbital Station, into the up-close-and-personal, in-your-face future full of people and events.

Now that they were here, with no turning back, now that they had crossed their Rubicon, and, at long last, had gotten to where they were going, Norla was eager to get off the ship and see what there was to see of this place.

Even the great Anton Koffield himself exhibited a bit of eagerness and impatience, and he even did something that was just microscopically irrational. While Norla was still completing her postflight checks, Koffield went into his cabin and brought out his precious secured container. He set it down by the side of the airlock. Norla watched him do it, and he caught her watching him. He smiled, and shrugged, and went back into his cabin without saying a word. It was quite absurd, really. How much time was he really going to save by having it that much nearer the airlock, once the lock opened? And for that matter, what point had there been in keeping the secured container in his cabin all this time? Had he expected her to try and steal it, or pilfer the contents?

At least it was proof, or at least strong evidence, that Koffield was indeed human. And proof that he, as much as Norla, was ready, willing, and eager to get on with it.

But SCO Station wasn't ready for them. Station Medical saw to that. Station Med did not volunteer explanations and refused to give explanations when asked. Station Med simply made it clear that Koffield and Chandray would not be allowed to enter the station until they cleared a much more rigorous medical survey than usual. A service robot wheeled over to the *Cruzeiro's* exterior airlock door and delivered two sampling kits.

Once they retrieved the kits from the airlock, both of them had to go through the unpleasant, undignified process of providing the required samples of hair, nail clippings, saliva, stool, urine, ear wax, a balloonful of exhaled breath, and even scrapings off the inside of their mouths.

Norla managed all of those on her own, but she knew not to try drawing her own blood if she didn't have to. It would seem Koffield's experiences had taught him the same lesson, and he was more than happy to trade help with the chore.

There was a peculiar sort of intimacy to the moment,

each of them rolling up a shirtsleeve and baring flesh for the other to stab, however carefully and gently, with a needle.

Norla felt strange, and a trifle uncomfortable, to have Koffield's hands on her arm, expertly massaging the flesh to bring out a vein. Neither of them had touched the other since the day he had revived her from cryosleep. There was something *dangerous* in the sensation of feeling his hands on her skin. The jab of the needle was merely cold, sharp, precise, rather than truly painful. The blood welling up in the sampling reservoir as he drew back the plunger looked redder than it should have.

To Norla, it looked too perfect and archetypal to be real. It looked like pretend blood, ghoulish makeup, rather than the genuine article. But blood and steel did not worry her. It was, some deep part of her knew, Anton Koffield who was dangerous.

Koffield cleaned and bandaged the needle mark on her arm, then unclipped the sampling reservoir from the needle. The needle went down the trash chute, and the reservoir into its carefully labeled niche in the sampling kit, ready to be set in the airlock for the service robot to collect.

"Now do me," Koffield said, rolling up his own sleeve. In the most literal way possible, he was placing himself in her hands, opening himself up to her, and she wanted to show herself worthy of that trust. It was the work of but a minute to draw his blood and pack the sampling reservoir into his sample case. It took not much longer to seal up the two cases, confirm they were labeled properly, and set them in the airlock. Norla sealed the airlock hatch and pushed the buttons to start the lock cycle. "That should do it," she said. "I wonder what they're afraid of catching from us."

"Or what it is they're afraid we'll catch from them," he said. "Disease vectors are two-way streets."

"I hadn't thought of that," she admitted. "And I can't blame them for being careful around people who could be carrying last century's plague, and definitely aren't carrying the antibodies to this century's. But I don't like being stuck here, waiting while they check."

"Nor do I," Koffield said. "All things considered, we've done all the waiting we should be expected to do, don't you think?"

Norla smiled at the small joke, then glanced down at the secured container that was still this side of the lock. The container Koffield had guarded so carefully still sat on the deck, ready to be moved out the airlock the moment they were allowed off the ship.

"There's some other waiting I've been doing," she said. "I've been waiting to hear the end of your story. What's in that Pandora's box of yours? What's it all about?"

"I read that story about Pandora, read all the myths I could, back when I was a boy," Koffield said. It was hard not to notice he wasn't actually answering her question. "The way I remember the story, all the evils of the world flew out of the box the moment she opened it," Koffield said. "Once the evils had escaped, she looked inside the box, and saw that the only thing still there was hope. That always bothered me. I couldn't help but wonder—who'd put evil and hope in the same box, and why? And why did hope hide in the bottom of the box, afraid to come out, when the evils were brave enough to rush out the first moment they could?"

"I assume you wouldn't pack a case full of evil and bring it all this way," Norla said. *Or would you?* she wondered. *Anyone from Glister would believe you capable of doing just that.* But she wanted answers to her questions, and she was damned well going to get them. "So if not evil, what is in your box? Is it hope?"

Koffield frowned, then shrugged his shoulders. It was strange to see any such sign of uncertainty from the man. "Perhaps," he said. "Hope, maybe, for some, anyway. Knowledge, certainly. And a warning, if anyone will listen."

"You said you'd tell me the rest of it," Norla said. Even to herself, she sounded like a petulant child demanding another bedtime story. "You said you'd tell me everything before I needed to know it. Once they give us med clearance and we open that hatch again, things are going to start happening. I don't think there will be time later on. I have to know *before* that hatch opens. Tell me."

Koffield looked down at his secured container, and then back at Norla. He nodded, in a way that seemed to signal if not willing agreement, at least acceptance.

But the last of the barriers was yet to come down. "It's not the sort of thing I can tell in two minutes standing by an airlock," he said. "They'll need at least several hours before they clear us. Tonight. Tonight, over dinner, I'll tell you the last of it."

Norla looked him in the eye and nodded back at him, she herself accepting, if not agreeing. She wanted to push harder, to make him get it all out in the open, once and for all—but she could sense that asking for more would likely bring her less. "All right," she said. "Tonight."

Koffield smiled stiffly to her. "Until dinner then," he said, turned, went back into his cabin, and closed the door.

Norla stood there staring at the closed door. It seemed as good a symbol as any for time spent with Anton Koffield. "Until dinner," she said to the door.

It was not a meal she was expecting to enjoy all that much.

CHAPTER FIFTEEN
DOMINO THEORY

"This, sir, is what did it," said Hues Renblant. He held up a standard-issue ten-centimeter archival program storage cube at shoulder height so Captain Marquez could see it. He held it the way a security officer might display his identity plaque, as a way of displaying his bona fides, his authority. "Or rather, the person who reprogrammed this cube did it."

Captain Felipe Henrique Marquez was sitting in the main command chair on the command level of the *Dom Pedro IV*, but there was very little commanding he could do at the moment. Half the ship's systems were down as the crew ran through exhaustive diagnostic tests on everything they could think of. It was no idle expression to say that they were working as if their lives depended on it.

Marquez held out his hand for the cube, and First Officer Renblant gave it to him, though both men knew perfectly well a naked-eye examination of the cube couldn't tell anyone anything. But Marquez wanted to touch the thing that had wrecked his ship, wanted to hold it in his hand and get a good, long, close-up look at the device that had betrayed him.

Not that it did him much good. It was a datacube just like any other. He set it down on the command console and looked at the two men, Hues Renblant and Dixon Phelby, who stood before him. "How?" he asked.

"Superbly," said Renblant.

Marquez looked at Renblant sharply. Up until that

moment, he would have said that the propulsion and guidance specialist had no detectable sense of humor—and he still wasn't sure. The man might have made a joke, but it was more likely he was offering an honest opinion of the skills of whoever had sabotaged the cube. "Could you be a trifle more specific?" he asked.

"Of course, sir," Renblant said. "Timeshaft ships use the most archivally stable memory and data systems possible. They have to have working lives measured in the thousands, or tens of thousands, of years, and they are built with a great deal of internal redundancy and designed to make it easy to recover from an accidental erasure."

"What of it? Everything was erased in any event," Marquez asked impatiently. After all, he knew the systems on his own ship.

"Yes, sir. But not accidentally. We've established beyond any doubt that it was done deliberately."

"Then why does the ability to survive accidental erasure matter?"

"Because our saboteur was unable to overcome those features completely. The cube there was the one that contained the entire program for retargeting the ship, and flying direct to Solace through normal space without benefit of a wormhole transit. But it had more than that on it. Once the ship had arrived, the cube activated a series of housekeeping commands—though housewrecking might be a better term."

"Then all the ship's memories and logs were intact up until arrival?"

"Yes, sir."

"I see," Marquez said, working hard to retain his composure in the face of such maddening news. For a hundred twenty-seven years the ship—*his* ship—had been methodically logging in a detailed and clear report of everything that happened to it, of what had happened, of what had gone wrong. And then, minutes, perhaps seconds, before he was revived, it had all been wiped clean. To say it was adding insult to injury was to understate the case by orders of magnitude. It was a slap to the face of a mortally wounded man. "Please go on."

"The last four commands in the housekeeping sequence were to erase the event-logging system, and all backups for it, to erase the main retargeting program, to set up a timed command to zero out the clocks, and then to erase the housekeeping series itself. The important point is that the clock-zero command had to run *after* everything else had been blanked, or else there would be a datestamp left on the event log, telling the exact time the clock was zeroed. Since the clocks restarted from zero, having a datestamp would be as good as knowing the exact time. All you'd have to do is add the two numbers. So the clock-zero command had to run last, direct from the main system sequencer."

"And that's where the housekeeping wasn't as thorough as it might have been," Phelby said cheerfully, speaking for the first time.

Renblant looked at the cargo specialist with quite obvious irritation. The two men might have turned out to be a good work team, but it was in spite of, and not because of, their personal relationship. "Yes," Renblant said. "Cargomaster Phelby located the one trace left by the sabotage."

"Well, Phelby?"

"Yes, sir. The whole ship-control system is designed to make it easy to recover from errors. It was built to make it impossible for any command or sequence or program to erase itself, and also built with the capacity for cascade recovery. Sort of like running a line of falling dominoes backwards. You put the last fallen domino back upright, and it pushes the one behind it upright. *That* pushes up the one before *it,* and so on. So I—we—knew that *something*—probably the zero-out-all-clocks command—still had to be in the system somewhere." Phelby glanced at his companion. "Our saboteur hid his work pretty well, but we knew it had to be there. We were both looking, and either one of us could have found it," he said. "It happened to be me. Once we found the clock-zero sequence, the rest was pretty straightforward."

"Very tedious," Renblant agreed.

"Boring as hell," Phelby said, smiling back at his partner. "But we managed to flip a lot of the dominoes upright. Not all of them."

"Please go on," said Marquez.

"Yes, sir," said Renblant. "We recovered a great deal of the sabotage program. Cascade-recovery has its limits, and some parts of it were irretrievably lost. But we did get enough of it to tell us a great deal. And the news is good."

"Good as it can be, under the circumstances," said Phelby.

"And that news would be?" Marquez asked.

"We believe the ship is now clean. Once we had the sabotage program to examine, we were able to find several characteristic patterns to the way the programmer, the saboteur, did things. You could say we learned what his or her handwriting looked like. We've done a search for the same patterns in other elements of the ship's systems, and they aren't there. All the other systems give normal diagnostic results. There is no further sign of tampering."

"So there are no further booby traps waiting for us?"

Renblant raised one eyebrow very slightly and shrugged. "A timeshaft ship is extremely complex. There will always be some way to conceal something on board, especially for something as microscopic and invisible as a bit of hidden computer code. But we have established there are no computer programs in the system that display any of the characteristics found in the sabotage program. Besides, the saboteur would have no reason to plant other traps."

"Why not?"

"The first one worked," Phelby said. "It did what the saboteur wanted it to do. Why plant a second one? I have no idea why the saboteur would want us delivered here a century and a quarter late, but that's what the program was intended to accomplish, and that's what the program did. It's gone now. We can start reloading the nav and propulsion control systems from the nonvolatile backups whenever you like."

Marquez nodded. He could see that logic. But all the same, he was not going to gamble his ship on the strength of it. "Very well," he said. "Good work, to both of you. But we'll work on the assumption that something else might be waiting for us. We'll continue with the full-ship diagnostic. Once it is complete, I still want full written reports from all sections—and a report from Koffield and Chandray about conditions in-system. Once I've had a chance to review all that material—we'll start thinking about doing system reloads, and about what we do next. What you've told me is most reassuring—but I see no reason to take chances."

Renblant displayed no reaction, but Phelby cocked his head to one side and shrugged. "We figured you've read it that way," he said. "Can't say as I'd disagree." He grinned, but there was something sad, and lost, in his expression. "After all," he said, "it's not like we're in a hurry anymore."

Norla should have been used to Koffield's surprising her, considering all the times and all the ways he had done so. "Expect the unexpected" was a clever-sounding slogan, but Norla had never seen any way to actually do it.

She could have spent the whole afternoon and evening expecting the unexpected and still been astonished by the meal put together by Admiral Anton Koffield of the Chronologic Patrol. She had known he was capable of commanding troops in battle, but she had not expected him to be able to cook. He certainly had offered no evidence of such a talent during their journey.

The *Cruzeiro do Sul*'s fold-away galley wasn't much, and it had not been stocked with any great imagination, but even so, the meal he set before her smelled wonderful, even if she had not the faintest idea what it was. But even as she was seduced by the delightful smell, part of her was wondering why Koffield was doing it. Was it an attempt to distract her away from her questions? But Norla couldn't believe that a strategist as intelligent as Anton Koffield would think for half a minute that such a gambit would work. He dressed for dinner in a formal tunic and kilt. Perhaps it was merely a sense of occasion that inspired him. Tomorrow they would meet with the Solacians, and who could know what their intentions would be? Perhaps it was merely a case of the condemned man eating a hearty meal.

Or perhaps—perhaps it was that Koffield felt that the end of a story, or at any rate the end of *this* story, deserved some sense of occasion.

They spoke of inconsequential things over dinner itself—technical aspects of the approach and docking, the two of them using the same hand gestures that pilots had used for millennia to describe planes and ships moving toward each other. They discussed SCO Station's physical appearance, the new and the old jumbled together like pieces of a life raft cobbled together out of whatever came to hand.

The main course was done. Koffield served a sweet cake drawn from ship's stores that tasted precisely as if it had been in cryostorage for a hundred years. At last the small talk petered out to nothing, and an expectant silence hung over the table.

"Very well," Koffield said, as if, instead of silence, the room had been filled with Norla's badgering demands that he get on with it. "I suppose I'd better tell you the rest of what I know. On this subject, anyway. As you'll recall, we left it with my discovery that someone had tampered with the Grand Library. That discovery hit me pretty hard, I can tell you. Even after everything I had seen, I still believed in DeSilvo."

Koffield thought for a moment and shook his head. "No. I have to go further than that. After—after Circum Central and Glister, I was still very close to low ebb. DeSilvo had been the one person willing to get near me, to have any faith in me, after that. It was desperately hard for me to stop believing in the one man who had at least seemed to believe in *me*.

"And yet I was already of two minds. I think, even then, I was starting to see, in the back of my mind, that he had seen in me a tool that he could get cheap, and get good use from. I have made use of many people in my life, and there are certainly worse things to be than useful—but I had always tried to be honest with the people I used, made sure they understood the transaction, and understood what was being given and taken by both sides."

Norla had to smile at that. She certainly felt that Koffield was getting use out of her, but she hadn't the faintest idea what the terms of the transaction were.

Koffield went on. "But DeSilvo did none of that. He pretended I was his great friend, his treasure beyond price, his indispensable man. Puffery, and fraud, all of it—and pretty transparent, as well. It was oddly insulting that he didn't even expect me to see through it.

"I suppose the normal, sensible thing to do once I discovered the missing books would have been to turn to a librarian, or perhaps to one of DeSilvo's archivists, or even to DeSilvo himself, and ask about them. But I realized that I could no longer believe that it would turn out to be some innocent mistake. It had gone past that point long before, about the time I noticed a pattern to what was missing.

"Perhaps, after that, the next most normal thing would be to conduct a computer search myself. There is almost always a way to track something down in a computer system after it has been erased or moved. But I already knew that someone—and I had a pretty good idea who—was playing games with the Grand Library computer system. I knew how sophisticated and secure the GL system was. It would take someone with great skill and knowledge, and very powerful access, to manipulate that system.

"Someone who could do that could also set up drop-traps and search monitors and other defense and detection systems in the computer system. I had to assume that, if I ran a search, DeSilvo would know about it almost at once. I didn't want to tip my hand too early.

"Besides, there was another thing I knew after my time in intelligence: A person who can manipulate a computer system that well tends to *think* in terms of computer systems and ArtInt operators. So much of what they know about the world comes to them through computer displays that they start to think that the world *is* what the computer and the ArtInt-ops tell them it is. If the computer records show that the book has been deleted, then it has been. That was something I could take advantage of—by doing a physical search. Not many people even realize that such things are still possible. They don't think of knowledge as having a physical location or existence. They think it's a cloud of invisible data that can be anywhere it is needed. But knowledge is still real, and still can be—must be—enshrined in physical objects, in books.

"There's an important rule of thumb it took the record-keepers of the near-ancient era a long time to learn. It is this: The more technically sophisticated a data-storage system is, the sooner it will become difficult or impossible to read and retrieve that data, once the technology becomes obsolete. We can still read the Rosetta stone, because it was carved on a rock. We can still read the nineteenth-century translations and commentaries on the stone, because they were printed on paper, and the facsimile versions of those books that we have today were printed on archival-quality flex-sheets that should last for thousands more years. But we *can't* read much of what was written about the Rosetta stone after the late twentieth century. We no longer know how to decipher the data in that era's storage systems, and their data storage has degraded over time.

"The obvious solution to this problem is to store vitally important documents in a way that will stay as legible as long as the Rosetta stone has, in the form of scrolls or bound books, or in permanent self-decoding systems.

"Knowing all this, I reasoned that if someone, at some time, had thought that Ulan Baskaw's work was important enough, and would have long-term importance, then Baskaw's work would have been put in the Grand Library's Permanent Physical Collection.

"I decided to try looking there, though just getting to the PPC was something of a challenge. There are actually two PPCs, one intended as a duplicate of the other—though of course it's impossible to keep the two collections perfectly synchronized with each other. The Main PPC is in an old deep-space orbital habitat, orbiting Neptune, though in a completely different orbit than the Grand Library habitat. The reserve PPC is buried somewhere on the Lunar Farside, I believe. They keep the exact location quiet. The idea is that no one catastrophe, short of the Sun somehow going supernova, could knock out the Grand Library and both permanent collections.

"I knew that I wanted to move carefully, and that it was important that I avoid arousing DeSilvo's suspicions. For that reason, I couldn't simply announce I was looking for Baskaw's suppressed works and hop a lift on a shuttlecraft over to the PPC habitat. I didn't want to do anything that would so much as remind DeSilvo that the Permanent Physical Collection even existed. To do so might remind him that he had failed to destroy any copies of Baskaw's work that survived there, and inspire him to beat me to the prize. I had to come up with a plausible cover story, an acceptable reason for me leaving the Grand Library habitat long enough to search the PPC."

Koffield paused again, and he grimaced unhappily before going on. "So I did something I'm not proud of. I told my superiors I needed to take medical-disability leave. I was entitled to it, after Circum Central, and the—difficulties—of our flight back from there. They had even urged me to take it. The doctors had gone on and on about mental and emotional exhaustion, the danger of a nervous collapse. But I had refused.

"Now I went back to them and told them they were right, that I needed a rest, a chance to get away. And it might have been true. Maybe I was about to snap. Maybe all my suspicions about DeSilvo were total raving paranoia. There's the old joke—just because you're paranoid, it doesn't mean they're not out to get you. It turns out that I was right about DeSilvo. But the fact that I was right does not prove I was sane. Especially as what he did, what I suspected him of, was at the very least something close to insanity.

"I got my leave, and told everyone that I was headed for a vacation in Nouveau Port-au-Prince, on the Old Haiti side of the island of Hispaniola, back on Earth. It was a plausible place for me to go. I'd always been interested in Caribbean history, the Haitian population crash way back when, and the ecorevival there. Some historians point at the rebuilding of Hispaniola as the real beginning of terraforming." Koffield was silent for a moment. "You might say that Haiti was the success that encouraged us to plunge into a thousand failures," he said.

Norla frowned. "I don't understand. What failures?"

Koffield looked at her sadly. "The ones all around us," he said gently. "The ones we've lived our whole lives in, without ever seeing."

It was not the clearest of explanations, but Norla let it go. "Maybe I'll understand that later," she said. "Go on."

"You will understand," he said. "Very soon. In any event, once I was officially on leave, there was no requirement for me to report my whereabouts or file travel plans. The privacy laws were strong and rigidly enough enforced. But I decided not to trust the privacy laws too far. I booked flights and ground transport and a villa in Nouveau Port-au-Prince, never intending to use any of them. I wanted to leave a false trail, in case DeSilvo did try to track me. I paid for everything in advance. Many businesses will try to track down a man who makes reservations and does not pay for them. Very few will try and track down a man who pays for, but does not use, their service. If the hotel room is paid for, the hotel manager ArtInt will not waste too much effort wondering if it is actually occupied.

"I used a lot of tricks I learned in my intelligence days, not only to create a complete false trail for DeSilvo to follow, but also to make it all but impossible for DeSilvo to track my real movements, if it entered his mind to try to do so. I still had no idea if he suspected me at all.

"The long and the short of it is that the ship back to Earth left without me, but any source DeSilvo would be able to check would show I was aboard. But I wasn't. Instead, I caught a local shuttle out to the Permanent Physical Collection habitat.

"I had never been to the PPC before, but I had done my homework well enough to be prepared. It's a huge place, twenty kilometers long, with most of it in a pure nitrogen atmosphere, to keep old paper from oxidizing. The station environment is designed for the comfort of the books, not that of people. I was ready for the low gravity, and I had my breathing mask and cold-weather clothing and camping gear and so on.

"I won't trouble you with all the details of the trip, but even once I was in the PPC habitat, it took me two solid days of travel to reach the proper section of the library, camping in human-rated environmental study habitats, called reading rooms, each night.

"It was not until the morning of the third day that I actually got down into the right section of shelved books, the stacks, as they are called. I walked for what seemed like hours along the endless shelves of books, with just a hand-lamp to light my way. They won't power up the stack lights just for a single freelance researcher.

"But then, at last, I was there, standing in front of the correct shelf, with the spines of three books by Ulan Baskaw right there at eye level. There was a certain strange pleasure in that moment. At some level, at least, I had proved myself right. I had more than half convinced myself, a couple of times, that what had set me off was nothing more than a clerical mistake, a typographical error citing misspelled titles. The books were missing, I told myself, because they had never existed.

"But they *did* exist, and I could hold them in my hands. I took all three books, and made my way to the nearest reading room, about fifteen minutes' walk from the shelves where I had found the books. I set up camp in the reading room, got the heat on, and powered up the air system. Then, at long last, I sat down and read what Ulan Baskaw had written, centuries before, trying to find whatever it was that had made DeSilvo want to make her books disappear.

"As I sat down to read, I found myself wondering if I were chasing after nothing at all. I had no real evidence. Suppose I was just a paranoid fool? Suppose Baskaw's books had been erased from the GL because they were boring, or useless, or inaccurate?

"I read straight through the first book, and by the time I had finished it, it was a lot easier to believe I was just paranoid. It was called *Statistical Analysis of Species Populations in Artificial Environments*. It was Baskaw's thesis, and, if I am any judge, an especially boring and pedantic example of a form of writing known for being boring and pedantic. The math in it was old-fashioned and convoluted, but still valid. The language was archaic, as was to be expected in a book that old. I needed a dictionary and a context interpreter to get through several passages. But there was nothing new in it. Maybe it was all groundbreaking stuff at the time. Maybe Baskaw was the now-forgotten founder of the whole field of population statistics. Or maybe she was just retreading ground that had already been walked over many times. I have no idea. But I could see nothing in that book that would be much of a skeleton in DeSilvo's closet.

"The second book, though—that one was pay dirt. *A Proposed New Method of Terraforming* was very plainly the basis for the whole Greenhouse-SunSpot system used at Solace. I was dumbfounded. Thanks to DeSilvo's promoting the idea, the whole of Settled Space knows about Greenhouse and SunSpot. They even named the technique after him: DeSilvo terraforming. But it was not DeSilvo. It was Baskaw. Detail by detail, it was all there. Ulan Baskaw had set down on paper all the ideas DeSilvo claimed as his own. I had incontrovertible evidence that the entire process used to terraform the planet Solace was one huge act of plagiarism. DeSilvo had claimed for himself ideas he had stolen from a long-forgotten source."

"So what?" Norla asked. "What difference could it possibly make who gets credit for the idea? So DeSilvo covered his tracks and hid the source matter hundreds of years ago. I guess it's the sort of thing that could cause a big ruckus in academia, but who else would care? It doesn't change anything. If that's what all this is about, it isn't worth it!"

Koffield looked at her with something close to annoyance in his expression. "Don't be absurd," he said sharply. "I would not have wasted my time or yours telling the story—or making the journey to Solace—if that were all there was to it." His expression softened a bit as he went on. "I admit that right then and there, at the moment I discovered that second book, I wondered if that was all there was. It was an anticlimax. You're quite right that it would not be enough to merit all *my* exertions. But, on the other hand, that second book *would* be more than motive enough for DeSilvo to suppress all mention of Baskaw in the library system.

"But from my—our—point of view, if that had been all there was to it—well, what point in pursuing it? Perhaps I would have turned my notes over to the Chief Librarian, and let her deal with charges against DeSilvo. But, after that, I would have turned my back on it, and gone on with my life. Or at least with what passed for my life."

"Sir?"

Koffield looked her straight in the eye, as if defying her to contradict him. "Would I have pursued *any* of it if life had left me anything else? I had no surviving family, no friends, no expectation of my career going anywhere but into dusty corners where no one could see me, places where my mere presence, my existence, wouldn't be an affront, an insult, a dirty word shouted in the midst of polite society. I had nothing left.

"But even in that state, I could only be drawn in so far by so little. Right from the start, I had gotten the sense that there was something seriously wrong, something more than DeSilvo merely covering his academic tracks.

"What he had done, in erasing Baskaw from the main records of the Grand Library, was a far more serious crime than plagiarism—and one that carried a greater risk of detection, no matter how great his skill in manipulating computer memory systems. He was, indeed, detected as a result of hiding his plagiarism, not by the plagiarism itself.

"It would have been far safer to conceal plagiarism by doing nothing. After all, the book that could betray him was one out of billions, and one that, more than likely, no one but himself had read in centuries. The odds against anyone reading it, and being able to connect it with his project, were remote indeed. No one else had made the connection—or at least reported making it—in all the decades since DeSilvo had started work at Solace. The erasure of Baskaw's book from the digital records of the

Grand Library, that was the clue that led to my discovering his plagiarism. If he had left the book alone, he would have been safe."

"So why did he do it?"

"That was my question. Why take such risks? Men don't overreact to risks and dangers they understand, and DeSilvo had been in academia all his life. He would have heard stories about plagiarists getting caught, and how it happened, and what the risks were—and he would likewise know how severe were the penalties for tampering with the Grand Library's records. He would know the difficulties he would face in trying to do it undetected. The gains and risks didn't balance out. Unless there was something else to it. Something more for him to hide. And there was.

"In the last chapter of *A Proposed New Method of Terraforming,* Baskaw discussed potential flaws in her idea—the idea that became Solace. She discussed weak points and unsettled issues that would have to be resolved before the ideas in one slim book could be turned into a way to remake worlds. And at the very end of that last chapter, she returned to the theme of her thesis, her first book: population statistics in artificial environments. It was just a few pages of material, a few relatively simple equations. But those equations had inspiration behind them. They *were* new to me. I've researched the literature, and they are new to everyone, down to our own time. They open new doors. More than that—they open doors that we did not even know were there.

"Baskaw used them to highlight potential flaws in the process she was proposing, having to do with problems in keeping initial populations of multiple species in simultaneous balance, without one species overbreeding or dying out and distorting the food chain. The mathematics she used was brilliant, but she put it to use in dealing with far too limited a problem. It was as if she used a hypersonic semiballistic transport to go from city center to the suburbs. Baskaw used her new mathematics to deal with questions that were not merely trivial in comparison to the power of her equations, but questions that actually *constrained* the power of her equations.

"But the questions she raised in those last pages were like a long-missing piece to a puzzle. Over the centuries since Baskaw wrote her books, and had her books ignored, and died as an unknown, we have assembled a great store of hard-edged, practical knowledge on the subject of terra-forming, and on the subject of multispecies population sta-tistics. But the pieces we collected never made a coherent whole. The facts never assembled themselves into real wis-dom, real knowledge. We have never had a systematic science of terraforming, only accumulations of empirical results and best guesses. But if you use Baskawian projec-tion mathematics, apply her math to the huge, convoluted, confused mass of data and projections and results and fail-ures in terraforming, suddenly things fall into place. I saw that at once. DeSilvo should have seen it as well."

Koffield rubbed his hands anxiously together. "And if he had seen it, as he should have, *must* have, if he read that book thoroughly, then his crimes are enormous beyond all calculation. The only possible way for him to have acted in innocence would be if he failed to read, study, and compre-hend the entire text, the one slim book whose central ideas he stole, the book upon whose foundation he built his en-tire life's work. Or else that he read those last few pages, and yet did not understand what should have leapt off the page at him. Otherwise, he is unquestionably guilty." And Koffield fell once again into brooding silence, staring out the wardroom porthole at the blank walls of the docking bay beyond them.

Guilty of what? Norla wondered as the moments slid past and Koffield said no more. How could reading all of the book make a difference regarding guilt or innocence? But she knew it would be best to let Anton Koffield tell things in his own way—if she could keep him talking. The question of DeSilvo's guilt or innocence, whatever the crime, seemed to weigh heavily on Koffield, and it had to do with this book. That was the tack she should take to get him to go on. "Do you think he *did* read it?" she asked.

Koffield glanced at her, then returned his gaze to the porthole. "It doesn't seem likely he'd rebuild a planet if he didn't read the whole book, does it? Occam's Razor tells us to follow the simple, obvious explanation," he said. "And yet." He did not speak again for a moment. "And yet, and yet, and yet. There are events in our lives, in our history, times and places where and when the most improbable explanations congregate, where the fate of millions is determined by some trivial and improbable event. One of the biggest wars of the mid near ancients, a war that killed millions, started because a groundcar took a wrong turn and then doubled back to meet the trap that had not been quite ready to spring when the car first went past. The decision to abandon Mars was made twenty years later than it should have been because an indifferent marksman missed an easy shot and later made a far more difficult one, killing the wrong man at the wrong time. Research into timeshaft wormholes went up a blind alley for forty years because no one realized that one measuring instrument had been installed backwards and so kept giving the expected answer, instead of the right one.

"Maybe DeSilvo read the book a dozen times or more, always excited by the possibilities in the early going, but never once getting all the way through the pessimistic bits at the ending. Or maybe he dismissed the last section as overcautious. I've dreamed up a half dozen or more such reeds I can cling to. Some of them are even believable. Because the alternative is that Dr. Oskar DeSilvo knowingly doomed the entire population, the entire planet, the entire future of Solace for the sake of his own ego." And once again, Koffield said no more, and simply stared out the porthole. But this time, there was something in his silence, his stillness, that suggested there was no more to be said, that his tale had reached its end.

But that couldn't possibly be the end. Unless she was expected to go the rest of the way herself. And, she realized, maybe she could. No need to have it spoon-fed to her. Suddenly, it all fell into place. *Connect the dots,* she told herself.

Then she saw it. "What the last pages of the second book said was that a Solace-style terraforming *might* not work," she said. "But put together with what we've learned since, the mathematics in the book was enough to tell anyone who looked that the terraforming technique *could* not work."

Koffield blinked in mild surprise and returned his attention to her. "Quite right," he said quietly. "Keep going."

"The third book," said Norla. "There was something more in the third book. What? Did Baskaw see in her own math what you saw? That it could be used for more?"

"Full marks," Koffield said. "Exactly right. Baskaw saw what I saw, and went farther down the path she had laid out for herself. She called the third book *Ecologic and Climatic Stability of Artificial Environments Formed by Certain Means*.

"I wonder about her at times, about Ulan Baskaw. There is virtually no information about her. Not so much as a biographical note in the back of any of the books. There's no mention of her date or place of birth, or of death. I am not even absolutely sure she was a woman. Ulan could have been a man's name. All we have to tell us about her is the books themselves, their dates of publication and other internal clues, the way things are phrased in the text. Probably there are experts in such things who could wring more information out of the texts, but I doubt there would be much.

"But the dates. The dates of the books. I came across all three of them, side by side, all together on the shelf, identical bindings and printings, as if they were all of a piece, and had been that way from the start.

"But the dates—and even the tone of the writing—tell a different story. She—or perhaps he—wrote, or at least published, the first in the year 4306, Earth Reckoning Common Era, and it was identified as her thesis from the University of Toowoomba—but for what sort of degree or certificate or whatever, it's impossible to say. And there's no University of Toowoomba anymore, anyway. Disbanded centuries ago. But she was young, and full of enthusiasm for her subject, even if population statistics seems dry as toast for us. The youth and enthusiasm shine through the pedantry here and there. She dedicated the book to a professor. That is something a young person would do.

"The second book is dated 4316, ten years later. The writing is more solid, more mature, more levelheaded. There is a confidence, a strength, a *pride* in the writing. She knows she has come up with something new and exciting, perhaps even important. She is pleased with that, but cautious, even restrained.

"The third book is dated 4359, fifty-three years after the first book, forty-three after the second. There was a time in human history when fifty-three years was considered a full lifetime. In any human life, fifty-three years is a long time. What happened in her life between the first book and the last? Did she publish a dozen works that did not chance to come down to us? Did she never write another word? Was her life full of happiness and contentment, or did one disaster follow another? Did she have a family? Children? Was she consumed by her work, in love with ecology and mathematics all her days, or was it but a passing fancy of youth she came back to on a whim in her later days? Did she write the third book to put to rest ghosts of doubt that had haunted her entire life, or simply to pass the time once she retired?

"How and when and why did she discover her mistakes? Did the errors come to light just as some forgotten terraforming project based on them was about to start up, and she or someone else chanced upon the truth? Was a whole terraforming project abruptly canceled when her mistake was found too late? There's no record of any such for the dates in question, but records get lost or erased or forgotten. Or was the question utterly academic, of no real-world importance? Did she write the third book simply because she liked to make things tidy? It's impossible to know.

"But I think I was able to read between the lines of that third, slim volume. There was guilt, and sorrow, and regret whispering through the stiff, careful, scholarly prose. I think the old woman—or man—who wrote that third book did so in search of some sort of absolution. The author of that book wanted to put right something that had gone wrong. What, exactly, we'll never know."

"Her mistakes. What were her mistakes?"

Koffield stood up, and turned his back on the porthole. He walked to the exact center of the deck and turned to face Norla. He spoke, raising his voice so it would carry across the distance he had put between them. "The center of it all," he said. Some trick of the compartment's acoustics put the slightest of echoes behind his voice. Norla could read the tension, the anxiety, in his expression. "The center of it all. In the second book, it seems that it never occurred to her to use the mathematics she herself had invented in order to explore her own ideas on terraforming.

"But in the third book, she does just that. The 'Certain Means' of the third book's title—by that she meant the ideas she herself had put forward. And in that third book she proved those 'certain means' *had* to result in an unstable planetary ecology. *Any* planet terraformed by those means would fail. Inevitably, and absolutely."

"And that was the method DeSilvo had used," Norla said. "He built Solace on the edge of a cliff."

"And now it's about to fall off it," Koffield said. "If we had gotten here when we were supposed to, there would have been time to warn them, time to evacuate them. But now . . . now it's too late. They might, or they might not, listen to me. Even if they do, it's hard to know what good could be done."

"Why didn't you go to DeSilvo?" Norla asked. "Obviously he wasn't entirely rational about Solace, but would he really have been willing to snuff out all those lives?"

"Probably not. Of course, he had to be at least somewhat delusional to go as far as he had. But yes, I think if I could have gotten him to understand, he would have stepped in—if for no reason than to save his life's work. He saw Solace as a monument to himself, and he wouldn't want it ruined. I wanted to go to him, once I was ready. I wanted to be sure, wanted to have a clear, cogent set of arguments that he couldn't refute. I was a long, long way from trusting him, but I realized that I was going to have to go public with the information if it was going to be of any use. Once I did that, he would know about it anyway.

"When I returned from the Main PPC, the first thing I did was book passage on the *Dom Pedro IV*, bound for

Solace, so I could present my warnings personally. Then I set to work on my analysis. I had only been at it a few days when I learned that the *Chrononaut VI* was in Earth orbit, and had changed her routing. She was headed for Solace, departing in five days' time. There was no way I could get a berth aboard her, and in any event, I wasn't ready to go. My work wasn't finished. I put together whatever material I could and sent a lasergram to the *Chrononaut,* for relay to the authorities on Solace. The 'gram contained the text of a quick preliminary report, and a cover message saying I would be traveling aboard the *Dom Pedro IV* some weeks later with more complete and detailed information.

"Then, three days after the *Chrononaut* left, DeSilvo died. Again."

"Again?" Norla asked.

"Medically dead, not legally," Koffield said. "DeSilvo was an old, old man, and he had died many times. But he was also a rich and influential man, living in a place with superb medical facilities. The Grand Library has—or at least had, a hundred years ago—its own hospital. For that matter, DeSilvo's research and archives staff members had their own private, and very advanced, medical clinic.

"They told me DeSilvo had had a new heart, a sprint-bud clone grown from his own DNA, implanted a few months before. It had been his third heart replacement. Apparently the new heart had failed in some way—not uncommon in a man that old who has had multiple organ replacements. And DeSilvo had had new everything at one point or another. Heart, lungs, liver, spleen, eyes. After a while, the stresses of the repeated surgeries can be too much. DeSilvo had collapsed. They drew fresh DNA samples from him, then put him in temporal confinement at maximum displacement—in effect stopping time for him while they grew him yet another new heart. It's a long, complicated process, and the medical people saw no reason to rush it. He was still in the confinement when I went aboard the *Dom Pedro IV.* I never had a chance to talk with him about what I had learned. I'll never know how he would have reacted."

Koffield lifted his hands to his face and rubbed his eyes wearily. He lowered his hands, and looked at them, as if expecting—or at least wishing—that they were not empty, that there was something he could do, something he could accomplish. "So I never got to ask him—did you know you doomed a world, and simply not care? Or were you just incompetent? Was it ego or stupidity?

"But even destroying a world doesn't get to the worst of it," he said. "It doesn't get to the depths of what DeSilvo failed to see, or refused to see. *Did* he read the third book? If he did, and then went ahead with the Solace project, blood is on his hands, a planet's worth, generations of it. And yet all that blood will be as nothing. Nothing at all, in the long run. It will be nothing more than a drop lost in the deepest of oceans."

Norla stood, and walked a step or two closer to him. Her own heart was suddenly pounding, her own blood roaring through her veins. There was something that scared Anton Koffield, and anything that scared him had to be terrifying indeed. "How could that be?" she demanded. "Losing a whole planet—what could make that seem insignificant?"

He moved a step or two away from her, not in any particular direction, but simply not wishing to be too close to her, to anyone.

Get close to something, and it hurts when you lose it, Norla thought, and drew back herself. "What is worse?" she asked again.

"Work the math," Koffield said bitterly, his voice quiet and cold. "All you need to do is work the math. Eliminate as many variables as you can. Simplify by canceling out whatever you can from both sides of the equation. Sometimes—not always, but sometimes—the more you can cancel out, the more generalized the equation, and the more things it can tell you. Sometimes it's all the things with meaning that cancel out, and what you end up with doesn't tell you anything at all. Sometimes the math is very elegant, very pretty and simple, and quite meaningless.

"And sometimes it takes fifty years, or a hundred years, to learn enough to let you spot the variables and values and whole subequations that can be done away with. Or it takes that long to see what the very pretty equation that seemed to say nothing is actually telling you."

Koffield looked hard at Norla, as if daring her to turn away from what he had to say. "Baskaw's commentary at the back of the second book used some complicated math to show that the techniques used at Solace *might* be unstable. The third book used some simplified and generalized—but still very complex—versions of the same math to demonstrate that Solace, or any world terraformed in the same way, *must* be unstable. Baskaw did not have a large enough base of knowledge and data to go further. Today we do. I did what any modern worker in the field would be able to do. I cleared a lot of the underbrush out of her math, eliminated things that didn't need to be in it, and brought it down to very simple terms.

"Among other things, what the Baskaw formulae tell us is that, all other things being equal, the period of stability for a given artificial ecosystem is a function of its inherent, internal complexity and the time it took to establish the ecosystem. Stability equals Complexity times Development Time. S equals Q times T(d). $S = Q \star T_{(d)}$. The simpler the ecology, and the faster it is created, the shorter the time it will last. Solace is a very simple ecology, and was created in a great hurry. Solace is doomed."

"But you already told me that. You said there was something worse."

"There is!" Koffield almost shouted. "I just told you! That same formula applies to *every* other artificial environment, and the value for complexity is not very high on any of them. There have been ecological collapses before—starting with the Mars disaster, right on up to the present day.

"We've always told ourselves they were one-off mistakes, caused by this or that specific failure. Fix this problem, enhance that system, try it again, and everything will be fine. But that's not true. The problem is systemic. It's inherent in the process. It's true everywhere, all the time. There are lots of ways to mask the problem, and lots of ways to fix things, at least for a while. You can double or triple the period of stability, if you try hard enough and get lucky. You can even do better than that by importing additional species and biomass. But absent that sort of manipulation, what it comes down to is this: Take five thousand years to build a completely isolated ecology, and it will last about five thousand years. Take five years, and it will last about five."

Koffield pointed out the porthole to the station outside, to Solace, to the universe. "*Every terraformed planet, every habitat, is doomed.* Sooner or later, they're *all* going to fail. All of them. And there's not a damned thing we can do about it."

SOLACE CENTRAL ORBITAL STATION

CHAPTER SIXTEEN

THE DEEPEST TOWER

Norla rolled up her sleeve and activated the subcutaneous injector against her right shoulder. The device shot its drugs and antibodies and pseudovirals under her skin. She didn't know, and didn't care, if the cocktail of chemicals in the injector was supposed to keep her from spreading a plague she carried out into the station or supposed to keep her from catching a plague that was already out there. Norla felt numb, lost, her spirit deadened. If she caught their plague, or they caught hers, what did it matter? They were all going to die. The planet was going to collapse.

Koffield used his own injector, then readjusted the sleeve of his tunic and needlessly straightened his collar. He looked every bit the ramrod-straight military man, emotionless, imperturbable. Norla envied him that. She had no such ready-built role she could draw on, or hide behind. She had only herself.

But if Koffield had his military persona to hide behind, to use as a shield between the outer world and his inner self, there had to be a cost. It had to eat at him. How much of the inner man still survived behind that shield-wall? How much of his soul had been hollowed out by the endless discipline, the rigid self-control?

"Ready?" he asked her.

"No," she replied, quite honestly. "Let's go."

He nodded and worked the airlock controls. The inner door slid open, and they stepped inside, Koffield hauling the secured container along with him, as well as a carrier bag packed with spare clothes, toiletries, and the like. Norla carried a similar personal effects bag, along with a small utility satchel, but the latter was more for form's sake than anything else. It held a pocket camera and a note recorder, but beyond that, she couldn't think of much she'd be *certain* to need. She had not the faintest idea what was to happen next. She could think of a thousand things they *might* need, from gas masks to assault lasers to ArtInt pocket translators to inertial trackers, more than would be possible to carry. But even given the evidence they had already seen that not all was as it should have been aboard SCO Station, it seemed to her it would be more diplomatic to assume—or at least pretend—that everything on board would be normal.

Norla stepped into the airlock, sealed the inner door, and reached for the button that would open the outer.

Assistant Station Operations Supervisor Yuri Sparten stood on the walkway inside the Personnel Access Tunnel, a meter or two back from the ship-end of the PAT, staring thoughtfully at the hull of the—well, *mystery ship* was probably the most accurate term. He had burrowed deep into the station's record archives and been able to confirm a number of details concerning the *Cruzeiro do Sul's* story, but the whole affair sounded too much like the sort of story invented to scare children sitting around a campfire. The ghost ship that came out of the past, the dead crew returned to life.

Yuri felt fidgety, anxious, as if he ought to be doing *something*. Acting more to use up nervous energy than because it needed doing, he stepped forward to the end of the PAT and started a hand check of the PAT's seal to the ship's hull. Pointless, of course. There was hard vacuum on the other side of the seal. If there had been a leak, he would have known about it without having to run his hand around the edge of the seal.

Yuri heard a clang and a thud from inside the ship. That had to be the inner hatch sealing. They'd be coming out in a moment. But now that he had started it, he felt obliged to complete his pointless check of the pressure seal. He knelt by the end of the PAT and ran his hand along the seal below the base of the hatch.

A low click and a slight hissing noise were all the warning he had that the outer hatch was about to open. He straightened up suddenly, almost toppling over in the low gravity of the near-axis decks. He moved back a step or two from the hatch, feeling strangely embarrassed, as if he had almost been caught at something untoward.

He managed to come to a respectable version of parade rest just a fraction of a second too late. That much he knew the moment he caught the man's eye. It plainly required an act of will on the man's part not to dress Yuri down on the spot. Never had Yuri seen a man who so obviously did not belong in civilian clothes. The man might as well have had the words SENIOR OFFICER stamped across his forehead.

Yuri was suddenly very self-conscious, as if the man were subjecting him to parade-ground inspection. "Welcome to Solace Central Orbital Station," he said to them, speaking a bit more slowly and carefully than he normally would. Accents might well have shifted a good deal over the last century. "I am Second Assistant Station Operations Supervisor Yuri Sparten." Unsure of what gesture—a handshake, a salute, a kiss on both cheeks—they might think proper, he offered none.

"Thank you," said the man. "I am Anton Koffield, and this is Norla Chandray. Our spacecraft is the lighter *Cruzeiro do Sul,* off the timeshaft freighter *Dom Pedro IV.*"

"Very nice to meet you," said Chandray, smiling at him mechanically, an insincere expression that did not reflect her feelings, but was merely meant to reassure Yuri.

"I am delighted to meet you both," he said, the words sounding awkward and insincere even to him. It seemed to him that Koffield was staring at him intently. He found himself fretting over whether his dark grey uniform was properly cleaned and pressed.

Yuri was suddenly acutely aware of his own youth, and felt embarrassed by it, as if it were a fault or handicap he had to overcome. He was dark-skinned, slender, long-boned. He liked to think he was capable of moving with remarkable grace, but knew how befuddled and clumsy he could be. Yuri had a long, angular face, and he practiced in the mirror to make sure his jaw was set, his eyes determined-looking. He kept his black hair trimmed so short that it looked from some angles as if he had shaved his skull.

But it was no time to worry about his own appearance. He was supposed to be evaluating the visitors. He forced himself to settle down. He decided to concentrate on Chandray for the moment, she being far less intimidating. She was as plainly civilian as Koffield was military. She was a rather nondescript sort, a little over thirty standard years or so, a kilo or two on the heavy side, pale-skinned and round-faced, with dirty blond hair cut so short it barely fell flat.

"Thank you for meeting our ship," Chandray said, and Yuri suddenly realized he had let the silence go on too long.

"It is my privilege to serve," Yuri replied, offering the formal phrase with a very slight, very correct bow.

"Thank you," Koffield said. "It is an honor to be so well received."

Not quite the conventional response, but they hadn't exactly had much chance to practice modern standards of etiquette. It would do. The two visitors both spoke with odd but perfectly understandable accents.

Chandray looked around the lock complex, and Yuri caught her wrinkling her nose and making a face. It was plain to see that the station's air scrubbers weren't doing a good enough job to meet with her approval. Koffield probably felt the same way, but there was no reading anything in that face. Well, if they thought the air up this way was a bit whiff, wait until they got down to Perimeter Level. Even Yuri thought Perimeter smelled like five thousand people who hadn't bathed in far too long—and that was not far off the mark.

Both of the visitors had the slightly sallow, wan-looking appearance of people who had not yet quite recovered from a long time in cryosleep. Nor was the slightly lost look on the woman's face all that unexpected. Yuri had seen the same expression on the faces of the abandoned and dispossessed who seemed to crowd in on every part of the station.

It was Koffield's grim features, his face as hard as stone, that surprised Yuri. The man looked not like a refugee, but like a man prepared to do battle.

"If there is anything you wish," Yuri said, "please do not hesitate to ask."

"Thank you once again," Koffield said. "And I trust you will forgive me if I take advantage of that gracious offer immediately. I don't know what the proper title might be, but I—we—would like to meet with the station commander or director, or executive, as soon as possible. It is a matter of some urgency." Koffield patted the handle of the large piece of luggage he had with him, and Yuri concluded that the contents of the case had something to do with the matter of urgency.

"No apologies required, sir. In fact, Station Commander Raenau asked to see you as soon as was convenient." That was understating the case by quite a bit. Raenau had bluntly ordered that the crew of the *Cruzeiro do Sul* be brought before him at once, whether they liked it or not. But Sparten could see no harm in being a bit more diplomatic, seeing how both sides wanted the same thing in any event. "If you would care to see him now, before being shown to your quarters, I'm sure I could arrange it."

Koffield raised his eyebrows in surprise. "I must admit that I expected to spend quite some time arranging things. I'm delighted by the news, but I must admit I didn't expect your commander to be quite so eager to see *us*. Might I ask if he gave you any reason?"

"No, sir, he did not." *Any more than you've given your reasons,* Yuri thought. "But if you'll allow me the chance to make a very brief call, we'll go straight to his office, and then take you to your quarters, where you will be welcome as the commander's guests."

It was a diplomatic way of saying they would not be expected to pay for lodging, and plainly Koffield got the message. "Excellent," he said. "We look forward to your hospitality."

The word *hospitality* gave Yuri pause. He considered for a moment, then decided now was as good a time as any for bad news. "Regarding that hospitality—I'm afraid it might not be up to our normal standards. In plain point of fact, we can't offer much in the way of luxury. As you might or might not be aware, the station is rather over-crowded at the moment."

"We didn't know," Koffield said dryly, "but we were beginning to suspect. The docking bays are remarkably full, and the ships in the bays do not appear to be in top-of-the-line-perfect repair."

Top of the line? It took Yuri a moment to figure out what the outdated idiom meant. "Ah, yes," he said. "Just so. But in any event, we can at least put you up."

"If the station is *that* crowded, Mr. Sparten," said the Chandray woman, "we could stay aboard our lighter."

Yuri looked at the woman in surprise—and noted that Koffield did as well. No doubt what she had said was quite polite and proper wherever—and whenever—it was that she came from. But Yuri could think of half a dozen cultures off the top of his head where to so much as offer to forgo hospitality was a deadly insult. There were certainly communities on Solace itself where it would have been a ghastly mistake. No one with any experience of other cultures would have made such a gaffe. Clearly she was far less experienced than Koffield.

"I'm sure that Mr. Sparten's offer was quite sincere, Second Officer Chandray," Koffield said. "And I have no doubt we will find the stationside accommodations more comfortable and more convenient than anything we could arrange for ourselves aboard ship."

Chandray reddened visibly. "Yes, yes, of course," she said. "Please forgive me," she said to Yuri. "If I have offended you, it was quite unintentional."

"Not at all," Yuri replied. He regarded the two of them thoughtfully for a moment. The brief exchange had told him a lot about these two strangers. One knew to be wary when approaching a new culture, and the other did not. It was the sort of thing that might be worth knowing, sometime down the road. "In any event, we *do* have accommodation for you, and the station commander is eager to see you. If you will both come with me, there's a free-runner waiting for us."

"A what?" Chandray asked.

"A free-runner. It's a small open car that isn't restricted to the transit-tube system, and can travel freely throughout the station. Could you come this way?"

"Certainly," said Koffield.

"Just a second," Chandray said. "I need to secure my outer hatches first." She stepped to one side of the hatch opening and flipped open a panel on the outer hull of the *Cruzeiro do Sul,* revealing some sort of keypad. Either deliberately or by chance, she moved to put her body between Yuri and the panel, and did something he could not see with the controls. The outer hatch slid shut, and Yuri heard a deep, solid *clunk, clunk, clunk* from inside the hatch. At a guess, the *Cruzeiro*'s hatches had triple dead bolts that had just slammed to. "All right. Locks set, combinations scrambled, and keys out," she said. "Let's go."

After the warning she had just received, it should have occurred to Chandray that locking her doors that completely, and that obviously, in front of your host, could be construed as one hell of an insult.

But then Chandray turned around and looked him right in the eye. No embarrassment there anymore, no apology. It was plain she knew exactly what she was doing. And, Yuri noticed, Koffield offered no objection this time, made no effort to smooth things over. Yuri smiled sadly to himself. He couldn't blame them. They'd seen what the docking bays, and the ships in them, looked like. They might even have seen the *Pilot's Ease* being jettisoned. They no doubt had guessed some, if not all, of what was going on aboard the station. Courtesy was one thing. Doing what you could to protect your only way out was quite another.

"This way," Yuri said. Koffield picked up the oversize hard-sided satchel he had brought out of the ship, and Chandray shut the access panel and stood by him, ready to follow Yuri. He led them down the Personnel Access Tunnel to the Gamma Docking Bays' airlock center, all three of them studiously ignoring everything that had just been revealed. He found himself wondering just how much else they would all need to ignore about each other.

Yuri gestured for his two guests to sit down in the rear bench seat of the free-runner. "You'll see more facing forward," he said. They got in, Koffield being very careful with his oversize case. Yuri got in himself and sat down in the front left-side swivel seat, facing forward. "Go to the Ring Park entrance to DeSilvo Tower, traveling via any convenient scenic route at observation speed," he said. Lights on the car's control panel came on, indicating that it had understood the instructions. A proposed route popped up on the main map display. "Route approved," Yuri said, then spun about in his seat to face his guests as the car started itself up. It rolled out of the Gamma Bays' airlock center, went down the vehicle-axis ramp, and took the side turning into the west-quad down-axis transit tube.

The transit tubes were utilitarian affairs, scruffy, windowless, dimly lit, and a little beat-up. The car turned on its headlight and interior lights as it rolled along the featureless tunnel.

"This is the scenic route?" Chandray asked.

Yuri laughed. "We're not quite to the scenic part yet. We'll come out of the transit tube soon, and you'll see— well, what you'll see. Quite frankly, even the scenic parts aren't very scenic at the moment. As it happens, the scenic route is probably the fastest way there, this time of day. But there's no sense hiding the situation from you. You might as well see us, warts and all."

Chandray and Koffield looked at each other for a moment. They seemed interested in what he said, but not surprised. "Why aren't the scenic parts scenic?" Chandray asked. She tried to make it into a casual question, but it was plain from the look on her face they had come to a subject of interest. Chandray would never get far in life if she had to rely on concealing her emotions.

But there was no sense trying to deny what they were

going to see for themselves in a moment. Some things, you couldn't even pretend to ignore. Yuri shrugged sadly. "The whole station is crawling with refugees, and we'll probably see a lot of them. It was a lot worse not so long ago, but it's still pretty bad. You'll see."

"We'd guessed something of the sort already," Koffield replied. "We picked up a few transmissions about some sort of evacuation panic on our way in. One is related to the other, I'd imagine."

Yuri nodded. "A story got started and it wouldn't die. A rumor about evacuating part of the population. Madam Kalzant—ah, Madam Neshobe Kalzant, the Planetary Executive, decided the only way to calm the situation down was to give everyone who wanted one a ride off-planet, demonstrate we could handle the traffic. I guess she figured that if she proved there wasn't a shortage or a traffic cutoff, that would kill the panic. And it did, pretty much. Even if it was awful hard on us, the plan worked. The panic stopped, outgoing traffic tailed back down to normal—or below. Incoming traffic back toward Solace went way up. Inbound traffic probably won't get back down to normal level for a while yet. But it looks like nearly everyone has decided to go back home to planetside."

" 'Nearly' everyone?" Koffield asked gently.

Yuri turned his hands up in a sign of helplessness. "We're a transit facility, a cargo-transfer point. We've got a fair-sized population, but this is a working station, not a resort hab with lots of excess capacity. We didn't have enough life-support service to handle everyone who came through.

"So we passed along as many people as we could to other stations and habitats, even to some of the domed colonies in the outer system. We were swamped getting them all processed through here. We're still keeping pretty busy getting them back to Solace. But some of the refugees could only get this far. No money, no equipment, no off-planet skills. They got here on ships that shouldn't ever have left the ground. Ships got here out of fuel, life support dead, propulsion out, some with nothing more than corpses aboard."

The free-runner shifted to an off-ramp and rolled itself into the waiting car of a cargo lift. The elevator car shut its doors and started to descend the moment the free-runner came to a halt. For whatever reason, the first half of the ride down took place in silence. What was there about lifts and elevators, Yuri wondered, that so discouraged conversation? Of course, to be fair, a ride in an SCO Station cargo lift could be a disconcerting experience. As one moved farther away from the axis of the station, the apparent pull of gravity increased dramatically. They would move from about one-tenth to nearly one-half gee in just over a minute. Yuri never enjoyed it, even if the normal operating speed of the lifts was kept low to try and keep the transition from being worse.

In any event, the lull in conversation offered up the perfect chance for Yuri to call ahead. He might as well take advantage of it. He pulled his pocket phone out, keyed a link to the commander's office, and put the device to his ear, so only he could hear the other side of the conversation.

"Answered by operations system, office, commander," the ArtInt on the other end announced. "Instruction to caller: Confirm caller identity via voice check as Yuri Sparten."

"Sparten confirming," Yuri said.

"Voice match," the ArtInt replied, then fell silent, waiting for Yuri to speak.

"Guests, two, from *Cruzeiro do Sul* arrived," Yuri told the machine. "En route with same to office, commander ETA approx twenty minutes. Immediate meeting with commander agreed."

"Confirmation is redundant. Confirmation noted and logged."

Yuri nodded to himself, then shut off the phone and pocketed it without speaking further. No point in courtesy hellos and good-byes with machines. Especially when, as the ArtInt noted, the call was utterly redundant. But then he had made the call for the benefit of his visitors, not the ArtInt. By calling in a confirmation, he had made the commander's summons seem a bit more like a social invitation rather than the peremptory order it was. Yuri spent a good part of his time on such smoothing-over maneuvers. Commander Raenau was not known for his skill at diplomacy.

Yuri glanced at the lift's floor indicator and saw they were getting close. He looked back down and noticed a quizzical expression on Chandray's face. "The way you were talking just now," she said. "I take it you were talking to a robot or some sort of machine?"

"That's right," Yuri said. "But why does that strike you as odd? Surely you had talking machines a hundred years ago."

"Oh yes, of course we do—we did," Chandray replied. "It's the syntax, the patterns of how you talked to it. It's almost like a distinct dialect. Now that I think of it, the traffic-control system had the same sort of odd speech patterns." She frowned thoughtfully, and then her eyes lit up. "Is that it?" she asked. "A distinct speech pattern when addressing machines?"

Maybe this Chandray woman wasn't much for questions of etiquette, but she clearly was nobody's fool. "Quite right," he said. "Supposedly it was Founder DeSilvo's own idea."

"DeSilvo?" Koffield asked.

The name drew a strong reaction from both of them. *Another* interesting detail to note down. "It's been handed down since his time, all through the Solace system. The machines can understand and use standard speech if need be, of course, but the convention is for them and us to use machine language whenever we interact. I think the idea is that if you speak to them in a way sufficiently unlike normal speech, you'll always remember, at a subconscious level, that they're not human. In a crisis, you won't waste time shouting at them, or offering arguments or reasons that would only make sense to a human."

"Subtle," said Koffield, half to himself and half to Chandray. "Interesting, clever, and subtle. He always did know his way around machines."

Which strongly implied that Koffield had actually known DeSilvo! Yuri worked the dates out in his head and concluded there was nothing impossible in that. Yet one more useful, even fascinating, item for the debriefers. "Supposedly it's a status marker as well," Yuri said. "As least that's what my social structure teachers called it. We use machine language to talk to robotic servants, but not to each other. It's supposed to be good psychology, according to my teachers."

The lift car came to a halt at Perimeter Level, the habitable level closest to the outer, perimeter, hull of the station. The lift car's doors opened, and the free-runner backed itself nimbly out, turned itself around, rolled down a side passage, and then out onto the Long Boulevard, the only route that ran the full length of the station.

Where once there had been bright light, laughter, and music, now there were only stripped-bare storefronts and the snarl of traffic. The smell, the stench, hit them as hard as a fist, and it would only get worse as they moved closer to Ring Park. The Long Boulevard had lost all her elegance, all her pride, all of it replaced by a wretched miasma of unwashed bodies and failed sanitation systems.

The Long Boulevard was no featureless transit tube, but the main thoroughfare for the station, the only one big enough and long enough to be considered a proper avenue if it were in a groundside city. It was so wide and tall in cross section that the station's girth was noticeable. Yuri looked straight down the Boulevard, and caught a glimpse of the Aft End Cargo Center at the far end of the station, more than half a kilometer away.

Shops and stores, shipping offices and cafes, theaters and nightclubs lined both sides of the Boulevard. Walkways separated the stores from the central transport road. A pair of glass-walled transit tubes hung from the ceiling, but the Boulevard was a route for more than closed-route transport.

Free-ranging vehicles of all sorts crowded the two narrow vehicular lanes of the Boulevard. Robotic cargo haulers, pedal-powered quadracycles, private free-runners, and taxibots came on and went off the main road to and from all the side and upper accessways. As always, the

Boulevard's vehicular traffic looked to be on the verge of chaos, but Yuri was not concerned about it. The automated road-traffic-control system was highly competent, and would see to it that all the transports got where they were going.

It was the walkways and the shops—and the people in them—that had him worried. Day shift and night shift, around the clock, the Boulevard was ready to boil over into new trouble at any moment. The closer they got to Ring Park, the denser, shabbier, and more surly the crowds became.

Once, not so long ago, the shops had been smart, the shipping offices bustling, the cafes and clubs alive with the sights and sounds of people enjoying themselves. Now half the businesses were shuttered, and a few had been wrecked or burned out in the riots. Most of the establishments that were still open had very obviously armed guards on duty, and very heavy, very utilitarian metal grilles fastened over the display windows.

Anything and everything of any conceivable value, anything even remotely fragile, had long since been removed. Some of it smashed, stolen, the rest put out of harm's way by the owners. All the signs, all the outdoor tables and chairs, were gone. Stripped of all decoration and on the defensive, the Boulevard was not itself anymore. It was nothing but a row of shabby little stresscrete bunkers barricaded against loiterers and malcontents, just barely hanging on. Business continued, but it was greatly changed and much diminished.

The free-runner slowed down in a particularly heavy knot of traffic. They came to a halt at the next intersection, and sat there, waiting to move again.

"Refugees?" Koffield asked, nodding toward a knot of grimy, bewildered-looking men huddled together on a street corner. It surprised Yuri not at all that Koffield had been able to pick them out. Everything from their haircuts to the style of their clothing, from the gauntness of their faces to the dirt on their skin, shouted out that these were people who did not belong, people who had no place, people for whom there was no room.

"Refugees," Yuri said, trying to keep the anger and frustration out of his voice. The shabby men looked harmless, even pathetic. But those pitiable men, and their wives and children, had, simply by being on SCO Station, put the station in mortal danger. It had been luck as much as anything else that had kept it from utter collapse.

The normal station population was about four thousand, a little above the official "optimum" population of thirty-five hundred. At the peak of the crisis, there had been two thousand refugees on the station, over and above the normal population. The air-recirculation system had barely held, and the food supply had reached critical levels. Water, waste recirculation, general sanitation, medical services—everything had been stretched to the limit. There were still close to a thousand refugees on board, and they showed no sign of leaving. Things had gotten better, but service and supply systems that had never gotten a chance to recover were still under strain.

"It's hard to explain to outsiders," Yuri said, "but for a lot of people, the worst of the refugee crisis wasn't that they came and took everything we had. It was that they took it all and made nothing, less than nothing, out of it. Our air reserves are down to zero, the whole station is on short food and water rations, we're completely out of all sorts of medicines—and it's all gone for nothing. They're still here, most of them no better off than the day they got here. It's as if we had done nothing at all—and we did so much it nearly killed the station and everyone on it."

"And you could do twice as much, and it would do no good," Koffield said. "I do understand. I wish I didn't. But I learned otherwise, when I wasn't much younger than you are now. I was just another junior officer on just another colony-relief mission. All of the rescue team went around wondering how we had come to be so angry at the people we were trying to save."

Yuri nodded eagerly. "That's it exactly, sir. Except that— well, you went out *intending* to rescue people. We just got the problem dumped in our laps." Yuri shrugged. "We're not angry all the time, of course. We feel for them. We care about them. I can't really blame them for trying to stay.

Most of them came from places on the planet that are bad enough that no one in their right mind would want to go back, places that make the mess we're in look like paradise."

"Why did you allow them here in the first place?" Chandray asked.

"It was out of our hands," said Yuri. "Orders from the planetary government. The official policy was that whoever wanted to go could leave the planet. Probably that was even the right policy, even if it wasn't too popular up here. It stopped the panic from getting worse. Most of the people who left the planet went back. But most of the ones who *didn't* go back are on this station, though there are a few refugees on other stations. But we're stuck with over ninety percent of them."

"And now you're stuck with two more," Chandray said, half under her breath.

Yuri wasn't sure if it was meant to be a joke, or even if he had been meant to hear it. For a moment or two, he considered treating it as one thing more that needed ignoring, but Chandray's words came too close to the truth. They had to deal with the issue. "If I can be a bit reassuring, at least on that point, I can tell you that the Station Administrator does not regard you as being in the same category as the gluefeet." He reddened as soon as the word was out of his mouth.

"You call the refugees 'gluefeet'?" Chandray asked.

"Ah, yeah. Gluefeet or gluefooters. Because they're stuck here. You can't get them to go."

No one spoke for a moment. Yuri was ashamed of himself. A fellow station-dweller would have understood and sympathized, but could these two? Yuri had started out believing, and wanting to believe, that the refugees were people just like anyone else. They might be displaced groundside peasants who had nothing in common with the engineers and traders who lived on the station, but people for all of that. But then came the endless trouble they caused, the crowding, the rationing, the riots—and the smell. There were times when Yuri felt he could forgive the gluefeet everything else, if only the camps didn't smell so bad. It was getting harder and harder not to think of the refugees as the enemy, as a willful source of trouble, as freeloaders who offered nothing and asked for everything. The station-dwellers equated the refugees with the squalor in which the refugees lived. It was hard, damned hard, to remember that the glue-feet had ever been anything else but a pack of filthy rabble.

And maybe that was what the station-dwellers hated most about them. Because the station-dwellers knew, Yuri knew, that the refugees were just like them, *were* human beings. The refugees showed the dwellers what they might become, if their luck went bad. If others could fall so low, then perhaps they could as well.

"I'm sorry," Yuri said. "It's not the kindest thing to call a group of people. But, well, that's the name they've gotten. The point I was trying to make, even if I did a bad job of it, is that for better or worse, you're not like them."

Chandray looked at him, her expression hard and cold, before she returned her gaze to the shabby men on the street corner. "I can think of things we have in common," she said. "They and we are both a long way from home—and neither they nor we can go back."

The traffic started moving again, and the free-runner rolled forward, leaving the little crowd of weary, defeated men behind.

Norla Chandray wanted to scream, wanted to cry. She had so long dreamed of seeing what people and places were like in other star systems. Now she knew. She knew the people on top were callous and angry at the helpless, and the ones down below had all life, all hope, crushed out of them. She knew this place was a bewildering, crowded, foul-smelling hell-maze. And she knew she was trapped here. She could see no likelihood of escaping this world, this future. Even if they did manage to repair the *Dom Pedro IV,* Norla doubted she could bring herself to set foot back in the cryo-can that had nearly killed her and had killed her two friends. Or perhaps risking cryodeath would be preferable to life in this nightmare. Norla shuddered. How had she come to be in a time and place where the choices were so few and so unpleasant?

The free-runner rolled forward through the thickest of the traffic. The signs indicated they were getting closer to Ring Park, whatever that was. Road traffic was thinning out, but the crowds of refugees on the walkways were growing thicker. Up ahead, the sidewalls of the Boulevard opened out, and the overhead transit tubes split apart, one to either side of the Boulevard. Both angled down steeply and vanished below street level. The rows of shops and buildings stopped dead. A flat, featureless blue wall on either side of the road marked the end of the commercial area, but the road and the walkways passed through a wide circular opening in the wall. The way ahead was clear, straight into what had to be Ring Park.

The road itself pointed straight ahead, toward another circular opening at the far wall, and the aft end of the station visible beyond. A huge green space—or at least space that had once been green—opened up on all sides of them as they moved past the barrier. Ring Park wrapped itself entirely around the Perimeter Level of the station. Norla looked up at the sky-blue ceiling, and estimated that the park took up three or four levels of the station. Beyond that ceiling there had to be several more decks, and then the central access tunnel of the station, through which the *Cruzeiro do Sul* had traveled.

There had been no attempt to make the overhead bulkhead look like anything but a high, blue-painted ceiling. Stations with similar parks sometimes used holographic projections and other tricks to simulate cloudscapes and sunshine and so on. Better to do what they did here, Norla decided, and let a ceiling be a ceiling. Here and there, flying figures and sky scenes from legend and history had been painted onto the ceiling. A dragon breathed fire here, an impossibly rickety wood-and-paper airplane from the near-ancient period struggled into a patch of painted sky there, but these were mere decoration, not intended to fool anyone.

Before her and behind her, the forward and aft bulkheads were painted in an abstract pattern of browns and greens that gradually merged with the overhead blue. It was enough to suggest and evoke imaginary forests, but not so much that it was an attempt to make anyone think there were forests instead of metal bulkheads. Perfectly normal direct lighting illuminated the park—no optical illusions of a simulated sun, or overly clever indirect lighting systems. The one lighting effect she could not understand was a sudden, brief, and faint pulse of light every three minutes or so, coming from off to the right.

The grounds of the park were—or at least had been—a fairly conventional approximation of open parkland. Broad lawns with small pools of water here and there, and small stands of trees dotted about the place.

But things were not as they had been. What little grass was left was brown. The water in the decorative ponds was a most undecorative greasy grey-green. Someone was emptying a slop bucket into the closest pond as Norla watched, while someone else was drawing water from the same source. Nearly all the trees had been cut down, leaving only a collection of ragged stumps. In among all the other odors that clouded the air, Norla identified woodsmoke. She could see the glow of half a dozen campfires.

The air was hazy with smoke and laden with the smells of unwashed bodies, rancid food, decaying feces, stale urine, burned food, and a dozen other things Norla could not identify.

And, everywhere, in groups of five or ten or a dozen huddled around a fire, wandering aimlessly or sitting huddled by themselves, were the refugees. Sparten's gluefeet. The people washed up on this noisome shore by a crisis that seemed to come out of nowhere.

The free-runner turned off the Long Boulevard onto a paved side path that led off to the right, toward the direction of the light pulses. "Vehicle command. Pause here," said Yuri Sparten. The free-runner slowed, pulled itself off to the side of the road, and came to a halt. "Well, here we are, Second Officer Chandray," said Sparten. "You wanted to see the scenic part of the scenic route. This is it."

"Damnation," Koffield said. It was hard to know if he meant it as a curse, or as a perfectly apt description of the place. The three of them just sat and looked for a long moment, the scene overwhelming them all.

"This is where you put them?" Norla asked. "In an open park?"

"The park is as closed-in as anything in the station," Sparten said. "There's no weather to speak of. We have guest quarters for two or three hundred to accommodate visiting crews—and those quarters are virtually at full capacity. Where else were we going to put two thousand people but here?"

Norla desperately wanted to have an answer to that, something she could throw back in his face, but she had nothing.

"I'm amazed your environment systems held together as well as they have," Koffield said. "With so many extra people on board, you must have been near the ragged edge."

"At it and over it. But we're coming back, starting to recover. Believe it or not, it was a lot worse than this. For one thing, the stink isn't nearly as bad as it was," Sparten went on with a studiously matter-of-fact tone. "Most of this is residual from when things were really bad. The air scrubbers are finally starting to cut into the worst of it. And we're actually a lot closer to being on top of the sanitation situation now. They were burying their dead for a while, except the soil's not deep enough to do it properly. We had corpses rotting under fifteen centimeters of dirt in here. We've disinterred them and put a stop to further burials. We think."

Norla stared at Sparten. He almost made it sound as if the refugees buried their dead as some sort of sport, or game, without realizing the nuisance it caused. She wondered what had happened to the disinterred bodies, and decided she didn't want to know. Besides, Sparten was still talking.

"The biggest problem we have now is getting them to stop burning fires," he was saying. "We can't afford to waste the oxy, and the smoke and soot are hell on the air scrubbers."

"Why are they burning fires?" Norla asked.

"To keep warm," Yuri said, as if it were obvious. "It gets cold here in the park during night shift. Most of the gluefeet are laboring class, not all that well educated, but still they should have had the sense not to set the fires in the first place. It was worse than useless. The park was actually built over the outer hull's thermal superconducting coils—the coils are right under the park surface. Heat-dumping was part of the idea designed into the park. The station air system drives warm air into the park. See that meter-high grey cube over there? There are lots of those all over the park, though most are better hidden by the landscaping. Some are air intakes, and the others are outlets. They connect to a convection pumping system that runs the air through the superconducting thermal coils, cools it, condenses water vapor out, then dumps it back out into the park."

"If the people are that cold, can't you shut down the coil coolers?"

Yuri shook his head. "They're an integral part of the station's cooling system. We generate a lot of waste heat here in this station. If we didn't dump the heat, the whole station would get above habitable temperatures in a few days and just keep going. We'd literally cook. We *have* to cool the station, and we use the park as a heat sink. So it gets cold in here, so the refugees cut down trees and light fires to stay warm, and pump more heat into the system right on top of the cooling system, so the system automatically compensates until we can correct manually, and then—well, I could go on, but it's a hell of a mess. The one bright spot is that they've just about run out of things to burn."

"So now they'll freeze."

"They'll be cold, that's all," Yuri said sharply. He frowned and shrugged. "I know how harsh it all sounds, but there's only so much we can do, and we're doing it. We're shifting machines off other work to make blankets and warm clothes and portable heaters and so on, but we don't have the manufacturing capacity or raw materials to do it very quickly. If we shifted enough resources to give them everything they need as quickly as possible, it would wreck the station. Probably kill all of us. That's the tightrope we're walking, in a dozen ways at least. Vehicle command. Drive on." The free-runner pulled itself back onto the paved path and drove on.

The path ran roughly at right angles to the Long Boulevard, following the inner circumference of the station, driving along on the inside of the huge cylinder. Norla's eyes insisted that they were constantly just about to start climbing a hill that grew steeper and steeper, while an equally steep hill was always just behind them.

What they had seen at first arrival repeated itself over and over again as they drove; the same destruction, the same huddled groups of people, the same dust and smoke and gloom.

At last the free-runner slowed down, and then turned onto a side path. There was what seemed to be another of the decorative ponds, a round dark hole in the lawn. But then Norla noticed one thing different about this pond—and then another, and another. The other ponds had all been artfully rounded abstract shapes. This one was perfectly and precisely circular. The others had no barriers between themselves and the surrounding lawns. This one had a quite substantial meter-high metal fence around it. And none of the other ponds had anyone watching over them. Norla counted six rifle-toting guards around the perimeter of this "pond."

And then came another of those pulses of light—flaring up out of the pond. It was increasingly clear that it was no pond at all—though what the devil it might be, Norla had no idea.

"What is this place?" Norla asked as the free-runner came to a halt by a footpath that led toward the whatever-it-was.

"DeSilvo Tower," Yuri said. "Come along." He stepped out of the free-runner and gestured for his two guests to do the same.

Koffield grabbed his secured container by the handle, lifted it, and carried it out of the vehicle. Norla got out after him. "Doesn't look like much of a tower to me," she muttered to Koffield.

"It looked like more of one when we saw it from the other side," Koffield replied with a chuckle.

It took a moment for Norla to understand. "Oh!" she said. "Of course." They weren't looking at the *top* of this tower. She walked toward the base of the tower with a more eager tread. For the first time since setting foot off the *Cruzeiro do Sul,* she was curious and eager to see something.

She followed Sparten up the path. He gestured to one of the guards, who nodded and signaled the others to let the party pass. Sparten stopped at the guardrail around the perimeter of what Norla had taken for a pond. Sparten smiled, and it was a faintly weary, tolerant expression: the local who had taken endless tourists to the same site, and knew exactly how the ritual went.

He turned his back on the guardrail and leaned against it, facing out away from the abyss behind him. "Take a look," he said. "It's worth seeing, even in its present state."

Norla moved cautiously over to the guardrail and looked down into the "pond"—and at three towers reaching down toward infinity. Beyond a massive slab of nonreflective and highly transparent glass, easily ten meters across, there was nothing but space itself. Space and—a structure. Three shafts of steel and glass, each hexagonal in cross section, stabbed up from beyond the edges of the huge observation port. They were equally spaced from each other, angling in to join far below, connecting with the base of a glittering steel-and-glass hexagonal *something* directly below. The sight was strange enough, bewildering enough, that it took her eyes a while to understand what she was seeing.

"DeSilvo Tower is really three towers in one," Sparten answered, before she could ask, in the faintly singsong cadences of someone who has said the same thing many times. "The three pylons form the three legs of a tripod. At their far end, as seen from the station, the three pylons attach to the base of the hexagonal structure you see.

Officially, that six-sided structure held in place by the pylons is called the Grand Pavilion, but some people call it the Outrigger, or Outrigger Pavilion. I don't quite understand that name, but I'm told an outrigger is a sort of auxiliary hull on some kinds of watercraft. Most people call it the Gondola, which makes a bit more sense to me.

"You're looking straight down at the base of the main structure. Depending on how you look at it, it's either the highest point or the deepest point on the station. At any event, the station commander's office is on the farthest-out deck of the Gondola, and is therefore the point on the station farthest from its center.

"The three pylons you see rise up out of the station's hull. They are ten stories high—or deep. You can't tell from this angle, since we're exactly face on to it, but the Pavilion is six stories tall."

"There must be a hell of a counterweight on the other side of the station," Koffield said.

"Well, obviously, we have to build all the extruded structures in tandem, or the spin would be thrown off completely," Sparten said. "There were questions of moment-arm and so on, of course, but naturally, if we hang a megaton of steel out this side of the station, we need to hang another megaton a hundred eighty degrees away. In fact, DeSilvo Tower is the real counterweight. One reason it got built was to balance off the bulk-storage towers on the opposite side of the station.

"You can see that the three pylons are not just support structures, but true buildings in and of themselves. Supposedly they resemble a certain style of antique steel-and-glass towers they used to build on Earth, though I don't know much about that. We're about to ride an elevator down one of those towers, down to the Pavilion, where your quarters are. Come this way."

Norla lingered as long as she could, fascinated by the incredible structure. It seemed a mad thing to build on a station that plainly had so many old, half-complete repairs on its outer hull, but that madness almost—almost—didn't matter. Its own magnificence was nearly reason enough for building such a thing.

As she watched, the heavens wheeled past the rotating station, and the surface of Solace hove into view beyond the fixed frame of DeSilvo Tower. The brightness of the planet flooded the huge viewplate with light, and seemed, from this vantage point, to light up the whole interior of Ring Park. At least that explained the light pulses.

Norla wondered why the station managers didn't opacify the viewplate in order to eliminate the pulses. Maybe there was such a mechanism, but it had been damaged. Maybe leaving the viewport transparent helped with the temperature management problem. Or maybe the station managers were hoping that a blast of light every few minutes would help drive the gluefeet away.

Norla shaded her eyes until the light pulse was over and watched again through dazzled eyes as the stars swept past the triple towers. She could see people inside the pylon buildings, moving around behind glass walls. A bit of movement at the corner of her vision caught her eye. She looked down one of the three pylons and saw what was plainly an exterior glass elevator car climbing from the Pavilion toward the station. She could see the people in the car, their faces close to the glass, staring at the view.

That was one elevator ride she just had to take. She looked up, intending to point out the car to Koffield, but he wasn't there anymore. She looked around, and suddenly saw that he and Sparten were already heading toward a low building set into an artificial hillside. Judging from the angle she saw through the viewport, it was the access point for the aft pylon.

She hurried to catch up.

Yuri Sparten paused at the entrance to the elevator, letting his two visitors go in first and get closest to the glass outer wall of the elevator car.

Koffield could not help but be amused at the way Norla eagerly moved forward toward the glass, even though they were still inside the station and there was nothing to see but the black wall of the elevator housing.

Koffield had been doing his best to hang back and

observe Sparten, along with everything else—but even the best human observer cannot watch in every direction. Sparten's behavior had told him a lot already, and no doubt the view out the elevator would be worth seeing. He turned his attention to the view out the car's glass wall just as the car started its descent toward the Outrigger, or Pavilion, or Gondola, whatever name they called it by. The car dropped out of the station's hull, revealing the universe beyond, dazzlingly brilliant objects—the planet, spacecraft on approach, the far-off stars—set against the jet-black skies of deep space.

The view from the elevator car was, of course, spectacular. Anton Koffield had expected nothing less. More than likely, the remarkable view had been one of the major reasons for building this whole absurd complex.

The two other pylons were gleaming blue steel-and-glass towers set into the station hull forward of their own pylon. They framed the view of the fleet of ships, functional and derelict, that orbited forward of the station and in formation with it. The ships, the stars beyond, the planet below, wheeled slowly, majestically, across the sky.

Koffield looked up toward the station itself as they fell slowly away from it. At first it was nothing but a huge and featureless plain of darkness, the blackness punctuated only by the massive viewport they had just looked through, a rounded pool of yellow-white light that seemed to drop away into the heavens as they descended from the station. But then the station's orbit brought it out of the planet's shadow, and into the sunlight. The huge mass of the station blossomed into brilliance, the complicated structures on its surface a sudden hard metallic forest of cranes and towers and piping.

Koffield had flown in an airship once, a lighter-than-air vehicle that was little more than a gondola suspended from a massive, rigid lifting bag. Looking up at the great bulk of the station looming overhead, it was impossible to avoid comparing the two images. He was in a car sliding down a guide wire connecting the gasbag and the Gondola.

He looked down and watched as the planet swept past and dropped behind, to be replaced by the wheeling stars of deep space. If he watched long enough, the disk of Solace would come into view again from the other side, but there was too much else to see now. The view was remarkable. Of course, one could get jaded about nearly anything. He glanced over at Sparten and saw that he was watching the elevator floor indicator, not admiring the view.

Koffield looked down. The main structure of this mad engineering folly was getting closer, the hard edges of its cold blue glass and steel gleaming in the sunlight. In its center, directly underneath the giant viewport they had looked out of at the station, was an oversize hexagonal viewport set into the top deck of the Gondola. He could plainly see people at the hexagon viewport looking up at their elevator car, pointing to it, waving at them. Koffield resisted the urge to wave back, but allowed himself a small smile when he saw that Norla did wave.

Their increase in weight was distinctly noticeable as they moved farther out from the central axis of the station. The increase in simulated gravity brought the matter of masses and stresses and loads to Koffield's mind. What sort of bearing members and structural reinforcement had it taken to suspend the monstrous load of DeSilvo Tower from the hull of the station? Surely the hull had never been designed to take such stresses. How difficult and expensive had it been to strengthen it? Had they done the job properly?

The sunlight struck the forward pylons, and then the forward end of the Gondola. Instantly, the cool blue of their exteriors shimmered into gleaming silver as the smart glass shifted from transparent to full-reflective mode.

But even full-reflective mode couldn't keep all the light out. Even if one percent of full-strength raw sunlight percolated through the glass hull of the pylons and the Gondola, that would represent a massive heat influx. Koffield couldn't even begin to guess at the energy cost for the Gondola's environmental control system.

Even assuming all that glass was tempered and insulated, and blocked nearly all the unwanted raw sunlight, an air-filled glass box like that would absorb and retain a tremendous amount of heat. And of course they had to keep the interior at an even temperature when the tower went into shadow. Perhaps they actually had to create heat to keep an equilibrium. The cooling and heating problems had to be enormous.

No wonder the station's air and thermal regulation were out of whack. The basic station structure had a solid, totally opaque, heavily insulated hull, in a shape that was relatively easy to heat and cool efficiently. Its environmental systems didn't have to be very large or powerful in relation to the station's size, and they could take advantage of economies of scale. The exterior structures weren't big in comparison to the entire station, but they had to be drawing on the environment systems out of all proportion to their size. The strain of keeping the Gondola and the other towers comfortable must have put a strain on resources long before the first refugees showed up.

Madness, from start to finish, but not in the least bit surprising, given everything else he had seen and learned so far. Perhaps even predictable, as depressing as that notion was.

The glittering six-sided jewel that was the Gondola loomed ever closer, until the car slipped down into the upper deck of the place. All of them blinked and widened their eyes, straining to make their eyes adjust to the sudden drop in illumination.

They had arrived at the Gondola, at a place that had no business existing to begin with.

Elber Malloon sat by his campfire, holding little Zari in his lap, and stared at the entrance to the Gondola elevator by the big viewport, the viewport they wouldn't let him use anymore. He had watched them come, and then he had watched them go. And now he stared at their point of departure, as if memorizing the place where they had exited would help fix them in his mind.

The young, hard-featured man in the Station Services uniform he had seen before. The young man had come and gone several times, ferrying these or those dignitaries or specialists through on the official tour of inspection, the scheduled viewing of the gluefeet. That one, he dismissed from his thoughts.

But his passengers this time, the older man with the military bearing, and the young woman with him—they were different, very different from the officials who came and stared, as if gluefeet were merely some odd species of animal life kept penned up for study.

Part of it was the shock on their faces. They were surprised. They had not seen this before, or heard about it, or had any expectations about it. Everyone else who came through on the free-runners was either a bored bureaucrat like the young hard-featured man, tired of seeing it all, struggling to turn a blind eye to what was right in front of him, or else they arrived on the scene with their minds made up. They were angry, or horrified, or dripping with sympathy, long before they got to Ring Park.

Not these two. They were astonished by what they saw.

But there was something more. It was not until his wife returned with their food rations, and he saw the look on her face, that it came to him. That look. No doubt he wore the same expression himself. That was the whole point. "It was the strangest thing," Elber said to Jassa as she sat down next to him. "Two more uppers just went by on the tour."

"What's so strange about that?" she asked, taking Zari from him. "They come and look at us all the time."

"Nothing," said Elber. "But it was the looks on their faces. They were uppers, all right, posh, clean clothes. They'd been fed okay—maybe a little thin and pale, but not much. And the free-runner's driver treating them right. Uppers, for sure. But—but the looks on their faces. They were like us. Like *us*."

Jassa looked at him and frowned. "What do you mean, 'like us'?"

"Those two. You could see it, in their faces, in their eyes, even from far off. Shocked, and scared, surprised—

and something more. It was there in their eyes to see. They'd lost everything, been lost to all, and got dropped into a new world they didn't know.

"Those two," he said again. "They were as lost and far from home as we are. Maybe more."

CHAPTER SEVENTEEN

CHAMBER OF THE CONJUROR

Sparten led them briskly through the glittering upper lobby and directly under the hexagonal overhead viewport. Norla had only the briefest of chances to look up at the massive bulk of SCO Station looming overheard. Even then, she had to break into a trot to catch up with the other two, nearly stumbling in the noticeably higher gravity. She had forgotten how much of a nuisance variable gravity was aboard a spinning station.

Directly below the overhead viewport was a circular open space in the deck, or floor, whatever one might call it here, with a low railing around it. The opening took up about half the space under the overhead viewport and was centered exactly under it. Norla looked down and saw a vast atrium, a great open space, circular in cross section. It extended five levels down. On each level below her there were people leaning on the railings, looking up or down or across, pointing things out to each other.

Norla looked straight down to the lowest level. She saw three wedge-shaped pools of still water, the barest of ripples ruffling their mirrored surfaces. She looked down into the pool directly beneath her, and spotted her own far-off reflection, framed by the view out the hexagonal overhead port above her. Down there in the still water, she could see the reflection of SCO Station looming up behind her. Between the water wedges were three walkways that met at a central circular dais, exactly in the center of the lowest level. Norla looked up, craning her neck to see SCO

Station overhead and figuring the sight lines. If one stood at that central dais on the lowest level, one could look straight up at the viewport in Ring Park through which Norla had seen the station.

Koffield glanced down at the atrium, but did not break stride. He kept right on, still with his secured container, and Sparten kept pace with him. Norla lingered at the railing for a moment longer, then hurried to catch up. She found them waiting for her in yet another elevator car.

This one was a more conventional sort of windowless box. She stepped inside, the door shut, and they proceeded down. No one spoke. As they moved still farther away from the axis of rotation, Norla's apparent weight increased still further, up to about three-quarters of Earth gravity. The sensation of getting heavier made it seem as if she were riding an elevator moving up, not down, leaving her more confused than ever by this inside-out, upside-down building. She watched the numbers on the display count down from *Upper Level,* to *5,* to *4, 3, 2,* and then *Main Level,* where the base of the atrium was. She expected the car to stop and the doors to open there, but instead it kept going. The display blanked out, as if the level they were going to had no name, no number.

The elevator came to a halt, and the door slid open. They stepped out, Norla going first.

She had only time to see they were in an office, with a man at a desk ahead and off to the left, before the fumes hit her. The pungent odor of burning leaves assaulted Norla's nose, and she blinked back sudden tears as a haze of smoke clawed at her eyes and throat. She sneezed twice, hard, then coughed violently.

All she could think of was that, somehow, the bad air caused by the refugee crisis had all somehow pooled down here, at the very base of the Gondola. Half-blinded by her tears, she turned back toward the elevator car. They had to get out of here, head back up, alert the life-support people—

"Sorry about that," a flat, laconic voice said. "I forget sometimes it hits some people pretty hard. Wait a sec while I jack up the air blowers and the scrubbers."

A low rush of cool, clean air enveloped Norla. She coughed once or twice more, then breathed easier.

She rubbed her eyes and blinked to clear them. The world blurred and shimmered before it settled down to reveal that the man behind the desk had stood up to face them. He glanced down at his desk and closed some sort of control panel, then looked back toward his visitors.

He was a round-faced, tough-looking, angry-looking man. Short, heavyset, almost squat. He was very dark-skinned and his scalp was utterly hairless. His eyes were brown, deep-set, and penetrating, the whites of his eyes oddly yellowed. He was scowling as he looked at them, but somehow Norla got the impression that it had nothing to do with them. A scowl was the expression that his face fell into naturally.

"Come on in," he said, and picked something up from a shallow container on his desk and stuck one end of it in the corner of his mouth. It was a brown cylinder about fifteen centimeters long and about a centimeter and a half wide. His face twitched, and the end of the cylinder glowed orange for a second. He took the thing out of his mouth, blew a stream of smoke out into the air, and put the thing back in his mouth.

Norla stared in fascination. She had heard of such things, but she had never actually seen anyone smoking a cigar before.

"I'm Commander Karlin Raenau," the man said. "They got me running this shop these days. Come on in and have a seat." Raenau glanced over at Sparten. "No need for you to hang around," he said. "You go get some real work done."

"Yes, sir," Sparten said, then saluted and withdrew. Norla watched as he stepped back into the elevator and the doors shut—and was startled to realize that the elevator shaft did not extend this far down. When the car rose into the ceiling, it left nothing behind but a blank spot in the floor in the center of the vast circular office. A ceiling hatch irised shut after the car was gone.

"He's a good boy, but he gets me nervous," Raenau said to no one in particular. Raenau sat back down behind his desk and gestured for Norla and Koffield to sit on the visitors' chairs facing him. Raenau regarded his guests thoughtfully and did not speak at first.

Norla took advantage of the moment to glance around the office. She began to realize that the vanishing elevator was far from the only strange feature of the place. The room was circular in its floor plan, half again as wide around as the main deck of the *Cruzeiro do Sul*. The ceiling was gunmetal grey, but the floor and walls were done in a single shade of flat matte silver. It was not until she noticed the faint image of a ship wheeling past under the floor and up one side of the wall that she realized the entire room, except for the ceiling, was made of adjustable-reflectance glass, smart glass, all of it cranked up to maximum opacity.

There was a woven decorative hanging, with an abstract pattern, suspended from a freestanding frame that stood behind her chair, where it was directly in Raenau's line of sight as he sat at the desk. What looked like a big decorative folding screen, with a fanciful pattern of swimming fish on it, stood to the side of the desk, opposite where the elevator car had been. It was too big an object, and too carefully positioned, in a spot too inconveniently close to the desk, for something just intended to be pretty. Norla guessed it was some sort of data display.

There was a thick, lush, intricately decorated carpet under Raenau's desk and the area in front of it, where she and Koffield sat. There were three or four groupings of furniture scattered about the open floor, each likewise with a decorative carpet beneath it, and with hangings or folding screens nearby. There was nothing actually hung from, or suspended from, the walls themselves.

The room seemed to take up the entire level of the building. There were no doors in any of the walls, and plainly there was nothing but stars and space beyond the opacified wall. Norla looked up into the ceiling and noted several other irised-shut hatches of various sizes. Some of the hatches were large enough to drop a compact kitchen or washroom into the room. Clearly the room was designed to be configured in a half dozen ways.

Big as the room was, it was nowhere as large across as

what she had seen of the upper levels of the Gondola. She realized that this one office was hanging off the underside of the rest of the structure all by itself, a blister set into the base of the deepest tower, with no way in or out but through the ceiling.

"Lots of toys in here," Raenau said, and Norla realized that he had been watching her as she looked around them. "I don't ever use them much. I needed a place to work, and they gave me a button-pusher's playground."

"That's all adjustable-reflectance glass, isn't it?" Norla asked, gesturing at the floor and walls.

"Multiglass, that's right. Hardly ever use that at *all*. Wanna see?"

Before either of them could answer, Raenau stabbed his finger down on a button and twisted a knob.

The lights died, dropping the chamber into utter blackness. Then the floors and walls faded away into nothing at all. Norla cried out in surprise and alarm. Even the unflappable Anton Koffield let out a faint gasp of surprise. Norla closed her eyes tight, held the arms of her chair in a death grip, and forced herself to calm down. She let go the arm of her chair and slowly opened her eyes, looking straight ahead at Raenau.

Or at least where Raenau should have been. There was nothing there but a small, faint dot of orange that flared and faded, flared and faded. Then she realized it was the end of his cigar, the ember glowing as he puffed on it.

She looked down, at the black outline of the carpet, and the planet swooping past it down below. The stars wheeled past, and a small orbital tug came into view. Norla stood up, swallowed hard, and walked toward the edge of the carpet, hesitated a moment, then stepped out onto the absolute nothingness beyond. She heard the click of her heels on the deck, and could feel the solidity of the deck under her. But for all of that, when she looked down she saw *nothing* there beneath her. She looked down between her feet and watched the universe, the stars, the planet, the darkness of the void wheeling past in stately procession.

She realized her hands were clenched into fists and

forced them to relax. She looked behind herself, at the decorative fabric on the frame, right where Raenau could see it from his desk. Now she understood the carpets and the carefully positioned hangings all around the room. Even when the glass was set at maximum opacity, there was a certain amount of see-through. No one wanted to see the ghost of the planet swooping past out of the corner of his eyes every couple of minutes. She noted there was no such hanging *behind* Raenau's desk. Either the man hadn't thought of it, or else he felt it would be to his advantage to have his visitors distracted.

Her eyes were slowly adjusting to the darkness. She looked around the room and saw the clusters of furniture on their carpets, seemingly hanging in midair. She looked down again, and watched as the orbital tug rolled back into view. She got her bearings, then looked out through the forward wall, at the fleet of ships, operational and derelict, that accompanied the station in its orbit. The room bloomed with light as the daylit planet swung past again.

Then the room lights came slowly up, though the walls and floor remained transparent. The people and objects in the room, which had been merely outlines and shadows, regained their solid forms. It was somehow stranger still to see brightly lit, real-looking objects seemingly suspended, motionless, in space.

Raenau stepped out from behind his desk and off the carpet onto the utterly transparent glass floor. He moved with a nonchalance that was a trifle overstudied, a sense of trying too hard to be casual about it.

He looked down at the stars beneath his feet and puffed thoughtfully on his cigar. "Here I am," he said, "master of all I don't survey."

"I beg your pardon?" Koffield asked. He still sat, composedly, in his chair, well over any momentary surprise or shock he might have felt when the floor vanished. An interesting note, that. Both Raenau and Norla had felt the need to prove themselves, demonstrate their courage, by stepping out into nothingness. Koffield had stayed put.

"Master of all I don't survey," Raenau repeated, and gestured downward with both hands. "I can quite literally see the whole universe from here, as the station rotates on its axis and orbits the planet. Sooner or later, every direction comes into view. The one thing I can't see, the one direction I can't look in, is toward the station I'm supposed to be running. *That's* always invisible. They built this office—the whole damn Gondola—mostly as a way of impressing people, for the psychological effect. Make it all look big and grand. Makes the symbolism of not being able to see it from here even stranger, don't you think?"

"To be frank," said Koffield, "I've been thinking on that and many similar points since the moment we came aboard. The Gondola is a shrine to the spirit of narcissism. It seemed to have been designed for the sole purpose of being looked at from different angles, built merely for the sake of being constantly admired."

Raenau nodded. "I don't know that the architect would *admit* any such thing, but it's probably true all the same."

"Who *was* the architect? I mean no offense, but it seems to me that the person who built the Gondola must have been extremely self-absorbed, and yet extremely self-unaware."

Raenau laughed out loud, took the cigar from his mouth, and held a most theatrical finger to his lips, signaling for silence. "Careful who hears you say that," he said in a loud stage whisper. "The Gondola and DeSilvo Tower are based on sketches left behind by the great Dr. Oskar DeSilvo himself."

"That," said Koffield, "does not surprise me in the least."

Raenau chuckled to himself once again and walked back to his desk. He sat down and twisted a knob on the recessed control panel. The nothingness, the stars and the sky under Norla's feet, faded away into the dull silver of the solid floor. If she looked very carefully, and very closely, she could still catch a glimpse of the brightest objects as they rolled past, but it wasn't easy.

Quite suddenly, she realized how foolish she must have

looked, standing there peering down at the floor between her feet. Blushing with absolutely pointless embarrassment, she returned to her own chair and sat down.

"Damned translucent walls," Raenau growled. "They drive me nuts. It's the same everywhere, in all the private areas on the Gondola. Everyone moves in, twittering about the view, the view, the view—and then they realize they can't stand having the universe wheeling past every minute of the day. The place is built for the sake of the views—and we've all put up shutters and screens and hangings to block it out."

Raenau stubbed out his cigar in the dish-shaped receptacle—an ashtray, that's what it was called—and pulled a box out of a drawer on his desk. He opened it and took another cigar from it. He was on the verge of putting the box back when he hesitated for a moment. Norla hoped that the man had realized how rude it would be to light another of the damned noxious things in front of guests, and would therefore put them away.

But Raenau's hesitation had another motive, albeit one still couched in manners. "Sorry," he said. "I should have offered these"—he held the box up—"to you people. I don't suppose either of you would care for a cigar?"

"No, thank you," Norla replied, hoping her tone wasn't too vehement. "I don't, ah, smoke."

"Hardly anyone does," Raenau said sadly. "Admiral Koffield? How about you?"

Norla had been expecting a refusal as firm as her own, if perhaps a more diplomatic one. Instead, Anton Koffield got a strange, faraway look in his eye. "I haven't had a proper cigar in twenty years subjective," he said. "Nearly a century and a half, objective time."

"Cuban," said Raenau, offering the box to Koffield. "Not Cuban seed grown twenty light-years from Earth, or Cuban-made from Texas leaf, or any of that nonsense. The real thing." The tone of his voice made it plain he was trying to tempt Koffield, but extolling the virtues of Cuba meant nothing to Norla.

"How the devil could you get true Cuban cigars out

here?" Koffield asked, standing up and taking the box. He opened it and examined the contents with an expression that was almost reverent.

"Let's just say I have friends in low places. And shipping techniques have improved some while you've been, ah, out of circulation."

Koffield selected a cigar and handed the box back to Raenau, who put it carefully away. Koffield held the cigar under his nose and sniffed deeply, then held it to his ear and seem to *listen* to it for some reason, as he rolled it between his thumb and forefinger. Raenau produced a complicated looking small gadget from his jacket pocket and handed it to Koffield, who used it to snip the end off the cigar. Raenau produced a second device from the same pocket, and Koffield had to puzzle over it for a second, before he got it to create a small jet of flame. He put the cigar in his mouth and played the fire from the flame-maker over the far end of the cigar, while studiously sucking in his breath through the cigar.

It took a good long while for this process to get the thing lit and burning to Koffield's satisfaction, and then, of course, Raenau had to repeat the entire procedure in order to get *his* cigar going.

It was plain that there was some sense of ritual about the whole thing, that Koffield had gained a lot of points with Raenau simply by understanding what to do, and because he appreciated the dubious pleasure of inhaling toxic fumes. Just as with making the floor vanish, the cigars had been a test. Of what, exactly, Norla was not sure—but it was clear that Koffield had passed with flying colors.

"I don't wish to be rude," Norla lied. She damned well *did* want to be rude, to both of them. "But you did wish to see us urgently, and we have traveled quite a long way to get here, on what Admiral Koffield said he thought were important matters. Perhaps we could begin?"

"You're right," said Raenau. "Let's get on with it, and get that agenda cleared. I guess I just wanted to enjoy the moment, now that you two finally made it on in. I don't know if you two realize it, but this moment, right now, marks the end of a mystery that's lived on for a very long time. And I get to be the one who hears the answer first."

"I've afraid we've got some bad news on that score, Commander Raenau," Koffield replied. "When we left her, no one aboard the *Dom Pedro IV* had any idea what went wrong, or how the ship malfunctioned. Nor do we understand how she could have made it here at all."

"No, no, you misunderstand me," Raenau said. "What made your ship malfunction isn't the mystery I care about, though others do. *You're* the mystery that interests me. You, and the message we think you sent."

"What's so special about us?" asked Chandray. "We were aboard a ship that never arrived, and we're certainly not the first ship that's happened to."

"True enough." Raenau shrugged. "There's no one good reason I can give you for it. Some cases get famous, and others don't. Something is strange enough, or bizarre enough, to seize the imagination. People invent conspiracies, or concoct explanations. There's a strange detail that intrigues someone. A rumor, a story, takes on a life of its own. Something gets blown out of proportion. Probably the *Chrononaut VI* never coming back, and because Pulvrick died before she could deal with the message. Anyway, there's a whole legend—a whole series of legends—that's grown up around the loss of the *Dom Pedro IV*."

"So we're famous?" Norla asked, amused by the idea.

Raenau hesitated, obviously not quite sure how to reply.

Koffield spoke into the silence. "Give it to us straight, Commander. Don't be polite about it. We need information more than courtesy. If we're supposed to be monsters with ten-centimeter fangs, tell us."

Raenau looked at Koffield in mild surprise. "Strange that being notorious is what you thought of first. Do you have a guilty conscience?"

Norla would have been fascinated to hear his answer to that question, but Koffield did not reply.

Their host laughed and went on. "Well, who doesn't have something to feel guilty about? But I can tell you it's nothing like that. Well, maybe with some people, the Glister refugees' descendants, it is, but never mind that."

Norla was more than a little taken aback to hear Raenau mention Glister, but Koffield revealed nothing. She wanted to take the bait, and there was something in Raenau's expression that told her he wanted to be asked, but now was not the time or place. There were other things they needed to know about. "Let's just stick to the point, Commander," she said. "We don't know much of anything. What is it you're trying to say? Who's Pulvrick, and what about the *Chrononaut*?"

"Of course. You don't know it. My apologies. Short and sweet: The disappearance of the *Dom Pedro IV* used to be well-known. It isn't really, these days. You're not famous any*more*. These days, you're part of an old story that most people know just a little bit about. People know there's a legend, or a mystery, but they don't know exactly what it is. Things have gotten mixed up and forgotten. I'm sure your arrival will spark a new flurry of interest, but I've dug around in the records enough to know that the versions of the story best known to the general public are way off the mark. I had to do a lot of homework before I understood the situation well enough to suit myself."

Koffield smiled. "You make it sound as if you've been expecting us for some time."

"That's a fact," Raenau said. "I have been. I'm one of those guys who *has* to know things. And you people have been driving me nuts every day since I took on this job. And every other poor bastard who ever held this job. You've been staring us all in the face."

"How could that be?" Norla demanded.

Raenau flipped open a panel on his desk and punched a few buttons. The image of swimming fish on the decorative folding screen by his desk vanished, the screen went black, and the upper half of the unit flashed up a text display instead.

"My daily agenda," Raenau said. "First item."

But Norla didn't need to have her attention drawn to it. It jumped out at her. All the other items on the screen were in normal-sized black or dark blue lettering. But the first item was displayed in bright red letters twice as tall as everything else. Even the shape of the letters for that first item was different. Everything else was in the same sort of ornate, fussy-looking type she had seen on most of the signs and placards around the station. But the first item was in the thick, blocky, simplified style of lettering they used aboard the *Dom Pedro IV* and the *Cruzeiro do Sul*. It read:

[EARTHSIDE STANDARD DATECODE 05FEB5213] TOP PRIORITY, PERMANENT STANDING ORDER, TO BE POSTED UNTIL COMPLIANCE: BE ON ALERT FOR ARRIVAL OF TIMESHAFT SHIP *DOM PEDRO VI*. ANY PASSENGERS ARRIVING FROM THAT SHIP TO BE CONDUCTED TO STATION MANAGER'S OFFICE AT EARLIEST CONVENIENCE. IF ANTON KOFFIELD ARRIVES, CONDUCT HIM AT ONCE TO MANAGER'S OFFICE AND ALERT MANAGER REGARDLESS OF TIME OR CIRCUMSTANCE. ATTACHED FILE WILL DECRYPT AT THAT TIME.

It struck Norla at once that the syntax of the instruction was relatively normal. Everything else on the board was in the same odd compuspeak Sparten had used.

" 'Posted until compliance,' " Raenau said. "I've been staring at those words since I took this job. So has every man or woman who's run this station since it was posted. Praise be, the great day dawns at last!"

"You couldn't erase the message?" she asked.

"Nope," said Raenau. "The station manager of the time, a woman by the name of Pulvrick, saw to that. I couldn't even change the typo and make it *Dom Pedro IV* instead of *Dom Pedro VI*. Probably they got it mixed up with the *Chrononaut VI*."

"Wait a second," Norla said. "Back up a little. We know something about the *Chrononaut,* but none of the rest of it."

"Sorry. I keep assuming you'd know this stuff, because it's all about you. Three days after the *Chrononaut VI* arrived in-system, Pulvrick told the station's artificial-intelligence system to burn that message"—he stabbed at the screen with his cigar—"into the station's core-memory systems. And every station manager since has had to see it every day."

"So why couldn't you just get rid of the message—or the system running it?" Norla asked.

"Because I don't really run this station," Raenau said "The station artificial-intelligence system does that. Has to be that way with a system as big as this station. The complexity of the station operation systems approach that of a human body. You can't yank out the brain and plug in a new one. You have to leave some systems running while you upgrade others. Backups in every subsystem, every sort of redundancy. I looked into it. There have been at least six replacements and fourteen major upgrades of the station's artificial-intelligence system in the last century And every generation of the station ArtInt has made sure that damned message popped to the top of the screen or the manager's schedule, no matter what."

"Pulvrick must have thought we had something important to say," Koffield said mildly.

"People have wondered about that, from time to time," Raenau admitted. "It was all the rage when the Glister refugees came in, back before I was born, and when I was just a kid. Not much anymore these days, of course, but there used to be a lot of theories floated about. It's always been assumed that the *Chrononaut* was carrying some sort of message from you, saying you were working on something big, or had vital news, or whatever, but no one's ever seen the message. *That's* what got people guessing. There were whole books just on that one subject, as a matter of fact. Have a look in the archives when you have a chance if you're interested." Raenau grinned suddenly. "But guess *you* know if there was a message, huh? I guess you don't have to read up on it."

Koffield looked intently at Raenau. "It's been *assumed* that I sent a message on the *Chrononaut*? Why assumed? How is it they didn't know? And if they didn't know, why did they speculate?"

Raenau pointed a beefy finger at the message display "Because of that. 'Attached file will decrypt.' It was posted three days after the *Chrononaut*'s arrival, and there's an encrypted file linked to it. Because of that, and because the message mentions you in particular, it's always been assumed that what Pulvrick had linked to that command was a message from you. People have tried to find it and crack it now and then, but the station's ArtInt was under orders to protect the message, and it always found ways to do it. Even the message's *location* in the memory storage system is encrypted."

"I did indeed send a message on the *Chrononaut* to the station manager—addressed to the office, as I had no idea who had the job. I never intended it to be kept secret," Koffield said. "Pulvrick should have unbuttoned the message once we were badly overdue."

"Right," said Raenau. "Except by then she was busy being dead. A bad virus ripped through the station, killed lots of people —including Pulvrick and most of her staff. And the *Chrononaut VI* never passed through the Solacian system again. It was years before anyone thought to track her down. She'd been sold for scrap by then, and the crew dispersed all over Settled Space. Just finding out that much took years. They traced one or two of the crew, but none of them knew anything. The captain was the one to talk to, but searching took a lot of time and money, and after a while, people gave up looking for him."

Koffield was staring straight at Raenau, and yet did not seem to see him at all. "Do you mean to say no one knows, no one in this star system has ever known, except this Pulvrick person, what was in my message?"

"Nope."

"For a hundred and twenty-seven years it's been in the station ArtInt's memory store, waiting for me to show up?"

"That's right. At least we think so. We *think* that when we give the ArtInt positive confirmation of your identity, it will deliver up the message. But we don't know for certain."

Koffield was plainly stunned. Of all the possibilities he had considered, this was clearly not one of them. "Then you don't know," he said. "You don't know."

"No, we don't," Raenau said. "And, well, I don't mean to be too hard-edged, but you two are quite literally history. Maybe that hasn't sunk in yet. Maybe your information was vital a hundred years ago, but, now, well—you're too late. The historians will want to talk with you, and I want to know myself, but, well—a long time has passed."

"If we're so unimportant, why did you bring us directly here?" Norla asked, a little belligerently.

"Didn't have much choice. Once your ship was identified as a lighter off the *Dom Pedro IV*, the station ArtInt systems started firing up every sort of alarm it had, insisting on compliance with its standing orders. Mind you, I was happy to cooperate. I want that message gone and my schedule board clear. Sick to death of staring at those big red words every morning. So—can we get you identified and get this over with?"

Norla was about to protest further when Koffield caught her eye and shook his head. "What we have to say, and what was in the message, are still quite important, Commander. Once you decrypt that message, and once I open this secured container, we'll prove that much."

"Hmmph. I suppose I have to admire your confidence, anyway. Lemme get the ArtInt into voice mode, and we'll get this done." He worked another of the controls hidden in his desktop.

A dull, expressionless, genderless voice spoke, coming from nowhere and everywhere in the room. "Voice mode, command systems, activated," it announced.

"I hate talking to this damned thing," Raenau growled. "Feel like I'm talking backwards to a smart-ass assistant who wants to show he's smarter than I am." He cleared his throat and spoke with exaggerated care. "Command ArtInt, receive command. Identity test, subject, seated in chair two. Compare results, standing orders, action list, item one, station manager schedule. Proceed."

"Subject, seated in chair two, state name, state personal identity phrase."

"Anton Koffield. 'I warn of things to come.' "

"Match, preliminary, formed. Stand by."

One of the ceiling portals, a different one than the one the elevator had used, irised open. A small wheeled equipment cart, held by a hydraulic arm, came down into the commander's office. The arm set the cart down and released it. It rolled toward Koffield and stopped in front of him.

"Fingerprint, blood sample, for DNA extraction, retinal scan," the dull voice announced. "Scanner-sampler active. Indicated slot, insert hand into, palm down." Koffield put his hand into the slot with far greater apparent willingness than Norla would have shown. She could see him flinch slightly, no doubt as the sampling needle drew its blood from a fingertip. "Hand to be withdrawn. Subject to stand by."

A second slot opened in the top of the cart, and a scanner mask raised itself up and out on the end of a telescoping arm. It positioned itself at eye level, a few centimeters from Koffield's head. "Face, press up against mask, eyes, align with scanners. Eyes open, looking straight ahead." Koffield obligingly leaned in close to the mask and pressed his face up against it. "Complete," the voice announced. "Identity, subject, established as Koffield, Anton. Standing orders, action list, item one, schedule, commander compared. Action, required, execute."

The cart withdrew. The arm came back down out of the ceiling, picked it back up, and withdrew. The ceiling port irised shut.

"It's gone," Raenau said, in a tone of wonderment and delight. "It's actually gone away."

He was, of course, looking toward the screen, and at the big blank space where the old-fashioned red letters had been for so long. The space on the screen was empty, and on Raenau's pugnacious face was the expression of someone who had just witnessed a miracle.

"Is the file there?" Koffield asked. "Did it decrypt the file?"

"Huh?" Raenau said, still all but transfixed by the sight of the message that wasn't there.

"The file. Has the ArtInt system released the decrypted file?" Koffield demanded. He was suddenly more alert, more animated than he had been a moment before.

"Oh! Yeah. Right." Raenau activated another screen, built into the top of his desk. "It's just coming in. Hell's bells, that thing must have been coded to the devil and back if it's taking this long to put it in clear."

"Very good," Koffield said. "What it says should match up with the files in here," he said, patting the secured container.

This is it, Norla told herself. Koffield needed that file to be there first, read first, before he could go further. If Raenau could match the encrypted file that had waited here all this time against the information Koffield delivered now, that would be prima facie evidence of the information's authenticity. No one would ever be able to claim it was planted or faked. Now he was ready. Now Koffield had come to the end of his long, long road. She could read it all in his face. A century late, perhaps, but now, at last, he was about to fulfill his self-appointed mission.

Koffield lifted the secured container up onto Raenau's desk, moving eagerly, hurriedly, nearly knocking over the ashtray that held his forgotten cigar. "The data in this secured container here will match what's in your file," he said. "Each will help prove the other is authentic."

"Hey! Careful you don't scratch my desk with that thing," Raenau warned, getting up out of his chair.

We're here to warn about the end of the world, and he's worried about his desktop. Norla found that she had to fight back a half-hysterical giggle.

"Your desk is perfectly safe, Commander," Koffield said with something close to sharp impatience. "It's your *planet* that is in danger. You need to examine the information in the file you have just decrypted, and the information I have in this container."

"Now wait a minute—"

"There is a two-page summary at the start of my message brought to you by the *Chrononaut VI*. Read it."

"I have got better things to do than—"

"My rank might be a hundred years out of date, but I am your superior officer. *Read it.* Now!"

Raenau stared at Koffield, and time froze for the space of a dozen heartbeats. Then, slowly, Raenau sat back down, stubbed his cigar out in the ashtray, and brought up the file on the display built into his desk. Norla watched him intently. It wasn't far from her mind that there were any number of ways for him to pull a stunt, to push a panic button and have armed guards drop out of the ceiling. But he did not. He sat, and he read, the glow of the display screen softly illuminating his expressionless face.

The room was silent, utterly still. Norla found herself holding her breath without knowing why. She forced herself to start breathing again. She stared at the station commander's face.

But Raenau was giving very little away. He frowned at one point and seemed to look back at something earlier on in the text before going forward.

At last he finished and shut off the screen. He sat there for perhaps half a minute, frowning down at the blank top of his desk. At last he spoke, still staring down at nothing at all. "My first instinct is to throw you both out of my office and have you locked away as a pair of lunatics," he said. "Your summary, Admiral Koffield, reads like a carefully reasoned, thoughtfully worked-out, hundred-year-old list of paranoid delusions and apocalyptic claptrap. I'm very much surprised Pulvrick took it seriously at all." He let out a weary sigh, then looked up at them. "Trouble is, everything predicted in your summary has come true. That makes it harder for me to think you're crazy. Not impossible. Just harder."

"Let me make it harder still," Koffield said. "Open this secured container, and then the case inside it. First detach the longwatch camera, and aim it so it can see what you're doing."

"This is what you do to help prove you *aren't* crazy?" Raenau asked. He glared at the impassive Koffield for a second, then shrugged. "All right. I'll go along with the gag. Quickest way to get this over with is to get this thing open and you out of here." He looked down at the secured container, saw how the longwatch camera was fastened, and removed it. He set it down on the opposite side of his desk so it would have a clear view of the proceedings, then turned his attention back to the secured container. "So how's this thing work? Not quite like what we've got these days."

"It's an open-once system," Koffield said. "Opening the main latches destroys the locking mechanism, so it can't be resealed. I believe there's a printed label by the latches, with instructions there."

"Ah, where—oh, okay, there it is." Raenau read over the instructions, then opened the seals and the latches, one by one. The container came open. He swung the lid open and revealed Koffield's personal pack, his Chronologic-Patrol-issue travel case. Raenau lifted it out, set it down on his desk, then took the now-empty secured container off his desk and put it on the floor. Norla could not help wondering if Raenau simply wanted more room to work, or if he was still concerned about marring the surface of his precious desk.

Koffield was visibly restraining himself, holding back from grabbing the travel case and opening it himself. But it would make infinitely more sense for Raenau to do the job. Koffield had done so much already to avoid any chance for trickery that it would be foolish to invent chances now. So long as he did not touch the travel case, there was no way anyone could ever invent a story about Koffield using some sort of sleight of hand to plant a newly written "prediction" of what had happened in the last hundred and twenty-seven years.

"Go ahead," Koffield said, his voice eager, his eyes bright. "Open it. Open it."

Norla stared at Anton Koffield, and for once the man was understandable. She could read his thoughts and feelings as clearly as if they were up on Raenau's display screen. It was the moment he had worked toward all along. Once his report was delivered to a high local official, and in such a way that no one could ever charge fraud, then the worst of the battle would be over.

"All right, all right," Raenau said. "I'm opening it." He broke the sealers on the personal pack, undid the latches, swung open the lid, and stared down at the contents.

The room was deathly silent for a time that could have been a single moment or a lifetime.

"Is this some kind of joke?" Raenau demanded. "Because I've got a station in crisis here. I've got no goddamned time for jokes and games."

Norla could see the age-faded, rust-stained interior

padding in the case, and the carefully carved-out niches in the padding that had been meant to hold books and datablocks.

But there were no datablocks, no books. Nothing but a melted, compressed-together, crumbly lump of ancient waste plastic and corroded scrap metal, no doubt put in the case to mimic the weight of the things taken out.

The report, the data files, the warning were gone, as lost as all the tens of thousands of yesterdays that had died since Anton Koffield had last closed his travel case.

CHAPTER EIGHTEEN

RUDE AWAKENINGS

Norla Chandray wandered the corridors of the Gondola, not knowing or caring where she went, so long as she did not return to her quarters. Her room was a tiny box of a place, but that was not the problem. She had lived half her life in space, in ships with all manner of small compartments. Small spaces did not bother her.

Her room had a massive wall-of-glass window that looked out on the stomach-turning gyrations of the universe spiraling past the station, but even that was not a problem. A space pilot had to be accustomed to disorienting views. Besides, she could always set the windows to maximum opacity and close the blinds that had so obviously been installed after the room was built, when it was discovered that the view drove too many visitors to distraction.

It was the sounds she could hear, and the sounds she might hear, that drove her away. Her quarters shared an obviously unsoundproofed wall with the next room over, where they had put Koffield. She had been with a shattered man when they left Raenau's office. Numb, lost, ruined.

It had been the quest, the crusade, the self-imposed mission that had propped him up and kept him going. It had kept him pushing forward in spite of all, and now it was gone. The task and duty that had been wrapped up into the center of his being had been reduced to nothing more than a crude practical joke, a travel case emptied out and weighted down for the amusement of some cruel and faceless stranger light-years away and a century in the past.

She had watched him stumble into his own room, plainly unaware of where he was or what was happening. She had gone into her own tiny room and looked out at the ships and stars wheeling past the darkness. And then she had heard the bumps, the thuds, from next door.

Maybe he was just been being a bit awkward opening up the fold-down furniture. Maybe he had tripped over something, or just slammed the bed open and then flung himself down on it a bit too hard, thrown off by the variable gravity.

Or maybe it had been the first sounds made by a man going to pieces. Maybe next would come cries of anguish, curses, shouts, sobs, or, even worse, a brooding, empty silence onto which Norla could write anything she wished. Would silence mean a man staring out into the infinity beyond the glass wall, contemplating his own doom, and perhaps the means of causing it to happen? Or would it mean Koffield was sitting down to work out a new plan, or write his report again? Or would it simply mean he had fallen asleep?

She did not want to know. Whatever sound or silence she heard from that room would be, at least to her, the most profound invasion of Koffield's privacy, and Koffield was the most private man she had ever met. Whatever torments he was feeling, he had no need for an audience, and she had no desire to be one.

And so, she had left. Now she wandered the glittering maze of corridors, the grand esplanades, the overdone public spaces of the Gondola, alone with her own losses, her own deprivations. This was not her world, or her time. All she had ever had, or had ever known, or ever done, and all the places she had ever been, were as lost to her as Koffield's precious report, drowned long ago in the ocean of years.

She felt herself adrift in that same ocean, and there was no safe harbor anywhere in sight. She felt half-drowned in time, adrift in the wrong world, the wrong lifetime, with no hope of rescue.

She found herself back on the upper deck of the Gondola, below the massive overhead observation port, standing by the atrium that opened out on the decks below. She leaned over the balustrade and stared down into the atrium and the people in the little park at its base. She caught a glimpse of herself, a tiny reflection in the mirror-perfect water in the pool below, with the massive bulk of SCO Station visible behind and above her, through the big overhead viewport.

She watched as a child knelt by the pool, stuck her hand in the water, and splashed it back and forth. The water-mirror warped and rippled and shimmered, and Norla watched as the image of her own reflection vanished into the suddenly chaotic surface below.

That was all it would take, she thought. A chance ripple on the water, a capricious act, here and now, or long ago and far away, and then the waters would close over her, swallow her up in that ocean of years, and it would be as if she had never been at all. A quirk of fate had thrown them a hundred years into the future. A sick mind had sent Koffield across the endless light-years carrying a sealed container full of recycling debris. What casual, cruel, deliberate act, what totally random chance, might utterly destroy them all at any time?

She turned away from the pool below, seeking a place where she would not see, or think, such things.

As he lay on his back on the bed, there was some part of Anton Koffield, some hunter's corner of his mind, that had noted the faint noises from the next compartment, and correctly interpreted them as Norla entering, then leaving, the room. There was even some tiny shred of his conscious self that guessed her motives, and was grateful.

But it seemed to Anton Koffield as if those tiny bits of awareness and rational thought were all but lost to view in a storm of shock, dismay, and disbelief.

how had it happened how had it happened how had it happened who did this who did this who did this why why why

The questions gibbered up from the base of his skull, and Anton slammed his hands over his ears in a futile attempt to avoid hearing the soundless cries of panic that came from inside him.

He let out a strangled moan and leapt to his feet. He kicked hard at the side of the bed, hard enough to set it swinging back up into its wall niche. He cursed loudly, so loudly that anger and frustration turned the profane words into little more than an incoherent howl of rage.

The warning he had struggled so long to construct was gone, stolen, lost in the depths of time. Millions of people, tens of millions, perhaps billions, here and on other worlds, would die if they did not get that warning.

He let it all out, let the emotions held in so long rip through him. He let the tears fall, let his arms wrap around his torso as if to ward off cold and danger, let himself slump to the floor and sit there, rocking back and forth, moaning.

He knew it had to come out, had to, or else he would go mad. The tiny bit of him that held on to rationality, that kept itself as a cool and careful observer, knew that rationality could not save him. He was drowning in a nightmare, and to struggle against it would only bring the end sooner. Only by giving way, by letting the nightmare work its will on his psyche, and then moving on, would he be able to survive.

Even as he sat, huddled in a corner, sobbing, rocking back and forth, crooning and moaning to himself, the cold, the hard, the determined scientist and tactician that was the core of Anton Koffield was operating by calculation.

Let the demons out.

Let them out, and then it will be time for you to move on, and fight and search again.

A mad figure whimpered in the corner of the room, and a sane mind waited for the madness to be over.

Raenau didn't realize at first that his cigar had gone out. That in and of itself would have been a sure sign, to anyone who knew him, of just how distracted he was.

But there was no one there to see. Raenau sat alone at his desk, in his absurd fishbowl of an office. The lights were low, and the chamber was deathly quiet. The recessed display screen set into his desktop had three or four items blinking, their priority codes flashing urgently. The screen built in the decorative room divider showed the same high-priority items, plus a dozen or more less pressing things.

Raenau saw none of the action items, saw none of the room, saw nothing at all.

Obviously the man was crazy. Brains must have frozen up for good in cryo. All that foolishness with the secured container. What the devil had he been playing at?

Maybe it was a hoax, a prank, a publicity stunt. Maybe the man was an impostor.

But if he had been a fake, the contents of that secured container would have been chock-full of all sorts of fascinating, believable information, instead of a decaying wad of compressed metal and plastic. Or was it all part of some deeper scheme, some wildly complex confidence trick that Raenau couldn't begin to unravel? But could that be?

Everything checked out, from the type, vintage, and serial number of the *Cruzeiro do Sul* to the retinal and DNA scans performed by Raenau's own equipment.

At last Raenau looked up, but only to see something that wasn't there. The blood-red, urgent notice that had glared down from the top of his action list, and from the action list of his predecessors for a century and more. Gone.

For a hundred and twenty-seven years, that message had shouted out that this man, this fossil marooned in the wrong century, was a person who should be heard. The red letters had urged generations of station managers to listen to Anton Koffield. Surely that was worth a certain degree of consideration.

Raenau worked his desk control and brought up a copy of the preliminary report Koffield had sent so long ago— or at least claimed to have sent. He scrolled through it one more time, though he barely needed to do so. He was close to having it memorized.

His office ArtInt controlled every copy of the report. Koffield had been too stunned even to think of asking for one. All Raenau had to do was enter a few commands and confirmations, and all the copies of the report, primary, backup, and tertiary, would be erased, purged. It would vanish as if it had never been.

It was a tempting thought. His hand moved toward the proper controls.

But damn all stars, it was too easy. Make the report go away, and pretend it never happened. Pretend things were as they should be. What sort of way to run things was that?

Pretending like that, generations of it, was what had gotten Solace into a mess in the first place. And, Raenau realized, he no longer wanted any part of the pretense.

He hadn't set his office walls and floors to full transparency for months, not until he had played his little games with Koffield and Chandray. Now he set them to clear for the second time in one day. The silver walls faded away, and the stars and the skies and the wounded world of Solace revealed themselves to Karlin Raenau.

He stood up and walked thoughtfully around his desk, to the edge of the thick carpet that surrounded it, and stepped out onto the solid nothingness of the floor itself. He had made a show of standing on nothing in front of Chandray and Koffield, but it had taken all his nerve to do it without seeming to be bothered.

Now, with no audience to play to, it was even harder. But Raenau was somehow certain he had to stand here on his own. He had to look down, to see what was there. He had to face it, and not pretend.

The universe rolled past beneath his feet. Once, twice, three times, the face of Solace wheeled past, and he looked on her, and forced himself to *see* what was there, and not look away, or tell himself that it was minor, was temporary, would heal.

He thought of all his trips to the surface, and what he saw when he let himself see what was honestly there. The stands of dying trees. The weed-choked parks overrun with destructive insects. The fields where no bird sang. The farms populated by spindly-looking cattle and undersize poultry.

Solace wheeled once more out of sight, and Raenau looked up into the black ceiling full of clever machinery and hidden devices. In his mind's eye, he saw his own domain. The station itself, forever hidden, always invisible from the office from which it was run.

"Master of all I don't survey," Raenau whispered to himself. "Ruler of all I don't see." The joke wasn't funny anymore. In his imagination, he swept away the madly extravagant Gondola, all of DeSilvo Tower, and saw the station itself. There she was, cluttered with the wealth of trade, commerce, industry, and yet overrun by the poor and desperate. He saw the jewel of Ring Park hidden by the smoke and dirt of the gluefeet, the refugees, the *people* who had fled something worse.

And if Solace was not in trouble, what the hell were all those people running from?

Damn all stars, but there it was. Maybe Koffield was insane. Maybe he was even a fraud, putting over an incredible con job by means and for reasons Raenau could not even imagine.

But, for all of that—Koffield was *right*. The planet was dying, and dying almost exactly on the schedule predicted by Koffield's preliminary report.

And *that* was the thing they all had to see. Raenau, Neshobe Kalzant, Jorl Parrige, the scientists on Greenhouse, everybody.

Karlin Raenau returned to his desk and sat down. A cover letter, an introduction. He had to attach something to Koffield's report to explain what it was and where it had come from.

It was something to work on, something to *focus* on.

Raenau noticed at last that his cigar had gone out. He relit it carefully, and then set to work, puffing on his smoke as he did.

Anthon the Terrible.

Yuri Sparten's eyes snapped open, and he sat bolt upright in bed. *Anthon the Terrible.* Of course. Every Glistern refugee, every descendant of folk from Glister, knew that name. Parents used it to frighten their children into behaving. Do as you're told, or Anthon will come for you tonight. There was even a nursery rhyme.

> Terrible Anthon closed up the sky
> Horrible Anthon made Glister die
> Closed up the sky, made Glister die,
> Made Glister die, no ship could fly
> Hideous Anthon closed up the sky

Anthon was a boogeyman, a monster made half from muddled history and half from legend. Yuri hadn't ever considered Anthon as anything more than that. Anthon was a piece of folklore, the past. Never had Yuri thought of Anthon as a real flesh-and-blood man.

Until today.

Anthon was a common name in Settled Space, and one with many cognates and local variants. Antonio, Anthonius, Nathan—and Anton. In similar vein, there were lots of Kerfields, Kolfeldts, Colfelts, and so on out there. Neither name, in any variant, was used among the Glistern community, of course. Not anymore.

But, throughout Settled Space, variants of a given name were often altered to match local usage, customs, and spellings. Histories tended to follow local variants.

Yuri got out of bed and went to his desk. He activated the reference links and searched the Glister history files.

Anthon the Terrible, see *Kolfeldt, Anthon.*

It could still be chance. Coincidence. He had to check more closely. He ran a further search and starting working through the results.

Yuri flitted impatiently from one reference page to another, starting down two or three blind alleys, discussions of the events, rather than the man behind them. At last he came to a brief biography of the man himself.

> *Kolfeldt, Anthon.* var. sp. for Koffield, Anton.
> Officer, Chronologic Patrol, final rank achieved,
> reserve rear admiral . . .

But Yuri read no more. A picture had come up with the bio, a head-and-shoulders shot, a slightly overenhanced, grainy, contrasty image from somewhere or other. A picture of the man who, thirteen decades ago, had stranded the ships whose loss had meant the immediate failure of a dozen terraforming projects, because the equipment and supplies to save them was destroyed along with the ships. The man who had prevented the rescue of thousands of innocents by destroying the ships that would have carried them.

A picture of the man who thus caused the ultimate collapse, five decades after the stranding, of Glister's entire ecology.

A picture of the man he had welcomed aboard the station not twelve hours before.

Milos Vandar tossed and turned in his bed, and moaned in his sleep. He dreamed of his work, of Lake Virtue and the fight against the algae. Some sort of buoy floated on the lake, ringing out with an echoing *bong, bong, bong* as it rocked back and forth. Milos was in the water, in the lake, somehow, fighting against the algae. He pushed it back, forced it away.

But the algae mats were fighting back, determinedly pounding their way back into the parts of the lake he had chased them out of. There was, somehow, a wall in the water. It was behind him, just out of sight, always behind him, no matter how he turned and looked behind himself. Somehow, the biggest algae mat had formed itself into a fist, a club, and was pounding against the wall.

Far off, above him, on the surface of the lake, he could still hear the sepulchral tolling of the buoy-bell, ringing its warning over and over. The wall he could not see was weakening, splitting open, and the killer algae that had choked all the life out of Lake Virtue were about to burst through it, pounding on his apartment door and leaning hard on the annunciator, just about ringing it off the wall, and the neighbors were bound to hear it, soundproofing or no soundproofing. . . .

Milos Vandar swam up from the depths of his dream-lake,

from the depths of sleep, toward the surface of wakefulness and a damnably loud pounding on his door. The annunciator went off again, and its mournful *bong, bong bong* echoed through the apartment. Milos swore to himself and made a mental note, not for the first time, to adjust the annunciator, and have it make some more cheerful sound than that. Every time it went off, it made Milos think of funerals.

He stumbled out of bed, found a lounging cloak to drape over himself, and walked, a bit unsteadily, toward the door. Whoever was pounding on it seemed to think something was dreadfully urgent. Probably some lab assistant in a panic because a sample had gone bad. He resisted the urge to mutter something along the lines of "all right, all right, I'm coming." No point in it, considering how thick the door was and how much noise his visitor was making out there.

He palmed the lock plate and the door slid out of the way. Milos was surprised and alarmed to find, not a panicked grad student, but a beefy-looking pair of men in severe-looking dark grey uniforms. Milos did not recognize their insignia.

"You're Milos Vandar," the larger of the two men said, as if that in and of itself was crime enough to justify arrest. "Come with us. Now."

"What?"

"You're to come with us. Now."

The bigger man took Milos by the arm, and pulled him forward. Not enough to hurt or enough to knock Milos off his feet, but just enough for Milos to know the other man's strength, and what he could do if he chose.

"But—I—it's—" Milos tried to speak, but could not find the words.

"Ease up, Wint," the smaller man—though he was only slightly smaller—said, speaking for the first time. "Let him at least get dressed first."

"Yes, please," Milos said. "Let me at least get dressed." Astonishing. He had heard of the ancient game of good cop, bad cop many times, and here it was. Even knowing it was, or at least probably was, just a trick, a way to intimidate him, it was still working on him.

"All right," Wint said in a grudging tone of voice, as if letting a man put his pants on was a vast concession, something that went against all his principles. "But make it fast. And keep an eye on him." He let go of Milos's arm and gestured for him to get moving.

"I, ah, ah, keep my clothes in the bedroom closet," Milos said apologetically, as if he knew it was rude of him not to keep a change of clothes handy there by the door, for the convenience of any secret-police arrest team that happened to stop by in the middle of the night. "I have to go get them."

"Go with him, Syd," Wint told his companion. "Watch him."

It was not until Milos had dressed himself, been led outside, and none-too-gently ushered into his visitors' waiting vehicle that it dawned on him to wonder what it was all about. No doubt that was part of their standard technique as well—keep the subject, or victim, as off-balance as possible. Get him to feel intimidated, and he won't have courage enough to cause you any trouble.

By the time he had recovered himself enough to ask what was happening, it was far too late. The two police officers—if they were police officers—sat impassively in the aircar, Wint next to Milos, and Syd in the forward, rear-facing seat. It was obvious neither of them was going to answer questions. Milos found he did not have the courage to ask them anything, in any event.

The military-grade aircar, its windows fully opacified, its blast shutters down, lifted off and flew out of the covered parking area by Milos's house, and on toward wherever it was going. The ever-present rain commenced banging and rattling off the roof of the car the moment it cleared the carport and flew off into the dark, but Milos barely noticed. His fearful imagination was too busy launching out on journeys of its own.

He remembered the stories of what had happened on planets that had gone through bad ecocrises—Go-Down, Glister, Far Haven, and even, in the dim past, Earth herself.

The same pattern held on the big habitats and domed colonies, for that matter. When the physical climate went to hell, the political climate deteriorated as well. When things started to go seriously wrong, sooner or later someone would decide the situation called for stern measures, powerful leadership, harsh discipline. In short, dictatorship. Arrest the dissidents, or better still, shoot the scientists, the messengers who brought the bad news.

Had it started here? Had he said something, found something, proved something that the authorities did not like? Was he the only one, the first one to be swept up? Or were the skies full of aircars like this one tonight, flitting back and forth between the homes of the innocent and the headquarters of whoever it was who had just retroactively declared thinking or speaking certain things to be crimes?

All questions he dared not ask. Milos rode in silence and waited for the trip to be over, and the nightmare to begin.

The aircar pitched its nose down and decelerated. They were about to arrive at their destination, wherever that was. It hadn't been a long trip. Was that a good sign, or not?

The deceleration stopped. As best as Milos could tell, the car had gone into a stationary hover. Then there was a shift in the low hum of the aircar's engines, and Milos felt the car moving slowly forward. The sound of the rain on the car roof faded away, and the timbre of the engine sound changed. They were in a covered, enclosed space, a garage or hangar of some kind, inside whatever sort of compound or complex it was.

Milos wondered if he had already seen his last of the outside world. Were they about to bundle him into some dark interior cell, never to be allowed to emerge?

Wint checked a status panel, nodded, and punched the open code into the door lock. The car door clamshelled up and out of the way, and Wint the bad cop stepped out. Milos followed, somewhat hesitantly, with Syd, the good cop, urging him on.

They were in a gloomy, anonymous, completely undistinguished covered parking garage for aircars. There were dozens just like it throughout the city. The place was utterly empty except for Milos, his guards, and the car that had brought them. A few lights gleamed here and there, and directory signs pointed to upper and lower levels. If there were any clues to his whereabouts to be gleaned from small details, Milos was far too distracted and disturbed to take any notice of them.

Wint and Syd gave him very little time to take in his surroundings. They immediately marched him off toward a passenger lift a few steps from where the aircar sat. The doors closed the moment they were inside, and the car started moving at once, without anyone pushing a button or speaking a command.

The lift car moved up, and that gave Milos at least some hope. They were not taking him down to any subterranean bunker. Up was good. Up at least meant the hope of windows and light.

Or else, of course, it meant nothing at all. Milos abandoned his effort to find meaning. Short ride or long ride, elevator up or down—such things were meaningless with no context. No sense guessing in the absence of data. He would know more soon enough—unless, of course, they never told him anything at all.

The lift came to a halt, the doors opened, and the three of them stepped out into a distinctly unsinister corridor. The lights were at a dim setting, and it was difficult to make out the placards on the doors. The two guards ranged themselves on either side of Milos, each holding him by a forearm. They led him down the hallway toward a pair of larger double doors that retracted into the walls before he could read the lettering on them.

They swept through a reception area and down an interior hallway. The guards stopped at a certain door that slid open at their approach. They shoved Milos into the room. The door slid shut behind him, leaving the guards in the corridor.

Milos was alone in a small, windowless box of a room. Even in his disoriented and terrified state, it was plain to him that the room had never been intended as a cell, or a prison. It had more of the look of a never-used storeroom, or perhaps a work cube for a low-ranking office drone.

But rooms had been put to uses other than those intended, now and again. Perhaps all the proper cells were already full to bursting, and the coup leaders were forced to use whatever rooms they could find to hold their numberless prisoners.

There was a plain, slightly battered-looking worktable in the center of the room, and two equally battered metal chairs, one positioned to face the door, the other facing the opposite way. For want of anything else to do, Milos sat down in the chair that faced the door. He folded his hands together on the tabletop and stared at the door, waiting for someone, anyone, to show up and tell him what was going on.

He did not have long to wait. Ten minutes after his arrival, the door slid open and then shut behind a thin, almost emaciated-looking man who stood there, staring at Milos. The newcomer was holding a flat-read panel in his hand. He had a strange expression on his face, almost as if he had caught Milos breaking some sort of rule, and was deciding whether or not to call him to account for the infraction. There was something familiar about him. He looked as if he belonged in the background, rather than front and center. Milos felt certain he had seen him in the back of a crowd, or with someone else.

"There you are, Dr. Vandar," the man said, as if he had been looking all over for him, and Milos had kept him waiting. "So glad you finally got here."

Milos looked at the man. He had come up against his sort many a time in the past—a petty functionary who worried about the rules more than the point of the rules. Milos had learned the hard way that the best way to deal with such people was to let them think they'd won. Quite automatically, he sat up straighter, took his hands off the table, and tried to look suitably apologetic. "I'm afraid I didn't know I was expected."

The newcomer looked irritated, and the lines of his face fell naturally into the expression. "How much did they tell you? The men who collected you and brought you here?"

"Nothing at all."

"You don't know why you're here?" the man asked, sitting down in the other chair at the table. It was plain from his attitude that he had seen Milos before and expected to be recognized. The two of them had met, and recently. Milos dared not risk insulting the man by asking who he was.

Milos shook his head hopelessly. "No. Perhaps something about my work met with your—disapproval?"

"Disapproval? On the contrary. You're here because of the high quality of your work at Lake Virtue." Suddenly, the light went on. Milos knew who his inquisitor was. Aither Friable—no, Fribart, that was it. Fribart, Jorl Parrige's assistant. Once he thought back to that day, Fribart fell into place in his memory. The assistant, the spear-carrier, the one at the back of the crowd.

What the devil was a nonentity like Fribart doing in the middle of a palace coup? And what did Lake Virtue have to do with it? What would a coup want with biologists? "Has—has Senyor Parrige taken over?" Milos asked.

"I beg your pardon?"

"Is it a takeover? A coup? Has your—ah, boss—taken over? Was he the one who ordered me to be arrested, or brought in, or whatever you want to call it?"

Fribart now looked not only annoyed, but confused. "Coup? Arrest? I don't know what you're talking about. I sent two men around to ask you to come down here and give us your opinion on an urgent matter, that's all."

"I see," Milos said, though he was far from clear on the situation. Either Fribart was being disingenuous in the extreme, or else there was a lot going on in Parrige's name that Fribart—and Parrige—did not know about. But at least it seemed there was no coup, and it was seeming a great deal more likely that Milos would be able to walk out of the room a free man. "The men who didn't arrest me likewise didn't tell me about any such urgent matter," he said.

"They had no knowledge of it," Fribart said impatiently. "But let us not get lost in side issues. Are you willing to help us or not?"

Milos Vandar thought of himself as a mild-mannered and reasonable person. But he also imagined that he had something of a spine—especially when facing a jumped-up bureaucrat, rather than the secret police. "You make it sound like you've asked nicely a dozen times already," he said. "What's really happened is that the two thugs you sent out woke me up, dragged me out of bed, scared the hell out of me, and brought me here without telling me where I was going or why. Then you come in and bite my head off for not performing a service you haven't even asked for. I don't call that the best way to convince me to help you. So unless you can do better, I'll be on my way."

He began to stand, and was already halfway out of his chair before Fribart spoke in a flat, hard voice. "Sit down, Vandar," he said. "Now."

"I have no intention of—"

"Dr. Vandar. *Please*. Sit down." An odd change came over his host. Fribart shuddered, visibly, and it was as if a wall had been knocked down, a wall of official conduct and hard-edged rules and disapproval of all nonregulation behavior. Behind all that, Fribart's face took on an expression, and his voice took on emotion, that had not been there before. Quite suddenly, Milos was looking at and listening to, not an annoyed clerk with too much power, but an intelligent, frightened, *alarmed* human being. "Please," Fribart said again. "Please accept my sincere apologies for your treatment tonight, but I must insist you stay and hear me out. Afterward, you can do what you like." Fribart gestured toward Vandar's chair, and waited until Milos was seated again.

"All right," Milos said, "talk."

Fribart paused for a moment before he went on. "There's an old saying, Dr. Vandar, that says you should never attribute to malevolence anything that could be caused by incompetence. Tonight we've gone one better. Please, I ask you—don't attribute to incompetence actions that were caused by blind panic. Something's come up. Something that's scared the living daylights out of everyone who has seen it. That is, I'm sure, why they pulled you in like a common criminal. The people who gave them their orders—including me—were scared silly, and made the mistake of letting it show."

He put the flat-read panel on the table, but did not take his hand off it. "SCO Station sent down this report about five hours ago. You're not alone. We've pulled in people from half a dozen disciplines to examine every angle on it. Linguistics people to match writing style. Nav and ballistics and ships' captains to see if this ship, the *Dom Pedro* whatever-number-it-is, could really have made the flight she's supposed to have made. ArtInt people to confirm that the report has been left unaltered since it was put in encrypted storage. We're checking every angle we can think of on it."

"On *what*?" Milos demanded. "Tell me what this is about."

Fribart looked at Milos and sighed wearily. "It's a complicated story, but what it boils down to is this: This report is supposed to be from over a hundred years ago. Maybe it is, maybe it isn't. Other people are checking that part of it out. In any event it was opened and read by the SCO Station commander today. It predicts the last hundred or so years of the history of the terraformed Solacian environment, and its current state, with alarming accuracy. More alarming still because of what it says will happen in future. What we need you to check is the science. The report describes the methodology used to derive the predictions. It involves some highly complex math, and specialized knowledge. The report, I might add, discusses further proofs and more detailed methodology that the writer would bring with him. Those proofs and details have been lost. This report is all we have, and all we're going to have. We need you to look at it and tell us if it's for real. Tell us if the math and the science and theory are legitimate, or just real-sounding fakes. Because unless they *are* frauds, this planet is in trouble."

Fribart shoved the flat-reader across the table toward

Milos and pulled his hand away from it sharply, as if he had been eager to cease touching it and was glad to get rid of it. And with that, whatever had changed in Fribart, changed back. The walls went back up, and the human personality was lost to view again. Whatever it had cost him to let down his shields, he did not choose to leave them down for long. "So," Fribart said, his voice back to its old tone of aggrieved bureaucratic virtue, "does all that meet with your definition of a *damned-good reason*?"

"Yeah," Milos replied. "Yeah, I guess it does." He took up the flat-reader, reluctant to take it up, just as Fribart had been glad to get rid of it.

He started to read.

SOLACE

CHAPTER NINETEEN

VIEW FROM A DIAMOND

"And that brings us to the last point," said Wandella Ashdin.

"Very good," said Neshobe. She was more than glad to hear the end was in sight. Ashdin was supposed to be a superb historian and researcher, but her technique for giving a report—if such massive disorganization could be dignified with the term *technique*—was enough to drive anyone to distraction.

"Yes," Ashdin said in vague reply. "The last point. Admiral Koffield reported Dr. DeSilvo's temporary death by heart failure. Now let me see . . . ." Neshobe Kalzant, and indeed everyone else in the room, watched with ill-disguised impatience as Wandella Ashdin searched through her excessively copious notes once again. "Yes. Here we are. Insofar as confirming Admiral Koffield's bona fides, it is a very useful detail. It dovetails very neatly with what we know of Dr. DeSilvo's movements and activities during that time, and indeed fills in one of the major lacunae in our knowledge of his life. Dr. DeSilvo was a most private person, and he kept his medical history as quiet as possible. I've learned that whenever I come across a period of his life that is completely blank, with no record of any kind of his actions, it almost always turns out that the doctor had been taken ill, and elected to withdraw himself from public view, quite often having himself placed in temporal confinement while treatment was prepared. The admiral's report exactly matches one of the largest remaining lacunae in the DeSilvo chronology. Even the mention of heart-replacement failure matches up with what I have from third-party and secondary sources of one sort or another. I could provide you with greater detail on those if you would like to—"

"I'm sure that's not necessary," Neshobe said hurriedly. "You've been quite thorough enough already."

"Why, thank you, ma'am," Ashdin replied, plainly missing Neshobe's not-very-well-hidden sarcasm.

"Not at all," Neshobe said absently. She let out a sigh and rubbed her face with both hands. Ashdin had been the last of the experts to report, as well as the longest-winded, and it had already been a long meeting, and a long morning, before Ashdin had started. "I don't know about the rest of you," Neshobe said, "but I need a break. Would anyone object if I ordered some refreshments brought in?"

No one, of course, objected. It was one advantage to being Planetary Executive. You could take your breaks whenever you wanted. "Service system," Neshobe said, addressing the Mansion's ArtInt network. "Meeting break refreshments, to be brought in, now."

A low double-chime indicated the Mansion's ArtInt service system had heard and understood.

Neshobe Kalzant stood up and stretched her arms wide, providing as clear a cue as possible to everyone else that it was all right for them to do the same. The conference table waited until everyone had gotten up, then extruded an arm that cleared its surface and stowed everything in a lower compartment. Then the table folded itself up and rolled out of the way.

Neshobe took advantage of the moment when everyone was getting out of the table's way. She moved to the far end of the room, folded her arms across her chest, and turned to look out the window, using her posture and body language to make it as plain as possible that she wanted a moment or two on her own. She did it so effectively that even Ashdin took the hint, after a moment's hesitation. For a second or two, Neshobe could see, out of the corner of her eye, that the woman was watching her and considering the idea of coming over for a nice chat. Neshobe turned more directly toward the window, and that seemed to do the trick. She watched the reflection in the window as Ashdin shrugged and turned toward the refreshment cart that was rolling itself into the room.

Neshobe had discovered shortly after taking on the job of Planetary Executive that very clear body language could often do what it had just done—stop an awkward social encounter before it had even begun.

Her desire to be alone with her thoughts having been established, she turned her back on the window for a moment and considered the other people in the room, each in turn, watching as they helped themselves to tea, fruit, pastry, and whatever else the ArtInt system had served up.

First off, the two visitors from long ago, and far away— Norla Chandray and Anton Koffield. Plainly neither of them was in very good shape at the moment. Not that she could blame them, considering the shocks and stresses they had already been through.

Then, Grand Senyor Jorl Parrige, who had, the stars bless him, left his assistant behind. Fribart always got her nervous. But Parrige was a rock. She needed him.

Then there was Wandella Ashdin. She was supposed to be a brilliant historian, an expert on the early years of the founding of Solace, and on the parallel subject of the life and work of Oskar DeSilvo. Neshobe's people had fished her up from the local university.

Ashdin was plainly overawed and overexcited by the situation—and, interestingly enough, it was Koffield, and not the local political heavyweights, who fascinated her.

Every time the man opened his mouth, Ashdin turned and stared at him, with every bit of the intensity her watery blue eyes could muster. At a guess, she was trying to memorize everything he said. It had pained Ashdin no end that this meeting was to be off the record. She had brought all sorts of recording and note-taking hardware, and had seemed near tears when told she was not going to be able to use it.

But Koffield's presence made up for that. Koffield, after all, had actually *met* DeSilvo, talked to him, truly known him. Ashdin had so far restricted herself to asking fairly sensible questions, but it was plainly a major effort of will for her not to pin Koffield to the spot and ask what Oskar DeSilvo was *really* like. Or maybe she was asking that very question now.

Then came Dr. Milos Vandar, the biotechnician who stood next to Ashdin at the refreshment table, trying to get at the samovar she was blocking as she nattered on at Koffield. Ashdin, busily monopolizing the long-suffering Koffield, was unaware of his presence.

Vandar had not been able to say, absolutely and incontrovertibly, that Koffield's work was accurate. But neither had he come remotely near saying Koffield had gotten anything seriously wrong. And Vandar was a man of enough imagination to understand the implications if Koffield's analysis was even close to the truth. To see a man like Vandar badly worried and distracted told Neshobe just how serious the matter could be. And Vandar seemed even more upset and distracted than Koffield.

Then, finally, pacing the far corner of the room, the only one besides herself who was taking no refreshment, there was Karlin Raenau. Neshobe and Raenau had worked together reasonably well over the years, but their relations had been correct and businesslike, rather than friendly. She had never felt any sort of connection with the man.

And yet, now, having heard his description of his meeting with Koffield and Chandray, and its aftermath, she realized that they did have something in common: They both hated their offices—not their jobs, but the actual, physical offices, the rooms where they were required to do their work. Both Raenau's office and her own had been designed by the same man. It was plain from what he had said that his workplace bedeviled him with the same sort of nuisances that beset her, and for that they could both thank the great genius Oskar DeSilvo.

DeSilvo. Damn the man. He seemed to be at the back of everything. Ashdin, along with most of the population of Solace, was quite sure DeSilvo had been a genius. But the more Neshobe learned about him, and was called upon to deal with his legacy directly, the more she doubted he was any such thing. If he had been a genius, he was one who seemed to have made nothing but mistakes. From his terra-forming the planet to laying out an office workspace, she could find nothing but muddle in his work.

The people in the story about the Emperor's new clothes had merely joined in *pretending* the Emperor was dressed in splendor. The people of Solace went one better. They were truly not aware that old Oskar was buck-naked. They genuinely *believed* DeSilvo had been a genius.

DeSilvo. The damned old man had been dead—truly and finally dead—for a hundred years or more, and yet it was as if he was in the room as well.

Well, that made sense. He had, after all, *designed* the place. Neshobe considered the office, the DeSilvo-designed room itself. The Diamond Room, they called it. The room was shaped, more or less, like an oblong, octagonal-cut jewel. The floor was white marble, and the ceiling was another of the damned skylights DeSilvo had put everywhere. But it was the walls—if you could call a system of concave-angled panels walls—that were the defining feature of the room.

Panels angled out from the octagonal ceiling and floor at about a thirty-degree angle, and between these upper and lower panels was a set of center panels at waist level. The center panels, at least, were at right angles to the floor, as walls are supposed to be. The eight sides of the room were aligned with the cardinal and semicardinal points of the compass. The west and east sides of the room were the longest, the north and south sides exactly half as wide, and the northeast, northwest, southwest, and southeast sides were narrower still, really nothing more than angles set into the corners of the longer sides.

The center and upper wall panels at the east, west, and south of the room were permanently transparent, like the skylight, and the room was positioned so as to provide dramatic vistas out three sides of the room. Neshobe wasn't entirely clear on the matter, but her understanding was that the clear wall panels and ceiling were supposed to symbolize open government. No doubt Ashdin could have told her, if Neshobe had dared ask. Neshobe did know that the splendid views from the windows were supposed to imbue the planetary leader with vision and ambition.

She also knew that it was by no means an accident that there was a lot to see—or at least there would be a lot to see, if the weather ever cleared. The Executive Mansion had been built on a bluff overlooking Solace City, and the sea beyond, on a carefully chosen and landscaped site. Supposedly, DeSilvo had picked the site for the Mansion first, and then laid out the city to provide an impressive view as seen from it.

The east side of the room presented one with a raw and barren rockscape, littered with craters: the unterraformed part of Solace. To the south lay Solace City itself: the signal achievement of the present age—at least in the mind of the architect who had designed both the city and the view of it. A grand highway, little used in an age of aircars, led from the city to the airport/spaceport complex, due south of town. Beyond the aero-spaceport was the seaport, and beyond that, the waters of Landing Bay stretched to the horizon.

Neshobe had read somewhere that a person considering the view south was supposed to reflect on the juxtaposition of land, air, space, and sea transport, and the part each had played in the history of exploration, expansion, and settlement. That notion had always irritated Neshobe. When she looked out a window, she wanted a view, not a lecture on high-minded notions written in visual symbols.

To the west lay lush and verdant parklands of Nova-terra Reserve, more than merely terraformed, but elaborately landscaped and planted, the old craters transformed into lakes and ponds: the radiant, living future of the world.

DeSilvo had, by all accounts, been much taken with the

conversion of dead craters into living bodies of water. For him, it had been a potent symbol of remaking the lifeless into the living, and he had used the motif in many ways, in many places. The unfortunate fact that there had been no craters to work with in Novaterra had been dealt with by digging craters and then filling them with water. A silly extravagance, it seemed to Neshobe, but one that hardly mattered anymore. Half of Novaterra Reserve had been ruined by mudslides, and the lakes and ponds had long since overflowed their basins. Flooded-out artificial lakes in artificial craters. *That* should have been a symbol of something, but Neshobe was not sure what.

The trouble was that, since the rains had come, the grand views and all their sanctimonious symbolism might as well not have been there. Whatever the character of the rain at any given moment—drizzle, mist, downpour—it cut visibility to only a few hundred meters at best. Besides, the transparent wall and ceiling panels, designed for the far drier climate that had once existed, tended to fog up. The Diamond Room was shrouded in mist and fog. And that was symbolism plain enough for anyone to read.

Neshobe hated the Diamond Room, but it was the most famous room in the Executive Mansion, and probably the most famous on the planet. She was more or less compelled to use it. People expected it of her. A meeting that took place in the Diamond Room was, by virtue of that fact alone, imbued with importance. The time or two she had tried to use a more practical and comfortable room, the participants had taken it as a sign that they, or the subjects of their meetings, were not important enough to rate the Diamond Room treatment. Getting into it, for whatever reason, was a great honor. Ashdin had nearly had palpitations at the mere thought of seeing it, let alone sitting down in it, no matter how grim the occasion.

And this extremely grim occasion was far from over. There was still a lot left to discuss. No sense denying herself the bite to eat the others were having. She'd need a little something to tide her over. Neshobe Kalzant forced herself to relax, willed a sincere-looking smile onto her face, and went over to join the others.

The refreshment cart trundled itself out of the room, and the doors of the Diamond Room folded shut behind it. The conference table had reopened itself, and placed everyone's papers and possessions precisely back in their previous positions. Neshobe took her place at the head of the table and waited for the others to do the same.

"Very well," she said. "We're back in session. Let me just go over what happened this morning, to be sure I have it clear. I've heard from all of you, all the evidence that's been checked, all the rush research that's been done, the navigational analysis of the *Dom Pedro*'s journey brought in by Commander Raenau, and so on. As you'll understand, Admiral Koffield, Second Officer Chandray, we had to find out as best we could if you were indeed who you claim to be, if you got here by the means you claimed, and if the warning you brought is authentically from the last century."

Neshobe turned to Vandar. "If I've got this straight, Dr. Vandar, you found the prediction highly, even frighteningly accurate, and that where it was in error, the errors of prediction seem to have been caused by unforeseeable events, such as the mass transport of refugees from Glister several decades ago."

"Yes, ma'am. It's difficult to quantify such things, but I'd estimate that the predictive value of Admiral Koffield's work, if we compare it directly to real circumstances, is on the order of about sixty-five percent accurate."

"That doesn't sound so startlingly good," said Jorl Parrige.

"Ah, no, Senyor Parrige, you're right. But I was about to say that it's more complicated than that. Admiral Koffield developed a sophisticated mathematical model and applied it against the real Solace of a hundred-plus years ago, and then projected forward, assuming everything would go according to plan. But, as the admiral knew at the time, things don't go according to plan. The unexpected happens, and the plan itself changes. We have to correct for those factors."

"So you change the model to fit the circumstances?" Parrige asked, the disapproval plain in his voice.

"No, sir, of course not," Vandar replied, sounding almost offended. "The model remains the same. It is merely a question of adjusting and correcting the data that we *feed* to the model. Now, I have to confess that I have had very little time to work with the Koffield model, and I don't pretend to understand it completely. But I have managed to plug in at least rough corrections for the two largest classes of major, unplanned, great-impact events: the influx of refugees from Glister, and the repeated restorations and repair done to SunSpot and Greenhouse. De-Silvo's original plan called for SunSpot and Greenhouse to be decommissioned over seventy years ago. With those corrections plugged in, I got a predictive value match of about eighty-five percent, on a first pass. I have no doubt at all that, given more and better data, I could get it up over ninety percent, perhaps even to ninety-two percent, or ninety-four or ninety-five. It's a strong, solid model. Far better than the tools we've been using up to now. But the model's ability to predict the present situation is secondary. Far more important is what it predicts for the future."

"And what is that?" Parrige asked. "In layman's terms."

Vandar shook his head sadly. "In layman's terms? Disaster. Absolute catastrophe. A collapse every bit as hard and deep as the one at Glister or Far Haven. The current planetary ecosystem is headed for sudden and drastic collapse that will make our present problems look trivial. If you want to be melodramatic about it, we're doomed."

"Just a moment, please, Dr. Vandar," Neshobe said. Damn the man. Melodrama, however accurate, was the last thing they needed at the moment. A situation this frightening, this emotional, absolutely demanded cold, careful, calm discussion. The people around the conference table were already close to the edge. There was no sense, and no purpose served, in pushing them closer to it, or over it. The best time to defuse panic was before it got started. "I need to take it one step at a time. All I need to know from you at the moment is that you are satisfied that the work presented by Admiral Koffield is legitimate. Is the math honest, are the assumptions valid, and so on. I take it you are satisfied?"

Vandar nodded vigorously. "Very much so. I feel certain that—"

"Please, Dr. Vandar. We will explore further in a moment. Right now I just want to be sure we have some sort of consensus. Commander Raenau, your people have examined the spacecraft our friends came in on, and run navigation checks on the course for the, ah, *Dom Pedro IV*, along with various other details, such as the identity match performed by your command system before it unlocked the report. Does their story hold together?"

Raenau limited himself to the briefest possible answer. "Yes, ma'am," he replied.

"Any sign of fraud or tampering? Any indication that this might be a huge trick being played on us?"

"No, ma'am. And believe me, we've looked."

"And what they've described is physically possible? The ship could do what they said it could do?"

Raenau hesitated just a fraction of a second. "Ye—es. The only questionable or implausible part is the failure of the ship. The chances against that sort of systems failure are so long as to be nearly incalculable. The chances against a ship's arriving at its destination, however late, after any major systems failure, are nearly as great. The chances of both failure and safe arrival are *beyond* astronomical. Unless, of course, we don't assume it was chance. And, obviously, the substitution of scrap material for the final report in the admiral's secured container couldn't be chance."

"Our ship was sabotaged," Koffield said. "There's no point in being coy about it. The information I was bringing to you was deliberately stolen. That much, at least, is obvious."

Koffield. Neshobe considered the man thoughtfully for a moment before she answered him. He had not spoken much, and reports from Raenau and other sources on SCO Station painted a picture of a rigidly controlled man who had snapped, quite understandably, under tremendous pressure. He was, in short, a man struggling to put himself back together. The signs were there if one looked carefully. The way his hands tensed, the way the muscles in his jaw flexed, the hunted look in his eyes. He was a man trying to appear calm and in control, rather than a man who actually was those things.

"I agree with you, Admiral," Neshobe said. "That is the obvious and inescapable conclusion. Who did it, and why, are vital questions—but they are not questions we are concerned with at the moment."

"Point taken, Madam Executive," Koffield said.

Neshobe nodded at Koffield and turned her attention to the historian. "Dr. Ashdin. You're intimately familiar with the historical record of the times and places and people in question. Is there anything in the record that would tell us that these people are not who they say they are, or anything that would serve to contradict or disprove the story they told?"

"There's a great deal of information to get through, and of course I'd like to interview both Admiral Koffield and Second Officer Chandray at great length. In particular, I'd like to learn about how the admiral and Dr. DeSilvo—"

"None of that," Neshobe said sharply. Let Ashdin get started again, and they'd all still be here when the planet died. "Not now, anyway. Later perhaps, if Admiral Koffield and Officer Chandray are willing to cooperate. Just answer the question. Do you have any reason to think these people are not who they claim to be?"

"Ah, no, Madam Executive."

"Do you in fact believe they are who they say they are?" Neshobe was quite deliberately presenting her questions in a form that made them almost a ritual incantation, a call-and-response of the age-old pattern. Neshobe wanted Ashdin, and all the others, to hear that formal tone, and understand the seriousness of the situation. "Answer carefully. Are they who they say they are?"

Ashdin swallowed nervously. "Yes, Madam Executive. They are. All evidence points that way, and nothing refutes it."

"Very well." It was time to move forward, but Neshobe realized that she had to give herself a moment. They were at a key branch point, a decision cusp. *If* Koffield was Koffield, and *if* the checkable parts of what he had to say about the past and present were true, and *if* his science and math were reliable, and *if* it all matched the climatic disaster she could see just by looking out of the Diamond Room's oversize windows, then—

Then it would be Glister all over again. She picked up her scriber and doodled a meaningless pattern of squares and inscribed circles on her datapage, then cleared the screen. She let out her breath, not realizing that she had been holding it in, and set down her scriber.

She looked up at the circle of expectant faces and nodded to no one in particular. "Very well," she said again. She looked toward Koffield and Chandray and smiled meaninglessly at them. "I'm convinced. You are who you say you are, and you're telling the truth. I have no doubt that the simple act of looking into everything you've told us will give us a great deal more opportunity to check your story, and we'll check it directly every way we can. On a matter this grave, this serious, that goes without saying. But I believe you, and I have no doubt that all our subsequent checks will confirm your information."

Neshobe paused once again and drummed her fingers on the table. Plainly she had to ask Koffield the next question, but she could not bring herself to do it. She needed to hear the truth, but she was unwilling to hear it from the oracle himself. It would be easier, at least a trifle easier, to hear it from the messenger, from the local man. She turned to Milos Vandar.

"Dr. Vandar," she said, "you have studied Admiral Koffield's material, and you are as familiar as anyone with the current health of the planetary climate. Not so long ago you seemed to believe there was at least hope we could repair the ecosystem, rebuild it, and move forward. But now you have seen the admiral's work. Has it changed your mind that completely? To the point where you are certain there is no chance whatsoever for the planet to recover?"

Vandar smiled wearily. "It used to be—last week, yesterday—that the scientists in the fields of ecologic management and climate research and biodesign and biomech and so on told each to avoid the word *certainty*," he said. "We tell ourselves—told ourselves—that all things—or at least many things—are possible, however unlikely. And, in a sense, that's still true. An ecosystem is a dynamic process. It ebbs and flows, weakens itself and renews itself over and over again. A fully robust ecosystem, such as Earth's, can recover, rebuild itself. Earth's ecosystem has the capacity to absorb change, survive it, rebound from it, and has done so many times. It is at least *imaginable* that Solace might do the same. But there is a big difference between something being scientifically possible on the one hand, and remotely probable in the real world on the other. Having seen the admiral's work, I'd have to say that the probability of climatic recovery is near zero, no matter how hard we try. I'd put the odds at about the same as this room being struck by lightning in the next ten minutes. *If* we restrict ourselves to reasonable, realistic possibilities, *then* we must accept that the planetary ecosystem of Solace no longer has the capacity for short-term renewal—if it ever did."

Jorl Parrige spoke up. "I gather, Admiral, that you're not simply talking about short-term renewal, are you?" he asked. Neshobe could not help but note that Parrige had no fear of facing the oracle directly.

Koffield shook his head. "No, I'm afraid not, Senyor Parrige. But if my model is reasonably accurate, and if the data is reasonably good, then what they tell us is that there no longer is a 'long term' to worry about." He lifted his hands off the table, and gestured with them, palms up, empty-handed, helpless. "I'm sorry," he said, looking at Parrige, then to Neshobe, then to the rest of the table. "It is a painful fact, but a fact nonetheless. You must regard the terraforming of Solace to be a failure. The planet is going to die."

CHAPTER TWENTY

FOR WANT OF A NAIL

Captain Felipe Henrique Marquez sat in the captain's chair of the *Dom Pedro IV*'s command center and glared menacingly at the message screen, as if scowling at the words presented there could scare them into revealing more information.

(1) Friendly contact made with local officials. Departing for groundside meeting with Planetary Executive, scheduled for 0900 hours tomorrow, Solace City time.

(2) Intended contents of secured container appear to have been deliberately removed prior to *DP-IV*'s departure from Solar System, motive and perpetrator unknown.

(3) Local situation difficult but peaceful, local officials cooperative. Estimate of danger to *DP-IV* in event that ship reveals itself: minimal. Estimate of general situation: short-term stable, estimate approx level four to five on Drachma pol-mil-econ stability scale. No immediate political, military crisis pending. Long-term prospects poor.

(4) Koffield badly shaken by learning of item (2) when container opened. His mental state could be of vital importance in discussions with PlanEx.

(5) Re: agenda: safety of ship and cargo. Estimate: low/acceptable risk of approaching inner system.

(6) Re: agenda: legal status of ship under current Solace law. Library search and legal services ArtInt referral confirm ownership and property rights undisturbed by *DP-IV*'s mishap.

(7) Re: agenda: market for goods. Unable to perform useful research thus far. Many items in manifest may have antique value. Your large-scale hardware likely to be quite valuable. Koffield speculates there may be need for rapid spaceside habitat construction.

(8) All systems nominal aboard Lighter *Cruzeiro do Sul*. Lighter docked and secured inside SCO Station, with result onboard comm systems are blocked by station itself. This message transmitted as omnidirectional radio blip patched through SCO Station Services. Estimate local crypto capability highly advanced. Must therefore assume this transmission monitored. Secure comm impossible at this time.

(9) Events moving fast. Will report as developments merit and opportunity allows.

Chandray

Damn the woman! A very nice, professional signal, sent in the standard top-down prioritized format, and yet she had still managed to fill the message with absurd melodrama and cryptic details that produced more questions than answers. What, precisely, were they talking about with the PlanEx? And how was it that Koffield's state of mind was so important? Marquez did not wish the man ill, but surely there were more important things in the world than what mood Koffield was in.

Or had Chandray learned something from Koffield, something Koffield had not seen fit to reveal to Marquez? Something that magnified Koffield's importance?

And how in God's name had they managed to get a meeting with the Planetary Executive so fast? Marquez checked the timestamp on the message. It had come in hours ago, while he was asleep. By now, if he had worked out the time zones properly, she and Koffield were already in their meeting with the PlanEx.

What were they doing there? Marquez felt frustrated, cut off—and it did his mood no good to remind himself that he had been the one who decided to have the *Dom Pedro IV* lie low and hide on the outskirts of the Solacian system.

And what of Koffield's secured container? Who the devil had pilfered its contents, and why? Marquez now had direct evidence of two separate acts of sabotage against his ship. Were they connected? Were more surprises going to jump out at them? Who had done these things, and why?

He needed to know more, a great deal more—but it was plain he wasn't going to find it out sitting where he was. And even if Chandray hadn't been clear on many subjects, it was plain she felt it at least reasonably safe to bring the ship in. It was time to start readying the *Dom Pedro IV* for a trip to the inner system. Marquez had known before Chandray's message that the ship would have to head in sooner or later, or else be permanently marooned where she was. But he was a merchant captain, not an explorer. He had no desire to venture into the unknown world of the future that waited in the inner system. Still, it was plain he had no other choice.

There was something else that had him agitated as he set about the job of ordering the ship made ready for the trip. Agendas. Chandray had mentioned several in her message, and all of them were Marquez's, things he had told her to look out for, and check on.

But which of those agendas, if any of them, were hers? What was on the top of her list, her priority? Marquez felt sure it was no longer the ship. That much was plain from the way she had ordered the paragraphs of the message.

So what was most important to her now?

When the time came for action, what, precisely, would Norla Chandray decide to do? And whom would she be working for?

"Next!" The clerk looked up from her desk to take a cursory glance at yet another freeloading gluefoot looking to leave SCO Station and run back home to dirtside, to the planet Solace. Policy was to send 'em back as soon as possible and give the tickets free. Much as the clerk wanted to get rid of all the gluefeet, making things that easy didn't sit right with her. They had messed up SCO Station—her station, her home. They ought to be made to pay for that, somehow.

The gluefoot taking his seat in front of her desk smiled at her. "Hello," he said. He was a young-looking man, and the gluefeet were nearly all farmers who aged fast. He couldn't be much more than a kid. His clothes were worn-out and shabby, but someone had made an effort to patch them up and clean them. His face had gotten a good scrubbing, and his hair had been more or less combed into place. He had tried. That counted for something.

"Name," she snapped, shoving all such gentle thoughts from her mind. No point in being sympathetic.

"Elber," he said. "Elber Malloon."

Her desktop ArtInt popped up his file on her screen. "Traveling with wife Jassa and daughter Zari?"

"That's right."

"And you want to go back now?" she asked, echoing the words she had heard a dozen dozen times that morning from the endless parade of gluefoot refugees. "As soon as possible, transport to spaceport closest to your home village?"

"No," said Malloon. "No, thank you, but that's not it."

The clerk looked at him sharply. "What? Why not? Why are you here then?"

"Well," said Malloon, "I want to stay, stay here on SCO. I want to see if there's a way to do that."

"We can't keep you here for free forever," she said.

"No. I know that," he said. "I'd work. Anywhere, at anything. Jassa and me, we've talked it over. Staying here has got to be better than going back home. Home isn't there anymore. And if we built a new farm, again—what about the next flood, and the next drought?"

"So you want to stay here," said the clerk, staring at him in wonderment. None of them wanted to stay. Home, home, home was all she ever heard. She wasn't used to finding one who asked to stay, let alone work. She wasn't even sure she had the right forms where she could get at them.

As for work—the gluefoot crisis had left SCO Station a shambles, and the labor shortage was bad, much as her department was unwilling to admit it. It was going to take a lot of work to clean it up again. Enough work for this fellow, and his wife, and his daughter, once she was old enough. "Any job you could get here wouldn't be pretty or easy. You know that, don't you?"

"I was a farmer," Malloon said calmly. "That's about as hard a job as there is. I can do your work."

Was a farmer. They all came through saying "I *am* a farmer," or "I *am* a grain shipper," refusing to let go of what they no longer had, no longer were. But this fellow said *was*. That counted for something too. Her sympathies were floating back up toward the surface, and this time she made little effort to force them back down. "If you get a work contract, it will be for two years at least," she warned. "You'll have to remain on the station until the contract is over. No changing your mind and deciding you just have to go home six months from now."

"I won't," said Elber Malloon. "That's why I'm here right now. Because I won't do that. Because I can't."

"Why can't you?" the clerk demanded.

"Because my home's not there anymore," he said quietly. "Even where it was isn't there anymore. It's washed away, a meter under water. We checked on the info-feeds. The waters never drained. They're never going to." He looked at her face, reading her expression. "You don't understand," he said. "We don't have a home anymore, and I don't think the uppers will let us settle anyplace good enough for me to start over. I'm not sure there are any places left on Solace that are good enough. So that's why we need to stay. For our daughter."

"Your daughter."

"Well, her old home is gone, and it's not coming back. So it's simple." Elber Malloon gestured at the clerk's office, at all of SCO Station. "We need to build Zari a new home," he said. "And not on the planet. Out here, where it's safe."

———

The planet is going to die. The words echoed in Neshobe's head, and in the quiet that filled the room. There was no sound except for the muffled drumming of rain on the transparent roof of the Diamond Room.

The planet is going to die. She had known it before Koffield had spoken, of course. In a sense, she had known it for quite a long time, deep inside. It had been so long since anything had gone right, since any victory had been anything other than brief, or transitory. But she had never dared speak the words, or even think them, until now. *The planet is going to die.* Now the words had been spoken. It was no longer possible to hide from them. Now her only choices were to deny the reality of those words, or else to deal with their consequences. "How long have we got?" she asked, her voice barely a whisper. "How soon until the planet is uninhabitable?"

She did not know Koffield at all. But his motionlessness was as expressive as any gesture could have been. He sat there, silent and unmoving as a tomb, as he considered his answer.

"No one knows, Madam Executive," he said at last. "My mathematical model is not wholly my own, as you know. The parts that deal with endgame chaos, the final dissolution of a system, and the unraveling of balances— those are based almost entirely on previous work. What I can say about them is that they are extremely sensitive to initial conditions—and the initial conditions will be wildly unpredictable. It is far easier to predict the behavior of a stable system. What you're asking for is the behavior of a system as it is becoming unstable, chaotic. The slightest change in any of a dozen variables now could have dramatic and unpredictable effects years from now."

"Don't just leave it at that," Neshobe said. "You've come here to tell me the planet is doomed. You've got to have some sort of idea, some gut feeling. Give me *something.*"

Koffield frowned deeply, then shook his head. "It's impossible to be definite. We did a quick estimate this morning, plugging Dr. Vandar's new data into my old model. It suggests that we'll start to see the partial pressure of oxygen decline rapidly. There will be a linked, though not precisely proportionate, increase in the partial pressure of carbon dioxide. The baseline projection is that it will start in something like ten Solacian years. That's an extremely uncertain number. It might start to happen in five years, or might not start for fifteen, or even twenty. Perhaps the process has already started, but we haven't detected it yet. We should be able to refine the estimate with better data. I can't give you a better answer than that."

Neshobe looked steadily at him. "Try," she said. "I'm not looking for absolute precision. I want a general idea. A drop in oxygen levels is bad, but how bad? Should we measure the time we have left in centuries? Decades? Years?" *Or months?* she asked herself. *Perhaps days, if word gets out and the exodus riots start up again.*

Koffield shifted uncomfortably in his seat. "The planet will certainly become increasingly inhospitable in the coming few years, and the process will snowball, feeding on itself and accelerating. That much is certain. What we don't know is how *fast* it will snowball. As to when the planet will become officially uninhabitable—well, it almost certainly will happen in our lifetime, and probably happen much sooner than that. In my opinion—and that's all it is, opinion—the planet will become unsuitable for unprotected human life within a few tens of years at most, under the most generous possible estimate—and perhaps far sooner than that."

"A lot of it depends on what definition of *uninhabitable* you use," Vandar said.

"I don't understand," said Officer Chandray. "It seems to me that either a planet is or is not inhabitable."

Vandar smiled slightly. "There are definitions for planetary habitability under which Earth herself doesn't qualify as habitable, because there are places a human could not survive, ah, I think the phrase is, *without the aid of technology*. You'd drown in the ocean, or freeze to death in the Arctic, or die of thirst in the desert. If you're willing to use technological means to build a robust enough life-support system, people can live just about anywhere. By that definition, just about any planet with a solid surface could be called inhabitable."

"It's not a time to be cute or clever," Chandray said sharply. "We all know what we mean by *inhabitable*."

"Forgive me," said Vandar. "I wasn't trying to be clever. My point is that we all *think* we know what we mean by *inhabitable*. If—if the worst-case scenario of Admiral Koffield's model plays out, the current trend of a very slight decrease in the levels of atmospheric oxygen will start to accelerate in the near future. Or maybe the drop won't speed up for a decade or more. But once the drop does accelerate, within about five years' time of that event, oxygen levels will be low enough, and carbon dioxide levels will be high enough, that humans will not be able to breathe the open atmosphere without some sort of respirator. Does that make the planet uninhabitable?

"Shortly thereafter, the greenhouse effect will reach the runaway stage, and it will become too hot for unprotected humans in most regions. We'll need cooling suits and respirators, but we could still extract oxygen from the air and find water to drink. Is *that* uninhabitable? About five to ten years after that, my hunch is that the weather patterns will have become so violent that only reinforced structures will survive for any length of time. But, inside such a shelter, people could live and work quite comfortably. Is *that* uninhabitable? You could define any of those stages as *uninhabitable*. Choose which one you will.

"We could maintain a human presence on the planet even if all the oxygen came out of the atmosphere," Vandar went on. "We could build reinforced domes over the cities and dig underground warrens. We'd certainly have to call the planet uninhabitable by then, but people could still inhabit this world."

"There's no way we can build enough domed cities in time," said Neshobe. "And even if we did, it would be bloody hell maintaining their internal environments."

"Yes, ma'am," Vandar said mildly. "I quite agree. Sealed domes and underwarrens are not sustainable unless they are very carefully managed. They are difficult to

establish and maintain even under the best circumstances—
and we will not have the best of circumstances by any
means."

"Where do you make your last stand?" Koffield asked.
"How long and how hard will you fight against an unbeatable enemy? And how much effort do you put into the final redoubt that might survive, and how much into the
outer defenses that will certainly fall?"

"You talk as if we are going into a war, Admiral
Koffield."

"You—we—are *in* a war, Madam Kalzant. A war against
a planet that was forced to support life against its will. It is
counterattacking, and it will, eventually, win, though it
might allow you to retain small enclaves, reinforced sealed
domes and warrens, here and there—if you decide it is
worth fighting hard enough, and intelligently enough,
merely to win such a limited and qualified victory."

"Madam Kalzant," said Parrige, "I think I see the point
that these gentlemen are trying to make. It is a question of
resource management and allocation."

Neshobe glared at Parrige, then back toward Koffield
and Vandar, both of whom were nodding their agreement.
They had gone mad. All of them had gone mad and decided to gang up on her. Oxygen levels, war, management
and allocation theory—it was all so much gibberish.

Ashdin cleared her throat timidly and spoke. "Madam—
Madam Kalzant, if I might?"

"Oh, please, go ahead." Neshobe slumped back in her
chair. If they were looking toward Ashdin as the voice of
reason, then things were becoming dire indeed.

"I know I'm not much at policy or strategy or any
of that," Ashdin said. "I get fascinated by old stories, people out of the past, that sort of thing. Oskar DeSilvo is
one of my interests. Another is the fall of Glister, the real
story behind all the legends and myths." She turned to
Koffield. "I doubt you've had the chance to learn much
about what happened on Glister. It happened decades after
your disappearance. The long and the short of it was that
Glister came up against the same sort of climatic crisis we
are facing here today. They had bad weather, extinctions

of species, algae blooms, air-quality deterioration, oxygen levels dropping. So they worked hard to stabilize the situation, as we have, investing a lot of time and money. Things kept getting worse. The planetary government announced a crash program, top priority, to provide respirators for every citizen, and sealant and partial-pressure-oxygen injectors for every building and residence, a stopgap until the atmospheric reoxygenation project could be brought on-line.

"But the reoxygenation program never worked very well. It slowed the decline in oxygen levels for a while, but never was able to stop the decline, let alone reverse it.

"So the government decided to build temporary domes over the largest cities and provide what they called enhanced sealing for outlying houses. And of course people weren't willing to wait for the government to do the job while the air itself was going bad—there were all sorts of private projects as well—all of them top priority, all of them rush jobs. Then the weather turned worse, and all sorts of corrosive compounds started precipitating out of the air, raining down on the domes, damaging them.

"There were unprecedented extremes of cold and heat, the weather patterns became completely unpredictable, and the storms grew more and more violent as the whole planet fell out of equilibrium. There were all sorts of plans put forward to build reinforced domes and underground habitats, all sorts of brilliant evacuation schemes worked out—but nothing could be done. The other, earlier crash programs and rush projects had used up all the money, time, and resources. They had expended all their energies before the *real* crisis hit."

"And we're in the first stages of doing the same thing," said Neshobe. "So what do we do? Yesterday we were trying to get through a spell of bad weather. This morning the planet is doomed. Yesterday we were going to have to work hard if we were going to get the climate back the way we want it. Now it turns out we can't repair the ecosphere no matter how hard we try. Even if we make an all-out effort, the best we can hope is to maintain the unsatisfactory status quo, at the cost of making the end come faster."

"Yes, ma'am. Those are the essentials of the situation," Koffield said.

"Then what?" Neshobe demanded. "What do we do?"

"Evacuate the planet," Norla Chandray suggested.

Neshobe looked at Chandray in irritated astonishment. How long had Chandray been on Solace? Twelve hours at most? Easy enough for *her* to suggest planetary evacuation. It wouldn't be her world, wouldn't be her family uprooted after a hundred or more years, wouldn't be her forced to abandon all her possessions without a chance to—

But then Neshobe remembered just how much Chandray and Koffield had been forced to give up, how much had been stolen from them. Not just their worlds, but their times. Their homes had ceased to exist, just as surely as the homes of the Glisterns had been destroyed.

Still and all, even if Norla Chandray was due a bit of respect, and even sympathy, that did not mean her idea had any merit. "Evacuate them to where?" she asked.

"To orbiting habitats, or maybe to Greenhouse," Chandray replied.

"All the orbital habitats are at or beyond their preferred population points," Raenau said. "Several are refusing all new arrivals. You've just seen what it's like on SCO Station."

"The habitats are at their *preferred* population points," Vandar put in, rapidly working his scriber over his datapage. "But that's not the same as their *carrying* capacity. Let's see." He brought up the data he wanted on his page and read it over. "According to this, there are just about three-point-two million people on the planet, and roughly the same number—about three-point-one-five million—in the various habitats throughout the Solacian system. They're the ones orbiting the planet, the asteroid miners, the free-stellar-orbit habs, everything. The combined certified carrying capacity of the various habitats is slightly over four million."

"That sounds as if there's at least some room for an orderly initial evacuation," said Parrige.

"And we can always build more habs," said Ashdin.

Neshobe struggled to control her temper. Parrige and Ashdin were the two persons at the table least qualified on the subject of space habitats. Ashdin she could almost excuse, but Jorl Parrige should have known better. "It's not quite that simple," she said.

"Obviously it would not be simple or easy," Parrige said, "but if we have excess capacity there, and people who need new homes here, surely it makes sense to match them up."

"No, it doesn't," said Raenau.

"Indeed?" Parrige asked, bristling a bit at the station commander's insolence.

Neshobe let out a weary sigh. Parrige was a valuable advisor, and a good friend, but the very traits that made him valuable often made him infuriating. When it came to policy, to big ideas, he thought in numbers, in theory, in absolutes. If the numbers said a thing could be done, he tended to assume not only that it could be done, but that it *should* be done—even to assume it *would* be done. But Raenau was out of line talking to a Grand Senyor that way. "Perhaps, Commander Raenau, you could be a bit *less* succinct," she said. "Explain, please, why doesn't it make sense."

"Carrying capacity means the maximum possible number of people that could be supported in an emergency, if another hab was evacuated, or whatever," he said. "It's the absolute, worst-case, brick-wall limit. Carrying capacity assumes all systems are functioning—no accidents, no breakdowns. It's how many people a habitat could sustain if everything worked perfectly and everyone went on short food rations, power rationing, water rationing, everything rationed. So you tell me, Senyor Parrige, how many habitats would be willing to take on their maximum possible population load in the form of half-starved, uneducated, indigent, disease-ridden dirtsiders who know nothing of habitat life and have no skills that are of much use in space? Could you force them if they refused? And if you used force on one hab, what would happen on all the others? And even if all the habitats *did* go along with you, how many would collapse because something *did* go wrong and there were no resources available to see the system through while repairs were made?"

"And there's the minor matter of transporting three million people from the planetary surface to orbit," Neshobe said. "Dr. Vandar, I expect you could pull up the figures the fastest of anyone here. What is the maximum daily capacity of our surface-to-orbit passenger fleet? Not the theoretical capacity, but the real numbers for the real ships that are operational and available."

Vandar scribed over his datapage for a moment, then looked up. "Approximately six hundred fifty passengers, ma'am."

"Well, then," Neshobe said, figuring quickly. "Six-fifty a day, times four hundred twenty-one days a local year. Just over two hundred seventy thousand a year. Assuming the entire passenger fleet works around the clock with no accidents or breakdowns, it will take just over eleven local years to transport the entire planetary population. As, according to Dr. Vandar's figures, the atmosphere might be getting close to unbreathable by that time, things could be a bit awkward for the last ones to get aboard."

"We can build more transports," Parrige said. "Enough to lift everyone—or nearly everyone—off the surface in time."

"At the same time we're working on an all-out crash program to build more habitat capacity?" Raenau asked. "If we commit resources to building ships, how can we take the same resources and commit them to habitat construction? And how long will it take to build more ships and habitats?"

"Ma'am, it will be difficult, and it will take time, and we will have to take great risks," said Parrige. "But surely it can be done."

"It is perhaps a minor point," said Koffield, "but the *Dom Pedro IV*'s primary cargo consists of fifty Habitat Seeds."

Raenau looked puzzled. "What's a Habitat Seed?"

"Mmmm? Oh. Perhaps you don't use them anymore. Habitat Seeds are habitat-making robots. Very large and sophisticated robotic machines that are programmed to mine the raw materials for a space habitat, process the materials, and construct the hab with little or no human intervention. They're one-shot items, and they don't always work. Sometimes a circuit blows out or a subsystem wears out and you're stuck with a half-built hab. But usually they do the job."

"So that's something close to fifty additional habitats that could be built," said Vandar.

"Possibly fewer," said Koffield. "And they won't be large or grand habs, and they won't be stocked with anything. Habitat Seeds produce just the bare bones. But they'll help somewhat, I expect."

"Every little bit is going to help," said Vandar.

"But even fifty extra habitats won't be help enough," Raenau said, looking at Parrige. "That moves the line up the chart, but not by enough. And life is not all lines on charts."

Parrige drew himself up in his chair and glared at Raenau, and then at Neshobe Kalzant. "I'm not a fool, Madam Executive. I realize there would be difficulties, immense ones. But all that is as it may be. It's plain to see that if the planet is dying, expansion of the orbital habitats only makes sense. We could start at once to transport those in most need—those who have been hurt the worst by this slow-motion grand-scale disaster—to the spaceside habitats at once. We can build habitats for the rest in the years to come."

"And the ones left behind will start to tell each other they're being abandoned while the lifeboats are pulling away," said Raenau. "How will you handle the panic that will start the second the evacuation begins? Go out to the next rumor riot with some charts and graphs and explain that everything is going to be fine?"

Parrige's eyes flashed at Raenau. "There will be difficulties, but—"

"Difficulties!" Neshobe half shouted. "You make it

sound as if the difficulties are nothing but minor inconveniences. Thirty-one people died in the last spaceport riot. We probably lost two or three times that many in groundside accidents caused by the panic at other ports. Space and stars know how many casualties there were in orbit. What sort of mob are we going to get at the spaceport when we announce that we have to evacuate the planet's surface?"

"Surely mob panic has no place in determining planetary policy," Parrige said snappishly.

Neshobe restrained herself, fighting off the impulse to stand up, cross around the table, grab her old advisor by the shoulders, and give him a good hard shaking. Instead, she held her voice in rigid control and spoke in words as cold and flat as she could find. "Senyor Parrige," she said, "it is time and past time for you, and everyone else here, to understand that we are dangerously close to the point where mob panic *is* planetary policy. People are frightened now. When this news gets out, they'll be terrified, and angry."

"Of course they will be!" Parrige half shouted. "*I'm* terrified, here and now. But as Dr. Ashdin and Admiral Koffield have just gotten through pointing out, if we approach things in a cautious, gradualist way, we are doomed." Parrige paused a moment, and took a deep breath before starting to speak again, in lower, calmer tones. "We will squander our time and resources on laudable but ultimately futile efforts like stabilizing Lake Virtue. Commander Raenau is right. We can't go to the ragged edge of carrying capacity on the habs. Admiral Koffield and Dr. Ashdin are right to say we can't proceed in a gradualist way. And *you* are right, Madam Kalzant, when you say that I am casually suggesting that we do the impossible.

"But *I'm right too*." Parrige frowned and shook his head. "I *know* how bad the orbital-habitat situation is. I *know* the risks of using all available carrying capacity. But we are growing weaker, not stronger. We are expending our resources, not marshaling them. If it is difficult to act decisively *now*, it will only become more difficult later on, and then more difficult still, until action becomes utterly impossible."

Neshobe looked at Parrige in surprise. It was nothing like him to express himself so emphatically.

Admiral Koffield cleared his throat and spoke in a quiet voice. "I've heard that politics was the art of the possible. But evacuating the planetary population is politically impossible. The people on the ground will panic. The more they understand they have to leave, the worse the situation will become. Panic, rumor, riot, profiteering, corruption—there will be no end to it. The people in the space habs won't want to let them in. But, even if evacuation isn't possible, it is absolutely necessary."

Neshobe let out a deep breath. "Then we must make it possible. Maybe, just maybe, if we educate the public, convince them that the situation is bad, but that if there is time, there will be a chance for an orderly evacuation."

"Yes," said Parrige. "That is the way."

"But before we start pointing the way," Neshobe said, "we must be sure we are convincing. We have to show them something we don't have. Proof."

"But, Madam Executive," said Vandar, "we have Admiral Koffield's preliminary work and my mathematical analysis of it."

"That's a start, yes, so far as it goes," Neshobe said, "but it is by no means enough. A crackpot admiral from a hundred years back—and one whose very name is, forgive my bluntness, a curse word for many of our citizens—appears from out of nowhere telling some crazy story about how his magical formula proves we're all doomed. No. I'm sorry, Admiral Koffield. We can't even begin to let the news out with your name attached to it. Our Glistern refugees and descendants would reject it out of hand."

Koffield shook his head sorrowfully. "It's incredible. I must admit that I thought the one bright spot in my being marooned was that people would have forgotten by now. A century and a quarter later, I'm still a monster to them because of Circum Central? Even after their planet died?"

Vandar looked at Koffield in surprise. "But don't you— no, of course, you've only been here a brief time, and it's not the sort of thing someone would tell you in casual conversation. The Glisterns blame you *for* the death of their planet."

Koffield stared at Vandar in astonishment. "But that's absurd! How could anything I did have caused the collapse of their climate?"

Vandar turned his hands palms up and gestured hopelessly. "You're quite right that it's absurd—but they blame you all the same. Someone on Glister dug up an old saying, a proverb, from near-ancient Earth: 'For want of a nail the shoe was lost. For want of the shoe, the horse was lost. For want of a horse, the battle was lost. For want of the battle, the kingdom was lost. All for the want of a nail.' The legend says that the ships you stranded were carrying vital supplies, special equipment, powerful terraforming technology that would have stabilized the climate and prevented the collapse. What, exactly, was aboard changes from one version of the story to the next. They call you the man who stole the nail."

It was plain to Neshobe that Koffield was struggling to calm himself. "I did—what I had to do," he said. "What I was ordered to do. I did what I did to defend against the very thing my garrison—and the whole of the Chronologic Patrol—were established to protect against—a violation of causality. There were people aboard those ships, colonists and their equipment. I had no intention of harming any of those people, and I will regret it to the end of my days. What I did will *haunt* me to the end of my days. Those people died as a consequence of my actions. If the Glisterns wish to hate me for that, then—then they do no more than I do myself, many a sleepless night.

"But after the ships were lost, I studied the records of those ships, their manifests, their histories, all I could learn about them. But there was nothing, *nothing* aboard those ships that was not replaceable, and, as a matter of fact, soon replaced. I killed those crews, and many more died because those ships did not reach Glister—but I did not kill a world. Glister died of the same illness that is killing Solace, and not because a few shiploads of equipment were lost."

The room went silent for a time. Even the rain spattering down on the roof faded away, and the people around the table sat, still as stone.

"That is true," Milos Vandar said at last, speaking quietly. "But what is true, and what people believe, are two very different things. I'd go so far as to say, what *people know* and what they believe are often two different things."

"I'm—I'm sorry, Admiral Koffield," Neshobe said. "From all I have ever read, and from all I have seen and heard here today, you are a man who did his duty and has suffered the torments of hell ever since as a consequence."

"Yes," Koffield said. "And neither you nor I nor anyone else can do the least thing about it. But—thank you, all the same. *I* killed Glister? Incredible."

Koffield shook his head again. "As regards the matter at hand—I must confess that, in spite of all the endless hours I have spent on this problem, the political angle never crossed my mind. I have lived in the military, where you give or take the orders and the orders are obeyed. But of course you are right. You cannot simply order the planet's population to do as you say."

"I *will* order them about, and I'll make my orders stick if it comes to that," Neshobe said. "I will do whatever it takes to protect my people, even if I have to protect them against their will. But it will be worse for everyone if it comes to that. I would prefer to persuade them. To do that, I need more and better proof."

"It's a hell of a shame the copies of your final report didn't get here," Raenau said to Koffield.

Neshobe looked at Raenau thoughtfully. Was there perhaps a slight hint of doubt, of accusation, in his voice? If Raenau did not completely trust or believe Koffield's information, that confirmed all her worries. If a hard-edged, rational, well-informed man like Raenau could not trust in Koffield completely, was there the slightest hope the general populace would?

"If you can offer up any sort of plausible story for why I would stage this whole catastrophe, what possible motive I might have for pretending to have proof of an imaginary disaster, why I might go to the incredible lengths that would have been required to fake the proof I have offered, I'd be glad to hear it," Koffield replied sharply, responding more to Raenau's tone than his words. "What possible reason would I have for stranding myself one hundred and twenty-seven years away from everyone and everything I know?"

"Escape," Raenau said, in a surprisingly gentle voice. "You yourself have just finished agreeing with us that your life back there was something close to a hell. You were a villain. Why not send a real-sounding advance message on the *Chrononaut VI*, put a heap of compressed scrap into a secured container, sabotage your own ship, and arrive a century and a quarter in the future as a hero, a savior, a visionary? It's obvious that your ship was sabotaged in a very precise way, and obvious that your tamperproof secured container was somehow tampered with—or else the tampering was staged. We have only your word that there *was* a final report, or that it was ever in that container."

"How dare you—" Koffield began, coming half out of his seat.

"I do not say I believe any of this," Raenau said in a firm, emphatic voice. "But you asked for a plausible story. I will not be the first or last to think of it, or of many other variants. You could say the theory I've offered is impossible. So it is. But it's plain that *something* implausible, something unlikely, has happened. I at least have offered a version of events, an explanation. You have not done so. You asked for a theory of how this could have happened. I have offered one."

"If it's a fraud, it's one damned hell of a good one," Vandar said. "I agree one preliminary report isn't enough basis for deciding the fate of a planet, but this"—he patted the datapage that held his copy of the report—"is solid work. Good math, good science. It's both self-consistent and consistent with the existing body of work. It's more than that. It answers nagging questions, ties together loose ends."

"Their being stranded in our time could have been staged, even if the report was not," Raenau said.

"Maybe that's true, but so what?" Vandar asked. "We can test the report, check it, take it apart, put it together again. We don't have to take the admiral's word for any of it. We can go see for ourselves."

"Great," Raenau said. "You go do that. I'll want to hear about it. But even Admiral Koffield has got to admit there's a problem when it tells me a big long story about how he's moved heaven and Earth to get a report to me— and it just so happens the only copy of the report we can get at has vanished mysteriously."

"It's not the only copy."

Neshobe had not heard the voice for so long that it took her a minute to realize who was speaking. "Officer Chandray? There's another copy? Surely if you knew that, you should have spoken up before now."

"There is," Chandray said. "There must be." She turned to Koffield. "You wouldn't have traveled with the only copy. You would have made sure it was placed in the Grand Library, or the Permanent Physical Collection, or hidden with some trusted friend or another. Something. You probably did all of those things, and more."

"I did," Koffield said. "But, assuming those copies even survived this long, they are light-years from here, back in the Solar System. What good do they do us here?"

"None, unless someone goes to get them," said Chandray. She turned to Neshobe. "You could send word back on the next timeshaft ship to Earth, and have a search performed."

"I could, and I will," said Neshobe. "But there are no timeshaft ships in-system—aside from the one you came in on."

"When's the next ship expected?" Chandray asked.

"I'm afraid that's something else that's changed from your day," said Parrige. "Timeshaft ships rarely call at Solace anymore. Trade has dried up."

"That's a polite way of saying we don't have anything they want, and we can't afford much of what they have," Raenau growled.

"True enough," Neshobe agreed. "But in any event, there's no way we can get a message back to the Grand Library, or anyone else, just at the moment. There's no ship to send it on."

"Except the *Dom Pedro IV*," said Chandray.

Aha, thought Neshobe. *There it is at last.* She had spent too many years in politics to be surprised by a show of self-interest masquerading as some sort of generous offer. It was a relief finally to have it show up. These two characters had seemed too good to be true. Neshobe had not the slightest doubt that Chandray had known ahead of time that there were no other ships in-system or expected. "You're suggesting that we might use your ship?" Neshobe asked sweetly.

"It at least seems a reasonable enough notion that it ought to be considered," Chandray said, offering an answer hedged in with qualifiers.

"According to what I've heard from you, that ship of yours is not in the best of shape," Raenau objected. "And it is a hundred years or so out-of-date."

"But it's what you've got," Chandray said, a bit too eagerly. She would never get far as a negotiator. "We need to get our ship checked over, and maybe repaired. And you need a ship."

"*You've* suggested a reason we might need a ship," Neshobe said.

"Officer Chandray's ship was crippled while attempting to bring vital information to this world," Koffield said. "None of her crew can ever return to their homes or their families. Two crew members died in cryosleep, apparently as an indirect result of the sabotage committed against the ship. Officer Chandray nearly died herself, and is only recently recovered. Precisely because the ship is an antique, it seems highly unlikely that there are any available qualified crew in this system, a fact which she knows perfectly well. If the *Dom Pedro IV* flies again, Officer Chandray will have to cross the starlanes on the ship that stranded her in your time, killed two of her friends, and almost killed her. She has no ownership stake in the ship, and won't gain anything from the repairs. Nor is the ship hers to command. Only Captain Marquez can make such decisions. Under those circumstances, suggesting that the ship be sent off after a misplaced book hardly seems like the height of selfishness.

"Unless you people wish to accuse Officer Chandray or me of any other frauds, crimes, shady deals, or dishonest acts, I suggest we take her suggestion at face value." Koffield glared around the table. "This isn't *our* planet. If you wish to take everything we say or do as a trick, feel free to do so. It will make no particular difference to us."

Neshobe spoke up before anyone else could, mostly to keep anyone else from speaking and making things worse. "Very well, Admiral. Point taken." The tension in the room was getting out of hand. There was going to be a fistfight in another few minutes—but she was not at all sure who would be fighting whom. She had to defuse this, and fast.

At that moment, the solution came to her. A way to buy time and get something useful accomplished, all at once. "It seems to me that your ship needs refitting, and we need to do a great deal more research into the whole question of ecologic collapse. There's a place where we can get both those things done. Officer Chandray, if you would be so kind as to contact your Captain Marquez, please invite him to bring his ship into Shadow-Spine Station. We will provide whatever service and repair the *Dom Pedro IV* needs at no charge. I would suggest you take your lighter, the *Cruzeiro do Sul,* and meet him there. It's quite convenient to your own destination. And perhaps Vandar, and a couple of others, could accompany you."

"To Shadow-Spine?" Vandar asked, and then smiled. "Ah, yes. That makes a great deal of sense."

Chandray looked from Neshobe to Vandar, clearly puzzled. "Ah, well, very good, ma'am. That's an extremely generous offer, and one that I'll relay to Captain Marquez as soon as possible. But, ah, well . . . Could you tell me where Shadow-Spine Station is? What's our destination?"

"Shadow-Spine Station in on the spine between Ballast and SunSpot, orbiting Greenhouse," Vandar said.

"I'm sorry?" Chandray said.

"Greenhouse," Vandar said. "Executive Kalzant is absolutely right. It's the center of terraforming and climate research for the whole Solacian system, and Shadow-Spine is our most advanced shipyard.

"Greenhouse," he said. "*That's* where you need to be."

SUNSPOT AND GREENHOUSE

CHAPTER TWENTY-ONE

GATEKEEPERS

"There he is on visual," said Phelby, pointing unnecessarily at the blinking dot that was moving slowly toward them.

"I see him, Mr. Phelby," said Captain Marquez. He watched the incoming flashing light grow larger, brighter, evolving into a constantly visible dot that flared brighter every two seconds, to a spacecraft with discernible features, and an acquisition strobe flashing beside the main docking port. Marquez had never much enjoyed being the passive target in a rendezvous and docking operation, and he liked it even less under the present circumstances. They were not in a comfortable sort of neighborhood.

Beyond the approaching tug lay the weird dumbbell shape of the SunSpot Construct. The SunSpot itself was the end of the dumbbell pointed straight at the satellite Greenhouse, while Ballast was at the spaceside end, with the Shadow-Spine forming the link between them. Greenhouse itself loomed behind the Construct, with the massive banded gas giant planet Comfort in turn swallowing half of the sky behind Greenhouse. A strange and disturbing vista of increasingly huge and foreboding shapes floating in the darkness.

As seen from this vantage point, the SunSpot itself was a gleaming silver sphere, five kilometers across, the Shadow-Spine rising up out of its perfect surface. The Spine itself was an arrow-straight shaft twenty kilometers long, with any number of complex extrusions and shapes and radiators and structures sprouting from it in all directions. Ballast sat at the far end of the Spine, a misshapen lump of sky-rock that served no other purpose than to provide sufficient deadweight to move the center of gravity for the whole structure out of the SunSpot and down to the center point of the Spine's length. Massive main trim and aiming thrusters were mounted on the rocky surface of Ballast.

But the SunSpot itself was very clearly the business end of SunSpot Construct. Marquez could tell that much by looking past the SunSpot, down to the surface of Greenhouse. The hemisphere directly under the SunSpot was brilliantly illuminated, and the illumination was very definitely not coming from the local sun.

From this vantage point, safely behind the shield-wall of SunSpot's outer shell, the shell appeared perfectly round. But Marquez knew that was not the case: The face of the shell nearest Greenhouse was sliced away, exposing the interior.

There, inside the truncated sphere that was the outer shell of the SunSpot, an artificial miniature sun shone down on the surface of Greenhouse below. The inner surface of the shell was coated with superreflectant material, and formed into a massive adjustable focusing mirror that directed virtually all the light down onto Greenhouse, rather than letting it radiate wastefully off into space.

The rest of SunSpot Construct was there to control, service, and maintain the SunSpot itself. Shadow-Spine's primary function was to serve as a radiator farm to dump waste heat energy from SunSpot. But one system's wasted heat was another system's free energy source. Only a fraction of a percent of SunSpot's power output went down the Spine, but that was enough to provide a large facility with effectively free and unlimited energy. Shadow-Spine Station had been built so as to take advantage of that power source.

It seemed to Marquez that literally living on the heat-dump spine for the largest artificial fusion reactor ever built was crossing well over the line into insanity, but free energy was one devil of a strong draw.

And part of that free energy went into running a shipyard. And the shipyard had sent out a tug to greet them and fit the *Dom Pedro IV* with an updated midship docking collar. That way the *DP-IV* could cozy up to Shadow-Spine Station and dock with the station herself. It was not a situation that made Marquez happy.

But at least it would mean he would get his lighter back. The *Cruzeiro do Sul* was already docked at Shadow-Spine, empty and waiting for him. Koffield, Chandray, and their party had already shuttled down to the surface of Greenhouse.

The only practical way of getting the *Cruzeiro do Sul* back was to dock at Shadow-Spine, but Marquez knew he would have probably agreed to dock at Shadow-Spine, despite all his misgivings, even if the *Cruzeiro do Sul* had not been there. A free comprehensive diagnostic exam and refit was every bit as strong a draw as a free power source. When PlanEx Kalzant had made that offer, she had revealed herself as someone who knew what motivated a ship's captain. The offer had been impossible to resist— but, on the other hand, Marquez could not help but wonder what Kalzant's motivation had been. Generosity was all very nice, but what was in it for her?

Or, to put it another way, to what use did Neshobe Kalzant want to put his ship?

The devil with it. He would find out soon enough, and worrying about it would not make that time come any sooner.

"I'll be in my quarters," Marquez told Phelby. "Advise me when the tug has docked."

Milos Vandar scribbled furiously on the board behind him, a perfect forest of incomprehensible symbols trailing behind his scriber. "And that *third* function can be further reduced *this* way"—he struck out half the symbols he had just written—"and, as you can see, that establishes equivalence with the sixth condition of formula six over *there*"— he jabbed his scriber toward another writeboard on the opposite wall—"which should serve as ample proof of

Baskaw's secondary population interference theorem." He set the scriber down on the table in front of him and folded his arms triumphantly.

The room was dead silent for five full seconds as the other scientists worked through the proof, and then the uproar started anew as they shouted their questions, their protests, their agreement, at Vandar.

Anton Koffield watched thoughtfully from a chair on the side of the room. He had been on Greenhouse less than a day, but that day had been decidedly fruitful. Vandar had brought Koffield and Chandray straight from the landing field to the Terraformation Research Center.

The symposium, if one could call it that, consisted of experts Vandar had pulled in from every terraforming discipline. Vandar had simply stood Koffield up by the writeboard at one end of a medium-sized lab-lecture room, and told everyone to sit down and listen to what Koffield had to say.

Koffield had long since finished talking and sat down to watch the seed he had planted as it began to grow. It was a scene that would have been familiar to any near-ancient scientist, and even to the natural philosophers and alchemists and theologians of the middle-ancient or far-ancient periods. They would have recognized the heated discussion, the frantic gesticulations, the formulae and diagrams and doodles being scribbled down and erased and rewritten, and understood what it meant: A new idea had gotten loose, a new way of looking at things that turned the old ways upside down and changed everything.

That was not to say a near ancient would have understood everything that was going on. Koffield himself was having a great deal of trouble keeping it all straight. Some of the doodling and figuring was happening on the writeboards that lined all the walls, in much the same way it had been done since the day when the first Sumerian drew a sketch in the dirt with a stick. But the way the doodles and calculations tidied themselves up, proofread and corrected themselves, would have given even a late near ancient pause.

Two or three of the scientists were arguing with their

ArtInts, while others were shouting at their datapages to get a move on and process the new data. Three-dimensional symbol-logic models popped into being in midair here and there, and then vanished again, or mutated and shifted until the boxes and spheres and log charts bore no resemblance to what had been there at the start.

More charts and diagrams and visual simulations were appearing out of nowhere. The images of heads, and whole bodies, of scientists popped into being in the middle of the room, and joined in the fray as their originals projected their images from elsewhere on Greenhouse. Display screens came to life and filled with text or images as other scientists linked in.

Milos Vandar was clearly in his element, but Koffield had no doubt that the other two members of their little traveling group, Ashdin and Sparten, weren't having much luck making sense of it all.

Sparten. Koffield looked over at him, on the opposite side of the room, leaning up against the wall, his arms crossed. It was a pose suitable for a prison guard. No one, his posture said, was going to move without his knowing it.

Sparten worried him. Why was he here? The others he could more or less understand. Obviously Milos Vandar had come to ease the way, to ensure that Koffield got the introduction and the attention he deserved. Wandella Ashdin was a far less logical candidate for the trip, but she had come along anyway. Koffield was willing to guess that Ashdin had talked her way into the group strictly for her own benefit, so that she could pepper him with endless questions about the great man, Oskar DeSilvo. He had done his best to avoid her during the trip, but she had taken every chance she had to learn more about her idol.

But Sparten. Koffield had no doubt that part of Sparten's brief was to keep an eye on one Anton Koffield—but who had ordered Sparten to do so, and why he had been so ordered?

If they—whoever they were—had to choose a watcher, the fact that they had chosen Sparten was informative in and of itself. It suggested that they wanted to keep things close in, tell as few people as little as possible. Sparten already knew a good deal about Koffield and Chandray and the *Dom Pedro IV*. Using him saved having to tell someone else—and also got Sparten and his knowledge well away from Solace.

They were *all* well away from Solace. Aside from Neshobe Kalzant, Raenau, Parrige, and his assistant Fribart, and probably a few other government officials, everyone who knew about Baskaw's work had been packed neatly aboard the *Cruzeiro do Sul* and sent well away from Solace. And the government controlled virtually all communications between Greenhouse and Solace.

That right there was probably the core reason for picking Koffield's entourage. Kalzant had said very clearly she needed to control the information until she had time to educate the public. Nor was there necessarily anything sinister about it. But still, Koffield told himself, it would do no harm at all for him to keep his eyes open.

Whatever one wished to call the gathering—conversation, symposium, heated argument, debate, near riot—it was getting more intense almost moment by moment, and more people were joining in by more and different means. Four separate 3-D cams lowered themselves on extensor arms from the ceiling, extended their twin cameras, and did their best to record and transmit the chaotic scene in three dimensions to remote sites, but Koffield couldn't see how any set of cameras, whether operated by humans or Art-Ints, could possibly make sense of the uproar.

And, come to think of it, neither could he. Koffield leaned over to Norla Chandray and smiled at her, feeling at least a whisper of his old sense of humor, lost for too many years, coming back to him. "Well," he said to her, "I'm completely out of my depth. I haven't understood a word in the last half hour. I'd say my work here is done. Let's get out of here." He got up out of his chair and slipped out the side door into the hallway.

No one noticed their departure but Yuri Sparten. Sparten was leaning up against the far wall of the room, and made a move as if to follow, but Koffield caught his eye and shook his head no. After a moment's hesitation, Sparten shrugged and slouched back against the wall. After all, they were in a domed settlement on an uninhabitable satellite. How far could they get?

Norla followed Koffield out of the room. She had to hurry a bit to catch up with him, but she got up alongside him before he reached the door to the outside of the building and followed him through as he shoved it open.

"Ah, sir, we shouldn't just leave like this. You shouldn't."

Koffield smiled. "Why not?"

"Well—because they need you."

"Not anymore, they don't," he said, and was surprised by how pleased that made him feel. "I've done my part. You can go back if you like. I meant 'let's get out of here' as an invitation, not an order. But I just thought you might care to join me for a stroll."

"Sir?" Norla looked at him in surprise. "What do you mean, they don't need you? We just got down here. You barely spoke ten minutes."

"Which was probably eight minutes too long. I wasn't getting much out of listening to the other speakers. I could barely understand a word any of them were saying."

"But it's all based on your work," she protested.

"Which *I* got from Baskaw," Koffield said, looking about the dome's interior with interest. There was a mixed stand of what looked like oak and pine trees a little ways off from the research center. The trees were at least ten meters tall, and clearly taking advantage of Greenhouse's low gravity to get in some extra growth.

Koffield decided he wanted a closer look and started walking toward them at a leisurely pace. He had meant it half as a joke, but his work *was* done, at least for the moment. It was a genuine pleasure to take a little time and admire the trees and the plant life. No question but that they knew how to make them grow, here on Greenhouse.

"Don't forget that what they're calling my work is all *Baskaw*'s work," he said to Norla. "I could follow the basics of what she said on the first try, but it took me endless study to get to where I was really confident and comfortable with her arguments and methodology. And *her* work was from centuries in my past, while these people are from a century in my future. They've had all that time to refine and improve terraforming techniques. Unusual sort of dome, don't you think? Usually they're all city with a bit of parkland, or all park with one or two maintenance structures. This one is half-and-half."

"If they're all that smart, how is it they never saw what Baskaw saw?" Norla demanded.

"Point taken. True, they missed what Baskaw found, but then so has everyone else in history. She is the only one *ever* to find those relationships and formulae and transformations. Her work is original and unique. DeSilvo found her work in the archives, and then I found it *because* he hid it. That's really all there is to my contribution. It took a genius unique in all of history to create the work, and I'm no genius. So why blame the scientists here for being like everyone else?"

"Even so, you should go back. They'll need you. They'll come looking for you."

"Oh, perhaps they'll look for me just to be polite, but they certainly don't *need* me. Not anymore. I'm just the gatekeeper, the man who found the key to a door that's been locked so long no one even knew it was there anymore. Then I came along and unlocked the door. Once the door's open, who needs the gatekeeper? The best I can do is get out of the way before they trample me in the rush to get through it."

Norla did not answer, and the two of them walked along in silence for a time. It was getting on toward evening as they reached the stand of trees. Koffield paused for a moment to look up, through the transparent dome, at one of the strangest skies he had ever seen.

The huge bulk of Comfort loomed directly overhead, right where it always was. Just as Earth's Moon always presented the same face to Earth, so too was Greenhouse tidally locked on Comfort. Comfort was in waning half phase at the moment, the darkened half of its surface blotting out a massive swatch of sky. The SunSpot was just setting in the west.

In the back of Koffield's subconscious, old instincts wanted a setting sun to redden and grow dimmer as it approached the horizon. The presence of trees, of sweet air, of grass under his feet, made the expectation all the stronger. But outside the dome was nothing but the near vacuum that passed for an atmosphere on Greenhouse, and the light of the SunSpot was scarcely dimmed at all by its passage through such insubstantial stuff.

The stars were lost in the SunSpot's glare, but if one turned around and looked in the opposite direction from the orbiting light source, stars, and even other satellites of Comfort, were plainly visible in an all but perfectly black sky. Stranger still, Lodestar, the true sun of this system, happened to be rising in the east just as the SunSpot set. Though the true sun was bright enough to cast a dim shadow, the SunSpot shone far brighter in the sky of Greenhouse.

And yet the SunSpot did not shed any noticeable light on Comfort. SunSpot was orbiting Greenhouse, while Greenhouse was orbiting Comfort. As seen from Greenhouse, the planet was behind the orbiting artificial sun at the moment. Besides, the SunSpot's focusing shield-shell directed virtually all of the SunSpot's light and heat on Greenhouse. SunSpot was quite literally a spotlight, aimed directly at the small world it circled.

The oddity of it all was if anything enhanced by the fact that the strange sky hung over a homey, comfortable, utterly familiar parklike setting. There were trees overhead, and a bed of pine needles and dried leaves and gently decaying humus underfoot. What looked and sounded suspiciously like a particularly arrogant male blue jay perched in a tree just ahead, scolding them loudly, and taking obvious pleasure in his own performance. A grey squirrel scuttled around the trunk of an adjacent tree, and the jay turned the brunt of his invective away from the humans and directed it at the new arrival with every bit as much zest and gusto.

The squirrel climbed his tree to a limb higher than the jay's level, then swarmed out the limb and leapt straight at the tree, and the limb, and the branch, that held the jay. The jay squawked in outrage, jumped off the branch to avoid the squirrel, and flew away, doing more gliding and less flapping than he would have on Earth, thanks to the lower gravity. The squirrel sat up on its haunches and started cleaning itself with a nonchalance so studied it was hard to believe it was not feigned. The squirrel had won, and the squirrel knew it.

Anton Koffield smiled, and even chuckled to himself, as he watched. He was quite astonished by how good he felt, how relaxed, even, strange to say, how happy he was. It had been so *long* since he had felt himself at ease, with no duty, no responsibility, no mission pushing him forward in directions he would not choose for himself.

Not since the moment, centuries before, back aboard the *Upholder,* when Alaxi Sayad had detected the intruder assault on the *Standfast,* on the downtime end of the Circum Central wormhole, had he truly felt himself this free of claims upon himself. Since then he had twice been marooned in the future, twice lost all connection to the people and events of his world, but always the weight of duty had pressed down upon him.

Even in the days after the *Upholder*'s return from Circum Central and before he met DeSilvo, when he had had little more to do than fill a desk in the Patrol's Grand Library offices, he had felt, not that he did not *have* a duty, but simply that he had no way to carry it out.

He, Koffield, had put on his own shoulders, and no one else's, responsibility for the destruction caused by the fight against the Intruders. He knew in his heart that it had been interference with timeshaft-wormhole travel that had caused that disaster. The Intruders' attacks on the future and the past had produced the chaos. *He* knew, *he* understood, even if no one else did, that it was the Intruders who had set it all in motion. But if all that death and loss were to have meaning, then the principles they had died for—defending causality, protecting the future from the past—would have to have value. And there *was* value, enormous value, in those things. But it was hard to devote one's life to a theory, an idea, that was by its very nature a negative, an absence. No paradoxes. A past not interfered with. He had found he needed something more, something nonabstract, something real to work with, rather than merely something theoretical to prevent.

It had been, in large part, Glister that had planted a

new duty in his heart. If not for Glister, and his connection to it, he would not have taken up the study of terraforming and its failures, certainly not with anything like the sort of zeal he had felt. It was, no doubt, his guilt over Glister that had driven him so hard, made him so determined to prevent a similar collapse at Solace.

But now. Now he had handed off his information to the people best qualified to use it. He had gotten past all the barriers, all the twists of fate and runs of bad luck and acts of downright sabotage, gatekeepers of another sort, that had tried to block the way.

Now he had done his job, and everyone else could do theirs. It had taken him a while, but he had come to realize that the data stolen from him meant nothing. He did not need the books and datasets that had been replaced by a suitcase weighted down with trash. No one did. The scientists and engineers on Greenhouse were experts in the field of terraforming, with resources, experience, and personnel Koffield did not have. They would be able to redevelop all of Koffield's work, and, more than likely, go beyond it, in a few days or weeks at most.

The blue jay suddenly swooped back into view and buzzed the squirrel, flying in close and fast enough that the squirrel jumped clean off its branch and barely managed to scramble to safety on a neighboring bough.

There was something wonderfully comforting and familiar in the sight of the bird and the squirrel teasing and chasing each other. The same scene had, no doubt, been played out a thousand, a million, a billion times in the past, on Earth.

Familiar. It was that, and no doubt. And, he realized, familiarity was something that had been bothering him, at the back of his mind, for quite a while now.

He had to laugh at himself. Three minutes ago, he had been congratulating himself on having no more concerns, no more worries, his tasks at an end. It hadn't taken him long to find something new to worry about.

But still, it was a mystery. He had been marooned in the future twice, once for nearly eighty years, and once for over a hundred. And yet, more than two centuries outside his own time, far too much was familiar, understandable, and easy. Or maybe he was seeing too much in too little.

"Officer Chandray?" he began.

"Yes, Admiral Koffield?" she replied, a smile on her lips.

There was just enough of a playful, half-sarcastic tone to her voice to make the message loud and clear. Here they were off duty, mission accomplished, walking in a garden, and he was calling her Officer. It was absurd. They had been through a fair amount together, and might end up going through a lot more. And, after all, the word *familiarity* had more than one meaning. "Message received," he said. "First names in private, rank and formal address in public?"

"Sounds like a fair deal—Admiral. But you go first."

"Very well—Norla." Koffield paused for a moment, surprised at himself. How long had it been since he had been on a first-name basis with—with anyone? How long since he had had anyone he could truly call, not a colleague, or a friendly professional acquaintance, but a *friend*? Even with two centuries of time-stranding figured into it, it had been a frighteningly long time. But his mind was wandering. "I wanted to ask you something. You're here from a hundred and twenty-seven years in the past. Doesn't all this"—he gestured to indicate not just the domed forest, but all of Greenhouse, all of the Solacian system—"seem just a little too *much* like home?"

"I'm not sure I know what you mean."

"I spent a little over a year in that time, in your time," Koffield said. "It never really occurred to me to realize just how little the time shift threw me off. Now I've made a second jump, twice as far as the first, and *still* I can recognize and understand the world around me. That just doesn't seem right."

"Why should you expect things to change?" asked Norla.

Koffield shook his head. "You're right. Maybe I shouldn't expect it. But there have been periods in history where two hundred years of history would leave society changed beyond recognition."

"And there have been times when the basic technology, and society, have remained mostly static for a long time."

Koffield nodded thoughtfully. "The theory is—or at least used to be, two hundred years ago, when I did my studies—that advanced, or rather advancing, technology, would force change, accelerate it. The more technology improves, the faster things change, the more technology improves. A positive feedback."

"But their technology isn't that much more advanced than ours," Norla pointed out. "It's got refinements, it's been improved, but it's essentially the same as what I grew up with."

"Maybe that's the explanation," Koffield said. "But even our clothing and hairstyles are similar enough that they fit right in. The local accents are not that different from the way some of the *Dom Pedro*'s crew speak."

Norla shrugged. "You're right. Now that you point it out, it is strange. I can't explain it, but it is odd." She turned and smiled at him. "At least it means they can understand us. Maybe we should just be grateful for small favors and leave it at that."

Koffield smiled back, but didn't reply. She was probably right. But he knew himself well enough to know he couldn't leave it at that. Now that he was aware of it, the mystery would nag at him until he knew, until he understood.

They walked on in silence beneath the trees of the strangely familiar forest and the utterly alien sky.

CHAPTER TWENTY-TWO
A THOUSAND TIMES

When they got back from their walk, Norla was both amused and pleased to see that Koffield had indeed been missed. A half dozen scientists pounced on him as soon as he came through the door, each with a complicated and obscure question to ask.

The questioning went on all throughout the evening meal in the refectory. How was this value derived? What further information did he have about Ulan Baskaw? Was he aware of the proposals for the latest Mars recovery project? How did he think his new mathematical models would affect that work? One working group had already applied the Baskaw-Koffield formulae to the available data for three historical ecocollapses, all of which had been explained away as freak accidents. The B-K formulae could have predicted all three of them. Did he have any comment? Several specialists were having trouble deriving useful data from sub-formula B of formula six. Would it be possible for him to look over their work and see if he could point out the difficulty?

The poor man scarcely had a chance to eat, but, if Norla had developed any skill at all in reading Anton Koffield, that very private man was extremely gratified—not because of the attention paid to him, but because that attention clearly signaled that all that he had done, all that he had sacrificed, had not been in vain. He had gotten the message through.

It was not until after dinner, when the locals started

slipping away from the refectory, that things settled down. But even then Koffield was the center of attention.

Norla, sitting next to him, watched as the last of the group settled themselves at their table, and engaged him in casual conversation.

Strange, strange, and strange again how people worked. Ever since Circum Central, people had pointed at him, whispered behind his back, because he happened to be there when the mysterious Intruders had wreaked their havoc. Koffield had done nothing but his job, and yet people had blamed him, and not the Intruders, for the disaster. Now here he was surrounded by admirers, not because he had made a great discovery, but merely because he had found it in a book, and read it, understood it, found a way to use it, and brought it to their attention.

"You come at a most fortunate time, Admiral," one of the group was telling him. Norla had to think for a moment to come up with the woman's name. Mandessa Orlang, that was it. The director of the Greenhouse Institute. "Or," Orlang went on in her somewhat booming voice, "perhaps a most unfortunate one. You and Officer Chandray will have the chance to see something quite spectacular and rare, if you wish to see it. Something we all wish was much rarer than it is. Something that is, unfortunately, closely related to the discoveries you have brought to our attention."

"What would that be?" Koffield asked.

"They are going to blow a dome," Vandar replied, before Orlang could speak. No doubt Orlang would have used three times as many words to relay the same information.

But Professor Orlang was not at all put out by Vandar's stealing her thunder. "Not just any dome," she said. "One of the oldest and most diverse domed habitats on Greenhouse." She paused, and spoke again, in grand and theatrical tones. "It is, in fact, *Founder's* Dome."

There was a moment's silence around the table. The solemn looks and the downcast gazes told Norla that Founder's Dome meant a lot to the locals. Of course, the name told her that much as well. Theirs was a people who set great store by their history, their heritage. Things would have to get to a sorry state indeed before they would be willing to destroy anyplace with the word *Founder's* in the name.

"I'm sorry to hear that," Koffield said, with obvious sincerity.

"It's not going to do much good for morale, that's for sure," said Vandar.

"I can't imagine that my showing up now, with all my warnings of doom and gloom, will make the situation any easier," said Koffield.

"No," Vandar said. "Not your fault, of course, but it won't. The ghost at the banquet, and all that. Before you showed up, we could all tell ourselves it was just bad luck that Founder's had to go. Now we know the problem is systemic. Now the death of Founder's will just serve to remind us that all the domes, all the habitats, all the *worlds*, are going to go."

"I am not sure I agree, Dr. Vandar," said Orlang. "Who can say? Maybe a one-two punch of hard-edged theory and grim reality will focus people's attention. Perhaps Planetary Executive Kalzant can use the failure of Founder's Dome to get the attention of the people, so that they can listen to the news you've brought us."

"Perhaps," Koffield said, plainly noncommittal.

"Excuse me, Dr. Orlang," said Wandella Ashdin. "Founder's Dome. That is where DeSilvo's Tomb is, isn't it?"

"Yes, of course. It is one of our most important heritage sites. There is a great deal of concern that it might be damaged when the dome is blown, but there is very little that can be done to get in and protect it, now that the dome is sealed down."

Koffield looked up sharply at Ashdin. "Wait a moment," he said. "DeSilvo's Tomb? He's buried *here*?"

"His ashes are here, in an urn inside the tomb. I suppose that means that *tomb* isn't exactly the right word, but that's what everyone calls it."

"How the devil did his ashes come to be here?"

"It was in his will. When he died for the last time, his

body was cremated, the ashes sealed in the urn and shipped to Greenhouse."

"Died for the *last* time?" Norla asked. "How many times *did* he die?"

" 'A coward dies a thousand times,' " said Koffield, half to himself. He was only half–paying attention to the conversation. It was obvious that something had caught him by surprise, made him see something. " 'A hero dies but once.' "

"What in the world is *that* supposed to mean?" Ashdin asked suspiciously.

"It's an old quotation," Koffield said absently, not aware that he had given offense. "It's from an early near-ancient poet, I believe. One of those things that's been translated over and over again across the millennia. The words change as it moves from one language to another, but the sense of the words stays the same. It means if you spend too much time worrying about the dangers, you'll never dare take chances or do what needs doing."

Ashdin sniffed audibly, and Norla could not help but smile. Ashdin took it hard when Koffield made it clear he did not share her affection for Oskar DeSilvo.

"Heroes and cowards to one side, how many times *did* DeSilvo die?" Norla asked.

"And when did DeSilvo die *permanently*?" Koffield asked, as if the question might be of special importance.

"*Dr.* DeSilvo was clinically dead at least five times, and subsequently revived," Ashdin said stiffly. "He died *absolutely*—that is, finally and without revival—thirteen years after your departure for Solace. However, he was not active during all of those years. He spent much of them in temporal confinement, and made at least one interstellar round-trip—presumably in cryosleep—during that time. No one has ever been able to ascertain where he went on that trip, but I suppose that is beside the point. He died in his offices, at his desk, at work, in the Grand Library. His remains were cremated and transported here, in accordance with his will."

Koffield stared intently at Ashdin, but, somehow, did

not actually seem to see her. His eye was focused on things unseen, things beyond the horizon and buried in the past. At last, he came to himself, then turned to address Orlang. "You said the dome was sealed. Is it no longer possible to get into the dome?"

"That is not precisely correct. Once a dome is sealed down, it is no longer possible to get *out* of it. It is sealed because we fear biological contaminants coming out through the airlock system and infecting other domes."

"So it is at least possible to go in."

Orlang was obviously baffled. "Theoretically, yes, I suppose. But whoever went in would have to remain inside until the dome was blown. It is a fairly complex process, blowing a dome. First they place powerful heaters throughout the dome and cut off the cooling system. They run the in-dome temperature up to one hundred twenty degrees centigrade and hold it there for twelve hours. Then they use shaped charges, strategically placed all over the surface of that dome, to produce explosive compression. That, plus exposure to near vacuum, provides near-total sterilization."

"But a man in a suit, an armored pressure suit, carrying spare oxygen and food and water, could go in, so long as he was willing to remain inside until the dome was blown?"

Orlang nodded vaguely. "I suppose. If he knew how to protect himself against the heat and the decompression blasts."

"Then I must go into that dome, now. I must see that tomb, and examine it carefully, before it suffers any damage from explosive decompression or heating."

"But whatever for?" Orlang asked.

"I'd rather not say," Koffield replied.

"But this is absurd," Orlang protested. "I can't just let you wander around a contaminated zone for a week without any explanation."

"I know it sounds absurd." Koffield paused for a moment. "I'm reluctant to discuss my suspicions because I could well go in there and discover nothing at all, and then I would have raised unreasonable, unfair expectations—or fears." Koffield shrugged. "Or it might be that I find something absolutely vital."

Orlang glared at him balefully. "I must say, your behavior is highly presumptuous, especially considering how brief a time you have been here. Why should I grant you special access to Founder's Dome when you will not extend to me sufficient trust or respect to explain why you want to go?"

Anton Koffield looked her straight in the eye. "I'm sorry," he said. "But I can say no more than I have. I do not ask you to put anyone else at risk, or to do yourself any harm. But I must get a look at that tomb, and do so before you blow the dome. Decompression and heat sterilization might—*might*—damage or destroy something vital."

Norla could see, if not what Koffield saw, at least the fire that was suddenly ablaze in his eyes. She could not see what it was that excited him, but she could read him well enough to understand the excitement, the need to reach out for—for *something* that had eluded him far too long.

"Why in heaven's name should I agree?" Orlang asked. "Just because *you* ask?"

"Because he's Anton Koffield," Norla heard herself saying. "Because he's crossed unimaginable distances of time and space to bring you a warning that only he saw, that only he knew was important. Because he risked everything, lost everything, sacrificed everything he had for the sake of getting the facts to you, for the sake of truth, and of doing what was right. Because before that, he did his job, and did it well, and his reward was being turned into a boogey man. Glistern parents tell their children the Koffield monster will get them if they don't behave. Because, after all that, he's still willing to take risks for others.

"And *because someone has tried again and again to stop him*." She looked around the table. "Have you thought to wonder why? *Why* would anyone try so hard to hurt him? Why sabotage his ship and steal his evidence? Why maroon him in the future a *second* time when he's already lost his own time into a still-more-distant future?"

"I don't know," said Orlang stiffly. "What do you think?"

"Perhaps," said Norla, "because someone is afraid of what he might find. Perhaps they think he's *still* a threat. And he is. When a man like that thinks he might find something worthwhile in Founder's Dome, I'd listen to him, if I were you."

Everyone at the table, everyone still in the room, was staring at her. Anton Koffield himself looked at her in more than slight amazement. In the sudden quiet, Norla realized she couldn't blame any of them a bit. If it were possible, she'd be staring at herself. What in space had pulled that impassioned speech out of her?

"Well," said Mandessa Orlang. "I am impressed. Anyone who can inspire that sort of defense certainly *ought* to be someone who should be taken seriously. And Officer Chandray does remind me that we do owe the admiral more than just a small favor." She thought for a moment. "Let me consider this," she said. "Maybe—just maybe—we can accommodate you after all, Admiral."

After a bit of negotiating, it was agreed that Koffield would be allowed in twenty-four hours before the dome was blown. It was obviously imprudent, from a safety viewpoint, for anyone to spend that long alone sealed in a pressure suit in a contaminated zone. Someone would have to go with him, and obviously enough, that person would likely be privy to whatever it was that Koffield hoped to find.

That last point was enough to explain why Wandella Ashdin volunteered to go with him, but even after repeated sessions with the suit techs, it was plain that, though she could probably look after herself in a suit, she was not anything close to mechanically competent enough to be much use to Koffield if his suit malfunctioned. Strangely enough, however, Koffield *wanted* Ashdin along, a quite remarkable development, given that he had next to no patience with the woman's fascination with DeSilvo. And, by virtue of some sequence of arguments, offers, bluffs, and counteroffers, Norla Chandray found that she had volunteered to make up the third of the party without exactly *meaning* to do it.

And so Norla found herself, five days later, her skin still raw and tingling from the ferociously hot and brisk shower that was going to be her last for a while, climbing into what she would have called a pressure suit. The local techs called it an environment suit, or e-suit. It had a number of modifications that made it more suitable for work in a contamination zone, but it still bore a close family resemblance to the sort of pressure suit she had worn all her working life. It was downright peculiar that her knowledge of suit design from the past century and another star system would be of any use at all to her here and now.

The main link between Research Dome and Founder's Dome was a nondescript underground tunnel, but that accessway had been sealed off some time ago. Orlang's people did not wish there to be any chance of blow-back contamination popping out of the airlock that sealed in Founder's Dome and then drifting down the tunnel into Research. The three of them would have to take the overland route, walking, not through pressurized domes and tunnels and corridors, but across the near vacuum of Greenhouse's surface, and making a shortcut through another dome that had been blown long ago. It was not likely to be the easiest or most pleasant of journeys.

"Ready?" Koffield asked her as the suit techs finished their last adjustments. Both of them were fully suited up, but their faceplates were still open.

"As ready as I'll be," Norla replied. "I think Dr. Ashdin is just about ready to claw the airlock open herself if we don't get moving soon."

"She does seem just a trifle eager, doesn't she?" Koffield replied. Ashdin had hurried through her suit-up and headed for the lock chamber five minutes before. "Let's go find her before she gets completely out of control."

The two of them said their thanks to the suit techs and headed down the hall to the lock chamber. Ashdin was there all right, her faceplate down and her suit sealed. Even through the bulky suit, even with her face half-hidden by the faceplate, it was obvious how eager and excited she was. She was pacing back and forth, peeking through the porthole by the airlock one moment, chatting with the airlock techs the next, and saying farewell to the Research Dome scientists who had come to see them off the next.

Mandessa Orlang and Milos Vandar were there as part of the send-off committee, and so was Yuri Sparten. Norla had been not altogether surprised that Sparten had tried to get himself included on their miniexpedition, and even less surprised that Koffield had kept him from going. There were undercurrents there.

"Good luck to you, Admiral," Orlang said as she offered her hand to Koffield. "Be careful, won't you? Things are likely to get a trifle warm where you're going."

"And the atmosphere will get a bit rarefied after that," Vandar said.

Koffield took Orlang's hand and bowed slightly. "Thank you, Director Orlang," he said. "Believe me, we'll be careful. I'm interested in gathering information, not taking risks."

"See you in a couple of days, then," Vandar said.

"Good-bye," said Sparten, and left it at that.

The three of them wrapped up their good-byes, and the visitors were herded out of the airlock operations room by a very polite, but very firm, no-nonsense, suit technician.

The tech then ushered the three travelers into the lock chamber proper. Norla noted that their equipment roller, in essence an oversize wheelbarrow packed with spares and supplies, was already in the lock. As soon as they were in the lock chamber, the tech got started with the final check-over. "Okay," he said. "Suits ready for check. Seal 'em up and turn 'em on."

Ashdin already had her suit sealed and running. Norla and Koffield closed their suits. Each then switched on main power on the other's main chest panels.

"Suit ready for check," Norla said.

"Ready for check," Koffield agreed.

"Um, ah, me too," said Ashdin, plainly both nervous and excited.

"Very well," said the tech. "Beacons are confirmed *active*," he said as he checked a small datapage. "Comm system *functional*. You have a short-range intercom channel linking your three suits. That's marked *chan 1* on the panel on the control panel on your suit's left forearm. *Chan 2* is the general operations channel. Lots of traffic on that channel, so it's not easy to hold a conversation. *Chan 3* keys you through to your base station here. We can patch you through to a private link to someone in another suit, or to pretty much anyone else." He consulted the telemetry display on his datapage again, and checked the readout on their suit panels. "Oxy mix and air pressure *okay*. Cooling system *up* and *running*. Suit integrity *confirmed* . . ."

The tech worked his way through the remaining steps of the checklist, then nodded in reluctant satisfaction. "The suits are all working fine," he said. "They can handle the temperatures and pressures you'll be going into—but don't push them too far. If you start to get too warm in the suits, *don't* just crank up the cooling. You might need that cooling capacity later on, and if you use it up the first time you break into a light sweat, it won't be there.

"Remember, once you go into Founder's, you can't come back out, no matter what, until they blow the dome. You can't break the integrity of your suit for any reason until the dome has been blown and you're out, clear, and have gone through suit decontamination. If you break your leg, or have a heart attack, or vomit your lunch onto the faceplate of your suit, or your suit plumbing fails and you're peeing into the suit leg instead of the collection system, that'll just be too bad. You can change your mind anytime up until you enter Founder's, but once you're inside, you are in that dome—and in that suit—until the dome is blown. No one's going to bend the safety regs, or abort something as complicated and dangerous and important as blowing a dome because someone who asked to go in and signed all the danger waivers calls for help. Is that clear?"

"Maybe a little clearer than we wanted it," said Norla.

"Good," said the suit tech. "Last chance to bail out. Any takers?"

Norla glanced at Ashdin, half-expecting her to change her mind about the whole thing. But Ashdin shook her head, and it was clear that Koffield was going to go, no matter what. Norla was almost tempted to wave off. She had experience in long-duration suited missions, and knew how rough they could be. But she was at least as curious as anyone else to find out what Koffield was after.

Silence gave the suit tech his answer.

"Hmmph," he grunted. "I was hoping at least someone would be sensible. All right then. Good luck, and we'll have the showers ready for you in a bit over two days. Off you go."

The tech left the chamber, and the inner door of the airlock swung shut behind him.

The lock began to cycle. Norla looked up to watch the force-filter field establish itself, masking the top of the chamber, and then begin its descent from the ceiling of the lock. The shimmering grey field moved downward, forcing the air out of the lock, through the floor vents below their feet. Norla could feel its static charge on her skin, even through the pressure suit.

The field sank lower, over her helmet, flowing down around her suited body. The comm channel filled with scratching and hissing for a moment as the field touched the top of her radio antenna. The radio static grew louder, then faded, to be replaced by silence. No, not silence—*exterior* silence. There were noises aplenty from inside her suit—the humming and clicking of the machinery, the sound of her own breathing—but there was no longer any sound coming from the outside.

She looked about herself, and at Koffield's and Ashdin's suited figures. Everything had taken on that extra-razor-sharp clarity produced by near vacuum.

Her pressure suit stiffened a bit as its flexible joints expanded against the near-zero pressure outside the suit. She looked down, watching the filter field drop toward the floor, forcing the air in the lock ahead of it. The grey field vanished, and then, after a brief pause, the outer lock swung open. The surface of Greenhouse lay before them, looking not the least bit green.

"Let's get going," Koffield said, his voice coming now, not from his direction, but from the speakers in Norla's helmet. He grabbed hold of the equipment carrier's pull bar and stepped out of the lock, pulling the two-wheeled cart behind him. Norla and Dr. Ashdin stepped out of the lock behind him.

Koffield stopped and turned back toward the others just a few meters outside the lock. "I want to move fast, but we'll probably make better time if we take a minute and acclimate first. Get used to the suits, get your bearings, get an idea of what the landscape and the footing are like."

Norla took a few cautious steps out onto the rocky, dusty ground. Somehow, being in a heavy pressure suit, out on the surface, made her more aware, rather than less, of Greenhouse's low gravity. Greenhouse was a small, dark lump of rock. Even with the outgassing caused by human activity, and the heating effects of the SunSpot, its atmosphere was far thinner than Mars's before the disastrous attempts to terraform that world. The air pressure at the surface of Greenhouse was only slightly thicker than the barely-there-at-all almost-perfect near vacuum on Earth's Moon.

The sky was black, the landscape a dirty, dusty grey, the big and small rocks and thick powdery soil all the same gloomy shade. This part of Greenhouse, at least, was not much at all to look at.

Research Dome rose behind them, and three other active domes loomed at various points on the nearby horizon. Seen from the outside, they glowed with the achingly lovely pure sky-blue of a perfect spring day, a color made only more intense by virtue of being the only color to speak of in the landscape.

It was just after local sunrise—or, more accurately, local SunSpot rise. Norla's helmet optics blocked out the image of the SunSpot itself when she turned to look at it. Comfort hung huge and aloof high in the sky, and the stars sprinkled the darkness beyond.

"All right," said Koffield, "let's get moving." He took up the pull bar of the equipment cart again and started heading east, toward the rising SunSpot. His shadow stretched far behind him as he leaned into the pull bar to get the cart moving over the loose sand that covered the surface.

"We're on the private channel now, right?" Ashdin asked.

"Yes, but I suspect we're all transmitting at the high-power setting," said Koffield. "I doubt anyone who took the job seriously would have much trouble listening in if they wanted to do so. I take it you want to talk privately, just among the three of us?"

"Yes, I do," Ashdin replied. "We're going to know more as soon as we get where we're going. We might as well know it now."

"I was expecting you to point that out," said Koffield. "Very well. Set channel one to minimum range."

Norla adjusted her settings. "Chan one, min power," she announced.

Koffield paused for a moment to adjust his own gear, but did not look back. "All right," he said, his voice suddenly made almost tinny by the power drop. "Channel one to minimum power."

"I'm, ah, having a little trouble," Ashdin said.

"Hold on, I'll give you a hand," Norla said.

"What? Did you say something?"

Norla resisted the temptation to let out a weary sigh. At least Ashdin didn't take more than a moment or so to figure out that Norla could hear her, but Ashdin could no longer hear her. She turned toward Norla, and Norla gestured for her to come over to her. She took Ashdin by the forearm, swung it around until she could see it properly. Sure enough, Ashdin had managed to zero out her receiver volume, rather than reduce transmitter power. Norla made the proper adjustments.

"Can you hear me now?" Norla asked as she peered through Ashdin's helmet.

"Oh! Yes!" said Ashdin. "Much better. And now, perhaps, Admiral Koffield, we are private enough for you to tell us what all this is about."

But there was no answer from Koffield. Norla turned around and looked in the direction they were heading. Koffield was already several hundred meters ahead. "Come on," she said. "We're going to have to do some catching up. They deliberately set the minimum range on these suit radios very low, so they won't interfere with other communications. I think we're already out of range of his suit. Let's hurry."

Koffield was walking hard, setting an impressively brisk pace, in spite of the fact that he was towing the equipment cart. It took several minutes for Norla and Ashdin to catch up with him.

"There you are," Koffield said, when they finally drew abreast of him.

"Yes, we are," said Norla, a little out of breath and just a trifle irritated. "You might have waited up for us."

"Forgive me," said Koffield. "I suppose I'm just eager." He slackened his pace just a trifle. "I suppose it can't make any difference if we get there ten minutes later."

"Eager for *what*?" Ashdin demanded, puffing a bit. "It is high time and beyond that you told us what, exactly, we are going to see."

Koffield chuckled. "I'm not sure if the joke is on you, or on me, but the honest answer is that I haven't the faintest idea."

Ashdin stopped dead and looked straight at Koffield. "You don't know? Then what in the name of stars and space are we *doing* out here?" she asked.

Koffield paused just long enough to look her in the eye, but it was plain that he did not wish to stop a moment longer than he *had* to. "I have no idea of the *what*," he said. "But I have a very strong idea of the *why*. But please, I am—or at least I have the sense that I am—near the end of a very long chase. A chase I did not even realize I was making, until very recently. I have been held back too long—centuries too long. I will answer all your questions and tell you all I know—but let us keep moving. I am too near the end for stopping long."

"All right," said Ashdin.

"Thank you," said Koffield, and immediately set out again, towing the cart behind him.

"You said you thought you knew the *why*," Norla said, addressing the back of Koffield's suited head. "What did you mean by that? What is the 'why' in all this?"

"Ego," said Koffield. "The 'why' is just one thing: Dr. Oskar DeSilvo's huge and insatiable ego."

Even after all her experience in pressure-suit work, it was strange for Norla to see the man up ahead, and yet hear his disembodied voice come from just by her ear. Perhaps it was because this was not the usual sort of conversation one heard in a pressure suit. This was no routine back-and-forth chitchat about adjusting a docking probe or recalibrating an out-of-whack antenna. This was Anton Koffield, that most private of men, rushing away from them, rushing toward the horizon, and yet revealing himself, explaining himself as he moved toward whatever it was that he sought.

"Dr. DeSilvo's ego?" Ashdin repeated. "I know perfectly well that you don't care for the man, Admiral—but I don't know why I needed to come out here in order to listen to yet more attacks on him. The man is dead. Does his ego matter now?"

"Yes," said Koffield. "Because he's dead once again, for what seems the thousandth time. He's cremated and interred. But interred *where*?"

"In Founder's Dome," Ashdin said. "Honestly, Admiral. I expected more than a childish question and answer from you."

"But consider the man," Koffield said as he strode along ahead of them. "Think about it. Think, not about what you have known all your life, that he died and left instructions in his will to be cremated and to have the ashes returned to Greenhouse. Think of the man, his pride, his need to be admired, to be at the center of things. Greenhouse? It's the back of beyond. Solace was the center of his triumph. Think of the oversize, overblown designs and impractical structures he built. All of them meant more to be wondered at than useful. All of them, in a very real sense, are monuments to himself. DeSilvo craved immortality, literal and figurative. Everything he ever did was a bid to be remembered forever.

"Would he really build himself a modest tomb holding a pathetic little urn full of ashes, and plant it on a world that even *he* knew couldn't last forever? Greenhouse will die and go cold and dark forever, once the SunSpot finally fails, and DeSilvo knew that.

"Wouldn't it have been more in character to build himself a vast memorial in the center of Solace City, or on some hillside by the town, where everyone who came to see his tomb would have to admire his brilliant architecture as well?"

Ashdin was silent. Norla glanced over at her, but their faceplates had mirrored themselves against the light of the rising SunSpot, and Norla could not see her face, let alone read her expression. But Koffield's logic held. It made sense. Something else occurred to Norla.

"Ulan Baskaw," she said.

Koffield stopped for a moment, turned and looked behind himself, his mirrored helmet revealing nothing of his expression. The two women paused as well. He nodded, exaggerating the move to make it noticeable under his suit. "Yes, yes. You're right, Norla. I hadn't even thought of that aspect. I've been so tied up thinking about why DeSilvo would have insisted on being buried someplace else, I forgot the one reason he would have flatly *refused* to be buried on Greenhouse."

Koffield turned back and started moving again.

"I don't understand," said Ashdin.

"Think about it," Norla said as they started to follow Koffield once again. "Think not just about what you knew before we got here, but about what the admiral told you about the Greenhouse-and-SunSpot technique—*it wasn't DeSilvo's idea*. He had to pretend to the whole of Settled Space that he had thought of it himself. But he knew, deep down inside, that he had stolen the idea, plagiarized it from a woman dead hundreds of years before. Solace was his. That he built in his own image. He knew it, and everyone else knew it—and it was true. But Greenhouse? Would he really want to be interred and memorialized on the one world that *had* to stand for all his lies and self-deceptions? Greenhouse was the world that reminded him he was a fraud."

"And that is all the reason you have for thinking DeSilvo is not buried here?"

"That's all," Koffield said. "Except for one thing. You assume DeSilvo died and stayed that way thirteen years after I left for Solace. Why?"

"What do you mean, 'why'? Every text, every source, every biography, every witness agrees on the day of DeSilvo's death."

"Were you there? Did you see it? He died and cheated death many times before. Can you *prove* he died then, for good and all? Or even that he is, in fact, dead? If we opened up the urn in his tomb, would you be able to say for certain the ashes in it were his?"

It was Ashdin's turn to stop in her tracks, Norla pausing alongside her, but Koffield did not so much as look behind. "You're not just saying it's not his tomb?" Ashdin asked. "You're saying that the man isn't even *dead*?"

Then Koffield did stop and look back. "Why not?" he asked. "I was born over three hundred years ago," he said quietly. "I have spent more than three-fourths of that time in cryosleep. DeSilvo had already been in and out of cryosleep and temporal confinement dozens of times when I knew him. He had only actually lived about eighty years of biological time by then, though centuries had gone by. I think it is at least possible that he either feigned death—or truly caused himself to be clinically, if temporarily, dead, merely to avoid confronting me before I left for Solace. Sooner or later, yes, he probably did have his final death. But how can we know for sure? When it comes to a man who has died and flirted with death that often, when it comes to a man who could and did manipulate and fake records in highly sophisticated data-storage systems, I will need something more than books that agree that he died before I believe he is dead for all time."

Ashdin did not answer, and the three of them started moving again, walking in silence for a time.

Koffield was the first to speak, though not about the matter at hand. "That should be Sunflower Dome up ahead, just to the left," he said. "Or at least, what's left of it."

Sunflower was not like Research Dome behind them. Sunflower was no gleaming swell of sky-blue. They had blown Sunflower a long time ago, and it was as dark and as grey and as dead as everything else on the surface. "Are we sure we want to go through there?" Norla asked.

"No reason not to. It's directly between Research and Founder's. It'll take us at least two hours to walk around it."

"Maybe I wouldn't mind taking up two hours of my time to avoid it," Norla said. But that sort of talk wasn't going to convince Koffield, and she followed behind without further argument as they bore toward the wreckage of Sunflower.

It took no great amount of time for them to reach the edge of Sunflower's debris field, the bits of blown-out dome, broken pieces of machinery, twigs, leaves, branches, whole trees torn up by the roots and thrown out onto the airless surface, and, worse by far, dead birds and small animals, their ruined, pathetic bodies mummified and baked down to nothing by the extreme cold and heat of Greenhouse's surface.

Norla spotted the twisted corpse of a squirrel lying in the dirt where it had been thrown by the blowout, its fur turned black by the unfiltered fury of the SunSpot's radiation. She thought of the jay and the squirrel doing merry battle in the trees of Research Dome, and could not bear to think that the wiry, stiffened, lifeless thing was the same sort of being at all. Was that what the future held for Research Dome as well? Was there no way to stop the inevitable collapses?

Perhaps, somehow, *knowing* they were inevitable, knowing that all domes and habitats and terraformed worlds were doomed was the first step. What was the term the terraformers had used over and over during that chaotic symposium? *Masked causality?* No. *Cause-pattern masking*, that was it. The deep connections between events got hidden behind the random noise of everyday life, so that twenty-three linked and similar events were seen as twenty-three separate and unrelated incidents. Maybe, someday, taking that mask off would lead them to a way to solve the problem. It was a faint sort of hope, but it was all she could find.

"Orlang told me this one went wrong," said Ashdin. "The idea of blowing a dome is to sterilize it so you can reuse it. You're not supposed to destroy the dome completely. But this was one of the first ones they blew, and they miscalculated the charges and set them wrong. Instead of getting some holes in the dome so it would decompress suddenly, they got a complete structural failure. They've learned to do it better since."

"They've had a lot of practice," Koffield said grimly. "This whole world is nothing but domed settlements and farms and experimental plots."

The debris got bigger, and heavier, as they drew near the perimeter of the dome itself. They walked around a fifteen-meter oak tree lying on its side. The decompression explosion had uprooted it and thrown it clear out of the dome. The ruined tree had leaves still on its branches, and dirt clumped to its roots. To see a once-living thing that massive, out in the hard vacuum, to see death in the landscape of the unliving airlessness, tore at Norla's heart. All was doom. All was death.

Picking their way through the debris, they came to the solid anchor wall, still intact, that had once held and supported the clear dome that was not there anymore. Someone had bulldozed the debris away from an airlock door that was the near twin of the one through which they had departed Research Dome. The rubble was shoved up against the anchor wall to each side of the lock.

Both the inner and outer doors of the lock stood open, and they stepped through, into the wreck of Sunflower Dome.

Apparently the wreckage of Sunflower was a convenient enough overland shortcut to merit bulldozing paths through the interior ruins as well. There were three paths cleared through the rubble. One led due east, the second bore off to the southeast, and the third went northeast. Koffield had studied every available map before departing, and led them unhesitatingly down the northeasterly path.

Having the rubble cleared out of their way only made the wreckage to either side seem worse. They walked past ruined fields, buildings with the doors and windows blown out, pieces of clothing, datapages, books, papers, a child's toy doll—small, personal things, abandoned by their owners, scattered by the decompression explosion, and then left where they had fallen. The wrecked buildings, stands of trees that, somehow, had remained standing after the disaster, loomed up ahead of them as they walked and then receded into the rear.

The scale of the place made it seem the ruin of a haunted mansion built long ago for a race of giants. It seemed unbelievable that any mere humans could be capable of building so much, of reaching for such great height—or of then letting it fall from so high, into such depths of loss and failure. Overhead, the Sunspot was rising steadily in the east, as the huge, dim, aloof bulk of Comfort remained frozen in one spot in the sky. But if the sky seemed strange and alien, the landscape was more so.

It was an incomprehensible place. Norla thought of barbarians walking through a once-mighty city, past structures far mightier than they could dream of, surrounded by evidence of a long-vanished power that had far surpassed their own abilities. Could the Solacians of today, the ancestors of the people who had made this place, build anything as grand as this ruin?

But the operative word was *ruin*. Today Sunflower Dome was like this. Tomorrow, quite literally, it would be Founder's turn. And then? This was the doom that awaited the trim, cheerful parks of Research Dome, and everyplace else, save Earth herself, that Norla had ever seen. Koffield had shown them that, shown that every dome and habitat and world would die. Past, present, future.

The knowledge seemed more curse than anything else. It did not bear thinking about.

"If it's not a tomb—*if* it isn't—what is it?" Ashdin asked, breaking the long silence that had held since they reached the wreckage of Sunflower's airlock.

"I beg your pardon?" Koffield said.

"The tomb. You've told us your reasons for thinking that's not what it is. So what do you think it is?"

"I haven't the slightest idea," Koffield said. But then, after a moment, he corrected himself. "No, that isn't quite true. I have ideas. But they seem absurd, even to me."

"What are they?" she demanded.

He paused for a minute, set down the cart handle, and flexed his hands, stretching the kinks out of them as he turned around. "Shall we rest for a minute?"

"Fine with me," said Norla. They were in the middle of what once might have been an ornamental garden, with large flat boulders, the right height to serve as benches, set here and there. She sat down on one of them, and Ashdin sat next to her. Koffield remained standing, and paced back and forth in front of them. "So," Norla said. "Tell us. What do you think DeSilvo built instead of a tomb?"

"And how you reached those conclusions," put in Ashdin.

"Very well," he said. "Start with the maxim *Think like your enemy,*" he said. "That's what I always heard from my instructors when I was learning to be an intelligence officer."

"But—" Ashdin cut in.

"Before you can launch into debate on the point," said Koffield, "no, I don't believe DeSilvo to be my enemy—at least I don't know it for certain. But he was, or is, certainly my opponent. I sought to uncover what he sought to hide. He wanted one thing, and I wanted another. Fair enough?"

"I suppose so," Ashdin said, not well satisfied.

"So I need to think like him, understand him, if I am to make sense of what he does." Koffield stopped pacing and looked directly at Ashdin, his face faintly visible behind the faceplate of his suit. "You still see him as a hero, a genius. I no longer do. Is he, was he, evil, or delusional, or insane? I don't think so. And yet, somehow, he committed a crime so vast that you, Dr. Ashdin, and I daresay most people, have trouble even seeing it as a crime. The only defense I can see is that, somehow, he did not know the consequences of what he was doing, but I cannot believe that. He *must* have known. He terraformed Solace with the certain knowledge that the terraformation would collapse and fail. He used a technique to make it happen faster, but he had to know perfectly well that the technique would bring the doom on faster. You have seen the evidence I brought, heard the story I told. What other explanation do you have?"

"We only have your word to go on concerning this Ulan Baskaw woman and her books," Ashdin said. "Her name doesn't appear in any archive, any history, that I have heard of."

"True. I hadn't considered that point. But there is at least evidence of the existence of Baskaw's work. I am no mathematician, but I brought your terraformers the work of a mathematical genius. It must have come from *somewhere*. It dovetails perfectly with the work DeSilvo claims as his own, and it has the merit of being true, and testable. Surely that gives me some credibility. And where you have been able to match my story against your records, it has checked out."

"But even so," Ashdin protested, "I can't believe it. He wouldn't do it."

Norla spoke up. "Just for the sake of argument, Doctor. You wanted the admiral's answer. Let him go on."

"Very well," said Ashdin, plainly reluctant. "For the sake of argument, let us say your story is true. But—but my point is that *surely* you can see that behaving as you said he did would be completely out of character for Oskar DeSilvo."

"Yes it would." Koffield turned away from where the two women sat, and considered the dead and ruined landscape that surrounded them. "It would be out of character—at least for part of him, the part he let be seen. He was kind, gracious, a gentleman—better liked, and more loved, than I will ever be. And yet he was a schemer, a manipulator, a user, a trickster, a plagiarist on the grandest scale. I have no proof—at present—of my stories of Baskaw and vanishing books, but they are nonetheless true. They tell me that Oskar DeSilvo was a whirling mass of contradictions. I am not the least bit ashamed to admit that I find thinking from his perspective, his point of view, difficult in the extreme."

"So what would a man like that leave in a tomb?" Norla asked.

"*Tomb.* I think part of the answer lies in that word," said Koffield. "A false tomb. Cryosleep chamber. Temporal-confinement chamber. All of them simulations of death.

And recall that, once I found Baskaw's books, he literally retreated into death, albeit temporarily, perhaps merely to avoid dealing with me. Tombs are safe, death is safe. No one can bother you, or challenge you, when you are dead. But he had an ego. A massive one. I don't think he could imagine that people would be fooled forever by his frauds and failures. And, of course, in some corner of his heart, *he* knew that Solace was going to fail, to collapse. DeSilvo, for all his flaws, was quite definitely human enough to be capable of feeling guilt—and he certainly had enough to feel guilty about. But death, real or imagined, would let him hide from the wrath of those he had hurt."

Koffield turned again, and looked in the direction of their travel, toward Founder's Dome and whatever was there. "He had to know that both frauds—his tomb, and Solace itself—would fail sooner or later. So why build a false tomb for himself on the wrong world—on the world dedicated to terraforming research?"

"An answer," said Norla. "An answer he could leave behind without getting near the people and the worlds he had hurt."

"*Yes*," Koffield said. "Precisely. Pride, guilt, ego, and death. A man preoccupied with those, a man who had vast resources at his command, who had perhaps decades to study the problem, rather than the mere weeks and months I had, or the mere days that our friends at Research Dome have had—such a man might have *found* something. A way out."

"And hidden it in his tomb?" Ashdin asked.

"Resurrection!" Norla said, standing up suddenly. "Out of the tomb comes life!"

"And the resurrection of his own reputation," Koffield said, the excitement in his voice barely controlled. "Precisely. It fits. It all fits his psychology far better than sticking his own real tomb on Greenhouse after his own real death."

"And you're worried that whatever that answer is, it might not survive explosive decompression," said Ashdin.

"Look around you," said Koffield, gesturing toward the hideous wreckage that surrounded them. "Suppose they get it this wrong again? Whatever the clue is that we're looking for, I doubt we'd find it in a place that looked like this."

Ashdin stood up as well, and looked from Norla to Koffield. "It's not enough," she said. "You might have something, yes. But it's too thin. Too clever. You're reaching too far. Maybe DeSilvo's Tomb is not what we all thought—but I don't think it's what you think either."

"Shall we go find out?" Koffield asked quietly, calmly.

"Let me pull the cart for a while," Norla said. "Come on. Let's get moving."

CHAPTER TWENTY-THREE
COLLATERAL DAMAGE

They moved on without saying much of anything. Maybe they had said too much as it was. They reached the far side of Sunflower Dome's perimeter and exited through another abandoned airlock with both doors left open. The same sort of debris littered the ground on this side of the dome. It was hard not to reflect on the notion that they were, quite deliberately, heading into a place that was going to have the same thing happen to it. In theory, the dome engineers knew better this time and could do an explosive decompression of Founder's that would blast the air out without tearing the roof off the place. All they could do was hope that Founder's Dome would be blown with a bit more care and precision than Sunflower, and that the precautions they had taken to protect themselves when the time came would be enough.

They spotted a work crew just coming out of the Founder's Dome west airlock when they were about a kilometer away. They could just barely see one of the figures waving its arms at them.

"Do you think they're calling us?" said Ashdin.

"Switch over to the general comm channel," Koffield said.

Norla switched her own comm over, and instantly heard a new voice.

"—ou the crazies going *in* there?" the voice asked, more quizzical than rude. It was a man's voice.

"That's us," Koffield replied, cheerfully enough. "We've got all the clearances we need."

"Fine," the voice said. "Glad to see you." Norla could just barely make out the tiny figures by the base of the dome. Her suit didn't have image enhancers, and she had to squint a bit to see them at all. A second figure turned to look at them, but the other three, busy packing up their open-frame roller transport, paid them no attention.

"Is there anyone else still in the dome?" Koffield asked.

"No, you'll have it all to yourselves," the man said. "We set up the last of the heaters and charges using remotes and ArtInts and robots. None of our team have been in the dome itself for a week now. Decontamination drills just got to be too much of a hassle. Maybe your crowd has the right idea. Stay inside until the blast."

"The hell they do," a second voice, a woman's, replied. "*I'm* not gonna stand at ground zero for a bake-and-blow."

"It shouldn't be that bad," the man said. "They put you through a standard blowout drill, brief you on what to do?"

"Yes," said Norla. "We spent the last two days on that kind of thing."

"Then you'll be fine. Keep anchored and sheltered, go easy on your suit cooling, and there won't be a thing to worry about."

"Speaking of cooling," the woman's voice said, "we've already shut down the interior cooling on the dome. It's middle of local afternoon now. The dome heaters won't kick in at all until sunset. There might be a minor spike in the temp uptrend then. But when the SunSpot rises tomorrow, you'll find out why they call it Greenhouse. With the SunSpot and the interior heaters going, the temps are going to climb like crazy, so be ready."

"We will."

"We're going to blow the dome just after sunset tomorrow to get the widest temperature gradient possible," the man's voice said. "You be ready. This thing is *complicated,* a whole sequence that started weeks ago. We can't stop it now if we're going to blow the dome right."

"Yeah, that's for sure," the woman agreed. "Sunflower is what happened back when we thought we could just abort a dome-blow and then just start over. Things went wrong. So we're *not* doing that again. Clear?"

"We're clear," said Koffield.

"And we're out of here," said the man. This time Norla was sure she could see him wave. He climbed aboard the transport, then helped the woman aboard. "So long," he said, "and good luck."

"Thank you," said Koffield. "Farewell to you."

The transport started up, its rear wheels rooster-tailing a plume of dust up off the ground as the transport started off. It turned toward the southeast, moving quickly across the barren land. It took no more than a few seconds for it to be lost to view behind a low hill.

They started walking again, on the last leg of the journey.

The inner door of the lock came open. The three of them stepped into Founder's Dome—and instantly understood why it had to die. A sealed habitat dome was supposed to be a controlled environment, but there was no part of Founder's that was even remotely under control.

The three of them had indeed been briefed before going in, and it was plain to see that none of the briefers' horror stories had been exaggerated. Founder's had started out as a crop development center, but had been converted into recreational space decades before. It was supposed to be parkland, but the manicured lawn and carefully tended glades had failed long ago. Uncontrolled organisms of every sort had invaded the dome. Mold and lichen covered virtually every surface. The trees that still survived were spindly, wretched things, barely capable of pushing out leaves. The ponds were covered by thick mats of brownish-green algae.

Roaches scuttled over everything, and termites were plainly at work in most of the trees, living and dead. But no other animals of any sort survived. The birds had been wiped out by a rogue virus months before. The fish had been simultaneously suffocated and poisoned as the algae sucked all the oxygen out of the water and excreted all manner of toxins, the same waterborne toxins that had done in the small mammals as well. Norla spotted a dead rat that seemed to have dropped in its tracks by the side of one small pond. Mold was growing on the fur of the rotting corpse.

Even the material of the dome itself had been corrupted. Some sort of slimy mildew had started to form on it. In some places the mildew was merely a thin, translucent layer, but in others it was several centimeters thick—so thick that it had started to buckle and peel off the dome under its own weight.

As bad as it all looked to the naked eye, the briefers had assured them, it was worse on the microscopic level. The bacteria seemed to be mutating into new and more deadly variants with every passing day. Even the roaches were succumbing to opportunistic infections. The entire dome was nothing but a tangle of disease vectors.

Koffield, Norla, and Ashdin walked along what had once been a tree-lined path of white crushed stone, and was now a dismal alley, the stone stained black with lichen, the path half-blocked by fallen tree limbs.

"Thanks be to the founders," Koffield whispered. "For look what they have bequeathed unto us."

"This is dreadful," Ashdin said. "I knew it was going to be bad, but I had no idea. I was here, years ago, before it started to go bad. It was lovely then. Just lovely."

They came to a big ceramic heater that had been set up along one side of the path. It was not powered up yet, but it would be soon. Norla checked her suit's outside temperature gauge. It was already warm out there without the heaters running, and the heaters were due to kick in at dusk. She glanced up through the mildew-fogged dome to the slightly blurry image of the SunSpot.

"We don't have a lot of daylight left," she said. "If we're here to get a look at DeSilvo's Tomb, maybe we should get there while we can still see it."

"You've been here before, Dr. Ashdin," said Koffield. "You lead the way."

Ashdin chuckled dryly. "Well, the place has changed just a bit since the last time I was here. But I believe if we bear off to the left at the next crossing, that will lead us there."

The tomb, Norla was not surprised to discover, was hexagonal, and stood in the precise center of the dome. She had seen enough DeSilvo designs to recognize his style at a glance. The man had used the same motifs and design elements over and over again.

This DeSilvo design, however, wasn't a glass-wall job, but simple white stone, marble by the look of it. At least it had been white marble, before it was blackened by the omnipresent mold and mildew. The entire structure was built on five low hexagonal platforms, each slightly larger than the one above it, so as to form a continuous stairway around the tomb, with the tomb itself at the top of the stairway. Five faces of the structure were stone. The sixth face stood open, forming the entrance to the interior. The tomb itself was about fifteen meters from side to side, with the outermost and lowest platform adding about three meters to that. Dead leaves and twigs littered the stairways, and a dead sparrow lay just outside the entrance on the stained and darkened marble.

"There it is," Ashdin said. "Your answer. A small six-sided building in the middle of a dome. If you can see a way that's going to solve the climate crisis on Solace, I'd be interested to hear it."

Koffield ignored her sarcasm. "I'm sure you know the tomb backward and forward. Walk us around it. Tell us about it."

Ashdin turned to Koffield and gave him a funny look. "Why not?" she asked. "We've got until tomorrow night before we can get out of here. Might as well fill the time up somehow. I don't even know why I came here in the first place."

"It'll come back to you," Koffield said mildly. "Walk us around."

Ashdin stared at Koffield for a moment, then shrugged. "All right," she said. "The marble itself was quarried on Solace, from the same quarries that built many of Solace

City's great public buildings. The six sides of the building, and the six levels formed by the platform stair and the tomb itself, recall the hexagonal shape of a honeycomb, and are meant to remind us that from the hard work of the bee comes the sweetness of honey. If you'll follow me around the exterior of the tomb, you will see that four of the five exterior panels bear carved quotations from DeSilvo's various speeches and letters and so on." She paused on the side of the building opposite the entrance. "This fifth panel, the one opposite the open side of the structure, and the one that, as you will see when we go in, is closest to the urn that holds his ashes, bears an inscribed reproduction of DeSilvo's design for Solace City, demonstrating that it is close to him and is the face he would best like to have presented to the outside world."

She led them around the other side of the tomb and came back to the front. "Note also that near the top of each panel is a glyph, a different one for each panel. The fifth panel's glyph is a stylized ray of light, symbolizing the sense of sight and the doors of the soul. The other panels display stylized symbols of the senses as well. A musical note to indicate hearing, a flower for the sense of smell, a loaf of bread and bottle of wine for taste, and a feather for touch. The five senses that are our gateways to the outside world are on the outside of the building, to remind us that buildings are the work of architects and should engage all the five senses. And, of course, the sixth panel, the one that is not there, and yet whose shape is formed by the presence of the existing panels, symbolizes the sixth sense, the passage that links the inner and outward life, and guides and shapes the actions of the artist."

"That doesn't look the least bit like a feather," Koffield said. "And I'd have never guessed that was a bottle of wine."

"A bit overly clever, isn't it?" Norla asked. "The symbolism is pretty forced."

"A matter of taste, I suppose," Koffield said. "But I must admit I don't seem to see any grand answers to the terraforming crisis."

"Thousands of people have visited here over the years," Ashdin said snappishly. "If it was there, surely one of them would have spotted it."

Koffield gestured, hands upturned and empty. "You've got a point," he said.

Norla gestured toward the entrance. "I suppose that, with the outer panels symbolizing outer life, the interior is going to symbolize inner life?"

Ashdin was plainly embarrassed by the degree to which Norla was unimpressed. "Yes," she said. "Come on." She led the way into the tomb, her e-suit making her move awkwardly as she went up the low marble steps.

The SunSpot was close to the horizon, and it was starting to get dark. But the entrance of the tomb was sighted to point due west, so that, as Norla could see from the outside, the setting SunSpot flooded the interior of the tomb with light. Light reminded Norla of heat. She checked her suit's exterior temperature gauge. It was already thirty-five degrees Celsius. That was nothing her suit could not handle, and it was far less hot than it was going to be—but there was no question that the dome's interior was heating rapidly. Ashdin walked inside the structure, and Norla followed, with Koffield taking up the rear.

The interior was on the grimy side, but in far better repair than the exterior. A marble sphere sat by the west wall of the tomb, and a golden urn, a cylinder of understatedly simple design, sat on the sphere. The single word *DE-SILVO* was etched into the urn, and the legend *THE FOUNDER* was carved into the floor beneath the sphere.

"The setting SunSpot illuminates the Founder's final resting place," said Ashdin—

"Just as his work illuminated all our lives?" Norla asked.

Ashdin turned and glared at Norla. With sunset coming on, their faceplates had adjusted their reflective coatings down to full transparency, and Norla could see Ashdin's expression quite clearly. "Something like that," Ashdin said. "He was a great man! Maybe not a saint. Maybe he made mistakes. But this is his tomb, his final resting place. It could do you no harm to show a bit of respect."

"I'm sorry," said Norla. "You're quite right. Please, show us the rest."

Anton Koffield came in behind Norla, and she turned to look him in the face. The disappointment was plain on his face. "I don't know what I was thinking," he said. "Madness. Hopeless optimism. I don't know. There's nothing here."

But now that Ashdin had started out to give the full tour, it was clear she was determined to see it all the way through. She gestured up. "The ceiling of the chamber is deliberately bare," she said. "It is the future, uncharted and unmade. An empty canvas upon which we draw what we will." She gestured at the floor. "The floor is the past, the tools and knowledge given to us. Note the single point inscribed on it just inside the entryway, and then, a little farther in, the line that runs the width of the tomb. Then, beneath our feet, an equilateral triangle inscribed in the floor. Around the triangle is a square, and outside that, a regular pentagon and a regular hexagon. Plane geometry. Note the crystal cube and the steel cone that sit on the floor in front of the side panels. Note also the marble sphere that supports DeSilvo's funerary urn. Solid geometry, and three dimensions, and the combination of materials, produce architecture.

"On the left side of the chamber, the wall formed by the two side panels is inscribed with a line of random numbers. On the right, it is inscribed with a line of random alphanumeric characters. The two lines point to the panel behind the funerary urn, just as the geometric forms of the floor move toward it. And on that panel, as you see, the letters become words, and the words poetry—quotations from noted poets on the theme of the natural world. The string of random numbers and letters form into the vital formulae that define the timeshaft wormhole that links the worlds, while the geometric forms are resolved, as I have said, by the sphere that holds the urn. But the sphere, as you will note if you look carefully, is lightly inscribed with a map of Solace. Mathematics, poetry, and geometry combine to form not only architecture, but the science and art of terraforming."

Norla shook her head. "I'm sorry, Dr. Ashdin. With all due respect, it's too much—and not enough. The symbolism is too heavy-handed. It's forced. It doesn't show us how noble and good it is to have aspirations. It *tells* us that we must be inspired. It lectures at us. It's as if there were something here that had to be in here, that didn't fit, so that everything else had to be bent out of shape to make it fit."

"What do you mean?"

Norla pointed at the side panels. "The random numbers and letters don't work in the concept at all. Everything else is so orderly as to be completely sterile. Lines, angles, geometry. It's all rigid and symmetrical. Randomness doesn't fit in."

She glanced behind her, at Anton Koffield, realizing that he had gone awfully quiet. She had thought he would be doing what she was doing—looking moodily around the self-important chamber for the clue that wasn't there, quite unaffected by the overworked good intentions, the naggingly virtuous tone of the place.

But Koffield was looking, no, not looking, *staring,* in one direction, and one direction only. At the left-hand wall. At the string of random digits that marched across the wall toward the unconvincing order and perfection of the west wall.

"I don't believe it," he whispered to himself. "I can't believe it," he repeated, shock and astonishment in his voice and on his face.

"Admiral Koffield?" Norla reached out and put her pressure-suited hand on the arm of his suit. "Anton? Anton? What is it?"

"It's too much," he said. "Too much."

"Too much *what*?"

"It's the answer," he said. "It's the answer, all right. But the answer to a very different question."

"What are you talking about?" Dr. Ashdin demanded.

Koffield pointed at the string of digits, his arm straight out, his forefinger stabbing at the numbers. "That is *not* random," he said. "It is the thirty-digit combination to my personal pack compartment on my cryosleep canister aboard the *Dom Pedro IV*."

"*What?*" Norla shouted. "It's *what?*"

"I don't understand," said Ashdin. "How could that be?"

Koffield ignored both of them. "*Damn* the man's ego. His arrogance." He spun around and studied the string of letters and numbers there. "It's got to be," he muttered to himself. "Backup. He would have needed a backup." Koffield punched commands into the comm panel set into the arm of his suit. "I'm switching over to the main comm channel. You two do the same. I—we—may need witnesses on this. Koffield to Research Dome comm central. Do you read me?"

"Research Dome comm central," a bored-sounding voice replied.

"Comm central, this is an emergency. More than a life-and-death emergency. Can you receive the signal from my suit's helmet camera and relay it?"

"Ah, yeah, I guess."

"Then get ready to do it. And locate Captain Felipe Henrique Marquez. He is most likely aboard his ship, the *Dom Pedro IV*, docked at Shadow Spine Station. Find him, get him to a comm station, and patch voice comm back and forth from him to me, and patch my helmet camera signal through to him. Make it happen *fast*. Did you get all that?"

"Yes, sir." Whoever was on the other end of that comm channel heard the urgency in Koffield's voice, heard the tone of command, and had the sense to take both seriously.

"Then do it, and fast. There's not a great deal of time."

Koffield turned to Ashdin. "Lights," he said. "SunSpot is setting. There are portable lights in the equipment cart. Get them. Fast."

"But what is it?" she demanded. "What do the numbers *mean*?"

Koffield shook his head. "Either I've gone around the bend just now, or else DeSilvo went mad before you were born. Maybe he and I are both mad." He gestured with outstretched arms to indicate the tomb. "Unless I'm insane, this entire place is—is a message in a bottle. And DeSilvo addressed it directly, specifically, to *me*. Damn the man! Go! Lights!"

Ashdin went.

Koffield checked his chronometer, then looked at Norla. "They're going to blow the dome in twenty hours. We have to be done and ready long before then. The heat might get bad enough to damage something."

"Done with *what*?"

"Taking this place apart and getting whatever we find into shielded, insulated containers. The urn, of course. That's obvious. We'll take it, but leave it sealed until we can get it examined."

"Sir—Anton—if I'm understanding you right, you're saying that up there is the combination you used to lock up your travel case? The one with your evidence in it?"

"That's right."

"Then DeSilvo is the one who—"

"Exactly. And that string of numbers on the wall has been there for a hundred years, waiting for me to get to this system and play tourist."

Ashdin came back in with the lights. "Did I hear that right?" she said. "You honestly believe this whole tomb was built for your benefit? To send *you* a message?"

"Yes, yes," Koffield said. "I know what it sounds like. Do you think it sounds any saner to *me*? But there it is, on the wall."

"According to you," Ashdin said. "Your memory could be playing tricks. Or maybe you're playing tricks."

Koffield nodded. "Maybe I am," he agreed. "I wish I were. But that's what the call to Marquez is about. Let's get these lights up and running."

The SunSpot was about to set, but they worked fast, and just about had the lights rigged when Marquez's voice came over their helmet radios. "Admiral? What's going on? We got some damned-fool call that there was an emergency."

Koffield nodded, though of course Marquez couldn't

see it. "And there is. But once again, my friend, I cannot explain what it is, for fear of prejudicing you."

"Prejudicing me? About what?" Marquez chuckled. "But it occurs to me you will choose not to answer that question."

"Let's see if you can answer for yourself. Are you getting the feed from my helmet camera?"

"They are just patching it through now—there we are. You're inside some sort of stone building, it looks like."

"Yes, we are. I am going to give you a look at some letters and numbers that are carved into the wall here. I want you to tell me if they mean anything, anything at all to you."

"Very well."

Koffield turned carefully, and pointed his helmet, and the camera, straight at the right-side wall. "Can you see clearly?"

"Yes, I can—I can—*meu deus*. Koffield. That's—that's—devils in chaos, we'll have to rebuild the whole security system. But how did it—"

"What *is* it?" Ashdin demanded.

"No sense worrying about security," Koffield told Marquez. "This cat is very much out of the bag. It's been on public display for about a century or so."

"A *century*? But then—then. Good God. Stars in the sky. So *that* is how it was done."

"Answer me!" Ashdin half shouted. "What is it?"

"It is my command access code alphanumeric for the *Dom Pedro IV*. With that access clearance, you could command or reprogram virtually every system on this ship. Admiral. Where are you? What place has this on the wall?"

"The same place that has my cryocan's personal storage combination on the opposite wall. The tomb of one Dr. Oskar DeSilvo. And it means that *he* was the one. He did it. *He* used one code to sabotage your ship. He marooned us all in the future. But that was just collateral damage that happened because *he* decided to make sure my warning got here a hundred and twenty-seven years too late to save anyone. Then he used the code on the other wall to steal my data, my evidence, and replace it with a wad of melted plastic and scrap, to try and make my warning not only too late, but too flimsy to be believed."

Koffield turned his head from the wall and looked toward the urn that might or might not hold the ashes of a megalomaniac. "Oskar DeSilvo. *He* did it. And for whatever bizarre reason, he left a coded confession that only you and I could read, on the walls of what is supposed to be his tomb."

"But *why*?" Marquez asked.

No one spoke. Not even such an expert in interpreting symbols as Dr. Wandella Ashdin could answer that one.

CHAPTER TWENTY-FOUR

BLOWOUT

"Damnation!" Koffield swore as he yanked again at the urn. "How in the hell is this thing attached?"

"Wait a second," Norla said from the other side of the marble sphere. "Pull it again, the same way." That time she had definitely seen a crack between the urn and the top of the globe of Solace. Koffield pulled again, harder, and the crack reappeared. She forced her improvised crowbar—which had started the day as the equipment cart's tow handle—into the narrow gap. "Okay, I've got the tip of the bar in under it. Keep up a steady pressure, and I'll rock the bar up and down, try and force it in farther."

"Okay."

Norla checked her outside temp gauge. It was showing fifty-five degrees Celsius, more than halfway from freezing to boiling, not quite halfway to the target temperature of one hundred twenty. But Norla was pretty sure fifty-five was already hotter than it ever got on the surface of Earth.

Didn't matter. Nothing mattered. Just get the damned urn off the top of the globe and into one of their cooling bags. Protect it so whatever the hell was in it wouldn't be destroyed by the max temps.

And what *was* in it? There was not a damn way in the world to know. Maybe it actually held nothing but DeSilvo's ashes, and if so, that would be good enough for Norla. The damned old ghoul had risen from the dead one time too many for her tastes. He had been there, in the

background, in the shadow, everywhere, from the momen
she had boarded the *Dom Pedro IV*, DeSilvo's sabotag
programs already preprogrammed into the ship's contro
systems. There in the sinfully self-absorbed Gondola, ther
pushing the refugees, the gluefeet, up off the planet he ha
built so shoddily, there humiliating Koffield in front o
Raenau.

No, ashes were too good for him. Norla would prefe
to see Oskar DeSilvo with a stake through his heart.

But if not ashes, then what? There was no way in th
world to know. She leaned in harder to force the tip of th
handle in deep. There. Yes. "It's definitely starting t
give."

"Good," said Koffield.

"Why isn't Wandella back yet?" Norla asked. "D
Ashdin, you back in radio range yet?"

She got an answer back this time, if a bit broken u
"—hear you,—ore or—ess.—idn't have much luck."

Ashdin had been scavenging the area for tools, or an
thing else that might come in handy. "Well, we're makin
progress as it is. I think. You might as well come back."

Norla leaned in one more time, and was rewarded wi
a distinct *crack* from somewhere under the urn.

"That sounded good," Koffield said.

"Yeah. It's coming." Norla was half-sprawled over th
sphere. She thought she could feel the warmth of
through her suit. Was that possible? The suit was superb
insulated, after all. Or was she just imagining things?
trickle of sweat ran down her forehead and down to th
tip of her nose. It hung there and refused to drip off. Sh
shook her head violently, and it fell. Wherever the he
was coming from, she knew she was overheating. Sh
knew damn well there were few worse things you could c
in a pressure suit. For the dozenth time, she resisted th
temptation to crank up her cooling. They weren't even
the bad part yet. She shoved on the cart handle again, ar
the urn came away from the sphere with a resoundi
crack.

"That's it," Koffield said, and lifted the bulky obje
down, and set it on the floor of the tomb. "Whatever it is

"Do you think there *is* something in there? Something useful?"

Koffield shook his head. "The one thing I've learned today is that my guesses and opinions aren't worth much. There could be anything in there, or nothing but ashes." Koffield knelt to examine the urn more carefully. "It's *big* for a funerary urn. Maybe—" Koffield stared at the urn, then shook his head. "Oh, to hell with it. I'm past guessing. For now, let's get it in a cool-down bag."

"I'll get one from the cart," Norla said, and walked out of the tomb. The radio link kept them talking in normal tones even as they moved around the tomb. "I wish *I* were past guessing. My mind is still whirling with it all. Why did he *do* it all? The cruelty of it all. Sabotaging the ship, destroying your evidence."

"To protect his reputation," Koffield said. "Or maybe he had even talked himself into believing Baskaw was wrong, that the fast techniques weren't flawed. He could have told himself that if I got to Solace on time I would cause a needless panic that could have wrecked the whole project at a critical time."

"But why leave a message for *you*?"

"I have no idea."

She stepped out of the tomb, and looked out into the blood-red night, the last night of all for Founder's Dome. The massive ceramic heaters dotted around the dome's interior were hard at work, glowing cherry-red, casting patches of dim, shadowless light. Fires were burning near a half dozen of them, but none seemed likely to get close enough to threaten the tomb. "What was so critical about that moment?" she asked as she knelt by the cart. She found the cool-down bag and headed back toward the tomb's interior.

"In a big complicated project, *every* moment is critical if you're looking for excuses to do what you want," said Koffield. "He stopped me causing that panic and did it without killing us all. He probably thought he was being clever and humane."

"Humane enough to get two of us killed in cryo," Norla said. "And none of us will ever see our families again. Our homes are probably unrecognizable, if they're still there and we can ever get to them. It would almost have been kinder to kill us all outright." She knelt next to Koffield and handed him the bag. "Which brings us to the next mystery, the next why. The codes on the wall of the tomb," she went on. "*Was* that just more cruelty, a nasty trick from beyond the grave? It couldn't be. He wouldn't have gone to all this trouble just for that."

"No. He couldn't have. The codes were here, for Marquez and for me. Were they a confession, a boast, the punch line to his joke? Some of each, is my guess. But they were more. The lines of numbers and characters pointed right *at* this urn. There has to be *something* in it." Koffield reached out and touched the urn, ran his fingers along its gleaming surface. "There *has* to be something that will make it all worthwhile." His voice faded away to a whisper. "Something, *something* that will at least give it all meaning," he said, and the words were nearly a prayer.

The SunSpot rose over Hell.

The old fires had died, after filling the dome's air with smoke. New ones were popping up everywhere as the howling winds scattered sparks and burning trash everywhere. But the dome's supply of oxygen was close to depletion, and nearly every new blaze guttered down to nothing almost as fast as it flared up.

The temperature continued to climb, reaching and surpassing one hundred centigrade shortly after sunrise. The filthy, algae-choked water in the once-decorative ponds was beginning to hiss and steam and bubble as it rose over the boiling point.

The plant life and algae were turning brown, drying up as the heat drove out their reserves of moisture. The last of the insects were dying, on their backs, writhing in agony as they were slowly cooked alive. Aside from Koffield, Norla, and Wandella Ashdin there would shortly be no creature larger than a cockroach still alive out there.

The dome's air pressure had already increased by a full five percent. The dome air had expanded as it heated, and smoke and steam were adding to the actual mass of gases in the air. The situation had reached the runaway-greenhouse stage. The thicker the air, and the more burn products in it, the better an insulator and heat absorber the dome became. Even if the heaters were shut down, even if they never detonated the decompression charges, the dome's temperature and air pressure would keep right on rising, powered by nothing but the SunSpot. It would likely blow all by itself in another day or so.

"I wish to God there was something to do besides wait," said Ashdin to Norla, as they stood in the doorway of the tomb.

Norla laughed. The tension between them had eased during the night, somehow. Maybe it was just that even Wandella Ashdin had now been forced to admit her hero was something less than a genius and a saint. It couldn't have been easy, sticking up for someone like DeSilvo as the evidence mounted against him. "Sign up for spaceside work if you want to find out what waiting is. All those years in cryo, just to make the time go past a little bit faster."

"I think we all could do with a bit of cryo just about now," said Wandella. "Or anything cold."

"Amen to that," Norla said without a trace of irony. Waking up in the midst of a literal inferno was enough to make a believer out of anyone. "I'm near to sweating to death."

"We're near death in lots of ways," Wandella said, looking out over the burning land.

They had spent a sleepless night searching over every square inch of the structure, looking for something, anything, that might be a clue, a lead. A hairline crack in a wall that might conceal a secret compartment, a hidden lever, an inscription hidden from view, a puzzle hidden in the pattern of shapes and lines that might tell them to look here. But there was nothing. In the end, even Koffield had been convinced of that.

They had searched as best they could. Others could do better job after the blowout. Prolonged heating was not the best thing for marble, and the place would no doubt suffer damage in the blowout, but it would survive. And when it did, it would, no doubt, be taken apart, practically down to the molecular level. Norla doubted they would find anything, but the search had to be made.

She turned her back on the flames and went to check on Koffield. Somehow, bless the man, he had found it in himself to rest, to sleep, in the midst of it all, there in his suit, on the floor of his enemy's tomb, his head propped on the cooldown bag that held DeSilvo's funerary urn. She checked his suit displays, the temp gauges in particular. Drifting toward the high end, but still in the safe range. The cool-down bag was doing better, showing an interior temp of twenty-five degrees, a pleasant day in late spring.

She looked to Koffield's face, and saw his features twitch, his eyes moving back and forth under their lids. Was he having the sweet dreams he deserved, or merely reliving the nightmare he had wakened to when the *Dom Pedro IV* arrived in-system?

So long as the man was granted rest, it almost did not matter.

"Sleep," Norla whispered to Anton. "Sleep."

"This is Research Dome Control. On my mark, three minutes to blowout. Mark."

"We read, Research Dome. Ready when you are," said Norla. "Boy, are we ever ready."

They would not have been able to hold out much longer. The sweat was pouring down their bodies. All of them needed water. Their suit helmets were starting to fog over. The low humming of their suit coolers had spooled up to a banshee wail that made it hard to hear or understand anyone else.

Norla checked her tie-downs again, and made good and damn sure she was strapped in tightly to the big marble sphere. Koffield, wide-awake and alert, was to her left. The cool-down bag with the urn inside was strapped down between Norla and Koffield. Wandella Ashdin, semiconscious and badly dehydrated, was on Norla's right. Their suits had drinking-water tubes and nutritab dispensers that could be operated by chin and tongue levers, but they had to use the food and water sparingly—and Ashdin was already close to depleting her water.

Staying in the tomb, and tying themselves down to the marble globe, had not so much been the best choice they could make, but merely the least bad. It seemed more prudent to risk the slight chance of the tomb collapsing rather than the near certainty of getting slapped around by flying debris outside. And if the roof did cave in, the globe itself would likely protect them. If nothing else, being tied down to a multiton stone sphere ensured they wouldn't be going anywhere when the decompression blast hit.

Norla was facing the east end of the tomb, the entrance-way that framed the swirling, smoking chaos outside. "I guess we've got a front-row seat to Armageddon," she said.

"No," said Koffield. "A front-row seat on the future. Unless, somehow, somewhere, we find some answers, some solutions, then out there, on the dried-out wreckage of Sunflower, is the future of every settlement, every habitat, every human world, aside from Earth herself."

"Do you think it might be that the answers are in here?" Norla asked, patting the cool-down bag.

"I wish I did, but no. I can't believe in magic, or wish fulfillment. Besides, can you imagine Oskar DeSilvo finding the way to save the universe, and then going to all this trouble just to see to it that someone else got the credit?"

"No," said Norla with a bitter laugh. "It does sound a trifle out of character."

"This is Research Dome Control. On my mark, two minutes to blowout. Mark."

"Message received. Two minutes," said Koffield. "Try to wake up Dr. Ashdin. She'll never live it down if she sleeps through Armageddon. Let her take some water. One way or the other, there's no sense in hoarding it now. An hour from now, we'll either be dead, or they'll be doing pickup on us and running us to the decontamination station."

Norla nodded, and took a sip of her own water. "Wandella," she said, shaking Ashdin to rouse her. "Wake up. You're going to miss it."

"What? Huh? What? Oh." Ashdin blinked, sat up, and looked around. "I'm sorry. I drifted out for a while."

"Anything that passes the time," said Norla. "Go ahead and take some water."

Ashdin nodded and sucked greedily at her suit's water tube. Norla looked at her worriedly. Wandella Ashdin was a mess. A dirty, sleepless, hungry, frightened mess. Norla knew she and Koffield didn't look any better. "We're going to get through this," she said. "We're almost there. Just a little while longer."

"This is Research Dome Control. One minute to blowout. Stand by for explosive decompression. Commence all safety precautions."

"Like what?" Norla asked.

"Just hang on," said Koffield. "Hold on and make it through, that's all."

"Thirty seconds."

Silence that surely must have lasted far longer than ten seconds.

"Twenty seconds. All charges primed and armed. All safety circuits off."

And again, a wait that lasted far too long.

"Ten seconds. Nine. Eight. Seven. Six. Five."

It was going to happen. Suddenly the moment they had wished for so devoutly these last twenty-four hours seemed far too close.

"Four. Three. Two. One."

"Ze—"

The world was shattered by a thousand blasts of thunder, booming, rumbling, roaring all around them. Even through their helmets, the sound was impossibly large. The ground shook, bucking and heaving. The sky outside the tomb lit up as if jolted by a sky full of lightning, as the dome was literally split asunder in a thousand places. The first of the shock waves hit them, a wall of compressed air that punched through the entrance of the tomb and slapped them back against the marble globe. Clouds of dust erupted from every corner of the tomb, and the globe itself rocked back and forth ever so slightly, just enough to provide Norla with the terrifying image of the giant weight rolling over on top of them.

The globe held steady, but the rest of the world did not.

Bits of marble bounced and pinged around the tomb as the walls and floors suddenly sprouted new cracks and stress breaks that were not part of Oskar DeSilvo's sterile, platitudinous geometry.

The explosions went on and on, and did not truly end, but instead were merely subsumed into a new and more terrifying sound, the screaming, roaring wail of megatons of air blasting its way out into cold space. New shock waves shook and rattled the tomb as jets of air went supersonic in their rush out of the dome. Norla watched in horrified fascination as cyclones sprouted out of nowhere and marched across the landscape, ripping up everything in their paths. Two of the twisters collided and blew each other apart.

The wind screamed and howled and bellowed, and the air was full of debris that flew in all directions. A massive tree dropped to the ground directly in front of the tomb entrance, and a violent gust of wind threw branches, sticks, mud, and gravel into their faces. They raised their arms to protect their faceplates. One piece of gravel zinged into Norla's helmet, starring the armored transplex, but not breaking it.

Water precipitated violently out of the air as the pressure dropped and the cold of space struck at the dome's interior. Sheets of rain slammed into the superheated ground and immediately erupted into columns of steam and water vapor.

Then, somehow, the terrifying chaos began to subside. The last of the wind and air howled away. Sound itself faded away as the air that bore the sound jetted out into space.

The violence of air in motion gave way to the stillness of vacuum—and the silence of the tomb.

CHAPTER TWENTY-FIVE

THE OCEAN OF YEARS

"Are we ready?" Koffield asked.

"Ready as we're going to be," said Wandella Ashdin.

"Not like we have much else to do for the next month," said Norla.

"All right then," Koffield said. "Let's get started."

In spite of the rigorous decontamination scrub-down they had gotten while still in their suits, and then once again when they were out of them, Koffield, Norla, and Ashdin had been put under a thirty-day quarantine. They had been shut away in a bioisolation bunker connected to, though at present sealed off from, Research Dome. None of them liked it, but there was little they could do about it.

The funerary urn itself, and everything else they had brought back from Founder's Dome, had been sealed in with them. The decontamination crews had run the urn through a chemical decontamination, but that could only sterilize the exterior. Obviously, since they had no idea what might be in it, they couldn't risk heat-sterilizing it. Just as obviously, no one could know for sure what was inside it, and after going through the trouble, expense, and trauma of blowing a dome, the good people of Research Dome were not interested in taking needless risks. If it were going to be opened, it would be opened in quarantine. After a day spent cleaning up and recovering, not only from two days in overheated pressure suits but from the decontamination process itself, it was time to do the job.

The urn was a simple cylinder about thirty centimeters in diameter and sixty centimeters deep. They had set it at the center of a worktable in Research Dome's quarantine facility. After a brief examination, it was obvious that the urn opened by simply unscrewing the flush-mounted lid. Anton Koffield carefully put his hands on the lid and began to turn it. It resisted for a moment, then began to turn smoothly, if not easily.

Koffield glanced over at Ashdin, standing on the other side of the table, ready to assist. Norla was working a long-watch camera, making a permanent, unerasable record of whatever they found, moving in and around the table to get close-ups as needed.

"It's coming," Koffield said. "The threading is very tight, but it's coming. Dr. Ashdin, if you could come around the other side and help me lift it off. It's quite heavy, and I want to do it carefully."

Wandella came over, took one side of the lid, and helped Koffield turn it through the last few windings of the thread. The excitement, the tension in the room was almost palpable. Koffield looked at Norla, and she looked back at him. He saw a strange blend of anticipation and fear in her eyes and had no doubt he wore the same expression.

"Here we go. That's got it loose," he said. "Lift it away on my count. One, two—three."

They lifted the heavy lid up away from the urn and set it to one side on the table.

They all three looked down into the urn. Disappointment slapped at Koffield. Ashes. After all that, nothing but ashes.

"Dammit!" Norla cried out. "It can't be."

"It isn't," Koffield said, holding himself calm. It was the slightest of setbacks, he told himself, and one that he had more or less expected. It had to be merely one more disguise, one more layer of trickery. He peered into the urn and saw what he was searching for. "Look more carefully. Those are ashes, all right—but they don't take up more than a quarter of the cylinder's depth. There's a false bottom. Dr. Ashdin, bring that bowl over here if you will. Set it down on the table, and help me pour out whoever, or whatever, these ashes are."

"You think those might not be DeSilvo's?" Norla asked.

"I've given up believing anything I can't prove," Koffield said. "Take the other side of the cylinder, Doctor. Easy now."

The ashes poured out into the bowl. For the most part they were fine and powdery, but there were a few bits of incompletely burned bone here and there, as well as a tooth. Koffield examined the ashes thoughtfully. "Very interesting indeed. Norla—Officer Chandray. Get a good close-up on that tooth. It's definitely not human. I'm no expert on animal dentition, but it looks as if someone cremated a large mammal of some sort—a pig, I do believe— and then failed to sift the ashes properly. Someone didn't cover his tracks quite as carefully as he should have."

Koffield ran a wipe-down cloth over the interior of the urn. It was plain to see now that the upper chamber took up very little of the volume of the urn.

Ashdin peered into the interior, then pointed at a set of five dark ovals that looked very much like blobs of near-ancient sealing wax, set into the base of the chamber in a radial pattern, each sealed across what might very well be the edge of an inner lid. "Those look like memory polymer resin thumbprint seals," she said.

It was the same sort of seal that had been used to seal up the personal property chamber on Koffield's cryotank. If the proper thumb pressed down on the resin, it would dissolve away, but it would only respond to the preprogrammed prints, or to whatever other criteria had been set into it.

"So they do," said Koffield thoughtfully. "So they do. I wonder if I could get you and Officer Chandray to try them."

Ashdin was obviously hesitant about putting her hands into a funerary urn, but it seemed she could not think of any logical reason for refusing. She tried both of her thumbs, and then all her fingers, on all five of the seals, without result. Norla handed off the camera to Koffield and tried herself, but nothing happened.

Koffield handed the camera back to Norla. "Let's see if I have any better luck. I wish we could get Marquez down here to try him as well, but I don't think anyone is going to be patient enough to wait for that. Make sure you have a good clear field of view with that camera."

Anton Koffield pressed his right thumb down onto the first seal and held it there for a few seconds.

And the seal crumbled away.

Ashdin gasped.

Norla let out a low whistle and shook her head. "I'd call that pretty convincing evidence that you were expected," she said.

"Yes," said Koffield. "Oh, yes indeed." Slowly, purposefully, he pressed his thumb down onto each of the remaining seals in turn. All of them dissolved as neatly and perfectly as the first. Koffield took another wipe-down cloth and cleaned the seal residue out and examined the interior again.

"See that?" he said. "Get a good shot of that. There were latches under the seals." He reached in and flipped each of the latches open, one by one. The lid popped up as the last latch came free.

And Anton Koffield lifted out the inner lid of the urn.

"It looks as if there's—there's a stack of things in here," he said for the benefit of the camera's recording. "Each in its own padded receptacle. The first is a datacube." He lifted it out, his heart pounding, his fingers trembling. He removed it from its padding, and read the label.

"*My* datacube," he said quietly. "The one I thought I was traveling with when I came to Solace." He reached into the urn again, removed the next item, and took it out of its padding. But the first had been more than enough to tell him what the second was. "The printed book version of the same data," he announced. "Again, the copy I thought I was carrying."

Koffield looked at Norla, holding the cube in one hand and the book in the other. "I don't know what to say," he told her. "Does this, do these *vindicate* me? I'm glad to have them, but why did DeSilvo—*send* them to me after stealing them from me?"

"I think it looks a great deal like he had a change of heart," said Wandella Ashdin. "It's a damned peculiar way to make amends, but I think that's what it is."

"What else is in there?" Norla asked.

Koffield pulled out a thicker, padded container, and opened it up. "Dear God in heaven," he said. "*Baskaw's* books. Hard-copy printouts of Ulan Baskaw's books. Either they're copies of the Grand Library Permanent Physical Collection file copies, or else DeSilvo simply stole the PPC's copies."

"Why send you Baskaw's books?" Wandella asked.

"It's proof," Norla said. "He's given the admiral proof that everything he said was true. And it's a confession as well. Of plagiarism and more. Baskaw's books should have told DeSilvo what he was doing wouldn't work. Oskar DeSilvo has just admitted his guilt. To Admiral Koffield, to you, and to all of Solace."

Koffield nodded. The *what* of it he could follow. But he could not see the motive, the *why*. "It makes no sense!" he protested. He set down Baskaw's books and opened one, and flipped through the pages. "Why did he do it? Why confess? Why confess to me, and in this way?"

"I don't know," Norla said. "I don't know."

Wandella looked into the urn. "Ah, Admiral, there's something still in there. It looks like a letter."

Koffield looked up at her in surprise. He looked around the room, his hindbrain telling him to scan the horizon, look to see what quarter of the horizon the next mad surprise would come from. But the room was quiet, calm, deadly silent. He looked down into the urn. An envelope, facedown, sat on the bottom of it.

A letter. A message in a bottle, thrown out into the ocean of years. Against all odds it had come to shore, and into the right hands, a century and a quarter later.

He reached in and took it out.

It was a most old-fashioned sort of letter indeed, on paper and sealed into an envelope, a form that was itself merely a fashionably old-fashioned copy of a technique used by the near ancients. Koffield turned the envelope over and read the writing on the outside.

Admiral Anton Koffield
18083-19109-SQN-115-APTO-205-APO-34030

"Oh my God," said Koffield. He slumped back and sat on the edge of the table. The hurt, the shock, was intense enough to be physical. He had been hit, hit hard, struck down by a mighty blow that came from nowhere at all. "Oh my God in heaven."

"What is it?" Norla demanded.

Anton turned the envelope over and showed it to her. "The code key under my name. The code key. It is—was— *the command-code prefix for the Circum Central wormhole.* This key, and the right command codes and suffixes, are all you'd need to control the Circum Central wormhole. DeSilvo is saying he could—and *did*—send ships through it."

"*What?*" Norla half shouted.

Suddenly his mind was reeling. It was madness. It was insanity. But it fit the pattern. "It's the same way he admitted to sabotaging the *Dom Pedro IV* and stealing my data," Koffield said. "He's saying he was responsible for the attack on Circum Central. Dr. Oskar DeSilvo is telling us he sent in the Intruders that jumped my wormhole. He's saying *he* killed my crew members, stranded the *Upholder,* and destroyed the *Standfast.*"

"That's impossible," Norla protested. "Only the Chronologic Patrol can—"

Koffield thrust the envelope into her face with a trembling hand. "Without this code prefix, yes. But if he could get this code, he must have cracked into the full command system. With these codes, he could control that wormhole."

"The letter," Norla said. "Read the letter."

Koffield nodded. He turned the envelope over, unsealed it, pulled out the letter, and began to read out loud.

" 'My Dear Admiral Koffield,' " Koffield began.

As you no doubt have already surmised, this letter is a confession. I write this some thirteen years after you embarked for Solace—that is to say, thirteen years after I sabotaged your ship and stole your documentary evidence that suggested that the terra-formation of Solace was doomed to failure. If you do indeed receive this letter, I would expect you to do so roughly one hundred and fourteen standard years from now. I imagine you visiting Green-house and touring the sites, or casually flipping through a book of notable monuments—and see-ing, in person, or in a photograph, the message I have arranged to leave for you. Or perhaps you will simply come to wonder what could have pos-sibly possessed me to place my tomb on Green-house, of all the unlikely and unpleasant places.

"He got that part wrong," said Wandella.

"We came damn close to never looking at the tomb at all," Norla agreed. "If Founder's Dome had been blown before we got here, would we have ever even heard of DeSilvo's Tomb?"

"Sooner or later," Koffield said. "But would it have dawned on me to realize how little sense it made for the tomb to be on Greenhouse? If we hadn't been on Greenhouse when we were—anyway, we did find the tomb, and we understood it. That's all that matters. He wasn't all that wrong." Koffield returned to the letter.

At the time you left for Solace, I believed in my own work, and thought your analysis to be completely—and dangerously—wrong. I believed that, if anyone listened to you, it would result in upheaval, panic, and economic collapse. Your warnings, I thought, could cause the deaths of thousands, perhaps millions.

It was not generally known at the time, but the terraforming project's finances were in a most delicate stage at the time in question. Controversy could have killed the project altogether. I thus had to find a way to stop you without confronting you, or starting a public debate.

Fortunately, as the head of a large enterprise,

great resources were at my command. At the same time, I have long been skilled in techniques of technical espionage, as you, by this time, clearly have reason to know. Not wishing to harm you, but not wishing you to be heard, I sabotaged the Dom Pedro IV *and abstracted your evidence from your luggage. The precise details of how I did this are unimportant.*

"And besides, he might want to use the same trick again sometime," Norla said bitterly. "Why tell how it was done?"

It was not until long after your departure that I returned and studied Baskaw's work again, and studied your own expansion of her argument, and your synthesis of it with the current state of the art in terraforming practice. It was only then that I began to see the truth. By then, the terraformation of Solace was too far advanced to be stopped without great loss of life and treasure. The main population of settlers were already on-planet in force. It was too late.

"Do you believe that?" asked Norla.

"I don't know," Koffield said. "I can't quite believe he wouldn't be able to make sense of Baskaw's work before then, but it might be possible. I'm sure that *DeSilvo* believed it by the time he wrote this letter." He went on.

You have likely guessed much of this already. What I believe you cannot have known before examining the envelope of this letter is that I interfered with you before.

I sent the robotic ships that later came to be known as the Intruders through the Circum Central wormhole. I will discuss the purpose of their mission in a moment, but I must emphasize several other points before I do so.

First and foremost, I never intended to harm

anyone, or damage any ship. But my ineptitude and ignorance of military matters, combined with a perverse streak of bad luck, were too much for my good intentions.

Second, and this, I believe, is the deepest irony of the entire matter, it was the injury I did to you, quite unintentionally, at Circum Central, and the guilt I felt, that inspired me to seek you out at the Grand Library, and, if you will, take you under my wing, give you a purpose in life. I had greater reasons than you yet realize for thinking that I had done you a grave injury at Circum Central, but more of that in a moment. It was my miscalculation, and mine alone, that failed to take into account your remarkable competence and relentless tenacity.

I have since had occasion to examine your military record in some detail, including your service in the intelligence department. Suffice it to say, that had I known so much about you before, I would have steered well clear of you, rather than inviting you to research the history of the Solace Terraforming Project. It was, of course, during that research that you discovered my academic crimes, my plagiarisms. And all spiraled out from there.

You will no doubt also have come to suspect already that my tomb was not my tomb. It is not. It is no one's tomb. The ashes are as false as the reports of my recent death.

What you likely have not yet divined are my reasons for this present, elaborately concealed, confession. One reason is obvious, so obvious that even I can now see it. I have failed. Failed utterly and ignobly, failed because I ignored facts I did not find convenient, failed because I believed I could make the world, the universe, fit the mold I decreed.

But I have accomplished great things, and learned far more secrets than those that Ulan

Baskaw taught me. There is much to be found in the most secret places of the Grand Library, and in other archives. Remarkable technologies of all sorts have been deliberately suppressed, by those who believe is it best for human society to remain nearly static, and progress with glacial slowness, if at all. Perhaps they were once right to so think, but their time is past.

You need only look to the events of the Circum Central incident to know that is true. The ships you called the Intruders did indeed exceed light-speed.

"Light-speed!" Wandella protested. "That's impossible. That's the whole reason for the timeshaft-wormhole system."

"I agree," said Koffield. "But the detection records from the *Upholder* showed otherwise, even if that point wasn't talked about much in public. The Intruders accelerated up past where we could detect them at all, and then just vanished. When they came back, they did the same thing in reverse. It looked a hell of a lot like light-speed to us."

"Read the letter," said Norla.

But failure is not mine alone, Koffield went on. *Humanity itself is failing. The enterprise of our interstellar civilization is subject to the same physical and mathematical laws as Solace. All our worlds are doomed. I share my crimes with every other terraformer in history.*

"That's special pleading if ever I heard it," said Norla. "Every other terraformer in history was ignorant of Baskaw's work. *He knew.*"

"He probably knew," Koffield said. "Maybe he was just criminally incompetent. And he does have a point. All of humanity is in big trouble." He went on reading.

I have done wrong. There is no question of that. But to whom would I turn myself in? What crime, in what jurisdiction, have I committed? What punishment would be meted out to me, and who would judge me? I believe the answer is that there is no judge, no court, legally competent to judge this case, and thus there are no legal means to judge me, or determine suitable punishment or re-habilitation for me. In the absence of such legal authority, if I were to go to the public, and tell all of Settled Space of Ulan Baskaw's work, I believe that it would be likely, perhaps even highly proba-ble, that I would fall to mob violence, or a re-venge bomb thrown by some relative or another of someone who died on Solace. How many oth-ers would be hurt or killed in the unrest such news would surely inspire?

If I exposed myself to a legal system that could not judge me, and was then thus killed, I could do no good to anyone at all. And I have great good to offer, prizes of knowledge and technology that I alone can give.

"In other words, he didn't just steal Baskaw's work," said Norla. "He found other discoveries he could grab. So what? And why should we believe him?"

"I can give one answer to both questions. He demon-strated faster-than-light travel," said Koffield. "That's what he's offering as a *sample*. It suggests that the main course could be impressive. If we believe him. It could all be trickery."

"He's done a good job of making his cowardice look like courage," Norla said. "He's not afraid to come out and face us, or the people of Solace. He's just afraid that if we kill him, someone else might get hurt, and he wouldn't be in a position to do nice things for us."

"I don't know if I'd put it quite that way, but it sure sounds like he's setting up his arguments for cutting a deal," said Wandella. "But what's the deal?"

I have much that I can offer, but much of what I can offer will not be accepted willingly. Drastic

*ideas will not be welcome until the situation is
desperate. Until then, the doomsayers will be ignored, shoved to one side, reviled and punished.*

"Fine and noble words coming from him," said Norla.
"*He* punished me, punished everyone on the *DP-IV,* because he was afraid of *your doomsaying.*"

Koffield nodded and read on.

*The collapse of Solace is coming. I believe that
now. But I also believe that it will serve as a wake-
up call, a warning to all the worlds. The more people that know about Baskaw's work, the more
likely that they will believe and listen. I believe
they will be ready by the time you find this letter.
At last, they will listen. At last, they can listen. I
have, therefore, enclosed copies of her work and
yours with this letter, that you might be better able
to communicate these ideas to others.*

"The son of a bitch!" Norla shouted. "He makes it sound
like the height of generosity to give back what he stole."

"Awfully decent of him," Koffield agreed. The madman! The self-serving madman! He realized that his skin
was flushed and his hands were sweating. But he had to
keep control, keep calm. His vision seemed a bit clouded
for some reason. He blinked and continued reading.

*Seek me out. I live, but slumber. I am hidden, but
hidden where you can find me. Find me, and together, we can do great things. With the knowledge I have gathered, and the skill, courage, and
determination you have so often demonstrated,
we can, I believe, defeat the doom to which Ulan
Baskaw has sentenced us.*

"Seek him out?" Norla shouted. "The man who wrecked
all our lives so completely? The man who made Solace a
shambles, but didn't have the courage to face the people he
had hurt?"

"Faster-than-light travel," said Anton Koffield. "Think of it. What would you not trade for that? Who would you refuse to deal with, in exchange for that prize?"

"Is there more?" Wandella asked. "Is that the end?"

"There's more," said Koffield.

I have much to offer, and many secrets I can reveal when you find me, though I dare not tell them to you in this letter. There is, however, one last confession I must make. You have been blamed for Circum Central. Not just for losing the ships, but for sealing the wormhole. In the time in which I write, you are still reviled for this crime. Perhaps, even a century hence, that is how you will be remembered.

"That's putting it mildly," Koffield said. "I'm not just remembered. I'm a monster."

"Only to some," said Wandella. "Most people have forgotten, or never knew."

"Is that supposed to be comforting?" Koffield asked her, his long-contained anger nearly breaking free. "It isn't."

"I'm sorry. Go on with the letter."

The time has come for you to learn the truth. I cannot now explain their mission in detail, but I must tell you one thing about the ships you called the Intruders. Much was made of the fact that they first went uptime *through the wormhole, from past to future. Why, many people wondered at the time, did they do this? Why run the risks and take the losses of sending robotic ships into the future, when all they would need to do is wait in normal space until they had reached the time in question?*

There are two reasons. The first is fairly straightforward. For various technical reasons, having mainly to do with their power systems, the ships would have deteriorated by then. The second reason was suggested now and then by the theory-spinners, but never much considered. The ships needed to do a calibration run, a passage through the wormhole that allowed them to get precise and detailed measurement of the wormhole's structure.

"Oh my God." Koffield stared at the page, read the next paragraph or two silently, and felt his knees buckle. Anger and shock swept over him. "This is the worst," he said, his voice suddenly no more than a whisper. "This next is the worst shock of all. Damn the man!"

"What is it?" Wandella asked.

"My life wrecked," Koffield said, anger helping him find his voice again. "My career wrecked. Marooned in time, not once, but twice, by Oskar DeSilvo. Pointed out as a killer.

" *'Terrible Anthon closed up the sky*
Horrible Anthon made Glister die
Closed up the sky, made Glister die,
Made Glister die, no ship could fly
Hideous Anthon closed up the sky.'

"That's about me. About me. Because I did my job. The Glisterns use my name to scare children. I am the criminal, the monster. And the great Oskar DeSilvo builds his own monuments, and they all tell me he's a hero. And now. And now—"

"Read it," Norla said. "Please. Read it out loud."

The ships needed this information in order to complete one element of their mission. I had sent them to perform several tasks—including the sealing of the Circum Central wormhole. It pains me to say it, but you must know, before you come to face me. If you had done nothing, nothing at all, if your ship had stood by, if your ship had not been there at all, my ships would have completed their work by entering the uptime end of the wormhole and sealing it, for all time. They were programmed to shut it down. In all truth, I believe it is impossible to say whether they did the deed, or whether the commands sent by your ship did the job. I cannot now tell you why the deed was necessary. But I assure you that, if you had not acted, the deed would have been done.

I could not reveal my part in the Circum Central incident without compromising operations of the utmost importance. It grieved me no end to see the punishment you took, and the guilt you carried in your soul because of deeds you did not do. It was my guilt on this point that led me to approach you, and invite you to join my staff. The sequels to that gesture are, as you will know as well as I, still being played out.

I am sorry. I offer you my sincere, heartfelt, and most humble apologies. Accept them or refuse them as you will. Hate me, forgive me. Feel what you will toward me, and I will accept it. There are larger matters at stake, and my own guilt and shame do not matter.

Only one thing does matter.

Seek me out.

With heartfelt respect, I remain
Your sincere admirer,
Doctor Oskar DeSilvo

Anton Koffield dropped the letter on the table, turned, and left the room.

CHAPTER TWENTY-SIX
THE DEPTHS OF TIME

Norla sat in the sterile, faceless compartment that served as her bedroom, there in the quarantine bunker, and debated with herself. Should she go and talk to Koffield? Three hours had passed since Anton had read DeSilvo's letter to her and Wandella. He had shut himself up in his room immediately afterward and not come out since. Would it be wiser to let the man be, let him wrap himself in privacy, in control, and deal with the shocks, the insults, the cruelty of it all that way? Or should she force him to engage in conversation, talk it through?

She had decided to let him be a half dozen times and changed her mind just as often. She did not know what to do, what was right.

But not to act was to decide. Settled Space was filled to bursting with the consequences of people who found reasons not to act, people who convinced themselves that doing whatever it took to avoid trouble was really the best, the wisest, the noblest course of action.

People like Oskar DeSilvo.

That notion was enough to decide her. She had stood up and was reaching for the door latch when the knock came on the door. Wandella, probably. Norla had thought the woman had gone to sleep. Poor Wandella. She had had her worldview turned upside down as well, if not as severely as Anton.

She opened the door.

"May I come in?" asked Anton Koffield.

"Oh! Yes, yes, of course. I thought you were going to be Wandella. Please, come in."

She ushered Koffield in, closed the door behind him, gestured for him to take a seat on the chair, and took a seat herself on the bunk. She was not particularly surprised that he didn't sit.

He stood before her, in the same style of shapeless plain brown coveralls that she wore, all they issued for clothing in the quarantine ward. Somehow he wore them with a brisk, military air. He folded his arms and smiled sadly down at her.

"It hasn't been an easy day," he said. "None of them has been easy. Not since we got to Solace."

"They haven't been easy for you for a lot longer than that," Norla said.

"No," he agreed. He turned and stared at the blank steel wall next to the door for a moment. "They haven't. And after what we learned, what *I* learned today, somehow now they seem even worse. I had just convinced myself that it was all blind bad luck, forces beyond my control. Now I know. Now I know what it was. *Who* it was. I have never been so angry in my life. I will go on being angry for a very long time."

Anton gestured upward with a grand sweep of his arm, as if to indicate all of space. "All the stories, all the lies are out there. They have a hundred-and-twenty-seven-year head start on the truth. And the truth will never catch up. When I go to my grave, the ancestors of today's Glisterns will not just believe, they will *know,* as absolutely certain fact, that *Horrible Anthon made Glister die.* And they'll raise a toast to Oskar DeSilvo, who built the planet Solace and gave them a place of refuge.

"But maybe even that isn't the worst. I thought I was a free man, acting as I saw fit. But all that time, I was a rat in DeSilvo's maze, walking in the path he set for me, falling into the traps he set. I was his puppet. Even now, he pulls the strings, from a hundred years and light-years away, and my muscles twitch, and I move in the way he bids me."

"You're going after him," Norla said. It was not a question. It had never entered her head that he would not go.

Koffield was not a man who found good reasons to do nothing.

"I wish I wasn't," Koffield said. "With every fiber of my being, I want to turn my back on him, on Solace, on the terraforming disaster. I want to say 'I've done my part. Leave me in peace. Let someone else do the work.' But I can't. I want to leave it be. But I *can't*."

"That's not DeSilvo pulling the strings," Norla said, standing up again. "That's *duty*. He has no claim on you, no power. You won't go after him because he asks. You'll do it because it's *right*. Because if he has stolen knowledge, science, technology that might save us, then someone has to take it back. Go. Find it. Take it back. Deal with the devil, because you have to—and see to it that he gets the worst of the bargain."

Koffield nodded. "Thank you," he said. "I learned very early that you knew how to see beyond what was before you. You have just demonstrated that skill again. It is one I value tremendously. And if I go in search of Oskar DeSilvo, I'll have need of it."

"Admiral? Anton? What do you mean?"

"I came in here to ask if you'd come with me. I am going to need your help. I'm sure of that. If I go after DeSilvo, will you go with me?"

Norla Chandray had not given a moment's thought to her own life, her future, here in the future. She had no doubt that she could build a life of sorts in the Solacian system. Someone always needed a pilot.

But it was not merely the future that she faced. From Ulan Baskaw's long-lost books to the collapse on Solace that was just gathering strength, forces were reaching up from the past, the present, the future, bubbling up from the ocean of years.

She could drift where she was on that sea. Find a way to live, eat, work, until it was time to die. If that could be called living.

Or she could set a course toward a goal that no skill of foresight could yet teach her to see, reach over the horizon for something worth doing, worth fighting for.

"Of course," she said. "I'll go."

Anton Koffield smiled, and somehow the room got brighter. "Good," he said. He laughed, and shook his head. "We make it sound as if we can head off right this minute and head straight for him. There are one or two details we need to sort out first."

"We'll get them sorted," she said, and there was no doubt of it in her voice, or in her soul. "We'll see it through. We'll find him. I'm sure of it. 'I am hidden, but hidden where you can find me.' We'll track him down."

"I'm sure you're right," Anton replied. "We'll find him." He looked at her, straight in the eye, and his voice grew far more serious. "And after we do," he said, "*then* will come the hard part."

Oskar DeSilvo's power reserves were great, but they were not infinite. Every temporal-confinement field consumed vast amounts of energy, but one could realize a substantial power saving by setting the field to a less extreme time-dilation effect. If one let a hundred years go by in an apparent week, rather than an apparent hour, one could stretch out the field duration almost indefinitely.

A smaller containment likewise consumed far less energy than a larger one. DeSilvo had therefore directed his ArtInts to construct the smallest containment possible. It was in truth no larger than a prison cell, and scarcely more comfortable. The food store, recycler, and sanitary facilities took up most of the compartment. He scarcely had room to turn around.

But the sacrifice of space and comfort might well turn out to be a most prudent precaution. DeSilvo was well aware that he could be in the containment for a long, and unpredictable, period of time. What if Koffield failed to reach Solace, or, having arrived there, did not, for some reason, visit Greenhouse or learn of the tomb?

DeSilvo had planned as best he could, but a thousand things could go wrong. If Koffield did not come, and did not open the confinement, the field was programmed to shut itself down after three hundred years of objective time had passed, but that circuit, and its backups, could fail. Then he would be held in the containment until the power system finally failed, or, perhaps, until he died of old age, or simply went mad from confinement. It was conceivable that he would be trapped in the containment for hundreds, even thousands, of years of objective time—months or even years of apparent time, trapped in a cell scarcely large enough to serve as a decent closet.

But he refused to believe in such things. Koffield would survive. It was obvious the man could survive anything. It was, after all, why DeSilvo had decided to make use of him.

DeSilvo thought about it as he made up his simple evening meal, then prepared himself for bed. He slept a lot while in temporal confinement. There was little else to do.

He entertained himself by imagining the scene in his head as he settled down to sleep. Koffield would find him. Koffield would shut down the confinement, and Admiral Anton Koffield would confront him, full of stern disapproval and righteous anger. Koffield would demand explanations, stand in judgment over all of DeSilvo's moral lapses and failures of personal courage. He would question DeSilvo, interrogate him, insist that DeSilvo tell all.

And then—

—And then, Anton Koffield would get one or two surprises. Yes indeed.

Somewhere and somewhen, hidden away in the temporal confinement that blocked out the passing years, Dr. Oskar DeSilvo smiled happily to himself, rolled over, and fell into a dreamless sleep, floating in the dark and quiet of the limitless depths of time.

GLOSSARY AND GAZETTEER OF TERMS, PLACES, SHIPS, ETC.

ArtInt—Artificial Intelligence. Any machine or device with sophisticated decision-making ability, and the capacity to interpret and execute complex orders. Generally speaking, ArtInts are deliberately built and programmed so as to be regarded as appliances and tools. Thus, while it is possible for them to speak and understand speech, they are usually designed to discourage any tendency to treat them as human.

Circum Central Wormhole Farm—The timeshaft wormhole linking Glister to other worlds, usable for transit to Solace as well. The name is an optimistic misnomer. Circum Central is not central to anything, and there is only one timeshaft there, though the term *wormhole farm* usually refers to three or more wormholes clustered near each other at a main transfer point. Circum Central was supposed to be much more important than it turned out to be.

Chronologic Patrol—The military organization assigned to protect the timeshaft wormholes, and to defend against any deliberate or accidental attempt to abuse time travel so as to damage causality.

Comfort—A large gas giant planet in the outer reaches of the same planetary system that holds Solace. The satellite Greenhouse orbits Comfort, and the SunSpot orbits Greenhouse.

Downtime—Referring to events in or travel toward the past as regards a timeshaft wormhole. For a hundred-year timeshaft connecting 5100 A.D. and 5000 A.D., 5000 A.D. would be the downtime end.

Glister—A terraformed planet near Solace that has suffered a climatic collapse.

Grand Library—The ultimate storehouse of human knowledge, housed in a massive habitat orbiting Neptune. Two Permanent Physical Collections, or PPCs, serve as backups in the event of the Grand Library's destruction. One PPC is in a different orbit of Neptune, while the other is buried in an undisclosed location on the farside of Earth's Moon.

Greenhouse—A rocky satellite of the gas giant Comfort, used as the research station and breeding support center for Solace. It is illuminated by the SunSpot.

Habitat Seeds—Large and sophisticated self-actuating robotic machines programmed to seek out the raw materials for a space habitat, process the materials, and construct the hab with little or no human intervention. Typically, a Habitat Seed is released near a suitable stony-metal asteroid, which it mines as a source of raw materials. Habitat Seeds are one-shot items and cannot be reused because they self-cannibalize certain parts of themselves during the construction process. Furthermore, the seeds cannot manufacture all the items needed to construct a habitat; for example, sophisticated electronics. Seeds carry such items as cargo, and cannot replenish their stores of them.

Herakles IX—Cargo ship, Ship One of the convoy caught in the middle of the Second Battle of Circum Central. The *Herakles IX* was the only ship of the convoy to make it through the timeshaft wormhole. She completed her journey to Glister, but her captain was detained, and all data related to the battle were impounded, in order to prevent a time paradox. Ships Two, Three, and Four of the convoy were destroyed. See *Stardrifter Gamma*.

Intruders—Name given, more or less by default, to the thirty-two ships that attacked and went through the Circum Central Timeshaft Wormhole, transiting from downtime to uptime, past to future.

Lodestar—Local name of HS-G9-223, the star around which Solace orbits.

Machine language—The name given to the specialized syntax and dialect used by Solacians when talking to voice-capable computers and ArtInts.

Near-ancient, near ancients—Referring to a period of remote human history, or the people of that period. The near-ancient period is considered to start roughly with the Enlightenment, and ends roughly with the establishment of wormhole transit. Thus, from about 1740 A.D. to 3000 A.D.

Objective time—The time or duration as measured by an outside observer. Typically used in regard to timeshaft-wormhole travel. A timeshaft ship might travel for one hundred years of self-chronologic time, and experience significant relativistic time dilation, but arrive only a week or so after departure in objective time, thanks to passage through a timeshaft wormhole. See *self-chronologic time* and *subjective time*.

Self-chronologic time—The accumulated duration or age of an object, a person's life, or an event, as it would be measured by a chronometer physically attached to an object or person, and ignoring the actual calendric time and date but accounting for relativistic time-dilation effects. Put another way, self-chron is a measure of how much an object or person has actually aged, regardless of time travel or cold sleep. A person who traveled, over the course of several trips, for five centuries in cryosleep, but traveled down five one-century wormholes, would have gone through five centuries of self-chron time, but have experienced virtually no subjective time, and might well end up in the same objective year from which he or she started. See *objective time* and *subjective time*.

Sirius Power Cluster Farm—A large Timeshaft Wormhole Farm, near the Sirius star system.

Solace—A newly terraformed planet.

Solace City—Capital of Solace.

C.P.S. Standfast—The downtime Chronologic Patrol ship attacked and destroyed during the Circum Central incident.

Stardrifter Gamma—A cargo ship, Ship Five in the convoy caught in the middle of the Second Battle of Circum Central. The *Stardrifter Gamma* was marooned on the uptime end of the wormhole and made her way to Thor's Realm Wormhole Farm. Ships Two, Three, and Four were destroyed in the battle. See *Herakles IX*.

Subjective time—The apparent time or duration as experienced. A passenger aboard a starship might be in cryo sleep for a century, but only be awake to experience a few weeks of subjective time. See *objective time* and *self-chronologic time*.

SunSpot—A massive fusion generator, in effect a miniature sun, surrounded by an adjustable reflector, which orbits Greenhouse in the same period as Solace's day, and thus provides simulated day and night to Greenhouse.

Thor's Realm—A large Timeshaft Wormhole Farm, near the Tau Ceti star system.

Timeshaft wormhole—A wormhole linking past and future. A hundred-year timeshaft would allow one to travel back and forth exactly one hundred years—no more, no less. In the year 5000 A.D., the downtime end of a hundred-year timeshaft would link with the year 5100 A.D. on the uptime side. A timeshaft experiences normal duration, such that both ends are moving normally through time, from past to future, at the normal rate. In 5001 A.D., the same timeshaft would link with 5101 A.D., and so on. A hypothetical twenty-four-hour timeshaft would link 4:15 P.M. Tuesday with 4:15 P.M. Wednesday. Two days later, 12:05 A.M. Thursday would be linked with 12:05 A.M. Friday. Move from the downtime to the uptime end of a timeshaft, spend five minutes on the uptime side, and then return to the downtime side, and it will be five minutes later there as well.

Upper—Slang term for members of the upper classes on Solace, used by the rural and lower classes.

Uptime—Referring to events in or travel toward the future as regards a timeshaft wormhole. For a hundred-year timeshaft connecting 5100 A.D. and 5000 A.D., 5100 A.D. would be the uptime end.

C.P.S. Upholder—The Uptime Chronologic Patrol ship, commanded by Captain Anton Koffield, that survived the attack of the Intruders during the Circum Central incident.